MW01230885

Marietta, GA 30066

Dedicated to C. C. J. & R. J. R

They have met only through mutual interest
to see this work completed.

BONDED

BY A

BLADE

GEORGE PETTETT

Chapter 1: An October Encounter

Caleb caught a glimpse of a man approaching from the woods but kept on with his whittling. He knew the nostrils of the hounds asleep at the steps of his cabin door would soon detect the presence of a stranger. The dogs weren't good for much except sentry duty. That quality made them valuable companions at Caleb's remote east Tennessee hillside.

Calhoun picked up the scent first and lifted his head. Scrambling to all fours, he jarred the older and slower Jackson awake and alert. The first tentative bark exploded into a chorus of threatening bays directed toward the oncoming stranger. With the younger dog in the lead, the sentinels leapt across the clearing and brought the man to a halt as snarls and lunges encircled him. He raised both arms high and called out.

His "H'lo, the house....h'lo..." was barely discernible above the dogs' barks.

Caleb could now see his uninvited visitor was an unarmed, bareheaded young man. "Deserter..." Caleb muttered to himself. "Confederate, most likely. Or somebody runnin' to keep from enlistin'."

He eased himself erect from the stool and took a painful step toward the spot where his dogs were in the midst of enacting all hell broken loose. Caleb's left hand grasped the crutch he had been whittling for support. The right hand held a foot-long knife.

"Jackson! Calhoun!" he yelled at the hounds, "hush up so I can find out what this feller's doin' here."

The dogs, assured their master paid attention, intensified their howls and flashed their teeth.

Caleb rested his knife on the cabin steps and picked up an egg-sized rock. He threw it and smacked one dog's skinny haunch. "Stay!" he bellowed. "Hush that racket, Jackson. *Stay*, I said! Shout your business, Mister. What do you want?"

The young man stood his ground. He raised his voice to make himself heard.

"I'm not lookin' to give anybody any trouble, Mister," he yelled. "Just wonder if I might do a little work for somebody in exchange for a meal."

Caleb leaned on the crutch with both hands and continued his shouts until he convinced the hounds their duty had been done. First Jackson, the older dog, lowered his head and stopped circling the prey. The younger dog kept barking but ceased his threatening leaps. The young man took a cautious step forward in the space yielded by the less noisy Jackson.

"That's far enough," Caleb called out, "I can hear you when you holler." He remained where the knife lay an arm's length away on the cabin step.

The young man lowered his arms and extended his open palms toward Caleb. "I got no weapon on me," he said. "If you let me come a little closer, we can stop yellin' at each other." He advanced a few steps toward the cabin, the dogs whining and sniffing his legs. "I could do some of your chores if you've got a bad leg. Won't cost you nothing... 'cept a little grub. Sound fair?"

"What you doin' so far off the road?" Caleb demanded. "Sneakin' out of the woods ain't a good way to come askin' about work. Guess you must have slept in them woods last night. You're mighty lucky them panthers wuzzent nearby."

The young man's face gave no sign the last remark had any effect. Instead, Caleb saw only the earnest eyes and calm innocence of a youth walking to meet an elder on even terms. Familiar, that look, thought Caleb. But from where? When?

"Why don't you sit back down?" the young man asked. "That don't look like much of a crutch." He moved within a few yards of the cabin door, where two small heads peered around the same side of a dark skirt. From the shadows above the skirt, the stock of a gun extended partway in readiness for the older man's grasp.

"First you say you're lookin' for work... then you start givin' advice," Caleb snapped. "I don't take kindly to folks comin' round uninvited. Especially them that start tellin' me what to do! Maybe you better git goin' before I take notion to use this knife on you."

"Suit yourself," the young man replied. "But I could swing that ax at that woodpile over there a whole lot better than you can on one leg."

Caleb shifted the chaw in his mouth and studied the tall youth's dark hair and broad shoulders. That sense of familiarity crossed his mind again. It's mystery bothered him. He tightened his grip on the crutch and spat at the hounds. From long experience, the older dog knew this meant his master was in firm control and wanted more room. He began to slink away. The younger Calhoun, sensing he now acted alone, lost confidence and retreated to the steps.

"What did you say your name wuz?" Caleb probed.

"Never said," came the reply.

"You got a home?"

"Used to be South Carolina."

The annoying fog in Caleb's brain thinned a bit at the words "South Carolina." Familiar ground. A long time ago. Before all the wandering. The bad whiskey. The lost years.

"What part?"

"Ever hear of Gowensville?

Mention of the town named after Revolutionary War hero John Gowen, where the Blue Ridge blends into the Piedmont, lifted Caleb's fog even more. He nodded and leaned heavily on the crutch.

"I grew up 'round there," the stranger said. "Now... you want me to cut you some wood? Or not?"

Desire to know more gnawed at the older man, but an uneasy feeling about what he might learn made him hesitate. The wrong question could expose his own past in that part of the country. A past never discussed with anyone. He needed to be careful with this young stranger who came poking himself into Caleb's life the first day of October 1863.

"How do I know..." Caleb considered aloud, "if I wuz to let you git your hands on that ax... you won't try and cut my head open?"

The young man looked him straight in the eye. "How do I know you got anything to eat?" He paused. "I'll say it again, Mister, I don't want a thing more'n a few bites to eat. If we can't make a fair trade, not much use'a my stayin', is there?"

The show of spunk persuaded Caleb.

4

"Well, if this ankle hadn't give out on me yesterday," he said, slumping to the stool," I wouldn't waste time with you. But I guess we can spare a little of what we got to eat if you earn it first." He nodded toward the woodpile. "Let me see you use that ax."

The young man crossed to the woodpile quickly. From a stack of split logs, he pulled one from the top, slid an end across the chopping block, picked up the ax, tested it for heft, and swung. His powerful stroke sent the blade deep into the wood. Again and again, he widened and deepened the cut until a two-foot section gave way. He repositioned the log and opened a second cut. First one oak, then another was reduced to fireplace fuel.

Caleb looked on with approving eyes. Years of memory rolled backward to a time when he saw another youth swing an ax and perfect the skill as he grew older. Together, man and boy formed a woodcutting team envied by neighbors. Caleb reckoned they cleared a mile or more of forest along the Middle Fork of the Tyger River, south of Glassy Mountain and the border between the Carolinas. Then problems mounted with Caleb's in-laws. Promises about crop divisions and the grant of a tract of land were postponed, then denied. Caleb took solace in his jug. Temperamental outbursts with his wife happened more often, and one night their almost-grown son came to her defense. Hot words flew and a fight soon followed. Just as Caleb's strength and experience gained the upper hand, something flat and hard crashed against the side of his skull. When he regained consciousness where he had fallen, he saw the youth's questioning eyes penetrate the dim light of the room. Caleb struggled to his feet, found his coat and hat, and left the house. He never went back.

"I sure could use a drink of water."

The words broke Caleb's reverie. He saw the young man standing by a mound of firewood, wiping sweat from his face with his sleeve. The older man turned his head and called inside the cabin. A minute later, a boy about five years old came down the steps slowly, a drinking gourd held between his hands. Caleb pointed to the woodpile, and the boy began to march cautiously in that direction. His hands cradled the gourd to prevent spilling its contents on the ground.

The young man took a couple steps forward to meet the boy. As the gourd was passed, the boy's shyness drew a smile from the young man.

"Thank you," he said and raised the gourd to his lips. He drank in long gulps, turning the gourd bottom up to drain while the boy watched. The young man handed the emptied gourd to the water bearer and turned back to the woodpile. The boy remained where he stood to watch the woodcutter select another log to be cut.

"Come on back, William," Caleb called from his position on the stool. "Don't git in the way. Bring that dipper back and give it to your ma."

As the boy returned to stand beside him at the steps, Caleb saw the young man take up the ax but then put it down. He tugged at the bottom of his shirt, lifted it over his head, and tossed the shirt aside before he reclaimed the ax. The strong arms and upper torso Caleb had suspected glistened from sweat. When the young man turned to attend to the log, something else caught Caleb's attention. Something not put there by nature nor hard work. Diagonal rows of red stripes crossed the bare muscular back, from lower ribcage to shoulder blade.

"He's been flogged," Caleb mumbled aloud. Was this fellow a deserter or an escaped prisoner? The latter possibility pushed thoughts about South Carolina aside. He tapped the shoulder of the boy beside him.

"Go in the house and tell your ma to hand me my gun."

The boy, who had been watching the woodcutter all the while, reacted with a puzzled expression but dutifully retreated into the cabin.

When the gun had been passed to him, Caleb placed the butt of the stock on the ground at his right side. He propped the barrel against the cabin wall, out of view from the woodpile. He sat still and tried to sort thoughts whirling too fast to make sense. Caleb then voiced more directions within the open cabin door. When satisfied his request would be met, he resumed watch.

After three more logs had been pulled from the stack and cut, Caleb yelled: "That's aplenty. Put the ax down and bring a few armloads of that firewood up here where we can git at it when we need it."

The woodcutter wiped his face on his shirt and slipped it back over his head. He knelt to gather an armload then staggered under its weight until the firewood had been deposited at the left of Caleb's stool. He returned for a second load, then a third, and a fourth to build a stack two feet high, two feet deep, four feet wide. He stopped, stepped back, and faced Caleb.

"Want me to get you a stronger treelimb for a crutch?" he asked.

"This'll do," the older man said curtly. He saw the young man's dark eyes had spotted the shotgun. Caleb lifted it and placed it across his knees. "It's just a bad ankle. My wife will bring some food out d'reckly," he said. "Sit down there at the end of the stack. You've done a sight of woodcuttin' so you've earned a share of such as we got. But we need to talk before you eat. Who... or what are you runnin' from?"

The young man looked down. "I 'druther not say," he said softly and seated himself..

Caleb glared at him. "I don't care about your druthers," he snorted. "I got a family to protect. I got a right to know. What brought you through them woods? This ain't the road to Knox-ville! I'm not keen about this crazy war, so it makes no differ-ence to me if you lit out. But them welts on your back must a' been put there by somebody you aggravated. A county warden, maybe?"

The young man winced, realizing his mistake in removing the shirt. He avoided Caleb's eyes and sat mute for a minute. He began to scuff the ground with the heel of his right boot. Finally, he answered.

"I left a few days after the Battle at Chickamauga Creek. I was a private in Company D, Greenville Hilltoppers, Tenth South Carolina Regiment... Manigault's Brigade...."

He stopped when a baby's cry sounded from inside the cabin.

"Go on," Caleb directed. "Baby's feedin' time, too. She'll bring your grub out before tendin' to the baby."

The young man studied Caleb's timeworn bearded face as if suddenly conscious of the older man's age bracket. His eyes shifted back toward the ground, then he faced Caleb again.

"We put the Yanks on the run that day, all right. Plenty of satisfaction to go around... all through camp. But the real trou-ble... for me... came three days later. Captain called for a pun-ishment detail because somebody above him claimed to have witnessed malingerin'. Sergeant grabbed two men... and had 'em taken away. I don't know why in God's world he picked me to tag along behind him, but he did. Ordered me to use a whip on the first feller they hitched up against a tree. I ..."

He paused, swallowed hard, and looked at the ground.

"I saw enough of his face to know it was Jacob Willingham... a cousin, from back home."

Caleb stiffened at the sound of the name, but the young man's eyes continued their study of the ground. He kept talking,"I couldn't do it. When they handed me the whip, I wouldn't take it. 'Do it,' the sergeant said, 'or it'll be used on you!' I tried to reason with him... 'I'm just a private,' I said... 'ain't this a job for a corporal or somebody higher?' I saw Jacob try to twist his head to see us... I know he recognized my voice. Sergeant motioned two fellers to grab my arms and... before I could stop 'em... they split my shirt up the back and roped me against another tree. I couldn't see which one of 'em used the whip... it got used all right."

He paused once more. "I thought our fight was for Southern independence. That sergeant was warrin' to look big... important... like a rooster in full strut. Don't know what they did to Jacob. Never saw him again."

Caleb spat the rest of his wad and wiped his chin. "Don't blame you for leavin'," he said.

"I didn't try it right away," the young man continued, "Sergeant took my gun. I did what they told me next day and made up my mind to go that night. Crept out of camp around midnight and walked north. Must have covered ten miles or so before daylight. I rested a while and walked some more... keepin' to the woods in daytime... til I happened up on a farm where a woman and a little boy was tryin' to chase some pigs back into a pen. I helped 'em out. She never said it plain, but... by the way she talked about the war... I 'spect her husband was off in some Union outfit. She didn't ask a bunch of questions, thanked me for helpin' with the pigs, offered me a big piece of pound cake, and I was on my way. Cake sure was tasty. I made it through the next two days on a pocketful of apples. Nobody around a big orchard... I figured they wouldn't miss a few."

He looked Caleb in the eye. "Sure hope you got something else to eat besides apples."

The older man called into the cabin. "Jen... 'bout ready?"

The long skirt on the steps signaled the arrival of a woman in her middle 20s, a plain but pleasing face above the thin blouse covering her full bosom. She carried a bowl in one hand and two hoecakes in the other. The boy with the refilled drinking gourd trailed after her. A little girl, about half as old as the boy, peeped from the doorway.

The young man stood to receive the bowl and the hoecakes. "Thank you, Ma'am," he said. The woman brushed a loose strand of dark hair from her eyes and backed away, her shyness evident. She directed the boy to place the gourd carefully on the stack of firewood then led him back inside the cabin.

"Eat up," Caleb said. "My wife makes a mighty good rabbit stew. I trapped two before I stepped in a hole and twisted my ankle." He fell silent and allowed the young man to devour the hot food without interruption. Once he saw the inside of the bowl wiped clean with what remained of the last hoecake, Caleb was ready with a question.

"Just where you figger on goin'?"

The young man licked the last crumbs of hoecake from his fingers then reached for the gourd.

"Thought I might try and make Kentucky," he said after gulping more water. "I hear folks up there don't run real hot or real cold on the war. Maybe I can blend in a while then go west. I know I'll be shot or hung if I'm captured. I can't go back to South Carolina anyway."

Caleb seized the opening.

"You got family back there... near Gowensville?" he asked.

"My ma... but she married again. Has more children, too. Her husband and me don't get along."

"What happened to your pa?" Caleb pressed.

The young man drained the drinking gourd and studied his questioner closely before he replied.

"Pa got killed in the War with Mexico. I was nearly three years old when he left, but I sure remember him. He used to ride me around on his shoulders. Once he took me fishin' with him."

A rush of recollection swept Caleb, strong and more painful than the others. Guilt welled up, and emotion burned his throat. He returned the gun to its former position, brushed a hand across his eyes, and looked away.

They sat without speaking. Then the young man stood and offered his hand to Caleb.

"I'm sure obliged to you, Mister... for the food. Hope you see that's all I wanted. I'll be on my way now."

Caleb tried to speak but a half-gurgle came out. The tough old man of the hills cleared his throat loudly before he rose and shook the hand extended to him.

"You take care, young feller. Keep to the woods... the high ground like you been doin'. Don't go down along the river. They's Home Guard rascals in every settlement. They'll turn you in faster'n they draw breath."

He leaned heavily on the crutch with both hands. "'Preciate all this wood you cut. This leg ought to mend in a day or so. I hope you make it... wherever you wind up."

He chose his next words carefully. He looked deep into the young man's eyes before he spoke.

"You keep standin' up for yourself. Don't let anybody break your spirit."

The visitor nodded in farewell and stepped past the hounds. He reached the trees and was out of sight in less than a minute.

Caleb slumped back to the stool. He picked up the gourd, the baked clay bowl, and small wooden ladle the young man had held. That man, Caleb felt certain, was his grandson.

So much needed saying to the young man, but Caleb's pride would not let him tell what went so wrong and led him to leave South Carolina. Men like Caleb expressed themselves through action and survival, dealing with life as honestly as they knew, paying little concern how others might interpret them. Moved though he was by the story he had just heard, Caleb could not bring himself to fumble for words that might give his own reasons for abandoning a family or persuade a grandson reared in that place and fed a different version of circumstances as they existed more than 20 years ago.

The young man had troubles of his own. Had Caleb asked him to stay and hear the long and convoluted story, it could have meant fateful discovery. The closest neighbor, the man who sold Caleb his 40 acres of hardscrabble farm and forest, held right of way to cross the property to reach fields beyond. The man could appear at any time and surely pass word of a young stranger's presence. Grandson or no, it would be best for the young man if he did not linger in any one place for a while.

The boy William reappeared on the steps. Caleb handed him the gourd, the bowl, and the ladle with instructions to take the items to his mother.

"She's nursin' Baby Thomas," William said.

"Well, she'll tell you what to do with 'em," Caleb said. "Y'all stay inside. I'll be in later." He needed time alone. The unexpected visitor set the wheel of memory turning to a walled off part of Caleb's life he no longer cared to remember. Painful as it was at the time, leaving South Carolina summarized so little of his story. More complex were the elements which brought him to it.

Chapter 2: Reverie

Sixteen-year-old Caleb Morgan was an unknown quantity when he showed up seeking work at Titus Willingham's place in 1821. His family's relocation from Virginia, he explained, brought him to South Carolina. With several younger mouths to feed, his parents had voiced no objection when Caleb chose to go out on his own. Harvest time approached. Customarily stern Titus decided to forego questions and put the willing hand to work.

The Willingham household included 10 children, four sons and six daughters. The six eldest had married, meaning the sons and sons-in-law formed a good-sized work unit to oversee and cultivate the cleared portions of a 12-hundred acre plantation. The only male exempted from labor was the eldest son. Thomas Sumter Willingham served in the War of 1812 –1815. He came home without commendation for heroism like that of the Revolutionary War figure for whom he was named, but his claim of a wound gave his father reason to make a show of having the son called Sumter ride beside him in the buggy on trips to the courthouse, the grinding mill, and other places men of some status gathered.

Titus put together his sprawling plantation at minimal investment through a series of land grants in the first years of statehood. He gained title by 1800 to one of the largest landholdings on the Greenville-to-Rutherfordton Road. When each son came of age, Titus deeded him 100 acres stipulating half of all production from crops, timber, and minerals would remain part of the family estate throughout the father's lifetime. He was not as generous right away with the husbands of his daughters, first assigning specific tracts for homeplaces in order to keep all of them close by and under his influence, then granting title to the land when his whimsy had been satisfied.

Young Caleb became a largely unnoticed member of this community, did the work assigned, asked few questions, and stayed out of family matters. A year went by, and he grew to like having a base without permanent sacrifice of independence.

He was very much aware of the three teen-aged Willingham daughters, but he kept respectful distance and spoke only when spoken to. That changed the day he worked in a crew harvesting wheat. Rachel, the second oldest of the three unmarried sisters, took a place behind him as a gleaner following Caleb's scythe.

He stopped wielding the mow blade and came back to her side when he saw her struggle with a wooden rake. By moving her hands down the shaft, he demonstrated how to control the long farm implement. He could not have known Rachel had gathered wheat and oats from childhood. She favored him with a smile, and big brown eyes expressed gratitude without a hint of pretense. She cautioned that he should not fall behind the pace set by her brothers and brothers-in-law.

"They might tell Pa," she said.

Pleased with that glimmer of personal contact, Caleb took her advice and returned to cut his assigned swath through the abundant stand of golden grain. But youthful magnetic attraction seized its opening, and Caleb responded by contriving to

16

work near this girl of his own age when most of the family members assembled for picking cotton, shucking corn, or when he was one of the climbers shaking limbs of apple trees to relinquish ripened fruit to those like Rachel filling hampers below.

He slept in the tack room of the barn and never took meals at the family table, so that avenue for conversation never opened. A trencher of food was handed to where he waited outside the kitchen. The meal seemed to taste better if Rachel was the one who passed the wooden platter to him.

The long nights of winter and the coming of spring brought brown-haired Rachel to Caleb's mind with urgency, and he began to pay attention to his own appearance. He had never had access to a mirror which left him unaware how others saw him. He recalled his mother's complimenting his dark hair, and he gave it a good brushing regularly. In rare time off from chores, he walked into Gowensville to exchange the little money Titus paid him for clothing from the village store. He did not want Rachel to turn away at any conversational opportunity, indefinite though it remained. Still he made no move that might raise suspicion from her father or brothers.

A warm Sunday afternoon in late March brought each of them by separate paths to the same bank of a creek. Caleb spent Sunday afternoons, weather permitting, aimlessly roaming trails of the plantation. He tamped feelings of loneliness as he wandered through the woods, stopping now and then to examine bark of a tree, to watch birds and squirrels, or stand and listen when winds sang through leaves far above him. He had not gone far from the barn that Sunday when he saw her seated on a quilt spread atop a grassy bank, a small parasol held above her head.

Caleb crept forward and took cover behind a cedar tree to admire the scene a few feet in front of him. Rachel's legs and feet were drawn up beneath long folds of her pale yellow dress. Her Sunday bonnet had been discarded, and chestnut brown hair hung loosely past a shawl spread atop her shoulders. Her eyes seemed fixed on something in the gently moving water. He stood motionless, holding his breath because he feared he might disturb the vision. Eventually he had to breathe, and the gasp gave him away.

"Is somebody there?" Rachel called, staring straight to the bushy cedar.

Caleb stepped into the open.

"Didn't mean to startle you, Miss Rachel," he said. "Never 'spected to find anybody out here. I ramble the backwoods when the weather's good. Sure hope I never scared you."

"Just surprised... not scared," she said with a smile. "It's such a sunny day I couldn't stay in the house. No particular place in mind... I didn't want to go too far. I just decided to sit awhile in this peaceful spot. You could come closer... if you want to."

He walked to the edge of the quilt and bent to inspect a honeysuckle bush. "Blooms comin' soon, looks like," he said. "Mighty purty along here last spring."

"Do you walk down here often?" she asked.

"Purty reg'lar," he said. "This here's my wash hole."

"You mean this is where you wash your clothes?"

Caleb nodded. "That, too....but I meant all of me. Glad you didn't walk up last night."

She giggled and covered her mouth.

"I'll find 'nother place down the creek next time," he said.

"Oh, no need for that, Caleb," she laughed. "I just happened to stop here today. No need for you to walk a mile from the barn."

"Well, I sure won't mind if you wuz to come back some other Sunday," he hurried to add. "I keep my clothes on all day. I'd like havin' somebody to talk to."

She smiled again and started to get to her feet. His outstretched hand steadied her rise to a standing position. He helped fold the light quilt and offered to carry it for her, but she declined.

"I'd better get back," she said and tucked the folded quilt beneath her left arm. "I'll have explainin' to do as it is." She rested the handle of the parasol against her right shoulder, head shielded from the sun, and faced him. "I'm glad you came by," she said, leaving him to watch the yellow dress and parasol weave in and out of trees along the trail to the Willingham house.

He did not have long to wait for a second serendipitous meeting at the same creekbank. She appeared the next Sunday and did not attempt to hide her pleasure to find him there, seated on the grass. In the third rendezvous, the creek lost its place in their attention to the hunger growing in their eyes. A first kiss ignited a passionate embrace. When she voiced fear they might be discovered, he led her into the dense cedar grove where fires of youthful desire could be kindled and nourished.

The secluded spot became their private hideaway.

On a warm June afternoon, Rachel told him she was pregnant, that it had been confirmed by her eldest sister, and she had confessed to her parents. Her father had threatened to run Caleb out of the county, she said, but her mother preferred a hasty wedding over family shame.

Caleb hardly had time to react in the blurred but lightning-quick sequence of her telling him, their exchanging vows before a justice of the peace summoned by Titus, and the entire family's swift raising of a cabin. Hand-me-down furniture, quilts, pottery, and odd items from the several Willingham households set the young couple in the homemaking business. While Caleb worked the fields with her brothers and brothers-in-law, Rachel begged portions of meals from kitchens of experienced cooks in the family until she learned to create meals on her own.

The baby, a healthy boy, was born after Rachel's daylong labor watched over by her mother and eldest sister in late January 1824. Rachel insisted the baby be named for Titus, as if that might bring forgiveness from her father. The senior Titus paid no attention. Caleb accepted that he had no say in the matter. However, as the infant grew, he began calling him Ty over Rachel's objection. A bond of father and son became set when Caleb placed the boy on his shoulders and pranced around, little Ty squealing happily throughout.

Another child, a daughter named Esther for Rachel's own mother, was born in 1826. The little girl's weak lungs did not let her mark a first birthday. The baby's death hit Rachel hard, and her grief could be relieved only through her attentions to their son. Caleb tried to be supportive, but she preferred the consolation found in hours spent with her mother. Prodded by his wife, Titus paid his first visit to Rachel and Caleb for the purpose of announcing he would one day grant them the tract of land where their cabin stood. He had already taken this step for all Rachel's married sisters and their husbands. Those grants were 100 acres each. But her father did not specify size in his vague description of a tract for Rachel and Caleb, implying the act to lift his daughter from depression did not mean he had completely forgiven her.

Titus never admitted it, but Caleb was a good worker and the best woodsman in the extended family. The prospect of having land of his own, even as an obvious gift to his wife at a date uncertain, drove Caleb to endure all that Titus demanded. He knew the old man could not live forever. The promise of land offered a way for Caleb to build something for his family and himself.

Titus Willingham showed no sign of slowing down, however, as the decade of the 1830s rolled forward His only outward concession to advancing age being increased reliance on his son Sumter as overseer of daily work on the plantation. Sumter took to his new responsibilities with zeal. He made the rounds on horseback, summoning a younger brother or a brother-in-law to stand at the horse's flank and explain why a planting sprouted poorly or any harvest might be delayed. Caleb escaped that wrath since he was never placed in charge of anything, but he sensed Sumter's cold eyes watching his work.

Ty Morgan grew to adolescence, and so did his admiration for his father. Caleb did not have spare time for leisure but tried to take the boy along with him whenever possible. They walked the woods in back of the cabin; Caleb explaining which trees were best suited for firewood or left for timber as well as those to be spared for the edible nuts they produced. The boy seemed happiest when he could spend an hour tramping the woods or fishing from a creekbank with his father.

Ty's early proficiency with an ax did not surprise Caleb because the boy begged to help bring in firewood once he grew tall enough to drag a stick from the woodpile to the cabin door.

Caleb came in from the field one sunset when Ty was seven to find his son flailing away in an effort to split a firelog as thick as the boy's own body. Rachel protested, but Caleb said the boy might as well be shown the right way to use an ax. Few demonstrations were necessary. Before he was 10, Ty had an ax of his own. By 12 he proved himself able to work alongside as his father brought trees to the ground then hitched teams of oxen to pull stumps and clear land for cultivation.

Rachel repeatedly drilled into the boy the importance of his being a member of the Willingham family. She pushed him to compete with other grandchildren for their grandfather's favor, although Sumter's son – also named Titus and blessed with the surname – had that honor locked down.

Caleb watched Rachel's futile efforts but did not dissuade her. Each year she seemed more desperate to regain her father's affection and less interested in overtures from Caleb. Titus said no more about the grant of land, and Rachel would not respond to any suggestion that she ask about it. She brooded in silence. Caleb sensed the blame fell on him.

When the plantation's land rested in winter, Caleb welcomed any neighbor's offer to pay him to cut timber for the sawmill or clear new acreage for planting. Word of his woodcutting skill spread for miles, and he had all the work he could handle from Thanksgiving to late February each year. Ty joined him many days.

On more than one woodcutting stint, Caleb overheard talk of a family who packed up for Georgia where land lotteries made grants as large as 160 acres to new settlers. Soon the destinations included a new place called Texas. Had the lure of Willingham land not held him back, Caleb would have been eager to join the exodus. He was willing to wait if gaining clear title to land of their own would convince Rachel her father had forgiven her.

As Caleb held onto hope, he discovered a thorn in his grasp.

Sumter rode up one day to announce new fields were to be cleared close by Caleb and Rachel's cabin. Those fields would become part of Sumter's adjoining parcel of the plantation. Caleb's questions were brushed aside.

"I don't care what notion you had," Sumter said, "Pa's left it up to me. He said he'd promised Rachel some land around the cabin. Seems to me five... maybe ten... acres is plenty. Depends how much I need for slave cabins." Emphasizing the last words with a smirk, he dug heels into his horse's flank and rode away.

The news left Caleb speechless. Dispirited, he went on with his work, but that night he told Rachel after Ty climbed into the cabin loft where he slept.

He spoke softly as they sat in front of the fireplace. She would not believe him.

"You must be mistaken. Pa won't allow that," she insisted.

"I tell you Sumter said *slave cabins*. He'll buy Africans...and bring 'em here."

"Pa's never liked slavery," Rachel protested.

That tempted Caleb to observe the Willingham hold on in-laws ensured a ready work force, but he chose to stick to the subject most important to them.

"Your Pa's purty old, Rachel. When he's gone, Sumter's bound to be in charge...executor of the will... all that. He'll do whatever he wants. Any land not deeded already will be his to control." He waited for a response, but there was none.

"Does your Pa know how to read?" he whispered.

She shook her head. "Not very well. He signs and reads his name," she said with hesitation. "He leaves the rest to Sumter."

"What's to keep Sumter from changin' whatever Mister Willingham tells him to write when he makes out his will?" Caleb asked.

She shushed him. "Don't accuse my brother of such a thing. Go to bed."

"If your Pa won't deed this homeplace and some land around it while he's still in charge," Caleb said fervently, "like he's done for all your sisters... even the one younger than you got a hundred acres... let's go on someplace that will truly be our'n... you, Ty, and me."

She buried her face in her hands and began to cry. "I can't believe you askin' me to embarrass myself like that," she whimpered. "Here I try so hard to gain his forgiveness for the pain we caused him..."

Caleb pulled her hands away and gently held them between his own.

"What did we do, Rachel?" he whispered softly, searching her eyes for his answer. "I loved you... I thought you loved me... we had a baby, a fine son. Rachel, I work like a dumb ox for that old man and the rest of your family. I don't think he's angry when he sees all the work I do for the little bit he gives us to git by on."

She freed her hands from his hold and wiped her eyes. "Well, I won't do what you say," she said firmly. "He'll decide... when he's good and ready."

Caleb said no more, banked the dying fire, and they retired for the night. He lay awake as he considered the dim prospect of their ever having anything to call their own. More than a sliver of Willingham land, anyway.

Year by year, he tried sparking Rachel's interest to move on but without success. A similar pall marked her reaction to his attempts to rekindle their once strong physical relationship. Occasional visits to Guthrie's Tavern led to woodcutting employment, and he began to drop in more often. Talk there often rehashed the opposite views of President Andrew Jackson and his former vice-president, John C. Calhoun, over South Carolina's nullification of her place in the Union but usually got around to someone's heading west or recent word from one who had done so. What he overheard gave Caleb an itch stronger than each shot of whiskey he could afford to buy.

The liquor warmed him inside where his wife's increased indifference left him feeling empty. With a pocket filled from another woodcutting payday, he bought jugs of whiskey and buried them to prevent discovery by Rachel. Except for the coins he gave Ty and a few for his own pocket, he handed the rest of the money to her.

Spring meant returning to the Willingham fields for a new planting season. Caleb did his customary yeoman's amount of work but burned inside each time Sumter rode up with unnecessary reminders about what had to be done before sundown. Titus was rarely seen, leading Caleb to suspect his health must be failing. But when he asked if Rachel knew more of this, she dismissed it swiftly.

Their conversations dwindled. He could not persuade her to consider relocation, and whiskey became his nightly companion. When she stormed at him for bringing a jug into the cabin, he stored it in a corner eave beyond her reach. Once he had a few swigs in him, Caleb could stare into the fireplace and ignore her prattle about his letting down her family, who had been so good to them.

Her words pierced deep within him one September night in 1840. She recited his shortcomings, some twice for good measure, and wound up with the blunt assessment "I should have known *you'd* never be worthy of the Willingham family."

Caleb allowed what she said to soak in then focused his eyes on hers. Several stout swigs had passed his lips that night, but his tongue did not fail to frame a reply.

"I'm a Morgan," he said with emphasis. "And you need to make up your mind if'n family means you, Ty, and me ... or just you, Ty, and your Willinghams."

Rachel fired back such a volley of loud accusations that Ty scrambled down from the loft in his nightshirt. He stood to the side as the verbal combat raged. Rachel stopped screaming to catch her breath and came at Caleb's face with clawing fingers. He pushed her away, and she staggered back on the hearth then mounted a new charge, the poker as her weapon. Caleb was sober enough to deflect her first wild swing. He disarmed her and pushed her away again. She fell to the floor in the center of the cabin, and Ty stooped to help her up.

When she was on her feet again, Caleb ordered "Go back to bed, Son."

Rachel squalled and launched another attack. She rushed at Caleb and pounded his chest with her fists.

Ty stood as if frozen, witnessing his parents' fury.

Caleb warded off Rachel's blows. She gave up momentarily and turned to lean on her son, who placed an arm around her.

"Pa," he said, "what happened?"

"I said go to bed!" Caleb commanded, with force he'd never directed at the youth before.

Ty bristled at being denied any explanation of what caused all the fuss. "No," he refused, "I'm stayin' here til y'all tell me what's wrong."

Caleb pulled the sobbing Rachel away and grabbed his son's shoulder. He pushed him hard toward the ladder. "I said go!" he yelled, but Ty resisted. When Caleb pushed again, the sturdy youth lowered his head and wrapped his arms around his father's midsection. They stood locked in an upright wrestling match until Ty's bare feet made him lose traction. Caleb pushed the advantage, and as the youth gave ground, Rachel reentered the fray. Caleb did not see her take up the iron skillet from the hearth, but he felt it make contact with the side of his head.

Chapter 3: October Encounter, continued

Jenny's voice called from the cabin door, "Will ye be eatin' now?"

Her words brought Caleb back to the reality he treasured until the visitor appeared. The life this young woman had awakened and shared with him was so much more to his satisfaction than hazy recollections. He reached for her hand and pulled her down to be seated on the step beside him.

"Not hungry now," he said, "but your touch is always welcome."

She squeezed his hand and studied his eyes as if she expected a sign posted there would identify the subject of his concentration.

"The way of it is, I need to make sure the wee ones eat" she said, "but I'll stay a minute. Do ye know that young lad?"

Caleb returned her even gaze. "No... never seen him before. He's on the run from the fightin'. Said he's from a part of the country I knew... long time ago..."

Jenny waited for him to resume, but his silence indicated his mind remained back in whatever place that hint implied. The older man and the young woman considered the past to be unpleasant ground, and neither wasted time exploring it. Life anew had been their joint discovery on this Tennessee hillside. What preceded did not matter, if it ever had. But something back there had resurfaced in him. She rubbed the back of his neck.

"'Tis more thinkin' ye have to do," she said when she removed her hand and rose to her feet. "I'll keep yer stew warm."

He watched her return inside the cabin. He heard her admonish the little boy and girl for eating slowly. Smiling to himself, he looked out beyond the woodpile and the earthen mound where he had stored potatoes safe from frost and the winter ahead, down past withered cornstalks in fields shorn of harvest, all the way to the last traces of green in the cabbage and turnip patch along the creek at the foot of the hill. Not much of a farm compared to the old Willingham plantation, he admitted, except he could call this rocky slope his own. His farm and new family were greater rewards than anything he visualized that night he left South Carolina.

Chapter 4: Reverie, continued

Caleb walked away and did not look back. He stopped a short distance from the cabin to dig up his one remaining jug then hit the road. His head throbbed for hours. The thick mat of black hair had cushioned the blow which knocked him unconscious, but the aftershock remained.

He walked north toward Rutherfordton. Caleb reckoned that Rachel, once convinced of his leaving, would tell her family of his talk about Georgia. Let the Willinghams think what they will, he surmised. They would be wrong. Once they stopped bothering sheriffs in Georgia, they might show Ty more Willingham favor without Caleb around. A price he was willing to pay.

He waded the south fork of Pacolet River at daylight and reached the north fork well before midday without seeing a soul. Once he convinced himself he was well out of South Carolina, he left the Rutherfordton road and veered northwest toward the mountains. Nights were not yet too frosty for sleeping outdoors, but the coins in his pocket did not go far in obtaining food. He lived off the land, such as it was. With the blade of his long knife, he whittled a chip of hardwood into a fishhook. He cut a strip from his shirttail and wove the threads into a stout line to control the hook. Using a bug or worm as bait, he managed to catch a fish once in a while and roast it on a creek bank. He helped himself to vines of wild muscadines, the fruits of apple and persimmon trees, and gathered nuts at every opportunity. When he did not find water to drink, he chewed leaves for their moisture.

He crossed the French Broad River and wandered farther into western North Carolina. One morning at a swift-moving mountain stream he happened upon a sawmill of good size. Short-handed, the operator agreed to put him to work. Pay included a noon meal for all hands, and that inspired Caleb to give it his all. The exertion and his weakness from hunger made him light-headed, and he came close to passing out twice before the dinner bell rang. He went at his ration wolflike and stuffed bread in his pocket for supper. By workday's end, Caleb's effort inspired the operator to insist he stay on and sleep in the barn.

Caleb settled in for a time, thinking of nothing more than the daily work with its reward of Saturday nights with money in his pocket. That meant finding a tavern where he slaked his thirst then spent Sundays sleeping it off. Weeks became months. A year passed, then another, and Caleb stayed put until the work ran out.

On the move again, he trudged deeper into mountainous country, working whatever sawmill or blacksmith shop offered coins or food for a day's labor. A tinker's wagon slowed one day and offered a ride. The skinny old purveyor of pots and pans to Cherokees, burrowed in their mountain retreats to escape forced resettlement in the West, looked as shabby as Caleb and as worn out as the rattling wagon he drove.

They did not make it very far before Caleb realized why the tinker was so generous to a stranger. A wheel gave way as the battered wagon bumped across a rocky creekbed. Caleb's strong back became the tinker's means for removing the useless wheel then cutting and fitting replacement spokes to outfit the wagon to roll again.

They camped by the creek where the repairs were made. The tinker warmed a pot of beans and a stale lump of bread over the open fire. He shared a few bites of supper along with several swigs from a jug drug out of the wagon's cluttered interior. Later, he produced a brandy flask and insisted his guest must take a wee dram or two.

Caleb woke the next morning with a splitting head and emptied pockets. The tinker and his repaired wagon were long gone.

Stumbling on, Caleb became obsessed with passage through Unicoi Gap, crossing into Tennessee, and finding some opportunity to farm on his own. Aimless drifting had grown tiresome. He craved something to call a base again. The solution to his quest awaited at an Hiawassee River sawmill.

Jesse Murdock took a good look at the undernourished man standing before him and recognized the strength those broad shoulders and rough hands once possessed. When he witnessed Caleb's skill at shaping and fitting replacement wooden blades for the all-important waterwheel which powered the saws, Murdock knew he had not misjudged. The kind-hearted family man offered employment and living quarters in a shed behind his home adjacent to the mill. Caleb welcomed being trusted again, but he was honest in making his real goal known. They struck a deal, whereby Caleb would work fulltime until the sawmill's next slack period, when he would set out to explore where a small piece of a farm could be secured before he was expected back in the month Murdock designated.

The established pattern flourished, and both parties felt satisfied to continue it as time passed into the 1850s. Caleb accumulated a little money for once, and he steered clear of tinkers' wagons when scouting farms on both sides of the river. It did not take him long to make up his mind when he found a farmer willing to sell a 40-acre strip even though it was almost a full day's walk south of the sawmill. Once he saw the hillside with a freshwater spring, a few fields already cleared and the adjoining creek below, Caleb agreed to meet the farmer's terms and began building a chimney for a cabin before he had to return to the mill.

Murdock's trust in him inspired a serious effort to cut down the drinking, but Saturday nights still lured Caleb to overindulgence at Bragan's Tavern, a short walk uphill from the sawmill.

If Bragan had a first name, no one used it. The proprietor was a husky Irishman, well-suited to knocking heads together and maintaining a semblance of order in his place of business so long as he limited his own sips from the barrel. But his considerable thirst grew on Saturday nights while the dingy tavern's first floor became crowded to capacity. By 10 o'clock, the barmaster himself was usually unconscious behind the makeshift bar of rough planks balanced atop two upright barrels. Patrons at tables or seated on the floor downed drinks, laughed or argued spiritedly, and pestered the two serving girls Bragan employed to continue pouring when he could not. Caleb habitually sought a stool by the wall and waited for the whiskey to deafen him to the noise and obliterate the presence of its creators. Mrs. Bragan came down from upstairs about 11 o'clock to berate her husband, yell "Last Call," and empty the money drawer. Pushed outside at closing time, Caleb reeled or tumbled to his shed in back of the Murdock house.

That routine was broken the night he stirred from stupor and went to the aid of the serving girl being pawed by two drunken loudmouths at a table in front of him. He reacted because the girl was Jenny.

She had shown up at Bragan's during one of Caleb's absences from the sawmill while building his cabin. Her shy manner, so out of place in the boisterous tavern, drew his immediate attention. Tish, who usually fetched Caleb's drinks, told him Jenny had been sent to the tavern when a band of stonecutters came from the Bragan couple's former village in Ireland to work marble quarries below the Tennessee-Georgia line. Instead of helping the girl find a housekeeping job, the Bragans used her skills for themselves.

Tish was a plump woman, sassy and experienced at holding her own with rough customers. Her big galoot of a husband came into the tavern often enough to pose a looming threat to anyone giving Tish a hard time. Sharp contrast to vulnerable young Jenny, who ducked her head at each liquored up suggestion from some rowdy who wanted more than a fresh drink. Caleb watched with sympathetic eyes as the Saturday nights went by but figured tavern girls learn to fend for themselves.

The night before departure for another stay at the farm, he dropped into Bragan's to spend a few hours and, before he had time to think about it, became drawn into Jenny's predicament. From his accustomed perch by the wall, he noticed the two strangers at the table in front of him paw at her each time she passed by. She dodged the swiping hands until one of them grabbed her by the arm and pulled her down across his lap. His table companion leaned in to give support. They pinned her arms quickly, and the one who yanked her off her feet began

35

to press his mouth on hers and to run his free arm beneath her skirt.

Caleb left his stool and towered over the aggressor. "Let her go," he ordered.

The man ignored the warning and pressed his mouth hard against the struggling Jenny. The man on the opposite side of the small table rose to his feet and glared at Caleb.

"What business you got, Mister?" he demanded.

"It's not my business, but it is hers," said Caleb, "She don't seem to like bein' pulled off her feet."

The man lurched around the table and took a wild swing at Caleb's jaw. Caleb punched him in the gut. The man sagged back against the table and his friend. The one who held Jenny raised his head to see what had interrupted his conquest. Caleb grabbed him beneath the chin and hauled him to his feet. "Leave the girl to her work and go on with your drinkin'," Caleb said.

Jenny bounced up and fled to the back of the tavern. Both men now came at Caleb with arms swinging from all directions. Caleb landed as many punches as he received. They knocked over tables and stools while spectators scrambled to clear the way as the brawl increased in intensity. The commotion stirred a semi-conscious Bragan into action, and the big proprietor rushed forward wielding the club he called "Shillelegh."

"Out with the lot of ye," he bellowed, and whacked all three combatants as he pushed them to the door.

They tumbled outside to continue the fight on the ground. With a pair of legs locked around each of Caleb's own to imprison him, their four arms eventually overpowered his two. They pounded him until they exhausted themselves. Caleb's body suffered a final round of kicks when the original assailant wheezed himself to a standing position and prodded his ally to do likewise. Both staggered away to the road.

Caleb refused to crawl. He lay where he had been mauled until he could struggle to his feet and wobble downhill to his shed. Once inside, he dipped a hand in the water bucket, splashed his face, and wiped blood from his nose. He fell across his bunk and passed out.

An irritating, irregular sound of knocking broke his spell. Uncertain whether he had slept for 10 minutes or two hours, he tried to ignore the rapping but failed. The noise made his head hurt more. From his last remnants of strength, he managed to stand, stagger to the door, and open a narrow space where Jenny's face appeared in the moonlight.

Her Irish brogue was not easy for the dazed Caleb to understand, but he thought he heard her say "Tish told me where ye live. Are ye hurt bad?"

He leaned against the door jamb and shook his head. "I'll be all right," he said. "Movin' on today. Bruises them fellers put on me will heal at my farmplace."

She began to talk rapidly, and Caleb made out what he thought to be "Take me wi' ye."

He stared at her with the best concentration bleary eyes would allow. "What?" he mumbled, and then he saw the bundle at her feet. A rounded lump in a blanket or heavy shawl. This young woman obviously intended to go somewhere.

"Hold on," Caleb said. "I got no place for takin' anybody in." He started to say more, but her pleading face added to the confusion in his swirling head. Before he could react, she joined him in the shed. First running a hand across his face, she drew a small cloth from a pocket of her skirt and looked around the darkened interior. Spotting the bucket, she splashed water on the cloth and wiped his swollen face.

"Tis rest ye need. Lie back down," she said. "I'll wait."

"No!" he protested. "The Murdocks will see you when daylight comes... maybe others, too. You've got to git while it's dark."

"I'll have nae more of that tavern, I tell ye," she interrupted. "Let me travel wi' ye. I'll nae be a burden. Tis yer help I beg to go away from this evil place. I know little of the country." And then, child-like, "Please?"

Caleb shook his head as if that would remove this additional ache. He was in no shape for clear thinking. He had to get rid of this girl and get some rest.

"Listen... do this," he said slowly to allow time to awaken his wits. "A short way up the hill past the tavern there's a fork in the road. Take the left, and go a half mile or so... you'll see a little waterfall comin' out the side of the hill and tricklin' 'cross the road. Go on past and wait in the bushes you'll see on the left side. I'll be along when it's good light. I reckon you can walk a ways along with me if you're so bound on goin'. But we can't be seen leavin' the community together."

He fell back across the bunk but issued one last instruction.

"You ain't stayin' with me. Understood?"

She picked up her bundle. "Understood," she said as she went out the door and closed it behind her.

Chapter 5: Reverie, continued

Aromas of hot coffee and breakfast preparations engulfed Caleb when the Murdocks' back door opened. He grabbed the handrail at the steps to keep from falling.

Jesse Murdock began his customary greeting, "Mornin' Caleb, good day to..." The sawmill proprietor stopped in mid-sentence after a close look at his top millhand weaving unsteadily before him. Disappointment spread across Murdock's face, but he withheld another lecture on Caleb's Saturday night habits and invited him into the warm kitchen.

"Another cup, Rhoda," Murdock requested of his wife, who looked up from stirring contents of a large skillet on the stove. "Sit here, Caleb. You look like you need coffee...and quick."

Caleb accepted the invitation to sit as well as the steaming contents of the cup his employer shoved across the table. Gripping the cup with both hands, he took a big swallow and avoided Murdock's eyes until he felt reasonably sure the first gulp would stay down. When that swallow had been followed by three more in rapid succession, Caleb eased the cup safely to the table.

He mumbled words of gratitude and explanation to his host and employer. "I 'pologize I look like this. Some trouble at Bragan's last night. Never started it, but I came out of it a little bruised up. Fresh air will do me good... I'll make it to my cabin 'fore dark."

Mrs. Murdock placed a plate topped by biscuits and gravy before her husband and turned back to the stove. Murdock insisted that Caleb must share their breakfast before he thought of going anywhere. The coffee and the aromas from the stove inspired a raging appetite, fed generously by the couple who valued Caleb's years of hard work at the sawmill.

After he cleaned the well-filled plate offered him, he shoved back from the table and savored the last sips of his third cup of coffee. Mrs Murdock brought out a jar of salve and daubed the raw broken skin of Caleb's face. He almost turned down her suggestion that he tuck a few biscuits in his jacket pockets before he remembered Jenny waiting by the road.

Murdock walked with him to the back steps. "The shape you're in, Caleb," the mill proprietor observed, "I'd feel better 'bout you walkin' that long way if you let one of the hounds go along with you." He pointed to a dog trotting toward the house from a shed where lumber was stored . "That one...Jackson... likes you. If you fall out on the road somewhere today, he'll wander back here and let me know."

Caleb looked down at the light brown dog approaching the steps. The name Jackson had been suggested by Caleb himself three years before, when Jesse Murdock showed a new litter in the family of dogs who inhabited the millhouse. "That one's bossy like a general" Caleb remarked on staring at the feistiest of a half dozen pups.

While the dog sniffed Caleb's boots to gain attention, Murdock reentered the kitchen and returned with scraps from the breakfast table. He tossed them out. Jackson devoured the bits of meat and table leavings as soon as they hit the ground.

"That'll get him set to cover some miles with you," Murdock said. He stuck out his hand to bid Caleb farewell. "I'll send word to that store near your place when business picks up again."

Caleb returned to the shed, the hound at his heels, and retrieved a sack of belongings left by the door. He was too sore to sling the parcel over his shoulder as called for by habit. He squatted instead, back to the wall, and pushed the sack against the shed until he could arch his body beneath it. Jackson followed his steps to the road up the hill and away from the river.

The morning sun was warm, and Caleb's movements grew less painful as he plodded along. Bragan's Tavern sat barren of any sign of the prior night's activity. Man and dog moved past without seeing anyone and reached the fork in the uphill climb where Caleb paused to catch his breath. The road to the left had been hacked into the side of the hill and offered a gradual descent for a quarter mile before the pathway climbed again for a hundred yards or so then began a second descent.

Once across the rocky bed of the thin runoff from the waterfall, Caleb began to scan the growth of fern, sumac, and bramble on the left side of the road where he told Jenny to wait. He hesitated to call her name aloud and chose to whistle instead. Repeats of the signal brought no response.

He left the road to push his way into the thicket. Jackson nosed his way ahead, being able to slip beneath entangling limbs that snagged the sack on Caleb's shoulder and slowed his advance. He was about to turn back to the road and search for a better way into the bushes when he heard a whimpering sound then Jackson's bark. Forcing his way forward, Caleb stumbled into a small clearing.

Jenny sat on the ground with the hound standing beside her. A heavy shawl covered her shoulders. Garments lay scattered about her, but Caleb's more immediate concern was the rock in her upraised hand and the wild look in her eyes.

Caleb dropped the sack from his shoulder and used his right arm as a shield.

"Wait, girl," he hurried to say, "you don't need no rock..."

The look of terror on Jenny's face softened when she recognized her defender of the night before. She dropped the rock and made a weak attempt to stand.

"Be they gone?" she implored.

"Who?" Caleb answered as he stepped to assist her.

"*Them* from the tavern," she said. "Scared the life out o' me, they did, when I came upon 'em. Sleepin'... out there in the road." She began to cry. "I stifled me scream... but one woke up and saw me before..." Her words became unintelligible sobs.

Caleb removed his hat and rubbed his sore head. He realized directions he gave Jenny failed to take into account her attackers might have gone the same way. Half-conscious when the two men left him in the tavern yard, he had no idea where they went. "Did they harm you?" he asked, dreading the reply he expected.

"They..." she choked out, "they... had their way wi' me." She covered her face with her hands and slumped to her knees. "I could nae get away."

Caleb placed a hand on her shoulder and sought to steady her balance between sobs. His own guilt hung heavily, although he wondered what else he should have done. Was he at fault, or were the Bragans and the parents in Georgia who sent this girl off on her own more responsible than he?

"How long ago, Jenny?" For the first time, he addressed her by name. A small effort at expressing compassion but the best Caleb could do. He waited while her sobs diffused into loud sniffles.

"I dinna know... before daylight," she managed to say between sniffles. She looked up, a plea for understanding in her eyes. "After they left me, I crawled back here. When ye came, I was ever so frightened it was...them." She wiped her eyes and reached for his arm to pull herself to her feet.

Caleb reckoned the men had a head start of three or four hours in whatever direction they headed. The road ahead connected with a number of trails and side roads, like the one Caleb used to reach his farm, before it wound up in the town of Cleveland, the county seat. The chance of following or ever seeing the men again was a slim one.

He reached in a pocket of his jacket and retrieved one of Rhoda Murdock's biscuits. "Here," he offered, "take a little food. Be careful with the crumbs, or that hound will be all over you to git 'em."

Jenny accepted the biscuit eagerly and stuffed a piece of it in her mouth.

"Maybe you ought to go back to Bragan's," Caleb suggested gently.

"*Nae!*" she sputtered in the midst of a second bite.. "I'll nivver go back there! He's bad, but she's worse. Nivver stops yellin'... 'Empty them slops...clean that floor....fetch me my knittin',' And if she finds out I've been ruined..."

The pained way she said the last word made Caleb shudder in sympathy for the way this young girl had been treated.

"What about Tish?" he asked. "She'd take you in."

43

Jenny shook her head. "She lives too close to the tavern. I'd soon be found out."

Caleb scratched his bearded jaw and considered his options. Leave the girl here and trust she'd change her mind about returning. Or go along a ways and search for a solution.

The second option won out.

"Do you think you can walk?" he asked. "If you can, we'd better git goin'. Mornin's half gone already."

"Don't leave me here," she begged. "I'll keep up wi' ye." She brushed her skirt and stooped to gather her scattered garments. Spreading her shawl flat on the ground, she piled clothing in the center, pulled the four corners into place, and fashioned them into a knot,

Caleb watched with disapproving eyes and took the bundle from her. "Let me show you a better way," he said and untied the knot, shifted the contents, and tightly fastened two shawl corners into a strap for each side of her shoulders. He walked behind her, slipped her arms through the straps, and raised the weight to her shoulder-level.

"There," he said, " it's a heap better way to tote that bundle."

He led the way to the road and turned back to the little waterfall.

"Might as well take advantage of some fresh water before we set out," he said. They took turns cupping hands into the rivulet to gulp several swallows apiece. Jackson did not waste the opportunity to lap his own supply down where the stream reached the road.

A sudden concern for what Jenny had been forced to endure overrode Caleb's thinking about his own aches. Man, young woman, and hound moved out in the sun-brightened road. One of the trio had a definite destination in mind. The others followed on faith.

They reached the cabin at sundown. Progress slowed each time he called a halt to allow her to rest. A long stop was in order where Caleb knew of a freshwater spring just off the road. They finished off the last two biscuits there.

The next to last stop came at Pickett's Store, a little over a mile from the cabin. Jenny and the dog waited outside while Caleb went in to pay what he owed for supplies bought on his last stay at the farm. He emerged with a peck of corn meal, a big chunk of streak o' lean, and sacks of dried beans and grits.

He unlocked the log cabin's one door and opened it wide to let in the daylight that remained. The cabin had no window. Interior visibility depended on the door being left open in good weather and a blazing fireplace in bad conditions or nighttime. A flagstone hearth served as the kitchen. Caleb had cobbled a stand of iron rods which fit within the fireplace and over the front burning log for a skillet to rest on top. A kettle hung from an iron hook, and an iron pot with cover sat on the hearth, ready to do its work in the ashes. A collection of jugs, clay bowls and small containers for salt and meager items in food preparation sat on a crude table in the corner beyond the hearth and opposite the door.

Caleb placed the goods from Pickett's on the table and went back outside to get water from the spring and wood for a fire. Jackson attempted to follow him inside but was quickly banished.

Jenny took silent inventory of the cabin interior while Caleb kindled a fire. The hearth was the only floor covering; the packed ground made up the rest. Furnishings consisted of a lone wooden stool sitting close to the hearth and, farther back, a wood-framed bunk. Blankets lay in a heap in the dark corner opposite the bunk. Clothing hung from pegs along the walls.

Caleb did not turn from his task at the hearth to speak over his shoulder.

"As you see, I'm not able to accommodate company. But I know you're tired, so we'll make the best of it tonight."

"Oh..." she hastened to reply, "I'm thankin' ye for kindnesses done me already. If I kin just rest here tonight, I'll be on me way tomorrow." She placed her bundle on the ground, sat on the stool, and watched him coax the first flickers of flame.

As the fireplace lit the room, Caleb's sharp knife sliced four strips of salt pork and dropped them in the hot skillet. He scooped up the cooked strips of meat, mixed grease, corn meal, and a little water in a bowl, patted out two flat circles of dough, and spread them on the hot hearth. Their simple supper materialized in a few minutes, and they washed it down with spring water. Crumbs were tossed out to the dog.

She almost fell asleep while they ate, and Caleb insisted that she stretch out on the bunk. "I'll make a pallet here by the hearth," he assured.

"All right... if ye say," she mumbled as she lay down. "I'll be up and on me way tomorrow... give ye nae more trouble, I vow..." Her exhaustion trumped her saying more..

Caleb slipped the shoes from her feet and turned back to attend to items used in the meal. He took the skillet outside and scrubbed it clean with sand. He checked on Jackson and found the hound had rooted out a resting place near the door. "Make yourself at home," he said to the dog.

46

He walked in back of the cabin and cut several low hanging branches off treelimbs to place beneath a blanket and cushion his sleeping pallet above the ground. He carried the armload to the cabin's door and stood awhile studying the clear night sky. A panorama of stars winked down on southeast Tennessee. Good weather for planting, he figured. He would see his neighbor early in the morning to ask when he might borrow the use of a mule, then go to Pickett's for supplies. In another year, he hoped, he'd be able to buy a mule to occupy the stable already built. One day he'd add a cow, and some pigs, as well. Farm plans always tumbled about in Caleb's mind faster than he could act on them. Inside the cabin another matter – someone, actually – made his jumbled thoughts turn even faster.

He knew the planting would be attended to in due time. He had returned to do just that, nothing more. He would not be distracted. In the morning he would suggest that Jenny return to Georgia and find her parents.

He left right after they breakfasted on grits and more fried streak o'lean. She said she would act on his suggestion about Georgia. "Sure, and I'll be off there before ye get back," she promised. "I'm rested now... I'll nae be a concern to ye. Tis long I'll remember the kindnesses of Caleb Morgan."

Jackson followed him on the way to neighbor Sam Greer's place. Greer, who sold Caleb the 40 acre tract, consented to an occasional loan of a mule or farm tool in return for Caleb's labor on some task the neighboring man found difficult to handle by himself. That very day he talked Caleb into plowing one of the mules in a field where Greer was planting corn, but he pledged Caleb could borrow the animal the following day. That meant a weary Caleb did not get back to the cabin until twilight.

Smoke rose from the chimney and the door stood open. As he walked up with Jackson, the strange sight of a woman's garments spread across his woodpile confronted him. He heard the humming of a tune. He stopped at the door and looked in at Jenny, kneeling at the hearth. A wad of cloth covered the hand she used to tug the cooking pot from its bed of coals onto the hearth. She raised her head when his shadow filled the doorway.

"I was about to leave when I decided to wash the clothes I had on," she hurried to explain. "I felt so dirty in 'em..." she looked down at the cloth she held, "because of what happened."

When Caleb did not speak, she began again. "I saw the wash-pot and that wooden tub and bucket out there... and the creek at the bottom of the hill. Didn't take long to fetch water. Used a few sticks of yer wood and boiled me clothes. Had meself a quick bath before I poured the water out. I hope yer not cross wi' me."

He walked in and hung his hat on a peg by the door. He was tired from a day of plowing and had no energy to spare on another surprise.

"I saw that sack o' beans," she said. "Soaked some all mornin'... simmered in the pot the rest of the day, they have. Yer supper's 'bout ready. Tis true me things will be good and dry after a day in that sunshine."

She slipped past him and made her way to gather the clothing from the woodpile. Caleb sighed and slumped on the stool, too tired to wonder what surprise might come next. The aroma rising from the pot of beans made him feel a little better.

A country-style chess match had begun. Except the players kept making feints instead of moves.

She vowed each morning at breakfast she would be leaving that very day. He said that sounded best, wished her well, went on to the task of planting his fields, and withheld comment when she appeared at midday bringing him food and a jug of water. As he worked through each afternoon, he glanced more than once to see if smoke continued to rise from the chimney. When he came in from his day's work, she chattered how starting a journey late in the day was bad luck or some other bit of Irish superstition. The meal she had ready for him became more important to Caleb than her excuses for staying or her daily attempts to neaten his cabin's drab interior.

She talked him into one such innovation the second night after they arrived. She held one end of a blanket against the wall a couple feet from the head of the bunk while he drove a peg into a log to secure it. They stretched the blanket to its full length, tied the far end to a clothes peg, and let it hang. The draped corner then gave shadowed privacy for dressing or donning her nightgown. To show her gratitude, she insisted Caleb take the bunk while she bedded down on the pallet.

All the years Caleb had been separated from intimate contact with a woman did not blind him nor immobilize his reaction to the presence of an attractive female. Seeing Jenny's fair face and slender figure, and the graceful way she glided through chores within his arm's reach, stirred Caleb's awareness of a part of life he had neglected. The difference in their ages, however, applied a brake to his pursuing such thoughts toward this young woman.

49

Her unfortunate experience after leaving the tavern was burden enough to carry, and he dismissed any notion of allowing his own physical desire to add to it.

Sam Greer came by one day and saw Jenny draping wet garments across a rope she stretched from the unoccupied stable to a sapling near it. He walked past without speaking and made a detour to Caleb, setting out potato plants.

"Takin' in boarders now, Caleb?" Greer asked.

Caleb offered the briefest explanation he could come up with on short notice. "That lass wanted to walk with me from Murdock's. She's goin' to her kin in Georgia... in a day or so," he said without looking up.

Greer glanced back at Jenny but shifted his remarks to Caleb's rapid planting accomplishments before he moved on to his own fields. "Bound to happen," Caleb muttered. "Word'll spread purty quick."

Two weeks went by, and then another. Caleb planted patches of both sweet and white potatoes and seeded three acres with corn. Jenny did not leave. When he finished putting in onions and beans in the garden spot by the creek, he decided to plant peppers as well. That meant a walk to Pickett's for seed.

Oliver Pickett hailed him as he stepped through the door. "Glad you came in, Caleb. Letter for you." The store served as post office as well as merchant to farmers in the vicinity. Caleb knew the letter had to be from Jesse Murdock.

He explained the situation to Jenny that night. Murdock wanted him back at the sawmill as soon as possible He would finish the planting in a couple days, then he would leave. From what Murdock wrote, more than a month's worth of work was underway at the mill.

He did not mention it again until the night before his planned departure. She busied herself more each day – washing his long-neglected clothing, scouring the woods for herbs for the cook pot, bringing shrubs and wildflowers into the cabin where heat from the fireplace wilted them quickly – without hinting of any preparation to go.

"I 'spect you could stay here..." he began in a low voice from his seat on a newly constructed second stool, "a while longer til you decide to go."

Her green eyes opened wide but she said nothing.

"The Greers know that you're here," he continued. "I reckon they'd...."

Jenny interrupted him.

"Tis a burden of confession on me heart, Caleb Morgan," she whispered, glancing down where her hands smoothed her skirt. She raised her head and her voice gained strength, "I di' nae go because I di' nae want to leave the kindest man I've met. I'll deceive ye nae longer... ye've been too good to me."

Caleb frowned and pretended to concentrate on the flames in the open fireplace.

He cleared his throat and faced her once more. "Is it true your people sent you to Bragan's?"

"Tis gospel truth, I tell ye," she replied quickly. "Pap's a stone-cutter, one of 'em workin' the marble. Mam's one of the cooks. Me sister Annie watches over the wee ones... five of 'em. I'm the oldest. They made me sail wi' 'em because, back in Ballycarry, they didn't like me seein' Fergus McCready. The Bragans left our village before the terrible hunger set in... 'twas Mam's notion I go to 'em for help findin' work as a housekeeper or scullery maid." She smoothed another fold of her skirt. "She'd nae want me back.... a failure."

Caleb could understand that fear of the unknown in strange and rough country may have added to her hesitation. However, she had assured him before they left Murdock's that his permitting her to walk with him a few miles from the tavern meant nothing more, and she would make her own way. Then she told him about the rape. At the time he took her word about that just as he accepted her promises to move on. The way she had extended her stay at the cabin from days to weeks made him wonder if bruises on her face the morning he found her could have been a self-inflicted act to gain his sympathy. Caleb felt he had a right to know if she had more to confess.

"Tell me, Jenny," he said softly, "did anything happen? Back there on the road?"

Her hands flew to her face, and a little gasp escaped her lips. She broke into tears and turned away from him.

He reached to remove her hand and lift her chin with his fingers. Her loud sniffs faded to whimpers, and she swallowed hard before she spoke.

"Them two," she stammered, "yes. *Both* of 'em, like I told ye. Right there in the road. Horrible, it was." She lowered her hands, crossed her arms, and leaned forward on the stool before raising her head to face him again. "I'd nivver lie 'bout that."

He placed his palm on her shoulder for a moment then rested his elbows on his knees and stared into the fire. He had no use for liars. His simple code for living expected the truthfulness from others that Caleb demanded of himself. Hard experience taught him to discard bad apples like Sumter Willingham and place his trust in men like Jesse Murdock, Oliver Pickett, and Sam Greer. The way it should be between grown men, Caleb reckoned.

But this lass seemed no more than a year or two older than he had been at the time he wandered onto the Willingham plantation. By then he had acquired a smattering of survival skills. She had been uprooted from all she knew in a land across the ocean and sent off to make her own way in rough country. The two men from the tavern were not the only wolves lurking along her path, and the Bragans were not the only creatures waiting to shear this lamb.

They watched in silence as the fire reduced itself to embers. Caleb's resentment of being victim of her little deceit about leaving waned as he realized his damages were slight. His pride would recover. She had the greater task recovering from her loss of innocence. He had no remedy for that, but he could offer shelter until the lamb felt brave again.

He rose to his feet, stretched his arms, and rubbed his back. "Then we'll say no more about it," he said. "But you must see I can't spare time to make this place comfortable to anybody 'cept me and that hound dog out there. I reckon there's no harm in you stayin' a few more days. Then you might try findin' work in Cleveland… somebody there who'll take you in. It's all right to walk the roads in daytime. The dog'll likely tag along with me. I'll stop at the store on my way. Oliver Pickett will let you have what food you need til you go. He'll mark it down in his ledger. Let's talk no more tonight."

Jesse Murdock had not underestimated the need for Caleb's help at the sawmill. The customary pace Murdock maintained with two fulltime employees could not cope with the surge of new business brought on after another mill on the Hiawassee burned to the ground. When Caleb arrived in late April, the reinforced crew needed more than a month to turn all the logs waiting to be cut into planks and joists for construction.

The hound's hanging about the shed was the only reminder of the farm. Caleb collapsed on his bunk each night, too tired to wonder about Jenny. He stayed away from the tavern or cut short Saturday nights there as a sacrifice to his need for rest. Bragan had not replaced Jenny, and that gave Tish less time to talk. Caleb did not ask questions nor volunteer any information.

The month of June was half gone before he could leave the mill to see about his crops. His dread of weeds choking the sprouts of corn made him hurry his walk back, or so he convinced himself. But thoughts of Jenny's whereabouts filled his mind as he moved farther from Murdock's and Pickett's store came into view.

The storekeeper continued serving a woman customer and scarcely looked up when Caleb walked in. Full eye contact and greeting had to wait until the two men were alone.

Oliver Pickett, ledger in hand, was ready to talk. "That young woman has been in a few times since you left, Caleb." he said. The storekeeper placed the ledger on the counter and thumbed its pages.

"I figured she'd need a little food 'fore she left," Caleb said as he bent his neck to see the page where Pickett's thumb rested.

"Not much in the way of food... she must eat no more'n a sparrow," the storekeeper confided. "You never said she'd be wantin' needles and thread... scissors... yards of cloth... candles and such, but you see what's listed here. Comes to twelve dollars and thirty cents. I done told her that's the limit til you got back."

Caleb glanced up from the ledger. "Is she still here, Oliver?" he asked hurriedly, seeking reestablished eye contact.

Pickett responded with a questioning frown. "Far's I know. Don't know what you expected."

Caleb reached in his pocket for money Jesse Murdock paid him and counted out what was needed to clear the sum. He thanked Pickett for trusting him to make it good and purchased a few items before he left the store. He whistled for the hound and resumed his walk.

The answer to his question appeared in a wisp of smoke rising from his cabin's chimney. The sight did not displease him although he had refused to anticipate it. Though short on comfort, the farm was important to him. He would spend his full time working the soil in harmony with nature if he could afford it. The money from Murdock's sawmill was essential until a fully producing farm could provide a living.

He did not see how anyone like Jenny, accustomed to being around others her own age, could tolerate the isolation. The young Irishman she mentioned – McCready – had no contemporary in these parts. In Cleveland, perhaps, but not out here.

To signal his approach, he slapped the hound's rump and sent him running ahead, barking all the way to the cabin. Caleb fixed his eyes on the open doorway.

Jenny appeared, wiping her hands on an apron and squinting into the afternoon sunshine. Jackson ran to her and received a welcoming pat on his head. Caleb walked up in silence.

"Tis pleased I am to see ye," she said with a smile.

She wore a white blouse above a long blue skirt he had not seen before he left. That explains the sewing goods he had just paid for, Caleb reckoned.

He made no mention of her purchases but commented on her appearance and good spirit before giving a brief recount of the work at the mill. After they supped on potato soup – made of ingredients she dug from the first products of his planting – he made a quick survey of his fields to determine where to start in the morning. When he returned to the cabin at dusk, she presented him with a surprise. A new shirt made from material like that of her blue skirt and another shirt of a black fabric.

"I took apart that ragged one ye left hangin' ," she spoke in a rush, "and cut cloth to fit. Tis little enough I kin do to thank ye. I hope ye don't mind me sewin' a few things for meself... when I go to that town ye spoke of... to seek work."

He accepted the gifts wordlessly except for an observation that her skill with a needle should serve her well when she went into Cleveland. He was ready to retire for the night in order to get an early start in the fields.

When he kindled a fire next morning, she was up and off to the spring to fetch water for the kettle. They soon had breakfast preparation well underway. Jenny fried strips of bacon while he sliced a cantaloupe brought from Pickett's until she suddenly let go of the hot skillet and ran from the cabin. He grabbed hold of the pan, scooped out the bacon before it burned, and sat down to eat. She returned a few minutes later, apologizing for a queasy stomach.

That first incident led him to suspect she had not been eating a sufficient amount, in line with Oliver Pickett's words. But a repeat performance the second morning spun Caleb's mind back through the years to a time he witnessed another woman's morning sickness before the birth of a child. He dreaded knowing whether this was Jenny's introduction to pregnancy. His appetite for breakfast vanished.

As soon as she came back in, he suggested she go across the fields to see Beulah Greer. Sam Greer's wife had borne children, he explained, and might well identify the cause for Jenny's upset stomach.

Jenny stared at him. Her pale cheeks flushed. She drew in breath and placed a hand on the wall for support. "*Nae!*...tis awful enough already," she cried in terror.

Caleb nodded. "You need to find out. Miz Greer can tell you more than I can. One of them fellers may have left you more than bruises and hurt."

She ran out the door.

Caleb looked up from thinning tender sprouts of corn and confronted the cause of a shadow above the spot where he knelt. The stout figure of Beulah Greer stood before him, hands on hips, face shaded beneath a broad sunbonnet.

"Unless I'm badly mistaken, that girl's pregnant," she said. "She told me you never touched her. Is that true?"

Caleb remained on his knees, uncertain what he should say. He had spoken brief words of greeting to Sam Greer's wife only in times when he went to see Sam on some matter. The first direct question she had ever asked him could be answered easily, but he did not know what else Jenny may have said.

"I swear that's the truth, Miz Greer."

The woman's eyes did not blink. Her stern countenance held as firm as her words. "Well, what else was a body to believe?

57

Her bein' under your roof all these weeks? I don't know what to make of all she said... sent off by her folks to be a slave in some tavern... rough sorts molested her... and then did worse to her on the road. Are you believin' all that?"

He rose to his full height and wiped sweat from his face with the back of his hand. "That's what she told me, too," he said. He vouched for the trouble at the tavern and explained how his intention to help her leave led to her being on the road where the assault evidently took place. "I felt sorry for her, Miz Greer. I meant to put her up a day or so... never a thought it would last this long. I 'spect she's skeered to go off on her own. Soon as I give these plants a better chance to grow, I meant to go with her to Cleveland one day soon where somebody might take her in."

"Well, whoever might have been willin' to do so before would put her out once she starts to show," Beulah Greer said in dry tones. "And that's not many weeks ahead. You'll have to see her through this, Mister Morgan. Nowhere else for her to go now. I'll be here to help when her time comes," she concluded.

Caleb thought he saw a sympathetic expression in her face before she turned to go. But her words weighed heavy on his conscience. The thing he dreaded had been confirmed. She spoke truth. If ever there had been another way to deal with the matter, that solution no longer existed.

"We'll have to make the best of it," he mumbled as he knelt again to pull the scrawniest sprouts of corn from each cluster and leave the sturdiest room to become an ear-producing stalk.

Jenny spent most of the following month in tears. She resented Caleb's attempts to console.

"Ye sent me out on that road by meself," she charged. "Why'd ye nae let me stay the night in that shed? And leave wi' ye? Tis yer own fault what happened."

"I'd lose my job if the Murdocks saw a woman leave that shed, Jenny," he said. "You could see I wuz in no shape to go anywhere that night. If anybody saw us leave in daylight, Bragan would know how to come after you. You left at night so he wouldn't. Don't you see?"

She cried louder. "Tis nae comfort to me now."

Caleb stayed busy in the fields and evaded saying more than necessary at mealtime. He talked Sam Greer into sharing a few pieces of scrap lumber so that a second bunk for the cabin could be built.

He returned to the sawmill once the corn grew tall enough to fend for itself. Storekeeper Pickett consented to again supply Jenny's needs and post them in his ledger. Caleb came back to the farm after an absence of six weeks driving a mule and wagon on loan from Jesse Murdock. The wagon bed held several planks of wood with a window featuring four small panes of glass, a handsaw, and other tools resting on top.

He stayed a week at the farm, checking the growth of his crop and using spare time to open a space halfway up the cabin wall opposite the door. Once he chinked the new frame to the wall with mud, he placed the window upright in the opening. Next he attached leather straps at the top and bottom of one side so the window could be swung back into the cabin, clear the usual smoky interior, and allow in fresh air. He stood back and admired the newly opened view of woods and sky.

Jenny had mumbled a few words of apology and appreciation when he built the new bunk, but her face lit up while she watched him work at the window.

"Oh, tis a lovely sight... blue sky, clouds, green trees, and growin' things," she sighed when he had finished. "Just like Ballycarry."

From that moment she seemed at peace with her situation. She had cried herself out. She could place her palms at her midsection without breaking into sobs of woe. What was to be would be, her actions began to say.

The window brightened more than the cabin's interior.

A relieved Caleb returned the mule and wagon to Murdock.

Beulah Greer supervised Jenny's delivery of a baby boy in January 1858. Mother and son came through their shared experience in good form, and Jenny's face beamed when she saw the well-used cradle brought over by Sam Greer.

Caleb kept a fire going and stayed out of the way. After Beulah Greer returned to her home at dawn, Jenny's knack of handling the baby surprised Caleb until he recalled her saying she was the oldest of several children. That meant practice tending to little ones, he reckoned, even newborns.

The sight that pleased him most was Jenny's unmistakable joy in holding her baby son. Her face had never shown such a look of contentment. She seemed to have dismissed all concern for the bad circumstances which led to her becoming a mother. This child had been given to her. Her actions showed there should be no doubt about his care or the love he would receive.

She coped with the baby's nights of colic and hummed lullabies to still his fretting in daytime. If anything looked more serious, she bundled him up and sought the advice of Beulah Greer. One such visit when the baby was a month old led the older woman to raise the subject of his need of a name.

"She said she wondered if I'd name him after Pap," Jenny told Caleb when she returned to the cabin. "Don't feel right 'bout that. Might be more shame than honor."

"Reckon you should suit yourself," Caleb volunteered. "And take your time."

Caleb returned to the sawmill once the baby's safe arrival and well-being were assured. April brought him back to the farm for a longer stay as owner of a mule and the two-wheel cart it pulled. A cupboard lay full-length across the bed of the cart with a wooden trunk balanced on top. He had cobbled both pieces of furniture by candlelight each night in Murdock's shed.

Jenny announced the baby's name was to be William. "'Tis a strong name," she said as she excitedly took charge of fitting the new furnishings into the cabin's cramped interior. While she moved things about and filled the new storage spaces, he borrowed a plow from Sam Greer, hitched the mule to it, and broke ground for planting to his heart's content.

At the early July "lay by time" – when farmers deemed crops hardy enough to grow on their own – Caleb went back to the mill for two months of steady employment. The pattern to his coming and going needed few if any words. He expected her to be there when he came back, and she gave him no reason to believe otherwise. Sam Greer agreed to stable the mule during each absence in exchange for Caleb's pledge of labor at harvest time.

By September he sensed an eagerness to get back to the farm that transcended the usual concern for the size his sweet potatoes would reach or how much corn and fodder the stalks should yield. He did not let on to anyone at the mill how or when he began to think of a home, not just a farm. Of the two settings – the near-emptiness of the shed in back of the Murdock house, and the newfound liveliness within the crowded cabin – his preference for the latter grew more dominant each day.

A thunderstorm broke long before he and the hound reached Pickett's Store. Sopping wet, he stopped to transact what business needed attention and continued on to the cabin. Jenny opened the door as soon as she heard the oncoming Jackson's bark. Caleb stumbled in, the uninvited dog right behind.

She took the items brought from the store and ushered Caleb to stand on the hearth. The hound's shaking water from his hide brought a cry of alarm from Jenny before she grabbed a piece of an old blanket she had turned into a throw rug and draped it over Jackson.

"Soaked through, ye be," she said as she pulled at Caleb's jacket. He tossed his dripping hat aside and seated himself on a stool. She tugged at the jacket until he slid both arms free and let her drop it on the hearth. She knelt to pull at his shoes. "Ye must get out o' wet shoes now," she scolded. "Put yer feet to the fire."

The disturbance woke the baby, whose cry demanded attention. Jenny began to rock the cradle and croon one of her lullabies. With the baby soothed, she began to tug at Caleb's wet shirt.

"Leave me be, Jenny," he protested. "I'll dry off here by the fire."

"Ye'll dry quicker wi' this shirt off yer back," she chattered and commanded him to raise his arms for her to slip the garment over his head and spread it across the foot of his bunk. She moved back to his side and began rubbing his chest and shoulders with a towel. She finished with a vigorous wipe of the towel across his damp hair and beard.

Jenny opened the trunk and withdrew a shirt she had washed and folded for storage. As she slipped it over his head, she kept one of her hands within the tail of the shirt and let her fingers slide up and down his bare back in a playful motion.

"That tickles," he said and grabbed for her arm. She laughed when he caught her wrist and pulled her to face him again. "Sit down and talk to me."

She smiled down at him. "Nae... yer to go back to yer bunk and remove 'em wet breeches. Dry ones on a peg back there. Methinks to see what you brought from the store to add to what I meant to have for supper."

He started to speak but something made him hesitate and look away. Without a word, he made his way to his bunk in the corner. It would not to be the only moment he considered that his own time for playful response may have passed.

Another year passed with little change in routine except that Caleb spent less time at the sawmill and stayed longer at the farm. He turned the makeshift stable into a small barn with a loft for storing fodder and peavine hay. A stall for the addition of a cow came next. Jenny willingly took on the role of milkmaid while Caleb built a split-rail fence around a small grazing area for the mule and cow.

An uninvited four-legged resident joined the farm population at Sam Greer's insistence. He called Caleb's attention to a new litter of pups. "I hold that dog of yours responsible," he said. "You ought to take at least one of 'em to feed." Caleb had to admit the pups bore a strong resemblance to Jackson, and he took one home with him.

"See what you've done," he scolded Jackson. The dog came close to inspect what Caleb carried but backed away when he saw the wriggling puppy. "I 'spect we'll call him Calhoun," Caleb said. "Serves you right to have something around to annoy you... like them old fellers used to pester each other."

Wee William, as his mother called him, and the puppy became fast friends.

One summer day they took the little boy and the dogs down to the creek for a picnic. Caleb and Jackson looked on from the bank as Jenny held the toddler to splash with the puppy in the shallow water. When she placed William on the grass, she settled beside him and began to wipe dry both her son and her lower legs with a towel.

"I loved playin' in the water when a wee lass," she reminisced.

The slender form of her bare legs became a magnet to Caleb's eyes. He forced himself to look away before she noticed. "Do you miss Ireland, Jenny?" he asked.

She lifted the boy to her lap and faced her questioner. "Oh, I loved our village... Ballycarry. Sweet, gentle folk. 'Twas so til

64

the crops failed... and nobody had enough to eat... and the land-lords..." Her voice faded to silence.

Caleb caught himself about to ask 'And Fergus Macready?' but he thought better of it. He did not understand why the young man's name intruded so often in his thoughts.

Seated beside him, Jenny slid a hand beneath the open neck of her blouse and lifted the fabric away from the top of her shoulder. She may have expected a cooling waft of air to reach the exposed skin, but the brush of Caleb's beard and touch of his lips to the base of her neck came instead. He sensed her shiver as she pulled away..

"I'm sorry, Jenny..." he stammered, "...I shouldn't..."

Without a word she sat the child on the grass until she could get to her feet and then stoop to reclaim him in her arms. When she turned to the path that led to the cabin, Caleb stood up, grabbed the basket, and walked behind them. All the way up the hill she did not look back.

Jackson followed, leaving the puppy to pad along for himself and wonder why no one stayed to play.

They passed the remaining daylight hours in chores without any mention of the scene by the creek. After supper, Jenny began to sing lullabies and prepare her child for bedtime. Caleb walked outside to gather his thoughts in twilight.

He knew he had broken dangerous ground. His impulsive action pushed their coexistence beyond the boundaries in which it had safely grown. He refused to relinquish the pleasant memory of a brief kiss of her bare flesh even though the difference in their ages hammered at his conscience. 'Old enough to be her father' and 'Don't be an old fool' competed for the upper hand in his self-scolding. He shook his head in frustration and seated himself on the stump which served as chopping block at the woodpile. He did not hear her footsteps when she came up behind him.

He felt her hand touch his shoulder. He did not turn but raised his own hand and rested it atop hers. She gathered her skirt beneath her, seated herself on a stick of wood cut for the fireplace, leaned her upper body against his knee, and looked up into his face.

He started to apologize again, but she interrupted. "Caleb, ye could nae know the why of me behavior when ye kissed me neck. Tender enough 'twas yer touch, but..." she stopped, looked down, and slowed her next words. "Twas the first time I felt a man's lips.. since that... awful night. Their breath... and rough hands..." She fell silent.

Caleb gently placed his arm about her shoulder and pulled her close. "Forgive me, Jenny," he said, "for failin' to remember what you went through. When I asked about Ireland... and you talked 'bout how you liked it there, I wuz just glad you came here. That's what the kiss meant to say. But no old man should expect a young lass could understand that."

As shadows darkened, they relied on senses of touch in the fading light. He stroked her shoulder and felt her slide an arm behind his back. The gulf of years between their ages gave him no peace, however, and he broke the silence.

"How old were you when y'all left Ireland?"

"Seventeen," she said quickly.

He pondered where to go with his next question, but she moved faster.

"I'm twenty now," she said with firmness but without raising her head.

"Well, you can likely tell I'm past fifty," Caleb volunteered. "Got no right to..."

Her head came up, and she stopped him in midsentence by placing her free hand across his mouth. "'Tis a well-known fact yer older'n me, Caleb Morgan," she said. "'Tis also true ye've got a heart o' kindness... and ye work hard... and ye give me a safe feelin'... the first since Ballycarry." She withdrew her hand, pressed her head against his chest, and almost caused him to lose his balance on the stump.

He tightened his grip around her shoulders. The closeness of her body revived that inner surge which prompted his attempted kiss earlier. He had not felt such a stimulating thrill in a long time, and he was reluctant to part with it. But the age difference again forced his hand.

"Well, you've not had much chance to meet young men," he cautioned. "Like that one in Ireland."

She lifted her head again and sought his eyes in the darkness. "Ye must mean Fergus," she said. "Fergus Macready. Aye, more'n one like him, I'll wager. Full o' pride and foolishness... and to a man they'd walk away once't they saw wee William."

Caleb broke eye contact because he did not wish to signal agreement or disagreement. He had not chosen this duty of an elder. Nor had he expected he would again experience feelings of desire as strong as those of his younger years. Jenny's presence at the farm began in innocent accommodation. One found a way to grant the other a bit of privacy when disrobing in the one-room cabin. Then her pregnancy and the birth of her child kept his own focus narrowed to that of protector and friend. That test of compatibility took new turns and intensified as the baby grew and her stay lengthened. Suggesting a course of action for her seemed simpler than overcoming the conflict within himself. But words did not come easily, and he could not look her in the eye when he spoke.

"Where one young buck might move on," he began, "in town, at least they's others who might not. And some young father left with a motherless child or two may not object to takin' in another. You should think 'bout that," he closed with a palpable drop in inflection.

Jenny's left arm tightened against his back, and she craned her neck so as to force his eyes to meet hers. "Methinks the man right here is worth more than all that," she said.

Caleb did not look away, but he struggled to speak. "I'm glad you felt safe, Jenny.... but you may not think that if you knew what's stirrin' in me. If you stay here, I can't promise that fool attempt I made to kiss you will be the last. I may be a durn sight older, but..."

Her right hand silenced him, quickly followed by the pressing of her lips against his mouth. She broke off the kiss and leaned back, facing him. "Does that prove I would nae want it to be the last, Caleb?" she asked.

Darkness did not conceal her broad smile, and he found himself matching it with one of his own. He got to his feet and took her in his arms.

Their feelings for each other flourished once freely expressed. The wall of mere coexistence fell away, succeeded by each one's open concern for the other. Caleb sensed the full pleasure of being attentive to her and seeing her respond with such cheerfulness. Jenny sang more. He felt 10 years younger and planned a return to Murdock's sawmill for lumber to improve their living quarters.

The subject of marriage was raised – not by anxious Beulah Greer – when a censustaker made his rounds in early 1860.

Caleb issued an invitation to the warmth of the cabin fire on the cold March day the enumerator rode up in his buggy. The visit was unexpected, and Caleb had not anticipated the many questions. His previous census experience was a dim memory – a simple count of numbers in 1830 and 1840 when only the head of household was identified by name. The censustaker explained the form had been expanded in 1850. "Must've forgot," Caleb pretended then supplied current but terse answers for himself.

The enumerator pointed to Jenny. "Is this your wife?" he asked.

Caleb looked at Jenny. Their eyes locked for an instant before he turned back to the questioner.

"Yes," he said quietly.

He went on to identify little William as his son and rushed through the remainder of the questions without another glance in Jenny's direction. The man hired to conduct a count of Bradley County's population folded his tally sheets, made small talk in order to toast himself by the fire a bit longer, and bade them farewell.

The lies had come easily from one who hated liars. The question of birthplaces had been answered truthfully – Virginia was a long way from South Carolina, and Ireland, in Jenny's case, even farther. The other answers, however, gambled that information given the censustaker would not lead to legal entanglement from his disavowal of a marriage broken long before he came to

69

Tennessee. The sudden confrontation made him state his allegiance to Jenny, openly within her hearing, but without considering how or when it would be solemnized. Caleb, a man who liked being left alone, never rushed to seek concern for society's approval.

Jenny came to his side as soon as the door closed behind the censustaker. "Did ye mean what ye told him?" she asked, eagerness showing in her voice.

Caleb smiled. "Course I did," he said. "We'll git around to makin' it legal some day soon. Jesse Murdock's a justice of the peace. I'll talk 'bout it with him."

She touched his arm. "And what ye said 'bout William?"

"The young'un needs a last name," Caleb said. "He can't hurt the name Morgan any more than I have." He paused. "Unless you object."

She embraced him. "Nae objection in the world!"

Jesse Murdock grinned while Caleb shifted his weight from one foot to the other.

"Friend of yours, you say?" Murdock asked, a hint of mischief in his eyes. "Wonders if a marriage broken long ago in a different state is any reason not to marry in Tennessee. Is that right?"

Caleb chose to nod his head instead of saying more.

"Well..." the sawmill proprietor said as he stroked his chin, "first let me say the changes in you have been something to see, Caleb. You got that drinking under control... we're proud of you, I might add. Then you worked night and day for that wagon load of planks to build onto your cabin... or so you told us. Next you say a woman's been staying there with you for over a year." He continued to rub his chin as if the action seemed to prolong his amusement. "And now... questions about marriage. Friend of yours, that is."

Murdock seemed in no hurry to put Caleb at ease, but he elaborated that his comments were "the views of a friend and not as an officeholder of the good state we live in."

He waited for Caleb's nod of assent before he said more. "The way this country's growing... people moving westward... new towns and counties... even states where none existed... old customs don't always keep up. I'm no authority on what the law may be in Georgia, or Virginia, or North Carolina. Tennessee's my concern. Why, I've heard South Carolina does not have a divorce law."

Caleb fought to control his facial muscles and silently prayed the look in his eyes did not give him away when Murdock said the words "South Carolina.'" If he saw Caleb flinch, the mill proprietor paid more attention to his own analogy. "I imagine more than two or three of the men coming across the mountains east of here left wives back there for whatever reason... and took new wives someplace else. Did the first wives give them up for dead... and marry again? Who knows? Besides the Almighty, that is. There's a law called bigamy which says either party in a marriage cannot be wed to somebody else while the other party of the first marriage is living and has not taken action to end that marriage. How much effort is made by either party to find out... I couldn't begin to guess. But somebody would need to try and find out. That's the way I see it, Caleb."

71

Once he reached the farm, unloaded Murdock's wagon, and gave a cursory glance at his fields, Caleb turned his attentions to the other members of his household. Jenny's cheeks glowed when Caleb explained his plan for expanding the cabin.

"A *floor*... truly?" she exclaimed. "And more room, too!"

"Yep... both of 'em," Caleb promised. "Soon as I tend to the corn and the garden... and return the wagon."

She reached for his hand and pressed it to her stomach. "'Tis almost as good news as what's inside me... a baby, Caleb! True on Beulah Greer's word... 'Tis yer child to come this fall."

Caleb blinked in surprise, but the joy in Jenny's face induced him to share her moment of exhilaration. He had no time to spare if the neglected crops were to be coaxed into a decent harvest and the cabin work completed before the baby arrived.

A baby girl whom Jenny chose to call Margaret was born in early November, fortunately two days after her father fitted the last floorboards in place and finished extending the cabin walls and roof.

Caleb surprised Jenny with a trip to Cleveland as soon as he finished the spring planting in May 1861. He hitched the mule to the two-wheel contraption he called a 'shay' and walked alongside while Jenny and the children rode the seven miles to the town's courthouse square. Securing a license to be married was the goal, but they could not get close to the courthouse because hundreds of men, women, and children blocked their way. Most of the men appeared to be shouting at each other. No one seemed to listen.

He tied the mule beneath a shade tree and left the little family there while he walked into the crowd. The noise intensified as he pushed through clusters of loud, gesturing men. Some of the women dabbed at tears. Somewhere a bass drum sounded an even beat, while from an opposite direction came infrequent blasts from a bugle. Boys perched on treelimbs surrounding the square yelled reports of what their better view provided. Caleb covered half the distance to the courthouse before he heard the words that explained the melee – "Tennessee has seceded!"

One faction in the vast crowd edged close and gave ear to an orator appealing for volunteers to join the Union army. His opposite, on another side of the lawn, spoke passionately for young men of Bradley County to enlist in what he called "the Army of the Free State of Tennessee." Supporters of each side looked about evenly divided. Some moved back and forth as if uncertain which cluster to join.

Caleb elbowed his way to the door of the clapboard court building and then learned all offices inside had been closed for the day. Oliver Pickett and Jesse Murdock had commented on the unrest aboil in the last election. Caleb avoided being drawn into a political discussion with either respected friend. He favored his isolation and wanted no part of other men's disputes. Pickett's excitement grew when South Carolina left the Union the preceding December,. The storekeeper – who journeyed into Cleveland frequently for supplies – posted a list as states followed suit in each passing month.

Thirty years earlier, Caleb overheard Titus Willingham praise South Carolina's nullifying a Federal tariff because of its effect on the price of cotton, but the state repealed its action before talk of separation from the Union became more than that – just talk.

"Now it's come to this," Caleb mumbled to himself as he made his way out of the throng and returned to Jenny at the shay.

"We'll have to come back another time, Jen," he explained. "They're all whooped up about makin' war on each other. May need to wait til this mess gits straightened out."

Jenny, who spent her early years where tensions from old wars simmered between neighboring families in the old country, nodded her understanding and returned full attention to the baby being nourished at her breast.

The presence of then one-year-old Margaret in Jenny's arms when they returned six months later may have influenced the county clerk to issue the license quickly. Caleb accepted his good fortune in so few questions being asked and posed one of his own: directions to the nearest Justice of the Peace. Clutching the hand of three-year-old William, he guided Jenny out of the courthouse and to a house just off the square where they exchanged wedding vows within the hour.

The radiance in Jenny's face pushed aside any concern Caleb gave to the likelihood he had committed what Murdock cautioned would be an act of bigamy. He hurried the little family to the shay and beseeched the mule he named Wayward to return them safely to the cabin.

War made even an occasional journey into the county seat unpleasant for Caleb. He felt uncomfortable in the midst of so many people. The apparently even balance of sentiment between townspeople openly favoring Union or Confederacy put an outsider on the spot. Eyes seemed to measure a newcomer's loyalty or looked away. When he had to enter a place of business Caleb steered clear of conversations and hurried back home.

His sympathy lay with his native South. Caleb put in his time with the militia company at Gowensville during the 1820s and 1830s, but he took up arms in drills then to defend his home community in the event of a problem created by the British or Indians. This time an independent South, free of dominance by the North, was at stake. Caleb liked that word 'independent,' especially if it meant a small farmer like himself could be left alone. He realized he was too old to go away to fight, but he vowed to do what he must to protect his family should the shooting come to Bradley County.

Jenny's excitement when she told him he was to become a father again before the end of 1862 lifted the weight of his 50-plus years for a spell. The cabin improvements had not been completed a day too soon. A baby boy they agreed should be named Thomas – honoring Caleb's father – was born the week before Christmas.

The following summer brought disturbing reports from places called Vicksburg and Gettysburg to all who believed the war was going well for the South. Caleb sought and obtained Jesse Murdock's agreement that his time at the sawmill be broken into three-to-four day stays so that he could keep a more watchful eye on his farm. All the while, he stalled at telling Murdock about his marriage and family because he did not know what to say should the mill owner recall the warning about bigamy. He stepped up his work effort on days he was present, and that trade-off satisfied Murdock.

Chapter 6: October 1863, continued

A burst of sound from quarreling children brought a quick end to Caleb's time for reminiscence. He heard Jenny's raised voice subdue the squabble for a moment then it began anew. She called to him from the cabin door.

"Tis their yearnin' to play outside, and I kinna rid 'em of the notion. Did ye forget to eat entirely?"

Caleb got to his feet. "Sorry, Jen... time just got away. Let 'em loose. I'll come in now and have a taste of what's left of that stew."

He had no idea how long his meditations lasted, and she did not make an issue of it. That was Jenny... patient, willing to wait when she sensed he had something on his mind.

He came in and accepted the bowl of stew she placed before him. She lifted the baby from the cradle then hurried William and Margaret in front of her into the afternoon sunshine. The pleasing sounds of their laughter at play soon shifted his attention from the event which stirred his mind to roam those trails of recollection.

While he ate, Caleb planned a return to the mill. The fall harvest was in. He, at Oliver Pickett's urging, had sold half the corn to Confederate Army foragers. The ankle injury had delayed him already, and he knew Murdock needed him.

Caleb departed at daylight two days later. He ordered Jackson to stay behind, folded an old blanket into a makeshift saddle, and rode the mule most of the way. He reached the mill a full hour before noon.

"Shed's in use right now," Jesse Murdock explained in greeting. "Deserter just brought in this morning."

Caleb glanced toward his accustomed home away from home where the familiar bulk of Bragan, the tavern owner, sat on the ground with his back against the shed door.

"Home Guard's gone to locate the nearest Confederate camp," Murdock continued as they crossed the road to release the mule in the pasture. "I expect somebody will come for him before the day's out, and you can move back in tonight."

Caleb nodded acceptance of the situation. On their return they passed two men who had the big saw in full operation. Chips and sawdust flew while the teeth of the giant blade separated a once solid pine log. When stripped of its bark, the squared-off log was carried back and guided through return engagements with the blade to produce inch-thick planks. The whine of the saw made conversation impossible, and Murdock motioned for Caleb to follow him on to the millhouse.

"Right now I need somebody to straighten this lumber, Caleb." The mill owner pointed to mounds of pine planks. "Won't put as much pressure on your sore leg as working the saw would do. The men piled things in here in a hurry, and if we don't get some order to it we'll have to stack outside. You know I hate that."

"Sure Jesse," Caleb agreed. "Let 'em keep goin'... I'll line up these boards the way you like 'em and make room for more." He set to work, and Murdock returned to oversee the sawing action.

From a pyramid of hastily-tossed lumber, Caleb kicked risers into place horizontally on the dirt floor and systematically began to place planks in vertical alignment across the risers, layer by layer. He worked steadily until a compact stack of lumber occupied less than half the space where disarray had ruled. A second orderly stack took shape faster than the first.

The clang of the big bell at the back steps of the Murdock house outshouted the saw's roar as Rhoda Murdock signaled her husband and the millhands to come to dinner. The big meal almost always included two kinds of meat with three or four bowls of vegetables and generous servings of coffee. The Murdocks believed in a well-fed work crew, an employment lure made more important in wartime when able-bodied men were in short supply.

At the table, the two men who operated the saw voiced opinions about the captive in the shed, but neither seemed to have gotten a good look. Murdock, who had unlocked the shed on request, simply described the fellow as "young... nothing unusual." Caleb concentrated on his meal, thanked his hostess afterward, and followed custom in accepting her offer of a biscuit for his pocket. He walked into the yard where he could stretch his arms and massage his sore ankle. While filling his canteen at the well, he spotted Bragan motioning from where he sat. Caleb walked over to see what concerned the tavern owner.

"I thought I recognized ye," the big Irishman said, "Ye've nae been in me place for a while now."

"Been workin' my farm," Caleb told him.

"Well, tis a big favor ye'll do this old friend if ye stay a minute here at the door while I go up the hill for the fetchin' of a bottle. This sun brings on a powerful thirst. I need a sip or two now and then while I keep watch over him inside." He rose to his feet and started for the tavern without awaiting an answer.

The circumstance suited Caleb so well he nodded agreement anyway. "Be right back," Bragan called over his shoulder.

When he saw Bragan enter the tavern, Caleb stepped around the corner of the shed and positioned one eye at a knothole in the wall out of view from the Murdock house. From long residence, he knew that hole would provide a limited view. Inside the windowless shed, the shadowy figure of a man sat on the floor beside the bunk, arms behind his back. The likelihood this was the same young man who appeared at his cabin two days earlier overcame Caleb's attempts to believe otherwise.

He sighed, backed away, and returned in front of the shed to await Bragan's return. The tavern owner soon came hustling down the hill, bottle in hand.

"Tis thankful I am for yer help," Bragan said hurriedly. "Let's have a look and be sure the rascal is there like he should be," he said as he unlocked the door.

The captive looked up when daylight flooded the interior. Peering over Bragan's shoulder, Caleb caught a full view of a noticeably unshaven young face and silently confirmed what the knothole view led him to suspect.

"I'd better go back to work," Caleb said. He started to move away.

Bragan slammed the door, clicked the heavy lock, and took a long swig from the bottle . He extended it in Caleb's direction. "Will ye join me in a taste before ye go?" he gestured.

"No time for that, Bragan. Got work to do," Caleb said. He returned to the millhouse and began to build a third stack.

The repetitive labor gave him time to consider options for what he knew must be done. Just what that responsibility entailed, Caleb was unsure. But the deadweight of his own past that surfaced in recent reveries had caught up with him and sat squarely on his shoulders.

Of this much Caleb Morgan was certain. That young man in the shed would not be handed over to any hangman or firing squad. The exact means of preventing it was unclear, and Caleb knew he must work fast before the executioners arrived. Somehow, some way, he would help the young man regain his freedom.

With each piece of lumber he fitted into place he developed a plan that called for a simple reverse action. As several wooden boards are needed to create an orderly formation, removal of a few can undo it. He would dismantle some part of what others had turned into a makeshift prison. Caleb's spirit rose as he envisioned a way to free himself from guilt long ignored.

The whine of the saw told Caleb work had resumed at the mill. He knew the hired hands would be on their own for a time because Jesse Murdock customarily took a nap after eating dinner. And the alertness of the millhouse hounds likewise lay numbed from devouring scraps Murdock tossed to them before he retired.

Caleb finished his stack and slipped out of the sheltered enclosure. He took the long way around to avoid crossing the open yard. That route brought him to the back of the shed.

He continued his stealthy move along the side hidden from view at the Murdock house, past the knothole, onward to peer around the front corner and observe Bragan. The big Irishman had obviously sampled the whiskey several times for his head nodded in a losing fight to stay awake. He would pass out in a few minutes, Caleb figured.

Another peek through the knothole determined the young man sat within a few feet of the back wall. That fit what Caleb had in mind.

Positioning himself outside the back wall, he searched for cracks a little below halfway up the boards that wrapped the old shed. Many nights inside he suffered the draft from winter winds whistling through cracks. He drew his knife and slid the long blade beneath an overlapped board where a once solid attachment had been loosened by time. He worked slowly and quietly to give the guard more time to slip into unconsciousness..

When the strong blade had disappeared all the way up to the handle, Caleb whispered aloud:

"Young man. Can you hear me?"

A second, then a third call was required to raise a grunted response.

"Slide yourself over here...or git to your feet if you can...back up, and rub your bonds against this knifeblade."

The sounds of scrambling and grunting convinced Caleb his instruction had been heard. He waited patiently, calculating the dim light inside meant the young man would need time to locate the knife. When he felt a thud against the wall, he knew the captive had begun to do his part.

"No noise," Caleb admonished in a loud whisper. He tightened his grip on the knife's handle to hold it steady.

The grunts conveyed the prisoner's repeated thrusts against the blade. An audible sigh signaled success. Caleb withdrew the blade and positioned the knife butt to pry upward against the overlap.

The young man evidently leaned his head near the opening because Caleb heard him whisper, "Who are you? Why are you doin' this?"

Caleb continued to attack the board but gave a terse reply. "Remember that farm where you cut wood two days ago?"

A pause preceded the next words from inside. "You're *him?*... the man with the bad ankle? How'd you get here?"

"I work at the sawmill, off and on," Caleb answered. "Keep your voice low."

"That still don't tell me why you're riskin' your ownself," came the whispered response. "But I'm mighty thankful."

"Back there at Gowensville..." Caleb continued in low tones, "anybody ever tell you 'bout Caleb Morgan?"

Caleb could not see the face, but he heard the gasp. "Caleb... *Morgan?*" Then quickly, "They told me he must be dead. Ma said Pa's father disappeared long before I was born."

Caleb pressed harder and felt the board begin to give way. He did not have to wait long for the young man to continue their whispered conversation.

"She said Pa named me after him."

Caleb caught his breath but did not lessen his effort to force fingers into the gap the knife butt created. "Named you after your pa?" he asked. When a response did not come, he rephrased his question. "Your pa *wuz* Ty Morgan... wuzzent he?"

The young man's eyes were now visible in the opened space. "Mister... you sure know a lot about me," he muttered. "I don't understand how..."

Caleb's eyes locked on the ones inside. "Well, I *believe* I'm your grandpa," he said. "Ty Morgan *wuz* my son... and I *know* I ain't dead."

Amazement and disbelief showed in the young man's eyes.

Caleb shook the loosened board and called for a push from inside. "Hurry," he ordered, and applied his knife to a second board. Seizing this chance at freedom, the captive pushed until the first board snapped and fell.

"Careful," Caleb hissed. He passed the knife through the opening. "Keep pryin' these boards loose so you can squeeze your head and shoulders through. But be quiet about it. I'm goin' back around front to see if the guard's still asleep."

He slid along the shed wall for a look at Bragan slumped against the door. Caleb stepped closer and, with his toe, nudged the bottle until it brushed the Irishman's meaty hand. By reflex, the big fingers closed around the neck in a determined grip of ownership.

Satisfied the sentry had not awakened, Caleb returned to find the young man's upper body wriggling through the expanded hole in the wall, hands clawing for support to bring his lower half into the open.

"Here, let me help you," Caleb whispered and pulled the young man's left arm. Their combined strength soon had the escapee tumbling to the ground. He jumped up and faced his rescuer.

"I'm tryin' to make sense of what you said," he wheezed. "If you *are* my grandpa, then you must be..."

"Caleb Morgan," came the soft words of admission. "You have to be Ty's son... no more Morgans anywhere 'round Gowensville when I left. Ty wuz full-grown by then... a fine young man. You look like him."

Caleb slid a strap from his shoulder and offered his canteen to the young man, who quickly drained its contents.

The intense inspection of Caleb's face did not cease The young man returned the canteen and the knife, brushed himself off, but he did not look away. "Why'd you leave?" he asked.

"Son, it'd take more time to explain than you have to wait," Caleb said. "I hoped my leavin' would make it easier for Ty... easier with his Willingham kin, that is. Now, you'd best git goin'. Any time now they'll come for you. And this time they'll use a rope on your neck."

Caleb waved an arm toward the thick grove behind the mill. "Through the trees, down to the river. Your best chance from here. Sneak down there and help yourself to the first skiff you find and head downstream in a hurry. Keep low in the boat and let the current carry you along. It flows north. Pull in to the bank on the far side when there's cover in the trees. Kentucky's up there somewhere, but you've got a long walk."

The young man did not move. Caleb cocked an ear to the welcome sound of the saw. He counted on the uninterrupted, high-pitched drone to serve as background music for Bragan's stupor. Still, the precious window of time was closing for this young man... his grandson.

"From what Ma told me," the young man said so low that Caleb strained to hear, "the Willinghams never had much use for Pa. After he married... and they had me... he went off to join the Army 'cause they could barely scrape by. Money he sent back kept Ma and me alive. Then he got killed."

"You mean Ty and his ma didn't git at least a piece of land?" Caleb interrupted.

"Not that I ever knew anything about. Ma said Uncle Sumter fixed it up so Grandma married a Greenville man... they lived in town. Ma said she died... while I was little."

The young man must have expected something besides Caleb's surprised look because he lowered his voice even more when he said, "Most of the Willingham land is Uncle Sumter's."

Caleb fought to control his anxiety to know more. "You can't stand here talkin'. Son, you got to *git!*"

"First, I want to shake the hand of the man I'm named after. I didn't know it when we met before."

"*What?*" Caleb sputtered.

"My name's Caleb, too," his grandson said. "Everybody calls me Cale... like Pa did. I'll never forget what you did for me today."

Tears welled in Caleb's eyes as he clasped the offered hand. In the same motion, his left hand drew the knife from where it had been tucked inside his belt. "You better take this," he said, extending the knife. "Got your initials carved on it."

Cale gave a quick inspection of the handle and smiled. "*Our* initials. Wish I could stay... Grandpa."

Caleb remembered the biscuit in his shirt pocket and handed it over. He fished in a trouser pocket for two Confederate dollars, all the money he carried, and palmed them into Cale's hand. Without another word, Caleb nodded toward the trees.

He watched his grandson disappear from view then returned by his own concealed path to resume stacking lumber.

He had completed four neat stacks with the fifth and final one almost finished when Jesse Murdock walked in.

"By Golly, Caleb, I knew you'd put things right in here," the mill proprietor said. "This place sure runs a sight better when you're around."

They talked while Caleb methodically finished his task. Satisfied all that needed doing there had been done, they were on their way to rejoin the other workmen when the sound of the saw stopped abruptly and one of the hired hands pointed excitedly across the yard at a commotion in front of the shed.

A man on horseback yelled at Bragan, who clung to the jamb of the opened door for support and jabbered unintelligible replies. Another man's voice from inside the shed added to the mix of shouts. Jesse and Caleb hurried over to investigate.

The mounted man prodded his horse closer and used his hat to swat at the cowering Bragan. "Fool! You let him escape!" were the words Caleb distinguished because the Home Guardsman shouted them from the saddle again and again.

Bragan, proclaiming his innocence, tried placing the blame on whoever tied the prisoner's hands.

"Rope was cut!" came a shout from inside.

"How in the name of all the saints in heaven could I know he had nae been searched when ye brung him in?" pleaded the tavern owner.

Seeing Murdock approach, the man on horseback called out. "Anybody else got a key to this shed, Jesse?"

"No, Abner," Murdock replied. "I let you all have the only key this morning."

The man called Abner jumped down from his horse and resumed berating Bragan. Caleb followed Murdock past the shouting into the shed. The second Home Guardsman's back was turned to them with his head stuck through the gap in the back wall. He whirled and hurried past them, then came in sight again a minute later when the crude opening permitted a view of him pacing around in back.

"Did you leave anything sharp in here last time, Caleb?" Murdock asked.

"No, Jesse. Just the quilts you loaned me... that water bucket and some rags over there... no tools of any kind." Caleb ran his hand over a stack of clay pots just inside the door. "None of Miz Murdock's flower pots got broke."

Murdock stepped outside and interrupted the accusations spewing from the man he had called Abner.

"Bragan, you were here the whole time?" the mill owner asked.

The denounced Irishman grabbed the chance to clear himself. "Aye... every blessed minute... " He halted when he saw Caleb. "Except when he," Bragan said as he pointed, "took over so I could hurry uphill and back. Gone nae more than a minute or two. I kept the key on me while I went. And didn't we look in when I got back?" he implored of Caleb. "And him inside sittin' there... right where he'd been put, was he not?"

When Caleb nodded agreement, Bragan directed his words at Abner. "And I stayed at me post all the while til ye rode up," he said.

"And found you *sound asleep!*" Abner bellowed. He faced Caleb and demanded, "Where wuz *you* all afternoon?"

"Stacking lumber over there at the mill," Caleb waved his arm. Abner snorted and stomped around in frustration.

Murdock motioned for Caleb to follow him around to the back of the shed. "Can't tell much back there," the second Home Guardsman said in passing on his way to rejoin his partner. "Some broken boards and weeds flat from where he must'a fell out of the hole he made. Likely went down through the trees and on the river now."

Silently, Murdock assessed the damage to his shed. "We have to patch and make do if you sleep here tonight, Caleb," the mill owner said. "I'll go to the house for a hammer while you get a few pieces of scrap lumber."

Starting across the yard, they caught sight of the Home Guardsmen leading their horses uphill with Bragan walking alongside.

"Guess they decided they'd settle it over some of Bragan's whiskey," Murdock sighed in resignation.

Caleb returned with an armload of boards to find Murdock waiting with a hammer. While Caleb held a suitable piece of wood in place, Murdock nailed each end with the least number of costly nails possible.

When they had finished, Murdock leaned an arm against the undamaged part of the wall. "I noticed... just now, Caleb, that big knife you always have stuck in your belt is missing. Did you remove it while you stacked that lumber?"

Caleb met his employer's eyes with an even, unblinking gaze.

"No, Jesse," he said. "Found another use for it."

Murdock's patient expression did not change as he waited.

"I slid the blade of that knife between these boards so that young man could cut his bonds on it," Caleb confessed. "Then I helped him break through this wall."

"What in the world caused you to do that?" Murdock asked. "Have you gone over to the Yanks?"

Caleb knew Murdock supported the Southern cause because his only son, a lawyer in Cleveland, enlisted early and advanced rapidly to become an officer in General James Longstreet's Corps. The great majority of the sawmill's patrons openly avowed loyalty to the South, and simple economic survival reinforced the senior Murdock's willing compliance in incidents such as the Home Guards' requisition of the shed.

"No, that's not the reason," Caleb said. "I've never lied to you, Jesse, and I ain't about to start now. I helped that young man because he's my grandson."

He gave a brief account of Cale's appearance at the farm and his reason for leaving his unit. That took Caleb less time than a summation of his own past never shared with Murdock before, but he felt the time to tell it had come. "When Bragan opened the door and the light fell full on him, I saw who it wuz," he continued. "I knew it wuz up to me to do something for the son of the one I deserted. My son became a soldier, too, I found out... gave his life in the War with Mexico."

Murdock did not interrupt, but his face showed concern.

Caleb took that as a signal to tell the rest. "I'm too old to take part in this war, and I just want to provide for my new little family as best I can. I favor whatever's best for Southern people. I know your son's puttin' his life on the line for what he believes in." He paused, then added, "Jesse, I don't think a son of yours would make a private use a bullwhip on one of his own."

Murdock cleared his throat. "Armies must have discipline, Caleb," he said. "What you describe expresses what happens when a few assigned to carry out orders take it upon themselves to go beyond what the officer directed. From what my son writes to us, our own army has to spend as much time clearing up misunderstandings within our own ranks as they put to fighting Mister Lincoln's Army. I'm afraid what we've witnessed here today is an example. The Home Guard was created with good intentions, but look what it has become... a bunch so eager to blame somebody else they go off to drink it over."

He gave Caleb a wry smile. "In this case, they didn't recognize a sharp enemy when he turned up."

"I'd never want to cause you trouble, Jesse," Caleb said. "I'm sorry it happened on your place, and all."

"That won't be a problem for me, Caleb, but it's likely to be a big one for you." Murdock allowed the words to sink in before he said more. "They're up there now looking for answers in Bragan's whiskey. Abner Suggins is a suspicious man... about everything I've ever heard him discuss. He'll make Bragan go over it again and again, and he'll ask more questions... how you happened to be nearby, and so on. The more they drink, the more they'll find reason to suspect you."

The mill owner cleared his throat. "They may not be able to do it when they finish with the whiskey, but they... Abner, at least... will be back here asking if anybody saw you all the time you stacked that lumber. Can you be certain Robert or Wesley down at the saw didn't notice when you came or went? One of them is bound to see you no longer carry that knife. They're your fellow workers, true, but who knows what Abner Suggins may twist out of anything they say?"

Murdock's right hand swung to rest on Caleb's shoulder. "I hate to say this, Caleb... but you'd better leave. After all the good work you've done for me, that's a hard thing to say. I can't fault you for what you did here today. Blood runs thick in all of us. But these men won't see it that way, not when their standing in the Home Guard could be at stake. If they don't get even with you now, they'll conspire... with others like them... to find where you live, take your crop, burn you out... or worse."

Caleb flinched. He realized his action could lead to harm for Jenny and their children. He did not regret risking his own neck, but they had no such duty to his grandson.

"I see what you mean, Jesse," he said.

"It'll be dark pretty soon," Murdock's hand dropped. "Wait til then, get your mule, and leave when no one will likely see you. Go into Cleveland and get what you can for your harvest. While you're there, see if the bank will give you something for your land, get yourself a wagon, get back home, gather your family, and go. If anybody has to know, say you're going west."

Caleb's mind reeled, but he saw the wisdom in doing what Murdock suggested. The safety of his loved ones demanded it because of circumstances he had created.

"I'm going to the saw," Murdock said. "Robert and Wesley must be dying to know what went on over here. Better they hear it from me..." he paused to assure himself Caleb saw his wink, "the necessary parts, that is. Why don't you put some of that newcut lumber under shelter, just to make the rest of the work-day look natural. I'll see you again before dark sets in."

The two men went their separate ways and did not meet again until dusk. Murdock came to the barn to feed his mules and found Caleb had taken care of it.

"I hope you won't mind my givin' Old Wayward here a taste of your fodder," Caleb said as he rubbed the neck of his own mule, bridled for departure.

"No objection, Caleb. That mule's got a night's work ahead," Murdock said. He extended a hand that held a biscuit stuffed with a piece of chicken. "Rhoda wanted you to have this."

"She's been mighty good to me... just like you have, Jesse," Caleb said in accepting the food.

"I told her what took place, Caleb," the mill owner said. "She understands... and she won't say a thing. She keeps a secret better than any woman I've ever met. Robert and Wesley went to their homes an hour ago. Neither one questioned the little bit I told, but we can't know what they'll say when Abner comes around. If he asks me, I'll tell him you were here just for the day to collect back pay." He withdrew from a trouser pocket the hand that had not carried the biscuit. "Here's that back pay. I told Rhoda, and she approves. We want you to have this money to see you on your way. Everybody 'round here passes Confederate, but you can't tell what may be needed where you go"

An astonished Caleb looked at the wad of Confederate paper dollars and two Federal gold coins Murdock placed in his hand. "Jesse... I don't know what to say," he stammered. "You've been the best friend I've ever had... and you've already done more for me than I deserve. I hate that it ends like this... but I see what you mean. It could be worse... for both of us... if I stayed. I'll never forget you."

They shook hands. Murdock prolonged the handshake far longer than customary.

"Wait til good dark before you leave, Caleb. God be with you."

Caleb led Wayward well past the tavern before he mounted. A saddled horse stood at a hitching post of Bragan's establishment and lamplight suggested a patron or two remained within, but no one appeared in front or along the road.

Once he swung a leg over the mule's back at the top of the hill, he had time to reflect on his years of friendship with Jesse Murdock. Caleb had never known such loyalty from another man. Deep within, he realized meeting the patient Murdock came in the nick of time and prevented the waste of Caleb's own life.

He had no regret, however, for action he had taken. His mood lightened as he felt a sense of pride in the grandson he barely knew. Likely resigned to fate in that dark shed, Caleb presumed, held there with hands tied behind his back. But the youth sprang to the opportunity to free himself, as any man should when just beginning to live. Hatred for a grandfather who vanished must not have been drilled into him since he had been given Caleb's name. There was no sign of resentment when he learned Caleb's identity or when he accepted the knife. Moreover, his refusal to let old problems with the Willingham family goad him into using that whip said a lot about his grandson's character.

"Ty, you sure produced a fine son," Caleb said aloud as if the spirit of his dead son would hear. "If that's not you doin' it, hope you've asked one of them guardian angels to watch over him."

Wayward's head jerked at the sudden sound of a voice. Caleb patted the mule's neck to slow the pace. They had miles to go. Caleb needed time to sort out what he would say to Jenny. By the time they passed a darkened Pickett's Store, he had decided to leave nothing untold. As much as she wished to hear, he would share.

The hounds caught scent and set up a howl. He knew Jenny would not light a candle when she awakened but would take the loaded shotgun from where it hung on the wall by the door as he had taught her, and she would wait to lift the doorbolt until the visitor's identity was made known.

Caleb shushed the hounds and called out, "It's me, Jen... I'm back early. I'll be in soon as I see to the mule."

He made his way from the barn and stepped into the light from a candle she held inside the open door. He swept her night-gowned body into his arms.

"'Tis an answer to me prayers when you come through that door any time, night or day," she whispered happily.

The October night was chilly, and he suggested a fire was needed because he had so much to tell her.

She huddled next to him while he coaxed the fire into life and began his lengthy explanation. Dawn had come with the fire reduced to embers before the telling ended.

"Methinks ye had nae choice but to help that lad," she said quietly.

Her calm reaction surprised Caleb. He had braced himself for a barrage of questions once his South Carolina past was revealed. He waited, more nervous than he wanted her to see.

Jenny looked toward the sleeping children before she spoke again. "She may have been forced by her brother, but she counted ye dead, and she married again... long years ago. We dinna know if she asked God's forgiveness... but we kin... for our own sins."

Witnessing the nightly prayers she taught William and Margaret to say as she tucked them in always won Caleb's admiration. But they had never prayed together or talked about religious beliefs. To be placed on the spot sent his mind racing back through time to his own childhood, where his religious instruction left off. He saw how much this meant to Jenny, whose patient eyes now searched his own, and he reached for her hand. "I'll need you to help me," he said.

She guided him to kneel with her on the hearth, and they opened their hearts in confession to the Almighty. First Jenny in soft tones of humility; then Caleb's voice, clumsy and indistinct to his own ears until he felt her hand squeeze his hand tightly. His earnestness poured forth. When their voices stopped, the cabin fell quiet.

Silence without movement complemented the peace made with the past. They remained where they knelt until the moment he helped her stand and enfolded her in his arms.

God must have heard, because the baby slept on another full minute before crying out for his feeding.

While Jenny nursed the baby, Caleb stepped outside for more firewood and returned to start breakfast preparations. He talked as he worked.

"First thing we'll do is find us a wagon and another mule, Take whatever we can git for this place, and dispose of what we can't take with us. Say goodbye to the Greers... see if Sam... or Oliver Pickett will take the cow." He faced her before he continued. "We won't head for some far off place like California," he assured. "Just a ways to start, where I can find a bit of work, Somebody ought to need a tough old woodcutter and sawmill man. Then we'll move on til we find some place we really like and want to stay, however far that may be."

"I'll nivver fear what's ahead as long as I am with ye," Jenny said.

Her shining eyes gave Caleb all the answer he needed.

Chapter 7: The Samaritans

Cale Morgan woke up when his bed began to sway beneath a roof that sprang a leak.

The young man on the run purposely chose a resting place above ground. He folded his body into the notch where a sturdy limb left the trunk of a big tree, pressed his back against the trunk, stretched his legs along the limb, and slept out of sight if Home Guardsmen or other living creatures moved on the ground below.

A miracle like that which freed him from the Home Guard's deathly intentions two days earlier could not be counted on again.

The leafy canopy overhead shielded him from sun since he traveled at night and rested in daytime, but the rainstorm that disrupted his sleep was borne on a wind that shook the limbs and twisted their leaves into funnels of falling water. With dampness coating his skin and clothes, Cale swung down to the ground and decided to seek better shelter even though daylight had vanished.

He had chosen the ancient oak halfway up a hill because going higher did not look inviting. What appeared to be an outcropping of rocks crowned the hilltop. But the sudden need for a place to keep dry made him wonder if some sort of cave formation might be found up there.

Cale stumbled through darkness and rain, dashing from the skimpy cover of one tree to another in a zigzag course up the steep slope. Soon he ran out of the treeline altogether, and his scramble became a frantic search through bracken and half-exposed boulders for something big enough to offer shelter.

His hair and clothes were soaked before he saw the huge over-hang that loomed above him. He lunged toward it on all fours, praying this was no shadowy illusion and would indeed leave room to wriggle his body underneath. He let out a shout when he discovered the shaft of solid rock protruded from the earth like a giant cannon barrel. A man could indeed crawl beneath it. Cale did more than that. He *tumbled* in.

The size of the hole he fell into surprised him. He was too thankful to be cautious until a troubling thought reminded him that four-footed creatures of the wild often made a home in caves.

He sat up, hugged himself for warmth, and tried to see about him. He slid his right hand to his waist for reassurance his grandfather's knife remained where it had been tucked. Armed with the knife, in one on one combat, Cale reckoned he stood a chance. He gripped the handle tightly and sniffed for trace of animal life or its droppings. If any existed, the odors coming from his own wet body and clothing exceeded them. Strange as it was, that made him feel a little better.

Cale rubbed his eyes as if that would speed their adjustment to the darkness and reveal whether he was in a pocket between layers of rock or a cellar nature hid away by sliding the massive slab over it. As he reached above to determine if he had room to stand, he sensed that his were not the only eyes probing the darkness. He shivered, lowered his hand, and restored his grip on the knife. Then he saw the eyes that studied him. They were big and open wide. Frightened eyes.

"That's no wild animal," Cale whispered to himself. The eyes of a mountain creature defending its lair would show deadly intent. These eyes belonged to another human being. Another scared one, at that.

"You there..." Cale called in a shaky voice.. "I mean no harm. Just gettin' out of the rain."

The eyes had not changed expression.

Cale managed to rise to a crouch and moved to give the faint light from the entrance a path to the figure. Then his eyes made out what had been indistinct. The seated figure blended into the darkness so completely because its skin was as dark as the night.

The deserter had stumbled into the hideout of a runaway slave.

Talk in Confederate camps included something about an underground railroad that helped slaves escape to the North. No one seemed to know much about the way it worked or whether any way stations existed in the mountains of Tennessee.

"How long you been in here?" Cale asked but heard no reply. "I'm not lookin' to turn anybody in," he added. "When this rain stops, I'll be on my way. Won't matter to me if you stay or go."

The dark figure made no sound.

"Had anything to eat today?" Cale asked and felt inside his shirt for the leather pouch he strung around his neck after leaving a backwoods trading post early that morning. He spent the first of the money his grandfather gave him for a block of cheese, stale crackers, and the carrying pouch. He knew he overpaid but chose to accept the terms and be on his way. He meant to hurry out from under the rock, too, but it seemed fair to offer a trade for the shelter he needed since someone else had claimed it first.

He withdrew the slab of cheese and cut a slice with his knife. He stuck the point of the knife into the slice and stretched out his arm. "No harm letting him see my weapon,'" Cale whispered under his breath, "in case he takes a notion."

The offer hung unaccepted until Cale drew back the knife and plopped the slice into his own mouth. He chewed slowly and returned the stare in the eyes that watched him. As he swallowed, he reached into the pouch, withdrew a cracker, and bit into it.

"I ain't got much to share, but I'll offer again," Cale said as he cut a second slice.

The black man reached out to accept the second offer. His hand swept quickly to his mouth.

Cale withdrew two crackers from the pouch and extended them in his open palm. The man took them and nodded his head to the provider as he ate. His eyes, however, still expressed fright, or perhaps it was mistrust. That did not stop him from accepting a thicker slice of cheese and two more crackers.

Cale crawled back to the entrance. He stretched a cupped palm beyond the overhanging rock to catch falling rain. After several swallows, he slid back to his former position and tilted his head toward the entrance.

"Them crackers is mighty dry," Cale said. "Help yourself to the drinkin' water at the door."

The suggestion went unheeded.

"Well, I won't trouble you if you change...," Cale said before his sneeze interrupted. He slipped out of his shirt and wrung as much of the wetness from it as his hands could manage. He slapped his palms vigorously against his bare chest and back for warmth before he slid head and arms inside the shirt and over the pouch suspended from his neck. He began to think how good it would be to feel sunshine on his back when words suddenly erupted from the black man.

"Boss 'cuse Moses steal. Say need 'notha whippin'."

The remark pivoted Cale's mind to his own day of punishment and made him stiffen.

"A'ready done twice. Moses slip off... swim big river. Go north... follin' Drinkin' Gourd."

The eyes that never seemed to blink remained fixed on Cale.

"How fah?" the black man asked.

Cale shrugged. "Well... if you want me to tell you how many days from here to the northern states, I can't help you. I don't know this country very well. You can tell I got lost huntin' shelter from the rain."

The one who said his name was Moses lapsed into silence again.

"Keep goin' the way you're goin'," Cale offered. "Follow that North Star of the old Big Dipper. I hear there's a big river up that way called the O-hi-o. Cross that, you'll be in Yankee-land."

"You own slave?" Moses asked.

Cale blinked. "Lord, no... I don't own...," he stammered.

"Solja?" came the next rapid question.

"You can say that," Cale answered. "But I've not been sent to bring in anybody. We both happened to find... you before me... a place to get out of the rain. Where you go's no concern of mine. We might as well make the best of it awhile." He felt another sneeze about to overcome him and scrunched his back tight against whatever rock or earthen wall was behind him. He hugged himself in another attempt to find warmth.

"Why you fight?" Moses asked.

Cale stared at his questioner.

"I joined up to defend and preserve the place I live," he answered in a flat tone. "So my home – South Carolina – could be part of a new country without northerners tellin' us what to do." He resented the question, but once confronted he realized the one who asked it expected a different answer. He posed a question of his own, "You think all Southern white folks keep slaves?"

Moses did not answer.

"Well, we don't," Cale declared. "Plenty don't even want to."

They sat opposite each other without further attempt at conversation as time passed. That suited Cale. The reason he happened to be in that hole instead of an army encampment was not a subject he cared to discuss.

He shivered too much to sleep but often caught himself at the edge of a doze, Each time he put a hand to his midsection to be reassured the knife remained where he put it.

He shook himself wide awake when Moses crawled past him to the mouth of their enclosure. A check on the rain, Cale presumed. He sat still for several minutes and listened for the sound of rain or Moses' return. Hearing neither, he crawled to the opening. The misty rays of dawn revealed the storm had moved on.

He stood and discovered rainwater collected in a cistern-like formation of rock nearby. He cupped a hand in it and quenched his thirst.

Moses had disappeared.

"My chance is slim, "Cale said to himself, "his a lot slimmer, I reckon." He patted the big shaft of rock in a thankful gesture of farewell and started for the hilltop. He crossed the ridge and started down the slope the other runaway may have taken earlier.

Unless, somewhere out of sight, Moses waited for the uninvited visitor to vacate his hiding place.

The morning mist hung tight to the hillside and shrouded the valley below, Cale swung his arms to stir his blood but could not shake the chill. The stout wind of the storm had been followed by a breeze that signaled the coming day would not be warm like the preceding one. October weather changed quickly in his native South Carolina, and Cale figured mountainous Tennessee to be even less predictable.

Although he tried to avoid traveling in daylight, Cale needed an hour or two of sunshine to dry his clammy skin and wet clothes. Thick clouds prevented that and buffered what sunlight the new day brought. He sneezed often and, without a warming sun, he knew that would worsen if he did not find some place to dry out and rest. A sneeze attracted attention. A man on the run did not want to be noticed.

He had no idea how far he walked or where his feet took him. With no visible sun position to guide him, he could drift east or west instead of north toward Kentucky.

He skirted fields of cornstalks stripped bare from harvest and caught sight of a river. A wide and fast-flowing river. If somehow he waded or swam across, another soaking was the last thing he needed. He turned away and trudged past a canebrake that led into the trees. He ran his fingers across bark of the bigger trees and trusted the old saying that moss grew on the north side.

His steps became more labored and his lightheadedness increased. He slumped down where the ground looked dry at the base of a huge oak tree. A search of the leather pouch revealed an inch-thick wedge of cheese remained with a few shards of broken crackers.

Cale broke the cheese, stuffed half into his mouth, and followed that with cracker crumbs. "Might have been too generous back there beneath that rock, I guess," he muttered aloud. He rested a short while until the sneezes began anew. He meant to keep the river at his left, but the thicket was so dense – unthinnned by a woodsman's ax – he was forced to sidestep and even circle occasionally.

Time and distance became, like the river's location, impossible to calculate. He grew feverish. Thirst drove him to dip his fingers in stumpwater collected in the uprooted base of a fallen tree. He licked his wet fingers and, immediately, started to shake from queasiness triggered by that he swallowed. He slumped on the downed tree in exhaustion.

Cale jerked awake when a haunting memory of capture by the Home Guard snapped him to consciousness. He threw himself into a new attack against the thicket until he came upon what appeared at first to be a small clearing but turned out to be an overgrown trail or wagon road.

What sky could be sighted through the narrow space above the stump-marked pathway suggested the glint of a star. Night had fallen, or delirium had such a grip on him that he could no longer tell day from night. He staggered along the trail that showed little evidence of recent use and seemed to wind around a hill until it led to a wider expanse of open country and a rail fence leading down to the dim outlines of a barn, sheds, and – just beyond – a house of good size.

The lure of shelter for his shivering body emboldened Cale to dare the risk.

Bracing a hand on the wooden rails for support, he stumbled toward the fence's destination at the barn. He crawled across a rail and halted a few feet short of the entrance. When assured his scent had not yet given him away to any dog or barn animal, he took a cautious step inside. Stables divided the interior, but only one had a resident – a cow, either asleep or uninterested in a nighttime visitor.

Cale slid a hand along the wall of the cow's stable until he felt a ladder that led from the ground. His boyhood years around barns told him what was likely to be found up there. He breathed deep to gather strength before he swung a foot onto the lowest slat and began a labored climb to the upper level. Once his head cleared the top of the ladder, he made out mounds of hay that filled the area below the roof. He crawled from the ladder to the hayloft floor and burrowed his body deep within the hay's inviting warmth.

Cale's delirium spun his disordered mind between highs of wild excitement to depths of desperation. He rode a seesaw, tilted first one way then the opposite. Exhilarating out-of-body sensations where he witnessed himself as a stallion running free across untrampled ground in glorious sunshine before his feet mired in the mud of a rainstorm. In another, he heard and smelled the gunfire of Chickamauga. He saw blue-coated men fall, others in their ranks turn and run, then the yells of celebration as the Federal army took flight. That darkened to a scene of a man at the foot of a scaffold while a crowd looked on. Had a trial taken place? Were those cheers he heard? Was the man Cale himself? If not, why did he feel stabs inflicted on his lower leg? Not once, but again and again as if he were being prodded to mount the scaffold.

He raised his head to learn what attacked his leg. Through the tangled hay, he made out the head and shoulders of a figure mounted on the ladder behind him.

The figure brandished a pitchfork. The tines aimed straight at Cale.

He was too weak to stand in spite of commands to do so. Was that a woman's voice? The commands ceased, and he lost all consciousness again. Then he soon felt more pricks to his leg, and the person who wielded the pitchfork seemed to be in conversation with someone below.

With great effort, Cale raised his head and rubbed his eyes, but he did not have the strength to move further nor could he understand what the voices said. He became aware someone in the loft began to pitch hay down below. He felt the rope as it was looped around his leg, then heard a voice command "Pull! Pull!" before his body was drug across the edge of the hayloft, flipped backward, and plopped onto a thin cushion of hay on the barn floor.

The landing knocked the breath out of the already weakened Cale and plunged him into the black hole of unconsciousness.

Sensations came and vanished as quickly in his trance. The voices moved closer. He was no longer in the barn but somewhere before an open fire whose welcome warmth lulled him to surrender rather than stir. A debate voiced over him became less relevant when he felt his clothes being removed while someone's hands began to apply a warm, wet cloth all over his body. The next sensation he felt was of being rolled into a quilt. Someone's arms drug the quilt across a floor, over a short stretch of ground, then upon another floor, a turn, and stop. He was lifted onto a bed, where water was spooned into his mouth, with that followed by bitter liquid until he gagged.

His captors left him to nestle in the cocoon that engulfed his feverish body.

When Cale awakened, a candle burned on the table beside the bed. His haze of consciousness opened and he looked up at the slender woman staring down at him. He blinked his eyes. That prompted her to speak.

"I am Miss Ada Pomeroy," said the woman. "I found you in my hayloft this morning. You are ill. My sister has been attending to you.... quite mercifully, I might add... after we dragged you in from the cold." She paused as if to be assured Cale paid attention. "But who *you* are, and why you have come here is unknown to us. Young man, you have explaining to do."

The word hayloft brought a vision of the pitchfork that had been thrust in his face. He tried to raise his head but slumped against the pillow. That slight body movement aroused acute pain from his midsection, and he sensed an immediate need to relieve his bladder. He caught sight of a second woman, who stood in back of the first. She presented a plumpish, shorter figure than the one who called herself Ada.

"Pardon me, Ma'am," Cale said with embarrassment. "I'm afraid I'm about to wet this bed. Will you let me get up and go outside to... uh ...relieve myself?"

Ada Pomeroy did not flinch. "That's not possible. Your clothes have been burned, and you have nothing on beneath the bedcovers. We've removed all clothing from this room."

Cale's eyes opened wide. His hands, already under the covers, reacted to her words automatically to confirm his naked torso and legs.

"We will leave the room for a minute and allow you to … relieve yourself in the chamber pot you will find beneath the bed. Replace the cover and get back into bed immediately because we will return."

The shorter woman opened the door and went out first. The one named Ada followed but turned for a final warning before she closed the door "I still have the pitchfork. Don't think I won't use it."

Cale pushed back the covers and slid his legs off the side of the bed. He rested there taking several deep breaths before he knelt to fumble for the chamber pot and the relief it offered.

Too weak to stand, he crawled back to bed and slid beneath the covers just as a warning knock sounded. The door opened, and he saw the tines of the pitchfork advance like four bayonets in perfect alignment. Ada Pomeroy marched in but lowered her weapon when she saw Cale had returned to bed. The shorter woman trailed again, a tray balanced between her hands.

"Now, young man," Ada said, "you *will* tell me who you are and what you were doing in our barn." She leaned the pitchfork against the wall, still within arm's reach.

"Can't that wait, Ada?" the second woman asked as she placed her tray on the candlelit table near Cale's head. She lifted a bottle and proceeded to pour a measure of its contents into a tablespoon. "He needs more of this tonic right now,"

She handed the bottle to her sister and slid her free hand beneath the pillow to nudge Cale's head upward then thrust the spoonful of bitter liquid between his lips. He sputtered in protest, but she forced most of it down his throat. The residue trickled into his growth of beard.

"Let him have some soup, " she said when she picked up a bowl and stirred its contents with the spoon. "Then rest awhile longer."

Ada Pomeroy's stern face had not softened. "Don't mistake my sister's kindheartedness, young man," she said. "*Who* are you, and why are you here?"

Cale could not answer because he had to open his mouth and accept a spoonful of soup or have it poured in his face. He swallowed and tried to lift his head.

"Hush now," the spoonwielder said with a smile. She stirred the contents of the bowl again and allowed the aroma to rise to Cale's nostrils before she held another spoonful to his lips. "Eat first, then tell us."

He found the warm potato soup more to his liking than the questions anyway, and he eagerly accepted each offer until the bowl had been emptied. The shorter sister stepped back.

"I'm waiting," Ada said.

Cale gave the briefest and clearest explanation his state of mind would permit. He must have been reasonably coherent because his interrogator did not interrupt. She looked on without giving a sign whether she doubted or believed what he told her. That is, if he were not too befuddled to notice.

A second matter of urgency came to his mind.

"If you burned my ragged clothes," he asked, " what about my knife?"

"In a safe place," Ada said. "You won't need it in this house. And the dollar we found in your trousers has been applied to what you will owe us for your care. We'll leave you to rest now and talk further in the morning."

She removed a glass of water from the tray, placed it on the table, and motioned for her sister to retrieve the tray while she reclaimed the pitchfork. Ada then turned back and blew out the candle before they left the room.

Cale found a pair of long flannel drawers with a pair of worn trousers and a thick shirt lying on the foot of the bed next morning. His head felt better, but he was so weak when he left the bed he almost fell to the floor in a first attempt to put a foot through a leg of the underwear. He sat on the bed to tug the trousers into place and slip the shirt over his head. The garments were too tight for a man of his size, but he was not about to complain. Barefoot, he tottered across the cold floor and opened the door.

He stepped into a hallway. A left turn appeared to lead past other closed doors to a glass-paneled door that he presumed meant the front of the house. Closer, at his right, a solid door beckoned him to believe it separated the passageway to the kitchen. Customarily, houses of this size had a kitchen located a few steps from the main house to lessen the danger of fire spreading from embers which rarely were extinguished in kitchen fireplaces. He chose the door at his right, crossed the short stretch of open ground, and opened the kitchen door. The sisters were seated on opposite sides of a long table before the fireplace. They turned to face him.

"Come in," called Ada. "You'll have to make do with some of our brother's old clothes. I see they're a bit small for you."

"Thank you. I can manage," Cale said as he moved unsteadily toward them.

The shorter sister rose from her chair. "How do you feel this morning?," she asked gently. "Would you like a bite of breakfast? Come sit by the fire while I fix you something." She turned to the fireplace and began to ladle contents from a big pot into a small bowl. Ada Pomeroy motioned for him to take the chair closest to the fire and between each sister's place.

Cale eased himself to be seated just before a filled bowl and a spoon were placed in front of him.

"Hominy," the friendlier sister said. "It'll warm you up."

She favored him with another smile but stopped talking at her sister's signal.

"I'll come straight to the point," Ada Pomeroy began. "Louella and I have considered all you told us last night, and we have a proposition to place before you. You may choose to accept our offer... or, if not, I shall go into Decatur... it's a short walk... and report your presence to the sheriff. "

Cale chewed his first spoonful of the hot swollen kernels of corn and nodded that she should continue.

"You see... we live alone now since our father passed away. He and Mother, who died before him, brought us here from

Virginia when we were children. Father established a bank for Meigs County and provided most of the merchants and farm families around here with their start. He had this home built for us and took pride in developing the farm until his health failed."

Cale savored his breakfast but concentrated on what she said. He guessed her age to be close to 50, likely older than the one addressed as Louella.

"We kept things together after his death because men were available to work for a day's pay in the fields or tending the stock," Ada went on. "But the war put a stop to that. The few able-bodied men left are either too busy with their own farms or too sorry to trust. We were able to purchase hay to feed our cow until spring brings new grass to the pasture. We harvested what we could from the garden. Besides the cow, we're down to a pig and some chickens. We're almost out of firewood."

She looked straight into Cale's eyes. "Are you willing to work for the shelter we can offer you in return?"

"I am," he said quickly. "I'd like to repay you for what you've done already. I'd prob'bly died out there if I hadn't found your hayloft."

Louella let out a satisfied sigh and jumped to take his emptied bowl.

"I don't want to cause trouble..." Cale began to say.

"It's to your advantage as well as ours that you keep out of sight," Ada interrupted. "The first work you can do, when your strength has returned, will be in the woods."

"I can swing an ax, " he said with confidence. "Soon as I'm steady on my feet, I'll lay in enough firewood to last you a week. I grew up on a farm in South Carolina. Barn chores come natural to me."

Ada's stern expression seemed to relax. "Finish your breakfast," she said as she rose and left the table. "I'll see if Euclid left any boots. They'll likely be small for you, but we won't know until you try them on..." Her voice trailed off as she moved to enter the main house.

Louella brought the refilled bowl to the table and reseated herself. "I'm pleased that you agreed," she said with another smile.

"Is that your brother's name... Euclid?" Cale asked before he spooned another bite.

"Yes," she said, looking down. "He went away before Father died. We've heard no more from him." She raised her eyes to give Cale's shoulders a close examination. "I believe I can take some stitches out of that shirt, resew it, and make it more comfortable for you. May be able to let out the waist of those trousers, too. If you'll go back to bed while I work, you can put them on again in an hour or so." Her smile accompanied a glow to her cheeks.

Ada strode in, holding a pair of woolen stockings in one hand and a weathered pair of boots in the other. "They look to be in better shape than what we took off your feet," she said. "Question is, will they fit well enough for you to walk?"

Cale pushed his chair back from the table and took one of the stockings. He slipped it on a bare foot then reached for the boot meant to match. The leather was cracked and stiff, and he tugged with all his strength while she pushed against the heel of the upraised foot. But when he stood and stamped his foot, the boot fit surprisingly well.

"I might be too big for your brother's britches," he laughed, "but his feet must be kin to mine."

Without comment, she simply handed the remaining stocking and boot to him.

"I'll wait to put 'em on," he said. "Your sister wants me to go back to bed so she can do some alterin' on what I'm wearin'."

Ada glanced at Louella. "Very well," she said. "Go back in, close the door, and hand the shirt and trousers to me when I knock."

In his refitted clothing, Cale felt strong enough next morning to take up an ax and pull a small sled into the woods adjoining the Pomeroys' pasture. Stumps marked places where thinning had taken place previously. A good-sized oak in front of him had a major limb evidently split and charred from a lightning strike. He chose it as his work for the day. Although he paced the strokes of his cuts at the base, he needed to sit down for rest several times before he made the tree fall into the clearing.

He trimmed limbs away from the trunk and reduced them to fireplace-size logs. He left the trunk to wait for a time when he regained more strength. When the sun's position showed noontime, he went back to the house to eat and rest an hour. He returned to stack firewood on the sled, fit its rope around his shoulders, and pull loads one by one until all the cut lengths were brought to the house and stacked at the kitchen door before nightfall.

That day's action established a pattern. In return for his work, he received a warm bed and hot meals the sisters prepared from dried and pickled garden products stored in churns beside a mound of potatoes in the cellar. The cow furnished milk and the hens gave eggs but meat was in critical supply. The Pomeroys' pig had not reached a size suitable for slaughter, therefore rare servings of meat came after Ada made one of her walks to collect mail or visit the bank on Decatur's square. She brought home what bits of pork or venison a storekeeper could furnish. The scarcity of salt meant freshly-killed meat had to be sold and consumed quickly. She returned empty-handed more days than not.

The first Sunday in November the sisters walked into the village to attend church. Cale busied himself with barn chores and was unaware of their return until Ada found him at work.

"I thought you should know we saw soldiers in Decatur," she said. "Word is, they're part of General Wheeler's cavalry. General Longstreet's about to move on Knoxville."

Things must have turned out well after Chickamauga, Cale reasoned, if Longstreet's army could be spared from the front at Chattanooga.

"You'd better come into the house and stay," Ada continued. "They might ride by anytime."

"I don't want to cause trouble, Miss Ada," Cale said. "I'll head for the woods."

"No," she countered. "They may come, and they may not. You stay inside. I'll talk to them... if they come."

He nodded and followed behind her to the kitchen. They found Louella Pomeroy bent over a cook pot at the fireplace, heating their Sunday dinner. She had her back turned, but Cale overheard her sing the lines "... when other helpers, fail and comforts flee... friend of the helpless, O Abide With Me."

The Confederate cavalry outriders rode on without calling at the Pomeroy homestead. November advanced into December without any change in daily routine which became familiar for the sisters and for Cale. He brought joy to the household with news he discovered a bee tree on one woodcutting expedition. Ada returned with him and supervised the taking of honey from the hive that bees had established in a hollowed out section of a tree deep in the woods. They carted the golden honeycombs back to the house in two wooden hampers. Louella excitedly promised to turn the sweet nectar into treats for their enjoyment in the Christmas season.

That excitement lost its edge when the sisters attended church the first Sunday in December and heard what had taken place at Missionary Ridge. A Confederate plan to use that stronghold on high ground and force the Federals to pull out of Chattanooga ended in disaster. Word did not reach Decatur until a few days before that Sunday service, where the alarmed flock's sttention strayed far from the minister's sermon.

When Ada and Louella returned home to share what they had learned with Cale, he did not hide his worry about the fate of his old company. Louella tried to persuade him that his presence would not have changed the outcome. Ada sensed his need to be left alone. He went to the woods and attacked trees with his ax in fury day after day until self-loathing yielded to exhaustion.

He realized that his sullenness spoiled Louella's talk about Christmas. To make amends, he brought in stems of holly and pockets full of nuts found at the base of walnut, pecan, and hickory trees. Her cheeks glowed brighter when, on the afternoon of Christmas Eve, he brought a sprig of mistletoe and stuck it in a small crack so that it hung just above the inside of the kitchen door. He did not detect any change in the set of Ada's jaw, but her eyes gave a hint of approval.

They ate supper earlier than customary that night. Ada asked him to push the table to the far side of the big kitchen then explained he would need to disappear into his room and refrain from lighting the candle. While she placed chairs and stools in a semi-circle before the fireplace, Louella cleared the table and began to arrange a platter of sweets along with cups and glasses for eggnog. As he closed his door behind him, Cale heard a knock at the front of the house and voices outside break into "Hark, The Herald Angels Sing."

Christmas carolers had arrived.

The sisters' feet rushed past his door as they made their way up the long hallway to greet their guests. The front door swung open and let the full sounds sweep into the house. Then a young soprano voice sang a passage in solo.

"Hail the heav'n born Prince of Peace, Hail the Son of Righteousness...."

Cale had never heard the familiar Christmas hymn expressed so sweetly. He pressed an ear to his door and strained to hear her, but the full chorus resumed for the conclusion.

Shouts of "Merry Christmas" rang in and out as the Pomeroy sisters welcomed the carolers in for refreshment. It sounded as if at least seven or eight pairs of feet trooped past Cale's closed door on their way to the warmth of the kitchen. Everyone talked at once, but Ada's distinct voice rose above the din as she directed the guests toward the bounty awaiting on the kitchen table.

Louella's voice then brought up the rear and offered a clue to the soprano's identity.

"Agnes, you always sing so beautifully in church," she said, "but tonight you sounded angelic."

"Yes... she surely did..." someone chimed in.

Louella again, "It might have been due to the stillness of the night. There's so much coughing and shuffling always within our congregation. It's distracting..."

The back door closed. Cale paced in darkened isolation, left to wonder what the possessor of that lovely voice must be like. His knowledge of music was limited to the lullabies his mother sang in his childhood, the usually discordant hymnsings at the little church he attended with her, and the tunes played at a raucous shindig at some neighbor's house or barn after he grew older. The Christmas Eve soloist did not fit in any of those places. He pictured her gracing some parlor, seated at a harpsichord or standing beside it while someone else played and an attentive audience looked on.

"There I go," he silently scolded himself, "thinkin' way beyond my reach again."

He liked most of the girls in his age group back home. The Willingham cousins, male and female, looked down on him. "Can't expect much from a Morgan," they chided. Sometimes the taunts helped him catch the eyes of their female friends when he danced to the fiddle. His grin and nimble footwork appealed to willing dance partners, and he found it easy to let go of innocence in the frolic that often followed. Betsy Gleason, his favorite, was destined by her parents for a future away from drab little Gowensville. A wall of society that Cale could not climb. That drove him to enlist on his 18th birthday before another late night frolic could change his mind. Then, hundreds of miles away, the voice of another young woman stirred a yearning he had tried to ignore.

Sounds again from the hallway told him the carolers must have concluded their time to refresh voices and warm feet for a return to the cold night air. He tiptoed to his door in hopes he might overhear some small bit of conversation that included the soprano voice. It was not to be. All the feminine voices ran together as they moved to the front door.

He did make out one short exchange. Most of the procession had moved ahead before Ada and one of the men lingered a moment outside Cale's door. The man must have inquired how the sisters found assistance with firewood or chores because Ada said "We're fortunate that others have been able to help out. We keep a fire in the kitchen only... spend most of our time there. Thank you, Horace, for asking."

Next he heard Ada and Louella call out "Good night... Thank you... Merry Christmas," and then, silence. He had moved away from the door when a knock sounded.

"Cale..."Ada called. "Everyone's in the wagon and they've gone on. Come have some eggnog."

He stepped into the hall and followed the sisters' candle. When they reached the kitchen, Ada motioned for him to help her slide the table to its original position. That done, Louella appeared at his elbow with a brimful cup of eggnog extended to his hand. She then retrieved Ada's cup, as well as her own, and drained the pitcher's contents into them.

"Merry Christmas, Cale," Louella said softly as she raised her own cup.

"Wait," Ada called from where she realigned a chair, "let me catch up." She took the cup Louella had placed on the table for her and lifted it high. "Eggnog at Christmas is a part of Father's tradition that we never want to relinquish," she said with pride.

They clinked cups before they sipped. The delicious milky concoction had obviously been laced with spirits. The late Mr. Pomeroy's formula left little room for doubt. And a grand tradition it is, Cale decided. He drained his cup and smacked his lips.

"I could hear them singin' at the front," he said. "Sounded real good. Especially the one who sang by herself. Thank you for leavin' the front door open so I could hear. Who is she?"

"Her name is Agnes Woodson," Louella replied before Ada cut in.

"She's a daughter of our county judge," Ada said. "Engaged to Joshua McAndrew, a local boy. He's an officer in the Tennessee Mounted Infantry, I believe they call it... Union."

Cale fought back a temptation to wish that ill might befall the fellow, but he did regret his own circumstance prevented an opportunity to get to know the young girl. He would have to content himself with the memory of that lovely voice. And his vision of a parlor, with a harpsichord, Agnes in a long gown, shoulders bare, head erect, lips releasing a tender ballad to the delight of all who might hear.

"Just curious," he said, "What color's her hair?"

Ada reacted with a questioning look, but Louella showed she understood. "She is blonde... with fair complexion."

Cale nodded to her in gratitude. She furnished what his vision had lacked.

Ada went back to finish her realignment of chairs then began to bank the fireplace embers. Louella carefully stacked the cups and glasses in the small wooden tub she used for dishwashing. As she placed her platter of sweets in the cupboard she took one of the honey-and-nut clusters and offered it to Cale. "If you like it, there's more for tomorrow," she said with her customary smile.

He thanked her and opened the door for them to pass through. Louella came first, holding a candle, and Cale moved swiftly. His quick peck on her cheek triggered her laugh.

"What?" Ada exclaimed before she realized what happened. He moved so fast from shadow she could not avoid receiving a peck on her own cheek beneath the mistletoe.

"You'd kiss half the women in the county if you could, wouldn't you Cale Morgan?" she pretended to protest and fastened the kitchen door behind her. Cale laughed as he caught up with Louella and opened the door for entry into the main house. He knew then he might never see another Christmas Eve. This one had been a gift in itself.

After breakfast on the day after Christmas Cale told the Pomeroy sisters of his decision to stop running. The Confederates' defeat at Missionary Ridge burdened his mind, he explained. He needed to return and face his punishment.

Both Ada and Louella – especially Louella – sat stunned, and then began to plead.

"You're not well enough.

"What good will it do?

"Do you realize what you're saying?

"Winter's no time to live outdoors.

"We need you to help put in the garden."

"I know what'll happen, most likely," Cale said. "They warned us over and over. Might just do it without a hearin' the day I come in. But I can't stop wonderin' what kind of terror caused 'em to run from Chattanooga. Boys I trained with... and took the fight to the enemy so strong at Chickamauga. One more gun in action on that ridge might have helped hold back the Yanks."

Louella stretched her hand across the table and placed it atop his. "Cale, we don't want to see you waste your life."

Seeing the fright in her eyes he mustered a confident smile. "I 'preciate that, Miss Louella," he said, "just like I'm so thankful for everything y'all have done for me... a total stranger. I'd never have made it to Kentucky anyhow. Not in the shape y'all found me."

He cleared his throat: "I'm carryin' a load of guilt because I left. I was so mad over the unjust way that sergeant treated me that I couldn't see straight. I forgot I was there to fight for homes just like this one, with good and kind people who've made their way by faith and hard work... who love the South like I do. Best thing about my leavin' camp came in discoverin' a grandpa I didn't even know I *had*. He really stuck his neck out for me. Then I got to know the two of you. I have to do what I can to keep this war from harmin' folks like you... and Grandpa Morgan. Seems the Yanks now control most of Tennessee. I have to see if my regiment will give me another chance to fight. We have to stop 'em and turn 'em back."

Louella's eyes had filled with tears. The lines in Ada's face showed the tightness of pain, but she sat in silence.

"I guess what I've realized," Cale went on, "is the danger I put you in just bein' here. You found out the Confederate cavalry rode through last month. The Federals might show up any day. And, since the singers of Christmas Eve, I've come to understand others will come by... for one reason or 'nother... and I might not be out of sight. Word could get out that you're harborin' a deserter. I don't want to let that happen. You've been too good to me."

"You're a brave young man, Cale," Ada said. "We've seen some of the good in you. If you must go, I suggest you go the courthouse and speak with the sheriff. He'll likely know how to locate the closest Confederate encampment. His sympathies lie with the South. Tell him what you've told us. I believe he will understand what is on your conscience." She paused. "He's a good sheriff, but he has acknowledged mistakes of his own when he was a young man."

She broke eye contact with her last words, and Cale sensed the time had come to move from the table.

"Thank you, Miss Ada," he said as he got to his feet. "Sounds like good advice. Means a lot to me that you understand what I tried to say. Yesterday, I took inventory of the firewood and pine knots stacked under shelter... believe there's plenty to last til spring. I'll check around the barn... make sure everything's where you can get at it."

While they talked, Louella bent forward and folded her arms atop the table. She pressed her forehead to her arms, crying softly. Cale walked to that end of the table, placed a hand on her shoulder, squeezed gently, and left the kitchen.

The sisters insisted he leave by the front door. Louella stuffed an apple and a corn fritter into a pocket of the jacket he wore and walked with him from the kitchen. A few weeks previously she had altered another of her brother's old garments to accommodate Cale's broad shoulders..

They found Ada waiting in the hallway. One of her hands parted the folds of her long skirt and presented Cale's knife. "You'll want to take this, I suppose," she said.

He accepted the knife and ran fingers across it to locate the initials carved into the wooden handle. He gripped the knife tightly for a few seconds then returned it to her.

"They'd take it away from me," he said. "I'd like you to keep it for me. If by some miracle I survive, I'll come for it some day when this war is over. If I don't, then I 'd ruther not let somebody get it who'd never know what them initials mean."

She clutched the knife and smiled. "Of course, Cale. Your initials mean something to us. We shall guard it for you and keep you in our prayers. You have a home here... if you need one." When they reached the front door, she opened it for him.

Cale kissed her cheek then turned to Louella. When she felt the brush of his beard and touch of his lips, her hand flew to grasp his sleeve as they stepped onto the veranda. Ada gently removed her sister's hand and embraced her. Cale descended the front steps but looked back when his feet touched ground. He saw Ada manage a brave smile in farewell. Louella wept against her sister's shoulder.

Chapter 8: Back to Battle

The Meigs County courthouse was easy to spot. The two-story wooden structure stood in the center of Decatur's square surrounded by seven or eight single-story buildings forming an outer rectangle. The nippy end of December weather discouraged anyone's lingering by the hitching rail or remaining in a wagon or buggy. Cale walked in unnoticed.

The foyer offered three closed doors identified by block letters burned into wooden strips that rested on pegs driven into each door's face. The "Courtroom & Chambers" option led straight ahead. "Clerk" marked the door at right. The door to the left read "Sheriff." Cale turned the knob and immediately drew the attention of a big man seated behind a desk in front of another closed door marked "Jail."

"What can I do for you?" the man asked.

Cale rubbed his hands and stepped close to the fireplace at his right, opposite the window.

"Are you the sheriff?" he asked.

"Yes," the big man replied as he got to his feet. "Sheriff Jefferson Tucker. What do you want?"

Cale swallowed hard and began. "I want your help. I want to find the closest Confederate camp... make things right... for leavin' my company." He swallowed again and watched the sheriff frown.

"You deserted a Confederate line?" Tucker demanded. "Where? Missionary Ridge?"

"No Sir," Cale said. "I left before that... shortly after we won at Chickamauga."

Sheriff Tucker's frown spread, "Chickamauga?" he blurted. "And you got all the way up here? Who's been hidin' you? You don't look like a body who'd been on the run for three months." He motioned to a chair in the corner between his desk and the door. "Sit down there and tell me everything," the sheriff said and reseated himself.

Cale did just that. The sheriff listened intently. The narrative moved swiftly through Cale's discovery of his grandfather and the narrow escape from capture by the Home Guard, but he began to ramble when he started to explain how he came to be in the sheriff's territory because he did not want to involve the Pomeroy sisters.

The sheriff was too quick for him. "Look here, Morgan... if that's your real name... you'd better tell me everything. You hear me? I'll lock you in that jail right now if you ain't truthful with me."

Cale glanced down but met the sheriff's eyes again when he resumed. "People who found me when I was awful sick helped me recover... and I stayed a while to cut firewood since they had nobody to do it. That's where I learned about Missionary Ridge and knew what a mistake I'd made. I didn't know where to go to give myself up to a Confederate camp. If they'll give me 'nother chance, I'll fight... just like I did at Chickamauga. That's why I came to you."

The sheriff leaned back in his chair but continued to look deep into Cale's eyes. "These people...," he said, "no menfolk about? Just women and children?"

"Yes, Sir," Cale said. His knee shook when he gave the half truth, and he hoped the sheriff had not noticed.

"How far away do they live?"

"Don't know what you'd call far...," Cale stammered. "But close enough I could walk in this mornin'."

Sheriff Tucker straightened and gripped the edge of the desk. "And I don't know what you'd call children, either," he said. His eyes bored into Cale's own.

The questioner rose and opened the door of the jail. "Sit down in there and wait til I come back," he directed.

Cale entered the small room and seated himself on the single article of furniture, a bench-like bunk anchored to a wall with a folded blanket on top and a wooden bucket below. The lock clicked shut behind him, then he heard the sheriff's grunts and dull clangs of metal. Cale presumed this meant the use of an iron poker to bank the fire before the door to the foyer opened and closed.

An hour passed and what had to be part of another before Cale heard the outer door open again. Movement around the sheriff's desk suggested the lawman had returned. The sound of a key turning the lock on the jail door prompted Cale to swing his feet to the floor and leave the bunk where he had stretched out for want of anything better to do.

The door opened and revealed Sheriff Tucker clad in a heavy jacket with a broad-brimmed hat on his head. "Come on out, Morgan," he ordered. "If you used that bucket, bring it with you. You'll empty it before we go."

Cale shook his head to deny any such use and fell in behind the lawman. Tucker talked as he led the way to the foyer and outside. "General Bragg's whole army went south in the retreat from Missionary Ridge, They'll be in winter quarters," he said over his shoulder. "If there's a unit left in east Tennessee, maybe someone over in McMinn County knows about it. We'll ride over there," he added as they approached two horses tied to the courthouse hitching rail.

They mounted and rode east at a trot until they had moved well beyond the village. The sheriff slowed his horse and Cale's horse, with its rein secured to the sheriff's saddle, slowed too . The gray sky and leafless trees by the roadside gave each mile a stark sameness, but warmth from the moving animal helped Cale dismiss the chill. They rode in silence with the only sounds coming from the horses' hooves.

Cale recalled Ada's remark about the sheriff's past. He could not help but wonder if the "mistake," whatever it was, involved the Pomeroy family. He also wondered if, in the time Tucker was absent, he had ridden out to the Pomeroy farm to check Cale's story. He could only hope the sisters had not been troubled. He had no doubt of the verification they would have furnished, but he trusted the honest account of it came without sacrifice to their own security and good standing. The slow pace of the horses and rhythmic motion in the saddle lulled him so deep in wonder that he hardly noticed the sheriff's hand grab the rein of Cale's horse until the sound of "Whoa." He jerked erect and saw they were about to share the road.

The sheriff halted the horses. They waited as two columns of blue-coated riders advanced to meet them. "Uh-oh," Sheriff Tucker said and rested his hand on the pommel of his saddle.

The blue lines extended far into the distance. Cale guessed they numbered 80 to 100 men on horseback, perhaps with supply wagons trailing behind.

Two riders spurred their mounts and hurried to close the 50 yards that separated the oncoming columns from the sheriff and Cale. "Don't make a move," the sheriff said out of the side of his mouth.

The soldiers' horses thundered to a halt and blocked the center of the road. "Good day, Sheriff" called a neatly dressed young officer who reined tightly to control his prancing horse.

"H'lo Lieutenant McAndrew," Tucker answered, "Hadn't heard you were back in these parts. Everything settled up around Knoxville?"

The Union officer stroked his horse's neck. "Everything's settled all over east Tennessee, Sheriff Tucker," he said in a confident tone. "And it's *Captain* now. Are you ready to state your loyalty to the Federal Union?"

Cale looked closely at the man the Pomeroy sisters described as Agnes Woodson's intended. Handsome, all right. In that uniform. He'd grant Joshua McAndrew that much.

Tucker took his time and shifted his stance in the saddle. "Congratulations on your promotion, Josh, but you know my loyalty is with the South," he said.

"I'm sorry to hear that has not changed," said the officer. "It means I must tell you that a new sheriff will be chosen for Meigs County... from those *we* can count on. I carry orders from the military governor in Nashville that all county officials loyal to the Confederacy are to be replaced."

"I'd like to see some proof of that," Tucker responded.

The captain raised his voice. "Then let's ride to the courthouse. I need to make the judge and other officials aware. You can read the order for yourself when we get there." He raised his sword arm high and addressed the officer who accompanied him to ready the columns to advance, then lowered his voice and his arm to point to Cale. "Who's this man, Sheriff Tucker?"

The sheriff busied himself in turning his horse around before he answered. "A soldier of the South who got separated from his own lines. We werc on our way to McMinn County... to return..."

"No Reb units in McMinn County any longer," the Union captain interrupted. "I'll take charge of him. Keep hold of his rein until we get to the courthouse." With that he prodded his horse forward and pranced ahead on the same stretch of road the sheriff and Cale had just traveled.

Tucker pulled on the rein of Cale's horse and followed. Blue-coated riders moved alongside, left and right.

The captain called for the ranks to straighten and present a stately procession before they entered Decatur. Somewhere behind him, Cale heard a beat commence, and the drummer kept the tempo going until the columns filled the square. Two supply wagons pulled alongside the well that furnished water for the courthouse. Doors opened. Heads popped out of shops and offices in the outer rectangle. Lamps glowed in a few windows, winter daylight having started its early decline. Three curious boys ran up for a close look at the uniforms and weapons of the many soldiers, but adult townspeople held back as if they sensed what they witnessed but waited for some authority figure to say it out loud.

Both the officers and the sheriff hitched their horses to the courthouse rail. Tucker led the way inside. Cale followed at their heels. They opened the sheriff's office, and Captain McAndrew ordered Cale into the jail. "I'll deal with you after we've seen the judge," the officer snapped. Beyond his own locked door, Cale heard the door to the foyer open and shut.

He sat down on the bench he left two hours earlier and took a few swigs from a filled canteen Sheriff Tucker had furnished before they rode out for McMinn County. The corn fritter Louella Pomeroy stuffed in his pocket that morning became his supper. Cale slipped out of the jacket and folded it into a pillow when he stretched full-length on the bench.

The jail cell had no window. The only light came through an opening at the top of the divide from the sheriff's office. With the fireplace unlit and dusk descending outside the one window near Tucker's desk, Cale meditated his fate in semi-darkness until he heard the door to the foyer open. Only one pair of footsteps, he determined. Someone muttered, and the footsteps ceased when the outer door opened and closed again.

When it reopened, a trace of light joined Cale in the cell, and a voice commanded "Turn the key and unlock that door, Sergeant." Cale sat up and listened to the key turn in the lock and the door open to reveal a blue-coated sergeant who stood in front of Captain McAndrew. The captain held a lighted oil lamp. He placed it on the sheriff's desk and seated himself in back of it. The sergeant ordered Cale to leave the jail and stand before the captain. Sheriff Tucker was nowhere to be seen.

The captain ordered Cale to identify his unit and state his reason for leaving. As he described the flogging episode, McAndrew interrupted.

"You ever have any problem following orders before?"

"No, Sir," Cale said. "Did everything I was told to do... through trainin' and the fight at Chickamauga."

"Why did you enlist, Morgan?" the captain demanded.

"'Cause South Carolina called her sons to fight, Sir."

"And why do you think South Carolina did that?"

Cale swallowed. "Why, for the right to go our own way, Sir," he said.

The captain removed his hat and brushed a hand through his hair. His hair was much lighter in color than Cale's, and neatly trimmed. "And you feel South Carolina owed nothing to the Union?" he asked.

"Well, Sir," Cale began, "I've not had a whole lot of schoolin', but... since you ask me... seems it was like a big family.. a big place with ownership spread out amongst a bunch of brothers. Some of the brothers disagree over how the land is bein' used.. or some other thing... and want to be separated . Other brothers don't want 'em to do it. If you ask me, Sir... looks like each brother should decide for himself. Them that want to go, well let 'em go. Them that want to stay, then stay. But if them that stay try to prevent the ones who want to leave from goin'... well, I guess the leavers have to fight for the right to do so." He felt shaken from the unexpectedly long speech and stiffened his arms to regain a soldierly position.

Captain McAndrew's eyes studied him throughout, but he did not interrupt.

"The Union is a big family, Morgan," he said. "You're right about that. The brothers you described as enforcers have the good of the entire family at heart, and the advantages to be gained by staying together. Without the practice of slavery."

Cale dared to raise a hand. "May I say, Sir, I grew up around a few plantations that did keep slaves, but I never worked on one. I did not want to then, and I don't want to now. Slavery's not why I fight." He fell silent again and struggled to keep from shaking before the eyes fixed on him.

The captain's mouth formed a thin smile. "I accept your word on that, Morgan. But, if we return to your analogy, let's say ... among the brothers who left, one or two want to own slaves, one or two do not. If you and other Southern boys fight for the right for all those who left the Union, then you're fighting to give the right to those who continue the practice of slavery... even if you don't wish to join them. Do you see?"

Cale feared whatever he said would come out wrong, but he had to say it."I went to fight for my people, Sir. Some of 'em think different from me. They're still my people. Same as my pa went when I was a little...."

The captain interrupted, "Your father went to war? When?"

"Pa was killed in the War with Mexico, Sir... place called Molino del Rey, wherever that is."

"That led our assault on Chapultepec," the captain said with obvious interest. "That victory brought on the end of the war. Morgan, former Sheriff Tucker seemed to believe what you told him. I know him to be a decent man, although I regret he cannot be allowed to remain sheriff. You appear to be a straightforward young man whose father died in the service of the Union. I have the right to offer you an opportunity to join the Seventh Tennessee Mounted Infantry and defend our Union... the big family," he said in a soft, matter-of-fact tone. "I make that offer now. Will you accept?"

Cale swallowed again. "I cannot, Sir," he said, "I could not fire a gun or use a bayonet on a Confederate soldier. I thank you, Sir, but I cannot accept your offer."

The captain pushed back from the desk and rose to his feet. "Well, Morgan, since there's no Rebel unit within fifty miles, the choice you leave me is to declare you a prisoner of war. You will be taken to McMinn County tomorrow morning and, with other prisoners, transported to Chattanooga. Someone there will decide what is to be done with you. Now return to the jail for the night. Sergeant, lock him in."

Captain Joshua McAndrew placed his hat on his head and strode from the room.

Cale and a half dozen Confederate captives in McMinn County were marched out in early January under a six-man mounted guard bound for a stockade in Chattanooga. They never made it.

A few miles south of the Hiawassee River, the same region where Cale met his grandfather, the guard grew complacent and failed to scout a defile before they rode into it. Too late, they discovered the tree-covered hillside swarmed with Confederate troops.

Shots were exchanged, but the lieutenant in command of the guard realized he was hopelessly outnumbered and surrendered. His onetime prisoners were told to mount the horses of their former guard and Union men ordered to walk while their captors, a party of Confederate cavalry, returned across the state line to winter quarters in Georgia.

A sergeant of the cavalry unit then rode with Cale to a larger encampment at Dalton, Georgia where he was reunited with the 10th South Carolina Regiment. Company D of the 10th had a new commanding officer.

"Another straggler, eh?" Captain Augustus Dunn sighed when Cale was ushered into his tent. The look on the officer's face grew more solemn as he listened to Cale's explanation. "Morgan, I say to you what I told the ones who've straggled in since Missionary Ridge. Our army needs men, but you're on trial. You'll be watched. The first sign of dereliction will end your trial, and you'll be found guilty. Now get out of here, go to the quartermaster, and get back into uniform."

The same day Cale learned the sergeant who ordered him whipped had been wounded and sent home.

For three months, Cale participated in his company's work details, drills, and reviews without a weapon. He set targets on the firing range and shouldered the dirtiest chores with the rawest enlistees. The constant scrutiny of superiors did not cost him a new friendship, however. One thin young man who became a member of Company D during Cale's three-month absence had a pale face and chin of light-colored fuzz. He appeared even younger than dark-haired, dark-bearded Cale.

"David Appleby's my name," the youth confided at a campfire they shared. "Heard some of 'em tell about what happened to you. I respect you for comin' back... lot more than the first ones who took off runnin' soon as blue coats started comin' up that ridge."

Appleby had enlisted back in Cale's home district before the battle of Chickamauga but did not reach the regiment until three weeks before they took up positions on Missionary Ridge. "Thought I'd gone to hell sure enough," he said so quietly Cale had to strain to hear. "If I survived that, I must be meant to last."

To Cale, the last words sounded as if the youth dealt with his initial panic when faced with enemy gunfire. It also brought memories of his own combat initiation when he fired his first rounds at men as his line advanced at Chickamauga.

Each young man soon proved to the other that he could be counted on when the Federals launched a new offensive to control the railroad to Atlanta.

Their first side by side battle experience came in the defensive line to hold a railroad stop named Resaca. Shells exploded above and around them. A deafened Cale flattened himself and fired his newly issued weapon into the wave of blue-coated infantry advancing under cover of smoke. A jab in the ribs from Appleby warned of a second wave that moved up to replace the fallen. The line held, and the Federals retreated.

Yells of "We showed 'em" rang out among the defenders but faded quickly when the order came to move farther south and defend another part of the railroad.

"I tell you, Cale," Appleby complained after they were ordered to fall back a third time, "we're givin' up too much ground."

"They're payin' a lot, too... only with them it's dead men," Cale said.

"They don't look any older than us, do they?" Appleby observed.

"Don't look at faces," Cale counseled, "fire at the blue coats. I don't 'spect they look to see if we're grinnin' friendly-like before they shoot."

They took heart when the commanding general ordered trenches dug and breastworks built around a natural fortress called Kennesaw Mountain. The 10th South Carolina, however, was sent to protect the southern rim of the town of Marietta. The terrain proved to be a second enemy. David sank up to his waist in a bog when the order came to move, under fire, to strengthen the flank.

"Good thing you're puny," Cale grunted as he lay flat on his belly and stretched an arm for David to grab. "Ten pounds more and we'd just as well leave you here."

The lines held, but the Federals decided to go around. In the middle of night, Cale and David marched south again with the rest of the Confederates' Army of Tennessee to cross the Chatt-hoochee River and fortify a defense of Atlanta.

They had one momentary burst of success. Spirit ran high as the 10th moved eastward across spread-out Atlanta and broke the Federals' grip on the railroad line to Augusta. In the fury of shot and shell, a minie ball winged Cale. He staggered and dropped from his place in the line, but a calm David reloaded and answered for him with a blast into the man who shot Cale.

"Now we're even," David said as tugged Cale upright. "But I won't mind if you care to take the lead again if I get knocked to the ground."

"You're too skinny for them to hit," Cale retorted. "But thank you anyhow."

Loud protests within the ranks followed yet another order to withdraw and spend the rest of the summer on the western side of town. The lull gave Cale the opportunity to seek medical attention for his wounded arm.

Sporadic outbursts of gunfire alternated with long interludes of uneasy waiting. The stifling heat as July yielded to August made conditions worse inside the barricaded area since so many shade trees had been sacrificed to build the encampment. When merciful evening coolness finally came a few hours past sundown, the Federals frequently launched an artillery barrage that made attempts to sleep fitful and short.

Picket duty gave the inquisitive David a chance to pester and joke when he found someone willing to talk among those who pulled similar duty on the opposite side of the hastily built complex of breastworks, felled trees, and trenches.

"Talked with a boy from Indiana while ago," he reported to Cale. "Said he wished we'd hurry and give up so he can go home to marry his girl. Abbie's her name."

"He can go right now, far as I'm concerned," Cale said. "Nobody invited him down here."

"I already told him that," David said between swats at flies. "Said I thought that's why they wanted the railroad so bad... to ride back home. He wanted to know if I had a girl."

"What'd you say?"

"Didn't see any reason to lie. Told him I want to see some of the country before I get serious. He said he'd never been far from home, either. Said his dog's name is Fearless. Good name, I'll admit. You reckon many of 'em are like that Indiana boy?"

"I 'spect they're a lot like you and me, Dave," Cale said. "Some of 'em, anyway." He had only one real conversation with a soldier from the opposing side to draw upon. Aside from a stiff neck and swagger, there must be some solid quality in Captain Joshua McAndrew if he had won the love of that sweet-voiced Agnes Woodson.

The relentless pressure the invader brought from so many directions forced the Confederates to abandon Atlanta in

September. After a losing battle a few miles southwest at a place called Jonesboro, the defenders marched up and down western Georgia and eastern Alabama in search of an opportune means to cut the Federals' supply lines. Autumn turned to winter and brought with it a plan to strike the enemy from behind in Tennessee. The numbers they faced proved far greater than believed and brought heavy losses of manpower. That attrition led to promotions to corporal on the spot for both Cale and David.

The South's once-proud Army of Tennessee was a fragment of its former self. A long retreat was ordered, but the wounds of war went too deep. The entire Confederacy lasted just four months longer.

Cale and David didn't keep track of what state they were in when the order came to push eastward to intercept Union forces who swept from the coasts of Georgia and South Carolina on a northward path to join their comrades in Virginia. Before January 1865 was out, the two armies faced off again at Bentonville, in North Carolina. Cale and David fought that day on little more than backbone and grit. Each man goaded the other and stubbornly refused to give in to exhaustion.

Appleby talked often of his determination to live to a ripe old age in Texas. He struck Cale as being well-read, and never seemed to run out of yarns fed from something he had read or heard. Railroads figured in most of them.

"Why I reckon there's a fortune to be made if a feller gets involved in connectin' the civilized parts of that wide open country," he boasted. "That part of the South's just brimmin' over with opportunity for smart fellers like us... more than what's already in somebody else's hands around here."

"I'm glad you've got a dream, Dave," Cale cautioned daily, "I just want to see the sunrise tomorrow mornin'."

Bittersweet assurance they would see more of 1865 came with word of General Robert E. Lee's surrender in Virginia. Confederate forces in North Carolina soon followed suit. Instead of celebrating the independence of the Southern nation they fought to establish and preserve, the defeated men were dismissed on the first day of May at Greensboro, North Carolina and began a long walk to their homes in South Carolina, Georgia, and beyond.

Unaware what account of his absence after Chickamauga had reached Gowensville, Cale requested and received a note from Company D's commanding officer stating he served until the hour of surrender.

Chapter 9: Aftermath

"How long you aim to stay?" David repeated the question every day once they left Greensboro.

"I can't say, Dave," Cale answered each time, but the question always resurfaced. "I'd like to see Ma, but I 'spect her husband will want that to be a short visit."

"I won't be around long myself," Appleby said. "We don't know what we'll find when we get there. These farms we pass don't look too hard up. Folks in these parts don't seem eager to see us linger for more than a drink of water from their wells."

Cale conceded the point. Rare was the occasion when one of the farmhouses offered as much as a piece of cornbread or a green apple when a soldier stopped at a residence along the road.

"Prob'ly 'cause there's so many of us," he said. "Remember, boys who served in Virginia walked these roads, too. These folks may have shared most of what they had with the first ones to pass by." He remembered the weeks after Chickamauga, when he survived by the grace of a few kind souls who shared a bit of food with a stranger. The miraculous discovery of his grandfather returned to mind, and he recalled how the meal he received that day came only after a lengthy test of intention.

David's chatter had resumed, but Cale's attention dwelled in memories of the two brief conversations with his grandfather. He wondered if he would ever see him again. He wanted to return to Tennessee to let the Pomeroy sisters know he had made it through the war and get the knife left in their keeping. "Need to accomplish that before I look up Grandpa Morgan," he said to himself.

"Are you listenin' to me?" his friend demanded as he jerked Cale's sleeve.

"I'm sorry Dave... been thinkin' 'bout something else."

"Well, pay attention," Appleby scolded. "I just asked if you'll consider settin' out for Texas with me?"

Cale had to smile as he glanced sideways at the gaunt face of his friend. Already skinny when they met, David Appleby became even thinner from countless miles of marching and infrequent and insufficient portions of food. The dirt-caked uniform hung on him and seemed to miss contact with any body part other than shoulders. The fuzz on his chin bore little resemblance to a beard. But he had shouldered a gun and kept his composure when the minie balls flew and shells exploded about him. He would be about the best companion Cale could think of should a man willingly head for the unknown.

"Well," David demanded, "what about it?"

"How you figger to get there? I hear it's awful far."

"Why, anyway we can, of course." came the irritated reply. "Walk a ways... we're used to that... maybe earn a little money somehow and board a train. We'll figger it out. Don't know if anybody will even care how we fought to make the South free, but we don't have to sit here under military occupation. We can go where we please... find someplace where it's wide open. No reason to stay in South Carolina, is there? Come with me?"

"I might go to Tennessee," Cale said.

David blinked. "Hell, that's partway," he said quickly. "I'll go with you!"

That told Cale his friend's spirit had come through the war undiminished. Suddenly, something his grandfather said popped in mind. After the admonition "Stand up for yourself," Grandpa Morgan had added "Don't let anybody break your spirit."

Cale enjoyed his heartiest laugh in months.

"All right, Dave, after we see what we find back in the old home district, we'll talk 'bout goin' to Tennessee. I'd like you to meet my grandpa. You two ought to hit it off real good."

Two young girls chased a little boy about the yard when Cale reached the house he left more than two years before. The eldest girl, about seven, stopped play and stared without giving a sign that she recognized him. She turned to face the house and called, "Mama, 'nother one's here."

A small woman appeared in the open doorway, wiped her hands on her apron, then raised her right hand to shield her eyes as she peered into the late afternoon sunshine.

"H'lo, Ma," Cale said quickly to put her at ease.

A smile crossed her face. She stepped off the small porch and ran across the yard to meet him. Both her arms flew to encircle his waist. "Cale, son... you're alive! Thank the Almighty God!" she cried and lifted her head from his chest to examine his face.

Cale bent to kiss her cheek. Her brown hair showed noticeable streaks of gray. He eased one arm free from her hug and placed it about her shoulders. "I'm proud to see you're well, Ma," he whispered. "Sorry I'm not much at writin' letters. No paper to write on these past several months. We stayed on the move."

She brushed tears from her eyes."We heard the army had moved this way to stop Sherman," she said in a choked voice. "I prayed you were still with 'em." She tightened her embrace again before she released him, took his hand, and led him to the shaded porch.

"Come, sit here and rest," she smiled and pointed to a wooden stool. "You must be so tired."

"I am that, Ma," Cale said as he dropped his pack and slumped to the stool near the door of the house. His mother, Millie Hunt Morgan Rainwater, called to the children who had forsaken their play to gawk at the stranger on the porch. "Children, you remember your brother Cale?"

"I didn't have this beard when I left," Cale interjected, "Susie might remember me." He studied the eldest of the three, who moved to the edge of the porch, sucking her thumb. "Susie, if that thumb's so good, I'd 'preciate a bite," he said. The girl's face reddened, but her eyes showed she recalled the way he teased.

"You've lost so much weight," Millie said. "We'll have supper shortly... soon as Noah and Eli come in from the field. You must be hungry. The boys who've come by all look about starved." She turned suddenly and hurried into the house. "Oh, forgive me Cale... I left something on the fire.. it'll be burnt..."

He leaned back against the front of the house and looked first left, then right, at the plantings of Noah Rainwater, his stepfather. Sprouts of corn extended in neat rows at his left. At right, beyond the well at the corner of the house and the packed clay of the yard, fields bore leafy evidence of peas, potatoes, and other vegetables.

He left the porch and walked to the well to draw a bucket of water. He drank long from the gourd that hung by the windlass, then dipped it in the bucket again and poured the cold contents over his head. He heard laughter behind him as he shook his wet hair and beard and wiped the back of his hand across his eyes.

"You can't believe how good that felt," Cale said to the children as he left the well for a better view in back of the house. Beyond the smokehouse and barn, cotton plants sprouted in fields spread between the pasture on one side and orchards that climbed a hill and backed up to the corn. Near the far end of a field, a man slowly followed a mule and plow in front of a boy in his early teens who walked behind and broke clumps of fresh-turned soil with a hoe. Freeing the young cotton from weeds, Cale remembered from his own experience before he left for war. He'd give Noah Rainwater credit. The man knew how to put each acre he owned into cultivation and coax it to produce.

Cale watched the plowman and the mule reach the end of a row. As Rainwater turned the animal and lifted the plow, he caught sight of Cale. He stared for a minute before he started the mule and plow down the adjoining row toward the house.

Cale walked to the barn entrance. He climbed the ladder to the loft, grabbed a bundle of fodder, and tossed it near the stable door. He scrambled down to fetch the big wooden bucket from the peg where it always hung. He walked to the well and filled the bucket before he returned to the barn where he waited for Rainwater to finish the row, unhitch the mule from the plow, and bring the work animal to be watered and fed for the night.

Rainwater nodded to him but said nothing while he attended to the mule. The boy's eyes lit up, and he dared to speak before his father. "Been hopin' you didn't let some Yankee take you down, Cale," he said.

Cale grinned. "Plenty of 'em tried, Eli, but I reckon I made it. Let me draw you a fresh bucket of water. Bet you could drink half of it yourself." He slapped the boy's shoulder as they walked together toward the well. Eli was the son of Rainwater's first marriage. That first wife's demise led to the courtship of Cale's widowed mother.

Once the filled bucket had been brought to the top, Rainwater joined them and put a stop to Eli's questions. Cale politely offered the first gourdful to his stepfather, who accepted and drank from it without a word.

"Looks like you've got corn and cotton off to a good start, Mister Rainwater," Cale said.

Wiping his mouth, the older man handed the emptied gourd to his son. "We need rain," he said. Not a word about Cale's arrival or well-being. Just "We need rain."

Millie's voice from the back door summoned them in for supper.

"I'm sorry I didn't have time to prepare much for you, Cale," his mother said. A plea showed in her eyes. "I'm so thankful you're here to share what we have."

Noah Rainwater seated himself at the big kitchen table and began to say grace before Eli had settled on the bench at his immediate right. Cale slid in beside the boy. The prayer offered several expressions of gratitude – none mentioned Cale – and rain was requested at least twice along with appeals for mercy upon the people of South Carolina before the "Amen."

"Too early for anything from the garden, Cale," his mother apologized from her spot at Noah's left. "Just what we can make do from that we dried and canned last year. Dandelion greens are all the new we have at this time."

Cale smiled to her across the table. He watched Noah ladle beans from a big pot onto his plate with one hand and break the pone of cornbread with the other.

"It's good to get to eat anything you cooked, Ma," Cale said. "Way better than the scraps I've been used to..."

Rainwater interrupted. "We've surely had to scrimp... on our vittles... so the army could be fed," he announced between chews. "And for what?"

Cale saw his mother divert her eyes, and he chose not to challenge his stepfather.

"I know it's been hard... on everybody," he said and turned his attention to the first tastes of his mother's cooking since he enlisted more than two years before.

The silent Millie favored him with a smile of gratitude.

On the other hand, Rainwater had more to say. "Well, we're worse off than ever," he continued. "Money worthless... notices posted at the mill and all over Gowensville... darkies set loose... Union officers sayin' what will and won't be allowed... dread to think of all they'll lay hands on now that we're under military rule."

He stopped rambling to look Cale squarely in the eyes. "Your mother is glad to see you," he said when another bite had been swallowed. "I know how she worried about you all this time. You left here of your own choosin', and you need to keep lookin' out for yourself best way you can."

Cale made sure they kept eye contact as he spoke. "That's what I mean to do, Mister Rainwater. I'm here just long enough to let my mother know I made it through the war. No more, no less. I'm glad your land escaped bein' torn apart by trenches, explodin' shells, fightin'.... you may not believe it, but you're a lot better off than... Well, I'd best not describe what I've seen and spoil your supper."

Rainwater went to bed soon after supper. Millie cleared the kitchen and reminded her young brood to prepare for bedtime.

"Ma, can I bother you for a towel?" Cale asked. "I'd like to take a good, long bath."

She went to the pantry and drew from a stack a rough but clean cloth sack that had been split and made into a towel. She handed it to him along with a piece of soap. "It's nearly dark," she said. "No need to move the tub far from the well... nobody'll see you. I'll meet you out there when you've finished."

Cale filled a tub halfway, stripped, and eased himself into the cold water. He shivered but rubbed himself hard with the soap to speed his adjustment then sat with knees drawn up to his chin to enjoy a long soak. His head had drooped to a nod when he jerked at the sound of someone's approach. He twisted position to see his mother with folded clothing in her arms.

"Some of your things I washed and put away," she said. "Perfectly good shirt and trousers. Might be a little loose on you now... some underdrawers and stockings. I'll put 'em here at the well til you're ready to dry off. Come round to the porch after you're dressed."

Cale found the old underwear and trousers still fit reasonably well. He left the shirt folded until he had soused the dirty uniform items in the soapy tub he had vacated and scrubbed them free of some of the accumulated dirt and sweat. Barefoot, he draped the wet garments and the towel across his mother's clothesline. Then he emptied and rinsed the big wooden tub, slipped into the clean shirt and stockings, reshod himself in beat-up shoes, and walked to the porch where Millie waited in the darkness.

"I'll take that soap," she said as she drew another stool alongside hers. "Come sit beside me. The others won't hear if we keep our voices low. My, you smell good."

"Lot better, I 'magine," he whispered. "I don't want to keep you up late, but I hoped we could talk a little."

"I want that, too," she agreed. "I've prayed this time would come."

Cale reached for her hand. "Tell me, Ma... is it all right... with you and him? I've thought about it so many times, and I regret leavin' you the way I did. I never could seem to please him. I did the work, you saw it... and I stayed out of his way. But he always looked at me with that distrustin' nature. His face showed that same old expression when he came in from the field this evenin'."

She placed her free hand atop his. "I won't ask you to forgive him, Cale. I've tried talkin' to him so many times. Tried to show him how much I loved Eli... thought that might help his feelin' toward you. To answer your question, yes... it's all right here. He's so different from your pa, but I believe he loves me... in his way. He's a good provider, and gentle with our children."

She squeezed his hand. "I realize that last part sounds hurtful to you."

Cale leaned closer. "Not any more, Ma. Only reason I came back was to see you. If you're cared for, that's enough for me.

The hurt I can't forget was seein' you have to go from neighbor to neighbor, askin' to do washin' or mendin' or field work... and earn a little or be paid in something we could eat. I'm sorry I couldn't grow up fast enough to be more help. If only Pa could have lived and come back..."

His mother rested her head against his shoulder. "Yes, Cale, if only. The few years of happiness I had with your father... why, that's a lifetime I treasure. Son, your pa was one of the finest, kindest men who ever walked this earth. Always be proud you are Ty Morgan's son."

He bent to kiss her again. "I am, Ma... don't ever doubt it. And I'll share a secret with you. I found *his pa!*" He whispered the last with such excitement it brought her quick reminder to whisper.

"You mean his grave, don't you Cale?"

"No, I mean *him... Grandpa Morgan*, in the flesh. Up in Tennessee less than two years ago." He told her of the chance discovery and the subsequent rescue. "He gave me his knife... got his initials... *his and my* initials carved in it. Some kind people I met later are holdin' it for me. I'm goin' back there, and I mean to find him again. But let's keep his secret."

She sat very still as if she needed time to store what he told her in some corner of her mind. "Oh, I wish Ty could have known," she said. "He said he came to understand how Mister Morgan must have decided he'd had all the Willinghams he could take. But Ty never wanted to talk about it very much. I could sense how it pained him. Of course, I won't tell now."

She stood and retrieved a folded quilt she had placed beside her stool. "I'm sorry we don't have a bed for you. Eli's in your old one, and the littlest one has the bunk Eli used to have. Will you be able to spread this and make do here… on the porch?"

He took the quilt and rose to stand beside her. "Porch will do fine, Ma. I'm used to sleepin' outdoors."

She kissed him goodnight. "In the mornin', I'll look to see if any more of your things are stored in the trunk. I'd best get inside."

He watched her enter the darkened house on tiptoe, then he spread the folded quilt full length and stretched across it. The May night was warm, and the non-warlike sounds from night creatures lulled his weary body to sleep.

A little past midday of the following day, a rested Cale hiked into Gowensville and stopped at the general store that filled one corner at the crossroads. Three Union soldiers waited beside four horses at the rail. Another horse stood hitched to an unoccupied buggy while a fourth soldier added an official notice to those already displayed on the storefront. Cale felt in his pocket to make sure the paper issued in North Carolina was in place.

"You belong here, Reb?" asked a sergeant who appeared to be in charge.

"I'm from this community," Cale said, "if that's what you mean." As he spoke, the sergeant's open palm stretched outward, and Cale presented the note issued in North Carolina. One of the blue-coated privates came forward and proceeded to see if Cale carried any weapon.

The sergeant read quickly, returned the paper, and walked to his horse. "Finish up, Jersig," he called to the soldier whose hands smoothed the newspaper-sized notice just pasted to the front wall of the store. "We've got miles to cover and more stops to make." The sergeant mounted, motioned for the men of his detail to ride, and the foursome left in a whirl of dust.

Cale glanced over the newly-posted "Notice to the People of South Carolina," but the many wherebys, therefores, and whosoevers demanded considerable patience to read. The door of the store stood wide open, so he chose to enter and speak to the proprietor.

The familiar half-light of the big store's interior made him feel right at home. When he was a child, the display of goods atop tables, in open barrels, and stacked on shelves along the walls introduced Cale to a wider world — merchandise he could admire but never afford. The ownership and operation of the store had been passed down through three, possibly four generations of the Gleason family.

A young Gleason female had been Cale's favorite dance partner, and they shared more than one moonlit tryst after the fiddler played his closing tune. Betsy benefitted from a secure family environment with social stature higher than his own. A finishing school was in her future, but it did not prove to be a barrier when Betsy saw his Willingham cousins repeatedly attempt to make him uncomfortable at social gatherings. She seemed amused. That did not set well with Jacob Willingham, who acted as if the prestige of his name entitled him to Betsy's attentions. She did not see it that way.

Their last night together lasted well past midnight. Cale had decided to enlist; Betsy was to leave for Spartanburg the following week. That night they did not have to hurry their acts of love. The full pleasure of body exploration and discovery of more ways to please each other made them reluctant to allow the night to end.

"I don't want to go," Cale had whispered in her ear when she sat up and put out a hand to retrieve her pantaloons from clothing cast aside in the straw. He reached to stop her. "We have to go, Cale," she had said. "We have to get away from here before anybody stirs." She laughed, and he joined in. The site mischievously chosen for their consummation was a Willingham grain shelter near the road they walked from the dance to her home.

They did not see each other again.

Memory of that night filled his mind as he moved inside the big store. He saw sixtyish Alexander Gleason, Betsy's grandfather, at his usual place behind the long counter engaged in conversation with a man who stood with his back to the door.

"I can't do a thing about it," Gleason apologized. "We're all under orders to use greenback dollars. I'm goin' to the bank in Greenville tomorrow to try for a loan on this store... don't know how I can stay open otherwise."

Cale stopped beside a stack of farm implements just inside the door and waited for the business discussion to end. The customer did not budge. His silence suggested he needed time to digest the words he had just heard.

"I'll give you as much time as I can to settle what's on your account," Gleason continued. "I just can't add much to it until I know how I'll pay my own obligations. Take the flour.. I'm sure your wife needs it... but I can't let you have anything more right now without Federal cash."

Still without a word the man shook his head, lifted the sack from the countertop, turned, and walked past Cale to his buggy. Gleason's face showed sadness as he watched the man leave. He did not notice the new arrival until Cale stepped closer to the counter.

"Come in, come in," the storekeeper called without a hint of recognition.

"H'lo, Mister Gleason," Cale said. "You prob'bly don't know me behind this beard... it's been a while."

Gleason's eyes narrowed then brightened and opened wide. "Why, I do believe it's young Cale Morgan!" he said loudly. "Another one of our boys made it through... and all together in one piece, looks like. Come here and shake this hand!"

Cale grinned and reached across the counter for the firm hand. "Had a long walk to get back to see Ma yesterday," he said. "How are you, Sir?"

Gleason insisted that Cale take one of the stools kept behind the counter. "Sit down here," he commanded, "and tell me as much as you want to. Got no business to transact anyhow. All I've done today is make folks mad. You must have heard what I had to say to that customer. We're all in a fix." He shook his head but dropped the despondent tone. "You boys didn't let us down. We just couldn't furnish the help you needed. It's over and done... we might as well talk."

And talk they did. At Gleason's urging, Cale began a short summation of his fight to stay alive but the storekeeper interrupted early on.

"Just remembered, Cale." Gleason said, "Mister Willingham said for me to tell you to come see him if you got back," he said.

Cale caught his breath. "You mean Uncle Sumter?"

"Yes... the head of the clan. He's mentioned it a number of times"

The news seemed less of a surprise once Cale recalled that Jacob Willingham was one of Uncle Sumter's several grandsons. That must be the reason his father's uncle wanted to see him.

Cale had never set foot in the big Willingham house, nor had he ever expected an invitation.

He resumed the hasty account of his part of the war then seized the opportunity to ask about Betsy.

"We haven't seen her in some time," Gleason said. "That Hawthorne School's strict about their schedules... so my son tells me."

Cale smiled as he pictured Betsy in the midst of proper young Carolina belles. She could pour tea in tiny cups and practice French with the best of them, he reckoned. And if war had deflated the gaiety, Betsy would somehow challenge those around her to enliven it again.

"If you think of it, Mister Gleason," he said, "tell her I got out alive."

"Of course, of course," the storekeeper said quickly. "She'll be pleased, I'm sure... any notion what you'll do now?"

Cale settled his elbows on his knees to rest his chin on his interlocked fingers. He liked Alexander Gleason and had no reluctance about confiding in him. "I intend to go to Tennessee... some people there I want to see. Then I might head for Texas. But that part's just a thought. I'll decide later on. By the way, Mister Gleason, my friend David Appleby may drop by in a few days and ask about me. He went on into Greenville to see his folks, but it's his notion to go to Texas. It's all he'd talk about the last few months."

"Why I'll be glad to take a message Cale," Gleason said. "Where will you be... if he does come?"

Cale ran a hand along the edge of the counter. "Mister Rainwater don't want me around," he said. "I don't want to cause trouble for Ma." He paused and studied the gray-haired

155

storekeeper's eyes. "I wonder if you'd let me sleep out back for a night or two, Mister Gleason? I won't disturb anything."

"Why, we can do better than that, Son," Gleason interrupted. "There's room for you at our house. If you don't have any place you need to go, stay around. When I close up, we'll go home to supper. My wife will be glad to see you and share what we have."

Cale's audible sigh of relief preceded his "Thank you, Sir... but that's too kind of you. I've not slept in a bed for so long, I wouldn't know how to act. I'll be comfortable enough out back." He liked the generous offer of a meal, but he sensed a need for caution about being in Mrs. Gleason's company very long. Betsy may have confided things to her grandmother that could be stirred by something he might say.

"Well, if that's your choice... you must eat with us, at least," Gleason insisted. "Fact is, you can sit out front tomorrow and explain to anybody who comes by that I've had to go into Greenville and won't open til late afternoon. If I left a note on the door, folks couldn't see it amongst all the notices pasted out there. I want to get an early start and see that bank."

"Glad to do that, Sir," Cale agreed.

Cale manned his post in the shade at the front of the store until the storekeeper returned in midafternoon. Gleason had dressed in his best suit for the occasion, but his face did not convey an outward sign of success. He shucked his coat and loosened his string tie as soon as he dismounted from the buggy. Cale jumped up and tied the horse's rein to the rail.

"Well, Cale, I've done something my father never had to do... and to the best of my knowledge, my grandpa didn't either," Gleason said. "I had to put up this store and property... everything but my house ... as collateral to apply for a loan. Money to stay open. And I have to wait to find out if it's approved. That application's got to go through more hands than them holdin' cards 'round a poker table."

"I hate to hear that, Mister Gleason," Cale said and shook his head in commiseration.

Gleason applied his key to the padlock and pushed open the door. Cale went inside with him and remained a while to allow the friendly storekeeper more time to vent frustration. At his first opportunity, Cale reported on the few who had stopped by during Gleason's absence. Two had promised to come back before the end of the day.

"I think I'll go on out to see if Uncle Sumter's at home, Mister Gleason," he said. "Might as well find out what's on his mind." Gleason concentrated on the thumb he ran through the big ledger on the counter and waved acknowledgment with his other hand.

Cale had two miles to walk along the road to the big house at the center of the old Titus Willingham estate. He was in no particular hurry to get there. As he walked, Sumter Willingham's summons took second place to concern for what would befall the Gowensville community should the Gleason Store be forced to close or change owners.

That issue still had not been sorted out to Cale's satisfaction when the two-story white house loomed on the horizon. The surrounding fields showed the customary plantings of cotton, corn, grains, sorghum cane, and tobacco. Large crews of fieldhands were at work in two different sections. Cale wondered if they knew they had been set free, or if they remained simply because they had no other place to go for shelter and food. "Doubt anybody else's got money to hire 'em," he said to himself.

The pebbles crunched beneath his feet as he walked up a pathway between boxwood hedges trimmed square. He climbed the steps of the wide front veranda, and stopped to catch his breath and dislodge small stones lodged in the soles of his worn-out shoes. Narrow strips of tinted windows ran up each side of the housing for the double doors, and Cale tried to peer through the left window as he shook the brass doorknocker. The sharp sound reminded him of a gunshot, but the lack of response from the quiet house convinced him to knock again with greater force. What seemed like a second full minute passed. He began to think he had been set up for another Willingham slight. He didn't hear footsteps, but the right door finally swung inward to reveal the dark face of an aged man in an equally dark suit. "Yes?" the man inquired.

Cale swallowed to calm himself. "Would you ask Mister Willingham if this is a convenient time for Cale Morgan to call?" he said.

The dark face returned a blank stare and a question, "Mista' Morgan?"

"Yes... Cale Morgan. I was told he wanted to see me."

The door closed. What seemed a good five minutes elapsed without a sound from inside. Cale tipped one of the veranda's several high-backed rocking chairs into motion to relieve his tension. The singing of workers in the fields drifted within earshot. Playfully, he tried to time the chair's rocking to the singers' rhythm. At last the door opened again. The servant beckoned. "This way," he said.

Cale followed the presumed butler down a huge hallway lined with mirrors, paintings in heavy frames, trunks, umbrella stands, and closed doors to the third door, right side. The servant tapped before he opened the door to announce, "Mista' Morgan, Suh!" He stepped aside and motioned Cale to enter.

Sumter Willingham sat in a high-backed leather chair by the window. The man's face always reminded Cale of someone who expected a sweet taste when he bit into a crabapple. The lines of age had not been kind to that face. Cale had never seen the man without a hat. The surprising sight of a bald scalp with thin wisps of white hair about the ears forced him to bite his lip as he advanced into the room.

"How are you, Uncle Sumter," he said and held out his right hand.

Willingham frowned at the greeting and made no effort to accept the offered hand. Instead, he motioned the visitor to be seated on the stuffed couch opposite his own position and in front of an entire wall of shelved books. Cale guessed he must have entered the old man's study, or office.

"I want you to tell me all you know about Jacob," said a firm voice from out of the withered body in the chair. No comment about Cale's safe return. "The army said his death was a suicide. We brought his body home for burial in the family graveyard, but it was badly decomposed."

Cale sat on the front edge of the couch and faced his questioner. He began to recount the episode which followed the fighting at Chickamauga, but Willingham's raised hand stopped him.

"I know that part. We heard about that from more than one source. And I was told you were punished because you refused

159

to take a whip to my grandson. What I want you to tell me is... what sort of soldier was Jacob before that day?" His narrowed eyes bore the bright gleam of inspection.

Cale shifted position to give himself more time to reply. "Well, Sir... Jacob was already there when I reported to the regiment in Tennessee. He was in another part of Company D... we had well over a hundred men at that time, and I didn't catch sight of him more'n once or twice a week... sometimes less. Everything was strange to me, and I spent my time learnin' what I was 'spected to do. My first fightin' came there at Chickamauga Creek.."

He swallowed and paused to regain confidence before that penetrating stare.

"The few times I had a chance to talk with Jacob he seemed like his old self." Cale hesitated when he realized what he had said. He did not want his less than flattering recollections of Jacob Willingham before the war to be so obvious. " I have to tell you, Sir, I never saw Jacob all through either day of the fightin' across the fields and up through the woods of that place. Hard to tell what others were doin', 'cept the ones close on my right and left... and all that enemy in front. My concern was... hold up my part of our line and force the bluecoats back. We did a good job of it, too..."

"Yes," the elder Willingham interrupted again, "the victory is well known. I don't doubt that you did your duty, Morgan. What I want to find out is, did Jacob do his? You were told he was... a malingerer... is that true?"

"That's what that sergeant said when he ordered me to follow him and shoved that whip at me," Cale said. "I never heard that from anybody else. And...I wouldn't know, Sir."

The stare lost intensity, and Sumter Willingham's face turned to the window. He held that pose in silence.

Cale clasped his hands to relax.

"What none of you will tell me," Willingham spoke to the window as if Cale had moved beyond it, "is that my grandson was a coward. Someone saw it in the heat of battle. My grandson... the youngest son of my dear late son Titus... and the recipient of a lifetime of favor endowed by his family name... disgraced it. My proud Southland is now at the mercy of military rule... our slaves taken from us... our honor blemished beyond..." The expressions of remorse trailed into unintelligible whispers.

Cale sat stunned. That name, that precious surname, meant more to the old man than the life of his grandson, and the lives of countless other young men of the South. Willingham honor and slave labor were all that mattered to the embittered shell of a man. He has more land than anybody else, Cale assessed, and far more ways to start over than any other family within several miles in all directions. He mourns for himself. Few, if any, others.

Sumter Willingham turned from the window and faced Cale again. "When I first heard of the punishment, the irony of your selection to wield that whip did not escape me," he said in the firm voice shown early in the conversation.

Cale was uncertain he knew all the word "irony" meant, but he waited to learn why this aged great uncle chose to use it.

"Perhaps you declined in order to turn the other cheek, so to speak," Willingham said. "If so, your gesture made its point. The end of my own life is near, and I wish to honor the memory of my late sister Rachel... the young Rachel, in her happiest times... with this gift." He lifted both hands from the armrests of his chair and grasped a small cedar box from items spread atop his lamp table. Unsteadily, he held out to Cale what appeared to be a miniature music box.

Cale fought an urge to seize the little box and throw it in the old man's face. It would serve Willingham right if he thought a trinket could make restitution for the years of slights and wrongs heaped upon Cale's father and mother. When he took it, however, the weight of the box surprised him.

"Open it," Willingham said as he leaned back in his brown leather chair.

Cale rested the box on his left knee and lifted the lid with his right hand. No tune began to play. Any mechanism could not have functioned because the space within the silken lining had been filled with an ivory cameo that rested atop a stack of heavy gold coins. At first glance, they numbered half a dozen. Still, the implication that money could compensate for things Cale could not forget bothered him. Then he thought of his mother. Whatever amount of greenback dollars he might secure in exchange could mean so much to her.

"Uncle Sumter..." he halted when he saw Willingham flinch.

"I'm sorry if that title of respect annoys you," Cale began again, "but it's what I was taught, and a lifetime habit's hard to break. I had a strong temptation to refuse this... but it may be put to good use for my mother. Pa could not do much for her besides give her me. Many times that proved a hardship. I don't know what you meant for me to do with this, but it will be of some benefit to her."

"That does not surprise me," Willingham said. He lifted a handbell from the table, and shook the clapper twice.

Cale clutched the box in his left hand and rose from the couch. "I offer my regrets for what happened to Jacob," he said. "So many families lost so many loved ones..."

Willingham waved a hand to silence him. Cale complied. So be it, he decided.

The hallway door opened and Willingham addressed the butler. "Show Mister Morgan out, Simon." A slight nod served as farewell.

"Good evenin' to you, Sir." Cale said as he crossed to the door. He had reached the hallway before Sumter Willingham spoke again.

"I believe Rachel would rightly be proud of you."

Cale turned, but the old man's gaze and attention were again fixed on the estate he could see from his window.

The reminder that a measure of Willingham blood flowed in his veins did nothing to cheer Cale's walk up the hallway. He passed through the door held open to the veranda then spun around to grab the surprised servant's right hand.

"Goodbye, Simon," he said with a shake.

Cale hurried down the front steps and the pebbled path to the road.

The next morning he showed the coins to Alexander Gleason. The storekeeper ran his thumb across the face of each coin and spread them one by one across his counter.

"Bechtler coined these pieces... look here on the reverse," Gleason said as he returned a coin for Cale's inspection. "'Carolina

Gold' inscribed above his name... 'C. Bechtler,' Christopher Bechtler founded a mint just across the North Carolina line nearly fifty years ago. The streams and hills 'round here, like the ones in Georgia, turned up considerable quantities of gold in the early years. It was safer to use Bechtler's mint than to travel the long and dangerous road to Philadelphia"

"Still good, ain't it?" Cale asked..

Gleason chuckled, "Son, there's nothing better in these times when Confederate paper's worthless and U.S. greenbacks are in the hands of so few. You've got six of Bechtler's five-dollar pieces right here."

He pushed the coins close to Cale's hands and picked up the ivory cameo. "What about this?" he asked.

"I think I'll give it to Ma," Cale said. "She's never had anything nice."

"That should please her," Gleason said. "It's a beautiful piece."

Cale put the cameo in his pocket and scooped the coins back inside the little box. "I need some boots," he said. "Might as well let Uncle Sumter buy me some. Think you can help me? And I want to pay you something for lettin' me sleep out back."

Gleason laughed. "You don't owe a cent for sleepin' in my shed." He motioned for Cale to follow across the store where he pulled assorted shoes from the shelves. Cale proceeded to try them on until he settled on a decent pair. When asked the price, the storekeeper mumbled "Half price... we'll call it even at five dollars."

Cale insisted on two gold coins, at least. Gleason gave in after he tossed two pairs of new stockings and a cotton jacket into the trade.

"Might be a good time to go see Ma now. Mister Rainwater's likely in the fields."

He left the store and started for the shed to place the new clothing in his pack when a distant voice called his name. Down the road which led to Greenville, the county seat, a lone man waved an arm overhead as he approached the crossroads. David Appleby had arrived.

Cale greeted his friend, "You tired of South Carolina already?"

"Never meant to stay long... told you that," David fired back. "If you're willin' to leave, I've got us a free ride as far as Anderson."

"Why should we hurry to Anderson? That's not even fifty miles."

"Miles we won't have to walk," David snapped. "A friend of my family needs to return a team and wagon. Said there'd be a good chance for us to join somebody crossin' the river to Georgia... then it's on to Tennessee and the West. But I have to tell him tonight."

They walked back to the shed where Cale folded the new items in his pack. The task gave him time to consider David's offer. To get to Tennessee, he realized, they'd need to resort to a variety of ways to travel and stay alive. There would be plenty of miles to walk, and he was grateful for new boots. He tossed the shoddy, worn-out pair aside and secured the straps on the pack.

"All right," he agreed. "First, let's tell Mister Gleason we're leavin', then I want you to go with me so I can tell Ma goodbye."

After his introduction, David seated himself on the porch to suffer the stares of the children while Cale went inside for a few minutes' private time with Millie. The midday meal had concluded. Rainwater and the boy Eli had gone back to their fieldwork.

Millie held his left hand tightly. The introductory words had conveyed this was a farewell visit.

"I've got some news, Ma," Cale said. "Uncle Sumter had left word at the store that he wanted to see me. I saw him yesterday... pitiful-lookin' old man he is. I believe all that's happened made him regret how he treated my side of his family, but he couldn't bring himself to say it. Instead, he gave me this."

He placed the box on the table between them. "There's three five-dollar gold pieces in there. I know you'll give 'em to Mister Rainwater, and that's all right with me. But there's something else I want you to keep. Wear it one day in remembrance of Pa." He produced the cameo from his pocket. "I believe he would have cut wood for a solid month to be able to buy something this nice for you, if he'd had the chance."

Millie's nervous hands accepted the cameo. She caressed the ivory profile with her forefinger. A quick intake of breath spoke for her.

"Must have belonged to Pa's mother," Cale ventured to say.

She nodded, then gave in to tears. "I'll wear it proudly," she cried.

"That's what I wanted to hear you say. I took some of the money to buy some boots. Old ones finally fell apart."

She choked back emotion to insist he should keep the gold in the box, but he refused. "Still got one," and he showed it to her. He took her arm and guided her to stand with him.

"I'm sure it'll take us a while to get to Tennessee. I'll let you know if I find Grandpa again. I hope Mister Rainwater has a good harvest this year and y'all won't be bothered much by this... occupation. I sure would like another hug before I go."

Cheeks coated with tears, she managed a broad smile. "You didn't think I'd let you out that door without one, did you?" she teased as she spread her arms. "Hold me tight just a minute, Son. I want the thrill of the Morgan touch one more time."

His arms pressed her close to his chest. They stood in silence until she looked up to his face, and he kissed her.

"I won't walk out with you, Cale," she said softly. "Let me remember my Morgan men like this."

Once he stepped onto the porch, he heard her call "I'm glad you're not goin' alone."

David jumped to his feet when Cale emerged and went ahead to wait by the road. Cale spent a minute in goodbyes with his small half-siblings then joined him.

"All right, Travelin' Man... let's be on our way to Tennessee."

Chapter 10: Autumn 1865

The Pomeroy house must have once appeared as a homestead of strength and stability. When Cale and David caught sight of it, the house offered instead the same tired look of faces they met all along their journey from South Carolina. Owners of those faces endured war only to become sufferers of the aftermath. The house simply fell victim to neglect.

The setting – beneath a cloudless blue sky with tints of autumn in the bordering forest – had retained its beauty, but the primary subject showed its age.

For the first time Cale gained a full frontal view where he could not fail to notice the absence of shingles from parts of the roof and walls badly in need of paint. Conditions of his previous stay required that he remain indoors or limit himself to areas in back and out of sight. That meant poor acquaintance with the overall size of the house or the position it commanded on a level above that of the village.

The memory of kindnesses shown him in that house surged, and the anticipation of seeing the Pomeroy sisters again quickened Cale's pace to a trot without so much as a signal to his road-weary companion. While Appleby stumbled and protested, Cale rushed to the edge of the untended expanse of front yard, cupped his hands, and shouted "H'lo Miss Ada! Miss Louella!"

He halted and listened for a reply then called the names again, louder.

"May not even live here any more," David wheezed. "Can't see any smoke comin' from a chimney, can you?"

Cale ignored his doubting friend and crossed between crape myrtles bare of blossom that flanked the steps of the front veranda. He was halfway up when he heard a voice from far to the right of the house. He hurried back down the steps and rounded the corner of the veranda. He spotted a bonneted woman standing erect facing him while a second looked up from where she knelt at work. The sharp repeat of "Who is it?" convinced Cale that Ada Pomeroy remained very much in charge of this house and lands surrounding.

He waved and broke into a run. "It's Cale, Miss Ada! Cale Morgan."

Ada wiped her hands on her skirt then raised them to cover her mouth. Her posture seemed to weave as Cale drew near. The other woman got to her feet and moved to Ada's side. The familiar gesture of following her sister's lead identified Louella Pomeroy to his satisfaction.

"Oh, Cale! We're so happy to see you," Ada cried through her fingers. "I regret you find us like this... scratching sweet potatoes out of the dirt." She brushed her wet cheek with one hand and adjusted her bonnet with the other.

Louella rushed to embrace him and knocked her own bonnet askew when she pressed her head against his chest. Sobs of joy served as her words of welcome.

Cale pulled Ada into the circle of arms. "Took three months to get here," he said, "but seein' you both again is what I wanted.

Why don't we go up to the house... let you rest a bit? We'll take care of these 'taters before dark sets in."

The trio moved toward the house, but their feet could not keep up with the women's words. "It was thoughtful of you to write to us, Cale," Ada hurried to say, "and let us know you survived the fighting."

"Oh yes." Louella gushed, "we've read your letter over and over It was such a relief to learn you were safe. Jefferson Tucker told us the Union Army took you. That frightened us even more."

"We knew you would keep your promise to come," Ada reclaimed the lead. "We've talked about it most every day."

Louella again: "'Cale will help us decide what to do,' we'd say."

"We'll tell him about that later, Louella," Ada directed. Their voices stilled when they caught sight of David Appleby, who had remained near the veranda corner. Cale kept an arm behind each woman's back and nodded to David.

"Miss Ada... Miss Louella... this is my friend David Appleby. He's heard me talk these past two years about how kind you ladies were to me. Dave kept me from gettin' shot more times than I could count."

Ada stepped forward, removed her bonnet, and smoothed her graying hair.. "Then we owe you our gratitude, Mister Appleby," she said. "Please forgive our appearance. We've waited so long to harvest our little crop of potatoes that we couldn't be cautious about dirty hands and skirts."

Louella clung to Cale's arm but greeted David with a welcoming smile.

Ada moved ahead to the steps. "Cale," she said, "why don't you take your friend around back to the well and draw a fresh bucket of water. We'll join you in the kitchen in a few minutes.""

"I like the sound of that, Miss Ada," Cale said. He freed his arm from Louella's hold, guided her to the steps Ada had climbed, and signaled David to follow him. "Come on Dave... you're about to taste some good Tennessee limestone drinkin' water."

The foursome reassembled a few minutes later around the big kitchen table. The women had shed the bonnets, brushed skirts free of dirt and dust, and cleaned their hands. Cale attributed their flushed faces to their work in the field, but the smiles were unmistakable signs they were happy to see him. The kitchen interior looked exactly as he remembered, and, as they talked he sensed a comfort not felt for a long time.

The spell ended when Ada's head jerked at some sound from the main part of the house. Cale was in the middle of a jovial account of an adventure on the road and did not hear what caused her reaction. Ada broke eye contact with him and glanced toward the door. Louella looked down at her hands, folded on the table top.

"That will be our brother," Ada quietly addressed Cale. "Euclid returned a few weeks ago. We were happy to see him, of course... but he's... different."

Her eyes kept the steady expression Cale remembered, but he saw in it a request for understanding without questions. He reached for her hand.

"I 'spect the war's responsible for changes in lots of folks," he offered. "He's your family. We don't want to cause any trouble, showin' up like this... but if me and Dave can help out anyway... like gatherin' them sweet 'taters... we'll get right to it."

"Oh, Cale," Louella found her voice again, "we've prayed for you to come." She sniffed loudly. Her eyes showed tears which she did not attempt to hide.

"We're thankful for your presence," Ada said. "So much needs to be done if we're to have any hope of surviving another..."

The kitchen door opened with a bang, and she stopped in midsentence. A suit-and-vested middle-aged man strode into the room. His shirt collar was open, and a loosened string tie hung beneath a shaven chin. He had a bushy head of brown hair and eyes of the same color made bold by their uncommon intensity.

"Who's this?" the man demanded when he saw strangers at the table. "Was company expected?"

Euclid Pomeroy in the flesh, Cale presumed.

"If you will lower your voice, Euclid," Ada said, "I will make the introductions. This is our young friend Cale Morgan..." she said, her open palm extended toward Cale. "We've told you of the great assistance he gave us one time during the war. He has come back this way along with his friend, Mister Appleby." She gave a brief nod to David. "Young Gentlemen... Louella and I would like you to meet our brother... Euclid Pomeroy."

Both Cale and David rose from their chairs out of Southern custom. Euclid ignored the gesture and directed his remarks to Ada. "You plan to board them?" he asked as he seated himself. "We have food enough for that? Too bad you didn't summon them sooner to put in a decent crop."

173

Cale cleared his throat and dared to speak. "I would have been here sooner if I could, Mister Pomeroy, but there was a fight to finish. Your sisters once showed kindness to me, and I'd like to do something for them in some way. My friend David and me just got here. We've come to pay our respects and help out however we can... like gettin' some 'taters out of the ground before dark. If you'll excuse us, Sir, we'll..."

Ada interrupted and took charge again. "They are our *guests*, Euclid," she said in her firm tone. "We are happy to share what food we have. We will see that your portion is not affected."

Cale motioned for David to follow him to the door. Ada caught up with them as they walked to the potato field. "I apologize for my brother's rudeness, Cale," she said with that steady plea in her eyes.

"That's all right, Miss Ada," he said. "Guess we surprised him just bein' here. Why don't you show us where you want the 'taters put once they're out of the ground."

"Thank you both for caring about us," she said. "Bring the hampers to the cellar... you remember where it is, beside the kitchen... inside you'll find the sacks we store them in." She stroked Cale's arm. "It's good you've come, Cale. I'll go now and work out some sleeping arrangements."

"The hayloft will suit us fine, Miss Ada," he said. "I speak from experience, remember?"

"That might be best," she said. "For the time being."

When she left, Cale headed to the spot where the half-filled hampers had been abandoned.

David followed but remained standing when he saw Cale drop to his knees and commence work.

174

"I got a notion this ain't quite what you expected, is it?" David asked.

"I 'spect you to fill that other hamper, Dave," came the answer. "And I 'spect you'll like a hot supper and a place to sleep that ain't on the ground as much as I will."

Cale savored his bowl of Louella's black-eyed pea soup alongside a roasted sweet potato slathered in butter and gladly allowed Euclid to set the conversational tone at the supper table. David, head bent low over his own servings, did likewise.

Euclid's tone became less hostile at table. His deference to Ada led Cale to wonder if she had had words with her brother. Before the meal concluded, however, Euclid could not restrain an urge to share his knowledge of the wider world. He spoke with a voice of conviction.

"Fools... in high places as well as low. We've not seen a leader in this country since Andy Jackson. Old Hickory could have outsmarted both the abolitionists and the plantation crowd at every jump. He knew... Andy Jackson knew... when to grab some ears, knock heads together, and make this country prosper. I tell you... I've traveled, been in many a city, met with real gentlemen... put up with some, too, who wasted my time."

He paused, got up from the table, walked to the hearth, broke a stem from a straw broom, held it to the open flame, and used it to light a stub of cigar he had fished from his vest pocket. "I saw the danger signs," he said after exhaling a second time and seating himself. "Years ago."

When Euclid replaced the cigar between his lips, Cale took it as a cue to speak.

"Were you in the war, Sir?"

Euclid puffed before he stretched out his arm for inspection of the two-inch long remains of cigar. "No," he said without shifting his eyes, "I offered my services to the South early on, but the damn fools could not see officer material right in front of them. Something about 'proper recommendations.' Just senseless evasion. I could have served in many capacities." He flicked ash from his cigar. "Too bad," he said.

He asked about the final action Cale and David saw before surrender but did not grant much time to hear it before he rose.

"I believe I'll take the air on the veranda if you'll excuse me, young guests" he said as he left the table. "I'll say good night at this time... Ada.... Louella... thank you for a nourishing supper."

"Good night, Mister Pomeroy, " Cale called after him. "Miss Ada," he said, "if you'll show us what needs doin' for the stock, we'll take care of it now."

Ada rose and motioned him to follow her outside. "I fed and milked the cow while you brought in the potatoes," she said when they were alone. "That's all there is, aside from that old rooster there... and five hens. Our orchard had a good year. We're putting up all the fruit in either dried or pickled form. We found help to plow the garden last spring... a half-acre of peas fared rather well... some good peavine hay, too. We planted what sweet potatoes we could... now with the cabbage, and turnips coming in soon, we're a little better off."

"You ladies know how to manage better than most folks," Cale said. "I want to see you're set for winter... plenty of wood...

anything else you think of. I noticed the roof needs some new shingles. We'll fix that before we look up Grandpa Morgan."

"Yes, we've had leaks in the front rooms," she said as they walked farther from the kitchen. "Cale, you cannot know what a blessing you are. I know you must be anxious to find your grandfather, but I'm so thankful you came here first. I'll get your knife for you in a few minutes."

She looked back as if to make sure they were alone before she spoke again. "First, I need to make you aware that Euclid wants us to sell this place. Immediately. He seemed alarmed when I told him that we were forced to sell our interest in the bank after Father's death. The Chattanooga newspaper lists so many places for sale... at most any price. I've told him it is short-sighted to sell now. Louella and I have no place to go But he is so determined,,, brings it up most every morning at breakfast. Everyone needs money in these sad times, but I fear my brother needs a great amount of money."

Cale put an arm about her, and she leaned her head against his shoulder. He did not know what to say but kept his arm in place until he felt her back stiffen when they heard the kitchen door open. She stepped away from him before David emerged.

"I'll get your knife... and bring a quilt for each of you," she said as she started for the house.

Cale was so glad to hold the knife again he kept a grip on the handle while he slept. Before they stored their packs and chose sleeping places in the barn loft, he allowed David a brief moment to inspect the treasured object.

177

"Right handsome old knife, I grant you," David said.as he examined it in the fading light. "Blade could stand sharpenin', don't you think?"

All other times, the knife became part of Cale's person, secured in his waistband while the two young men applied muscle and will to work sorely needed around the place. They cut trees and split logs for the fireplace. Cale stuffed his pockets with nuts found on the ground in woodcutting expeditions and delivered them to a delighted Louella. They cleaned the barn. They split hardwood and used a rusty saw to cut shingles to fill holes in the roof.

Euclid watched them begin each day's work but did not offer to take part. At midmorning he left on a daily journey to the village and did not return until late afternoon.

Cale and David were perched on the roof, fitting new shingles into place one afternoon when they heard a shout from the road.

"Is this the Pomeroy place?" yelled a man from horseback..

Cale knew Ada and Louella were at the washpots in back of the house and likely beyond hearing range. "Yes," he answered for them. "I'll need to climb down and summon the ladies for you. It'll take a while."

"No need," the man said. He jerked the rein and rode off.

Cale broke the news at supper.

Louella suggested the visitor likely was a neighboring farmer, but Ada overruled. "Our neighbors and most everybody in the village know full well who lives here," she said with customary firmness.

Euclid did not react outwardly until he finished his meal. His eyes studied Cale's face as if he had it under examination for the first time. Then he leaned back in his chair, and his lips formed a thin smile. "I don't suppose you saw what direction that man came from?" he asked.

Cale shook his head. "Didn't even know he was around til I heard him yell."

"Well, did he appear to be a gentleman? Clothing... decent saddle... trappings on the horse? You must have been able to tell," Euclid pursued.

"Ordinary feller, I'd say. Dave, did you see anything to remark on?"

David looked up from where he sat, alongside Cale, both opposite Euclid. "Just the hat," he said. "Big, black hat. Looked new... nice wide brim. Like to have one like it myself."

Euclid pushed his chair away from the table and stood. "Sisters, I've enjoyed my meal. I'll retire to my room now. Good night, All," he said and left the room.

Cale saw an opportunity to turn the subject. "Tell me again... the name of the young lady who sang the Christmas Eve I spent here. Did she stay around after the war?" He tried to make it sound like a polite inquiry but realized he probably fired the question too fast after the slow start..

Louella nodded. "Yes... Agnes Woodson is still part of the community. It upset everybody the way her father, Judge Woodson, was dismissed. That broke his health. He did not live out the year. Poor Agnes. Joshua McAndrew had the responsibilty to replace all the county officials... her feeling for him must have been strained... terribly.."

"Joshua came back from the war badly wounded," Ada contributed. "Agnes devotes a lot of time to him. I believe the engagement still exists."

179

Cale tried to hide his disappointment.

"Why don't you accompany us to church next Sunday?" Louella suggested. "Agnes sings, almost always. Perhaps we can introduce you after the service."

" I sure would like to see who has that beautiful voice," Cale confessed. "But I wouldn't want to embarrass you... or her... the way I look..."

"You won't embarrass anyone," she assured. "I'll see that your shirt is fresh and ironed."

"Several in our congregation don't even bother with that," Ada joined in. "But it is the Lord's house, and I'm sure He welcomes us in whatever we wear."

On their way to the hayloft, David poked Cale's elbow with his own.

"I'm gettin' a notion our journey to look up Grandpa Morgan will be put off a ways," he teased.

Cale grinned. "I 'spect Grandpa would understand."

David chose to stay behind when they left for church. Cale entrusted him to look after the knife. Euclid returned to his room after breakfast.

The little stone church occupied a position near the courthouse square. About two dozen worshipers had been seated before Ada, Louella, and Cale walked in. He started to take a seat at the back, but they insisted he join them in a pew two rows from the altar and pulpit – space evidently reserved for the Pomeroy family. The sisters acknowledged welcoming nods from others and directed that Cale should precede Louella down the pew so that Ada might be seated on the aisle. That reversed the order on other pews with men seated on the aisle. Cale presumed it maintained a traditional place for the senior Pomeroy in attendance. He liked the arrangement because it allowed him to feel less conspicuous.

After much shuffling of feet and clearing of throats, a man not much older than Cale walked to the side of the pulpit and announced the first hymn. He spoke each line and led the congregation to sing that line in unison until "The Old Rugged Cross" had been sung in its entirety. Louella's voice rang in his left ear, but Cale sought to single out a voice that might belong to Agnes Woodson. He failed, as he did in the performance of the second hymn when off-key voices of several men increased in volume and made it hard to distinguish even that of the song leader.

A silver-haired man in a black frock coat left his chair in back of the pulpit, knelt beside it, and commenced to pray aloud. He began with the needs of the flock and local community then moved on to the state of Tennessee and her place in the reconstructed nation. The preacher got to his feet when his prayer concluded. "We'll now honor the glory of God through the voice of Miss Woodson," he said and sat down.

Cale's eager eye caught stirring across the aisle where a petite young woman rose from a position at the song leader's left on the front pew. A dark bonnet trimmed in white lace concealed her hair but framed the fair face. She chose a position in front of the altar and faced the congregation. A pitch pipe sounded, then she began to sing.

"Rock of A-ges, cleft for me... let me hide, my-self in thee...."

The clarity of her voice took Cale back to that Christmas Eve of 1863. But he much preferred the second hearing when he could see *and* hear. What he saw complimented the vision he imagined at that first event as surely as the shade of her dress matched the equally dark bonnet. She raised her clasped hands in front of her bosom and, with an upward tilt of chin, looked straight ahead while she sang.

Cale's stare remained unbroken as she moved through all the verses. He strained to establish eye contact but had to settle for a shy smile of appreciation – directed first to all those applauding on his side of the aisle and then the other – before she returned to her pew.

The rest of the service was an anticlimax. The silver-haired preacher launched his sermon and compared the suffering of the Jews under Pharoah to Meigs County's circumstances in what had been given the name Reconstruction. Frequent shouts of "Amen" came from segments of the congregation, but an occasional loud cough meant a nerve had been struck in an occupation loyalist.

When the lengthy service ended, the Pomeroys exchanged pleasantries with both men and women who had been seated nearby. That trapped Cale in place, and he lost sight of Agnes while a mass of bodies clogged the aisle. Ada insisted that Cale be introduced to the preacher who had moved down from the pulpit. They did as she wished until he found a way to whisper in Louella's ear. "Do you see Miss Woodson?"

They left Ada immersed in another conversation and moved out into the churchyard; Louella in the lead, Cale obediently in tow. He heard her bid farewell to several departing worshipers, then suddenly a loud whisper meant only for him, "There she is... come with me."

She pulled Cale along behind her to the spot where Agnes and another woman conversed. Louella joined their conversation and soon took control. Cale's ears may as well have gone stone deaf until he heard, "Agnes, I'd like to present our young and good friend Cale Morgan."

He willed himself to speak. "I want to thank you, Miss Woodson... for the pleasure of listenin' to your lovely voice."

A hint of welcoming warmth showed in her eyes. "Thank you, Mister Morgan," she said. "I'm glad you could attend our church. Will you worship with us again?"

He liked the suggestion but fumbled to answer because a grunted "Agnes" sounded loudly from behind her where a man sat in a waiting buggy. He was well-dressed with a hat pulled low so that it shaded his forehead and concealed most of his blond hair.

"I'm coming, Josh," she said to him before she turned back to Cale and Louella. "Forgive us, Miss Pomeroy, we must be going."

Louella gave soothing assurance she understood as Agnes placed a foot on the buggy step. Cale sprang to offer a supporting hand. As she settled on the seat she murmured "Thank you, Mister Morgan" but did not look at him.

The man's stormy expression lingered after Cale withdrew his arm from her elbow.

"Captain McAndrew," Cale said. "No reason you'd remember, but we met...."

McAndrew's right arm jerked the rein sharply and used it to slap the rump of the horse. "Adieu, Miss Pomeroy," he called. Before the buggy rolled out of the churchyard, Cale grudgingly conceded to himself that the captain still presented better than average handsomeness in civilian clothing.

Louella waved her handkerchief as farewell.

"Was Captain McAndrew in the church," Cale asked.

"He comes in after the first hymn," she said, "sits on the back row... close to the door... among the first to leave. Poor man..." she touched the little kerchief to her face and dabbed an eye. "He hates if folks see him crawl in and out of his buggy... and him so young, too."

Ada caught up with them. A tall, broad-shouldered man followed her. "Cale, do you remember Sheriff Tucker?" she asked.

The big man stuck out a hand. "Ex-sheriff." he said with a grin. "Miss Pomeroy can't break the habit. I'm just a blacksmith and harnessmaker these days. Glad to see you again, Morgan."

"I'm not on the run this time, Sheriff," Cale said with a laugh. "I 'spect you heard how our Union guards rode into a big surprise in that valley south of here. My old company took me back, down in Georgia."

"Yes, "Tucker said, "news travels slow in these parts, but word about that did make its way. Drop by my place any day you feel like it. It's right across the square. Miss Pomeroy will tell you how to find it. I'll bid you all a good afternoon and let you be on your way," he said with a tip of his big hat first to Louella and then Ada. He held the second gesture noticeably longer than the first.

"And to you, Jefferson," the sisters said, almost in unison. Ada's fingers tightened the strings of her bonnet as Tucker walked away. Louella gave a knowing smile to her sister that caught Cale's attention.

Something Ada said on the day he left "...good sheriff..... mistakes of his own." came to mind . Had Tucker's "mistake" involved one or more members of the Pomeroy family? Could the passing of time have healed whatever scar the "mistake" inflicted?

The incident of years past was not Cale's concern, but customarily solemn Ada's light spirit on their walk home fed his belief that she must have played a part.

The sisters entered the house to remove their bonnets before the preparation of Sunday dinner. Cale walked to the barn. "We're back, Dave," he called to the loft, "you asleep up there?"

Hearing no answer, he climbed the ladder for a look around. The loft was as still as the stables below – the cow having been released to graze the pasture after the morning's milking. Cale jumped down and returned to the barn's front entrance.

He cupped his hands for a louder shout that died in his throat when he heard the scream.

"Cale! Cale!" It was Ada's voice. "Come quickly!"

He crossed the back yard on the run and almost collided with her as she dashed from the kitchen, a half-filled washbasin between her hands. "You're old room..." she gasped once they were inside the hallway.

Cale ran ahead and saw, through the open door, Louella's back. She knelt on the floor at the foot of the bed. When Cale stepped past her left side, he saw that she held David's head against her knees and wiped blood from the base of his neck. His eyelids flicked open irregularly.

"He's alive, ain't he?" Cale blurted from a crouch.

185

Ada knelt at Louella's right. "Here's hot water... straight from the kettle," she said, the pan placed on the floor within her sister's reach. "I'll get more clean cloths,"

"And salve!" Louella called over her shoulder, then to Cale, "See if you can lift him to the bed."

Cale slid one arm beneath David's shoulders and the other under his thighs. But when he tightened his own back muscles to start the lift, he saw the wrecked bed. With quilts tossed aside, the mattress overturned and slashed, wads of padding exposed and scattered, the bed was in no condition to receive a patient. He withdrew his arms from underneath David and rose alone.

"That bed's in shambles, Miss Louella," he said. "Let me drag a quilt over. We can rest him on a pallet."

Ada hurried in again, cloths and a jar of salve in hand. "Father's room has been burglarized," she cried. "Desk drawers open, trunk contents scattered, closet door wide open... someone's raided this house!" She bent to offer the medicinal items to Louella.

Cale folded a quilt lengthwise before he placed it alongside David. He slid the inert body onto it, then tucked a folded end of a second quilt as a pillow beneath David's head. Louella's hands continued their ministrations. Cale stood erect again, "Any sign of your brother?" he asked Ada.

She shook her head and began to pace the room. "The bed is ruined," she sighed. "Euclid's closet is in disarray," she added from in front of a chifforobe with door ajar. "Clothes on the floor... it's hard to tell what's missing." She turned back to Cale. "Will you go and tell the sheriff?"

Cale nodded, but a second thought made him kneel again, place a hand at David's waist, and run it along each side. The knife he expected to find was not there. He got to his feet quickly and started for the door.

"Cale..." Ada called after him, "after you notify the sheriff, see if you can find Jefferson Tucker. He lives in back of the harness shop... you can see the shop from the well at the east side of the courthouse."

Cale ran to the hayloft for his jacket and hat. He jumped to the ground and began a trot to the village, thoughts a-tumble with each step.

"Somebody beat and left my friend for dead.

"And the devil took my knife, too.

"Where was Euclid in all that?"

Tucker answered the knock at his door and invited Cale inside.

"Hate to bother you, Mister Tucker," Cale rushed to say, "but something's gone bad wrong at the Pomeroy house. Miss Ada suggested I tell you after I reported it to the sheriff. Nobody there but a deputy... sheriff's at Sunday dinner."

"Most everybody is, this time of day," Tucker said. "What happened? Are the ladies all right?"

Cale hurried through an account of what they found. Tucker's eyes narrowed when he learned of David's wounds then became a squint when Euclid's disappearance was mentioned. While Tucker heard him out, Cale shifted balance from one foot to the other. He wanted Tucker to respond faster than that deputy at the courthouse and suggest a plan of action. The way officers were expected to react when told a line needed to be reinforced or abandoned. Cale had witnessed failure to make decisions too often on a battlefield. He prayed silently that was not about to happen again.

Tucker did not let him down.

"Come with me," the ex-sheriff commanded with a grab for the rifle mounted on the wall. He stuffed ammunition in his coat pockets then fixed the big hat on his head. "We need horses," he said. "Stable's close by... if Sheriff Early wants deputies for the search, we'll join. If he doesn't, we'll go anyhow."

They went by the courthouse first, where Tucker bullied the deputy he addressed as Gibbs into riding out to inform the sheriff. By the time Tucker and Cale roused the keeper of the livery stable and secured horses, saddled up, and rode back to the courthouse they did not have long to wait before the deputy returned with his superior. The first words of conversation hinted that Sheriff Early did not like Tucker.

That was proved when the four men rode to the Pomeroy house. The sheriff made a rapid assessment that a fight between Euclid and David had taken place. "You don't know the young man very well, now do you?" he goaded Ada in the hallway. When she turned to Cale for support, which he gladly supplied, Tucker remarked that David was the one found beaten and cut. "If Euclid won the fight," the former sheriff asked, "why would he leave his own home? Seems he'd stay... and bring charges."

Sheriff Early frowned at logic that interfered with his theory. "Well, I don't believe a man would tear his own mattress apart like that. What was this young fellow doing in this room... answer me that?" he demanded.

"He could have heard the commotion and hurried to help," Tucker offered quietly.

"That's what he began to tell us," Ada said, "once he regained a little consciousness. Something about men who threatened

Euclid. You really should let him tell you in his own words, Sheriff."

Early ignored her condescending tone and returned to the bedroom. "Let that go Miss Pomeroy," he said to Louella seated on the floor beside the semi-conscious David. Deputy Gibbs assisted Louella to her feet and motioned that she should leave the room. But he did not close the door to the listeners in the hallway..

David's voice was weak, and he managed to say no more than two or three words at a time.

"Head injury," Ada whispered to Tucker and Cale.

The sheriff's interrogation did not last long. He would return to the courthouse, he told Gibbs. The deputy should ride to alert the sheriff in neighboring Rhea County. "Witness said two men attacked Mister Pomeroy," Sheriff Early instructed Gibbs to report. "Demanded money... witness says he heard shouting and came to help... they overpowered him, too. Said, before he passed out, he heard one man use the word 'ferry.' That puts a chase out of our jurisdiction, unless the sheriff of Rhea is willing. Before you go, get this man on his feet."

"Miss Pomeroy, Miss Pomeroy," he said to each of the sisters as he rejoined the group in the hallway, "I will remove the witness and take him with me to the courthouse."

"No!" Louella screamed. "He's been hurt! He should not be moved."

Ada quickly echoed her sister.

"He is our only witness," the sheriff insisted. "If he didn't make up the whole thing to cover his own self. He can't remain here. He could escape." With that he returned to the room and, with Deputy Gibbs, began to force David to sit up.

Tucker chose to intervene again. "Sheriff Early, the man can easily be secured in this house until he is able to travel. Put whatever bonds on him you think necessary, then remove him to the courthouse tomorrow. I'm sure the Pomeroy sisters will agree..."

"Oh, Yes," Ada concurred. "He's been cut badly... we've not finished his bandages. And he's obviously been beaten as well."

The sheriff bristled with resentment at his predecessor for making sense and at Ada for raising a subject beyond his depth. He made sure both saw his displeasure before he addressed his deputy.

"Tie that man's arm to the bedpost, Gibbs. If he's not here when I come back tomorrow, somebody else will take his place in my jail." He grabbed for the hat he had placed on a hall table on arrival and marched out the front door.

They persuaded Deputy Gibbs to shackle one of David's feet and leave his arms free after Tucker whispered, "He can only use one arm, Gibbs... a man has to use the chamber pot now and then." Cale lifted what was left of the mattress to the bed and made David a bit more comfortable before they left the room.

The sisters clung to one another as Tucker tried to give assurance that the lawmen would do their jobs. "I know *you* would, Jefferson," Ada said. "We'll try to be strong, but it appears we may never see our brother again." At the last words, Louella's sniffles became sobs.

"I'll ride in and offer my services to Sheriff Early," Tucker said. "Maybe he's calmed down and will realize he needs all the help he can get." He turned to Cale, "I'll need to return your horse... that is if you don't want to ride along."

"I surely do, Mister Tucker," Cale said.

"Then let's water the horses out back before we start." Tucker gave tender pats of reassurance, first to Ada's arm, then Louella.

They moved the horses around to the empty wooden trough in back of the kitchen, and Cale drew a bucket of water from the well. Tucker's eyes scanned the horizon on both sides of the barn. "Used to be an old trail back there along the fence," he said.

"Still is," Cale said as he splashed water in the trough for the waiting horses. "That's how I stumbled in here the first time. Cut many a tree back in there afterwards."

"Smoke's rising from somewhere back there now," Tucker said and pulled his horse's head away from the trough. "Better take a look," he said as he mounted, "...fire in the woods is always trouble.... spreads fast."

Cale jumped back on his horse to follow Tucker. They had not gone far when Tucker pointed to the ground alongside a section of rail fence. "Look there.... ground's been pawed up, like somebody left some horses tied. And there's the proof." He called attention to a recent horsedropping near the fence.

"If they approached on foot," Cale joined in, "then Dave wouldn't know they were on the place until he heard some sound from the house... or the snicker of a horse."

They rode on slowly because the trail into the woods was thick with bushes and vines that had taken over since the days Cale drug the sled back and forth. Hanging twigs on broken bushes proved the trail had been traveled recently.

Cale saw Tucker's right arm suddenly go up. He brought his own horse to a halt and peered around the horse in front to see what held Tucker's attention. Straight ahead stood a massive oak tree that he once judged too formidable for one man's ax. Tucker's left arm motioned Cale to draw alongside him. The obedient horse pushed forward as commanded.

The lifeless, naked body hung from a limb of that giant tree.

Cale witnessed death many times over on battlefields, and the experience hardened his outlook on what men could do to each other. What had Euclid Pomeroy done to deserve such a fate?

Tucker dismounted and pushed forward until he found the source of the smoke. The remains of a pile of cloth smoldered near a patch of dry grass that had begun to blaze before Tucker's feet stamped it out.

"You ride to the courthouse and tell the sheriff," he yelled. "I'll stay here. Don't stop at the house. I'll tell the sisters."

"What if they see me ride past?" Cale asked as he turned his horse.

"They won't if you're quiet," Tucker answered. "Hurry!"

Sheriff Early's eyes twitched when Cale broke the news. He bolted from his office and hurried across the street to the tavern. "I need deputies," Cale heard him shout. "There's been a lynchin'!" Two men stepped forward, and Early swore them in on the spot. He handed badges to both but ignored Cale. "Saddle up, men," he commanded.

Cale caught up with the sheriff's horse and conveyed the need for quiet when the party neared the house. "The Pomeroy sisters ain't been told yet," he said.

Sheriff Early allowed Cale to lead, and they kept far to the side of the house until all the riders had passed. They found Tucker on guard, rifle in hand.

The sheriff and his new deputies recoiled in their saddles when they saw where Tucker's rifle barrel pointed.

"They burned his clothes right over there," Tucker pointed in another direction. "Some tatters ain't completely burned up yet."

Early dismounted unsteadily.

"If you approve," Tucker said, "we'll cut the body down now that you've..."

"Yes, Yes," the sheriff stammered, "Get it down."

From that moment, Early did not appear to resent a suggestion from Tucker. A scrap to be taken from the burned clothes to serve as identification and spare the Pomeroy sisters from having to see the body – "Fine idea." The choice of the oak tree and the signs of horses tied at the fence as indicators these raiders approached, and likely departed, from the woods in back of the house – "Good thinkin'."

"And look here," Tucker called the sheriff to the base of the tree. "Here's what they used to cut that young man and slash that mattress."

Cale recognized the object instantly. His knife.

"They couldn't know whose knife it was," Tucker continued, "but the initials on it sure might be used to frame someone else." He pointed to Cale. "This young man in particular. His initials are on it."

Sheriff Early looked to Cale for confirmation.

"That's my knife, Sheriff," Cale said. "I left it with Dave when we went to church. They must have taken it away from him."

Early's hand scooped up the knife. "Evidence," he said as he stuffed it in his pocket, "I'll secure it." He backed away from the tree while his deputies, with Tucker's assistance, lowered the body. They draped it face down across the back of Cale's horse.

"Mister Tucker," the sheriff's voice showed he wanted to sound authoritative again, "you and the young man go on to the house, secure the body, and inform the ladies. Tell them I will come by shortly after I've scouted a bit more of this trail with my deputies."

They found Ada and Louella in the kitchen. Cale entered the main house and collected one of the quilts from the room where the tethered David lay asleep. He returned outdoors and walked to the barn, where Euclid's body had been placed in a vacant stable. He rolled the body into the quilt then went back to the kitchen.

He found the sobbing Louella, forehead pressed against her arms folded on the table. Ada stood nearby, encircled within Jefferson Tucker's right arm. Her eyes revealed weariness, but the calm set of her head and shoulders affirmed her control of the situation. Cale crossed to her without speaking. He slid his left arm below Tucker's arm before he leaned close to Louella and stroked her shoulder with his right hand. She pressed her cheek against it. Her cries quietened to sniffles.

Ada's voice broke the silence, "He must have owed someone a terrible amount of money."

"I'm sure Sheriff Early will ask for your ideas where Euclid may have traveled," Tucker said softly.

Ada shook her head. "Why, he must have named every city of any size from Savannah to Saint Louis, didn't he Louella? And two or three steamboats. But he never told us why he went to any of them. I fear he spent a lot of his time in card games."

The sound of a knock at the kitchen door preceded Sheriff Early's entrance. Tucker and Cale stepped aside.

"Please be seated, Sheriff," Ada said.

Early did not hide his obvious relief that Tucker had performed the harder duty already. He held out a charred piece of cloth for the sisters to inspect.

Louella spoke first. "His trousers..." she managed to say before she buried her face in her hands.

Identity established, the sheriff kept his questions short – whereabouts, acquaintances, past trouble – to which Ada supplied one word answers in most every case until she remembered the stranger seen by Cale and David.

The sheriff beckoned, and Cale stepped forward to tell about the man on horseback as best he could recollect. "When Dave's head clears, he can tell you more than I can about the man... his hat, especially. Dave was quite taken with that hat. Said he wanted one like it."

"Good...Good," Early said and rose from his chair. "I'll want to talk to him tomorrow... at the courthouse. I'll send a buggy out for him. I think you ladies should prepare a list of items you believe were taken from the house. Get it to me as soon as you can. Now, I'll just look in on the young fellow... Dave, you say?... before I go. My deepest sympathy, ladies, for your loss."

Ada led Cale along a well-worn path to the family burial ground some 200 feet from the house. The rectangular plot had been selected by her father at the time of her mother's death – a small clearing tucked within a little grove, where trees filtered the sunshine and softened the wind to whispers. The stones that marked the corners and the flat, full-length marble covers on graves of the senior Pomeroys might be overlooked if someone hurried past.

He dug a grave at the place she specified. "Mother spoiled him. He'll be back beside her," Ada said in a dry tone.

When they returned to the house, Tucker had arrived on a wagon with pine boards for a coffin. The two men built the burial box while Ada and Louella dressed the body. Cale begged them to let the quilt suffice, but they insisted they would not only look at the corpse but clean the caked blood and force some of their brother's clothing onto his rigid form. "Father would demand it," Ada said.

The preacher responded to his summons the following day and conducted a brief service at graveside. Cale, with Tucker's help, filled in the grave while the preacher comforted the weeping Louella. Ada stood aside with bowed head, but her tears had been shed. When they all returned to the house, Deputy Gibbs sat in the buggy he had driven out to collect David. Two ladies then arrived in a second buggy. They brought bowls of food and delivered them with obvious affection for Ada and Louella.

Cale entered the house with the deputy and found a restless David hungry for attention. "'Bout time somebody looked in," he griped. That told Cale his friend was more like his old self.

"They say you're the only witness to what happened, Dave.. Deputy's been told to bring you to the courthouse so the sheriff can watch over you."

"Damnation!" David exploded "Didn't I answer his questions yesterday?... or whenever that was?" He twisted the leg bound at the bedpost. "Git this blasted rope off me... who said I was 'bout to run off?"

Deputy Gibbs proceeded to remove the bonds. David tried to stand too fast and would have fallen on his face if Cale had not been there to brace him. "Easy now, go on with the deputy. I'll drop by the courthouse and bring you back when they've finished their questions. We found Mister Pomeroy's body and buried him a while ago. What the sheriff don't tell you, I will... later."

"I heard noise in the house, Cale, when I came to the well for a drink of water. One of 'em jumped me while the other was beatin' Mister Pomeroy..."

"Save all that for the sheriff," the deputy ordered. "Come on with me... don't make me have to restrain you again." He pulled David up the hallway to the front door but could not keep him from one more question.

"What happened to your knife?"

"Sheriff's got it," Cale answered.

Chapter 11: A Growing Awareness

The next morning Cale started to leave for the courthouse. Louella rushed after him, "Wait, Cale... let me get some things. I want to go with you and change his bandages... in case they insist on keeping him longer."

She chattered while they walked, first about how long it might take to get the judge to allow David's release. "Finding that man is not easy. Judge Woodson would never have tolerated the way that courthouse is run now."

Cale tried to seize mention of the Woodson name to talk about Agnes, but Louella was off on her second topic: the sheriff who got on her nerves. She swiftly put that in contrast to the kindness of friends who brought food and sympathy. "And whatever could we have done without you," she squeezed his arm. "And Jefferson Tucker." She came to a complete stop in the road. "I'm sure you must have noticed how attentive he is to Ada," she said as straight out as the look in her eyes.

Cale put a tentative step forward before he answered. When he saw her do the same, he began to talk as they walked.

"Yes, I thought talkin' with him at church seemed to refresh her spirit... most lighthearted I believe I'd ever seen her.... on our walk back. Then we came in on that awful sight. She's held up real well," he patted Louella's arm, "you both have... and Mister Tucker's been right there for you."

He hesitated for a second then continued. "Something Miss Ada said on the morning I left to go back to the fightin'... she suggested I see him about locatin' a Southern outfit, and she said something like 'he's a good sheriff, but he's made mistakes of his own.'"

Brightness flickered in Louella's eyes. She slowed her steps, saving energy for what she wanted to confide. "She was talking about the time Jefferson oversaw our farm for Father. Father liked him very much... young and strong, hard worker. I believe he fell in love with Ada then, and she with him. But Mother did not approve. She had already been disappointed when Ada chose to help Father at the bank rather than go to a finishing school back in Virginia. Then when Euclid was about sixteen... he's two years older than me... he grew envious of Father's reliance on Jefferson. Euclid thought he was big enough to be in charge of the farm. He didn't know a thing about it. Hired men would never have taken orders from him. He didn't know they whispered behind his back, but I heard it more than once. Euclid tried to talk Father into buying slaves, but Father would have none of it. He despised the practice."

She paused for breath, then rushed on with her narrative. "When Mother became ill, Father wanted Ada to stay with her constantly. He was busy at the bank and in a poor mood to confer with Jefferson about needs of the farm. Poor Ada was caught in the middle – Mother needing attention, Jefferson impatient that decisions of the heart, as well as the farm, were hard to come by. I remember them in a long conversation at the grape arbor. I believe he wanted Ada to agree with his asking Father for her hand. She's never said as much to me, but I think she asked him to wait. He resigned after that year's harvest and left the county. He worked several years in McMinn County, where he met the young woman who became his wife. I've been told she was a lovely little thing but ill-suited for childbirth. Their first child was stillborn, the second lived a few days only... the mother... did not survive. Jefferson came back to Meigs County close to ten years ago, got himself a small farm and, a year or so before the war, some men urged him to run for sheriff. Father had passed before then, Euclid left before that, and Ada had to devote all her time to settle our interests at the bank. Took years. That must have seemed like another wall to Jefferson. The courtship did not resume."

They walked on in silence for a minute. It gave Cale time to absorb what he had learned. When they came in sight of the town of Decatur, he had another question.

"That day I left... did Sheriff Tucker come out to your house and ask you to vouch for what I told him?"

Louella smiled, the first Cale had seen since the tragic Sunday.

"Yes. We gave him an earful, I'll tell you," she said, then added with a hint of a giggle, "Perhaps it took *you* to get them talking again."

Cale laughed out loud, and she joined in.

Solemn faces had been restored before they passed the houses at the edge of town and entered the courthouse square. They found the sheriff seated at his desk.

"Can we see David, Sheriff?" Cale asked.

"Don't you get excited now," Sheriff Early replied, "I've had enough out of him. I have to..."

"That you, Cale?" David yelled from the same holding cell Cale occupied two years earlier.

"Start raisin' hell til they let me out of here!"

The sheriff raised his own voice. "I've explained to you, Son, and I will to Miss Pomeroy and this young man here... because you are the *only* witness to a high crime... and a temporary resident of this county, I cannot release you until the judge says so. You may decide to run off somewhere. We've got criminals to catch and a trial to prepare for."

"He'll be with us, Sheriff," Louella hastened to say.

"That don't change it, Miss Pomeroy. He could leave before you know it. I'll keep him here tonight. Surely the judge will come in tomorrow, and, if he approves, the young man can return to your place then."

"Well, let me see to his wounds," she insisted. "His cuts need to be cleaned, and I've brought fresh bandages."

"Well... all right," the sheriff gave in. "The young man with you will have to fetch water from the well." He called in to David to hand out the drinking gourd kept inside, unlocked the door, stepped aside, and allowed Louella to enter.

Cale reached the well just as a horse and buggy went by. Ample time to identify the stiffened back and stern jaw of former Captain Joshua McAndrew and the poised young woman seated beside him.

Once Louella attended to David's wounds, they left the sheriff's office and entered the foyer. The door to the county clerk's office stood open. The man recognized Louella and came out to offer his sympathy. She thanked him but did not bother to introduce Cale.

"Your brother sure spent a lot of time in here in recent days," the clerk volunteered. "Searched the deed books back to the time records started being kept. Was he always so interested in land records?"

"I wouldn't know," she answered as Cale opened the outer door. She questioned Ada immediately when they reached the house. "Do you have any idea why he did that?"

Ada shook her head. "I showed him the papers from the final transactions with the bank. He saw there was no unfinished business there... that may have caused him to look into all Father's land records. Could be he thought something was overlooked and might give him the basis for a claim. I'm convinced he was desperate for money... for some reason."

David was set free the next day on condition he remain in Meigs County until the perpetrators were caught and tried. That did not satisfy the young man who yearned to go west. "Fought and survived a bloody war... finally able to go where I want... and look where it's got me! Stuck at the mercy of a cranky sheriff and a lazy judge."

Cale allowed his friend to vent his inner turmoil on their walk from the courthouse in the hope David would calm down a few notches before they reached the Pomeroy house.

Ada and Louella came to the rescue as soon as Cale and David stepped inside. They welcomed David with such concern for his well being that he swallowed his sour mood and let sheepish grins speak for him. "We'll never forget that you risked your life coming to help our poor brother," Ada said. David's pale face turned red.

The sisters had restored some order to Euclid's old room and insisted Cale and David should move in. The bed was a wreck, so folded quilts were substituted as pallets for sleeping. David kept to light duties around the house and barn with Louella's constant watch over the healing of his wounds.

The next afternoon Cale drug a sledload of corn to the grinding mill in town. Since the miller needed time to crush the kernels into corn meal, he decided to walk around the square to Jefferson Tucker's harness shop. A glance in a storefront window brought him to an abrupt halt.

Inside the store, Agnes Woodson pointed to a ruffled bonnet on a stand. An older woman beside her lifted it carefully for Agnes' inspection. Cale stood motionless while she placed it on her head. He grinned in approval. She must have sensed eyes watching her and looked out the window. He nodded three times quickly to encourage her selection. She recognized him and smiled.

He stayed rooted to the spot until she finished her shopping and left the store.

"That bonnet sure looked pretty on you," he said. "Did you buy it?"

She smiled again. "No, silk's too expensive," she said. "It just appealed to me so much I couldn't resist trying it on. Thank you for the compliment."

She wore a chocolate-brown dress with an even darker shawl draped at her shoulders. Her blonde hair was uncovered with a rust-colored bow tied at the back of her neck. A string shopping bag hung from her hands.

"I just happened to walk by," Cale said in explanation. "Left some corn at the mill... thought I'd go 'round and see Mister Tucker while I waited. May I tote that parcel for you?"

"Thank you, no," she said, keeping a tight hold on the strings. "I'll wait right here. Please tell Miss Louella and Miss Ada that I want to come out to offer my condolences one day soon. They've been so kind to me since my father passed. I would have visited them already, but Mister McAndrew needs my help... and my mother has not been well...."

Her words faded beneath the sound of an oncoming horse and buggy. Dust flew as the big animal's feet stomped to a stop in front of the store. In back of the horse, the frowning face of Joshua McAndrew looked down from his perch on the buggy seat.

Agnes lifted a hand to her shawl to raise one side of the garment from shoulder level to the top of her head. Cale quickly stepped in back of her and lifted the entire shawl high so that she could position it as cover for her hair as well as shoulders.

"Thank you... Mister Morgan," she spoke in a lowered voice as she placed her foot on the buggy step.

He steadied her elbow until she had settled beside McAndrew. "I'm pleased you happened to be here when I walked by, Miss Woodson. Think about that bonnet," he said softly. Then, with full volume, "My respects to you, Captain."

McAndrew's eyes showed his impatience. He said nothing and lashed out at the horse with the end of the rein. The buggy sprang into motion, and Agnes' shawl-enshrouded head disappeared from view .

Cale leaned back against the storefront. His parting comment about the bonnet may have sounded mischievous, but he did not regret it. He wanted Agnes to remember what he said about the way she looked in it.

He found Tucker out back at his forge, shaping replacement shoes for a horse whose bridle rein had been tied to a post.

"I don't keep a horse of my own any longer," Tucker said. "I trade out with the owner of the livery. He lends me a horse when I need one... I keep his horses shod or mend some harness for him." He plunged the redhot iron into a cooling tub. "What brings you into town?"

"The ladies needed some corn meal," Cale said. "I was amazed to see they 'bout filled that corn crib somehow... just the two of them. Somebody must have lent a hand with the plowin'."

Tucker walked over to the horse and coaxed it to allow him to bend one leg and hold position on three while he turned his back, straddled the upraised hoof, and braced it between his own knees to remove the old shoe. Cale watched in admiration. The challenge of learning the farrier's craft intimidated most men. Tucker appeared to be the sort of man who could master most anything he set his mind to do.

"I went out there with a mule and plow a couple times in the spring," Tucker said as he fitted a new horseshoe on the hoof. "They won't accept any help unless they can repay it some way... I took some corn when it ripened, a few tomatoes, and some onions in return. They may have told you I used to look after that farm for Mister Pomeroy." He hammered a nail into the thick hoof. "Are the ladies holding up well?"

"I would say so," Cale replied. "Miss Ada's the stronger one, and Miss Louella recovers a little more by the day. She's been nursin' Dave's wounds 'bout as well as any doctor could." He began to explain the judge's order, but Tucker interrupted.

"I heard about that. Judge Haynie likes to apply the law to mean what he says it does. This military occupation put him in office and lets him get away with it. Was your friend able to describe the attackers?"

"Dave's pretty sure one of 'em was the same feller in a black hat who hollered up to us when we worked on the roof a few days before. Dave would like a hat like that. But a new hat's the least worry we got right now... what we had in mind changed all sudden like..."

Tucker must have sensed the words Cale couldn't finish. "Were you about to say you two were ready to leave before all this happened?"

"Well... Dave was ready, all right," Cale admitted. "He's got a constant itch to head out west. For over a year he's talked about goin' to Texas. I agreed to go along, after we came here first so I could see Miss Ada and Miss Louella, then we'd head down below the Hiawassee to look up my Grandpa Morgan. I sure want to see Grandpa... "

"Why can't you?" Tucker asked. "You're not bound by the judge's order.

The question surprised Cale. "But I wouldn't run out on Dave," he said.

"You wouldn't run out," the older man argued. "A couple weeks, maybe."

Cale needed a minute to grasp all that he had just heard. Unexpected suggestions that made sense.

Tucker finished with the horse and tossed his hammer aside. He stretched his back and shoulders. "Be sure you're back well before Christmas. I hope there'll be a wedding about that time.

You know the bride." He winked and added, "And I don't mean Agnes Woodson."

David launched a new round of self-pity when Cale mentioned his plan.

"I won't stay long," Cale vowed. "Just spend a day or two with Grandpa, and see how he's doin'. Then I'll head straight back."

They were in the woods, where David sat on the sled and watched Cale trim limbs from a hickory tree he brought down with the ax.

"How you goin' to explain about your knife?" David demanded. "You said that's why we came here first... so you'd have it when we went to see him."

Cale rested a moment. "I'll tell him how you fought off five men with it, and the sheriff's got it as evidence."

"Bull!" David roared. "What about sayin' you wanted me to meet him? Ain't that worth waitin' til I can go with you?"

"We'll still do that, Dave... later on, soon as that judge says you can leave the county. We'll spend more time around Grandpa then. This time I just want to find his place again... let him know I never went to Kentucky but made it through the war anyway... and see if riskin' his neck for me caused him any trouble."

David kept his sullen expression, but he listened.

"You can be a big help to these ladies, Dave. I'll see there's firewood to last a month before I go, but you can help with other chores as you get your strength back. You've got a dry bed to sleep on... food to eat..." He broke the list with a question, "Have you ever seen anybody make as many good things to eat. out of *black-eyed peas* as Miss Louella?"

He waited, but when no response came he swung the ax into action. A few minutes later, David walked over and, using his good arm, began to pull severed treelimbs out of the way.

The Pomeroy sisters were more enthusiastic when they heard Cale's plan.

"You certainly should go, Cale," Ada said as they sat at the supper table. "I'm sure he worried about you. Just as we did."

"Promise you'll come right back though," Louella urged. "Winter's on its way. That's no time to sleep out in the woods. And we need you to bring in the holly and mistletoe to trim the house for Christmas!"

Cale laughed heartily. The big house would need a lot of holly and cedar branches as trimming if wedding guests were to be hosted.

Chapter 12: Return to the Scene

The walk into Decatur placed Agnes Woodson forefront again in Cale's mind. He surrendered to fascination every step along the road to Athens, the next town. Without her knowledge or consent, Agnes had become his forbidden fruit – appealing, as lusciously tempting as an apple on the highest branch of the tree A tree might be climbed, however. A long engagement to another man was a more complicated barrier.

They were on opposing sides in wartime, but Cale could not bring himself to feel hatred for Joshua McAndrew. The man had suffered lasting wounds. He won the girl's heart before Cale ever set foot in Meigs County. That is, the man McAndrew *used* to be had done so. Her loyalty must have been tested when her father was removed from his judgeship. Had that been smoothed over before McAndrew came home with infirmities? Still, he appeared to be a man of some means and able to provide for a wife. Granting that snapped Cale's mind back to his own footloose state in the harsh conditions of the time.

He entered Athens, where the Union Army escorted him on the first stop to a prisoner of war encampment. That experience provided his bearings southward to Hiawassee River country, and he walked on for a few miles before he made camp for the night.

He was up and on the road again with daylight. A wagon with high sideboards bulging with cotton soon clattered up behind him. The driver halted the mules to welcome Cale aboard.

"You can rest your feet to Riceville," the friendly farmer said. "I'm headin' to the gin."

In the half-hour before they reached the small town, the farmer had learned Cale's general destination and purpose. A grandfather himself, he proposed that Cale help unload the cotton in return for a seat at the table where the farmer planned to share a midday meal. That provided the nourishment Cale needed to hike on to the northern banks of the Hiawassee before sunset. He studied the river's current until the light failed then settled in for the night, confident the sawmill where he last saw his grandfather was somewhere across the river.

When morning came, he walked upstream and asked himself aloud "Where would I find current fast enough to power a sawmill... if I wanted to build one?" Two hours farther along, where the river narrowed, he soon realized the current rushed to meet him. He stumbled and almost fell into the river when he saw, beyond a zigzag formation of exposed rocks, a waterwheel on the opposite shore.

"If I'm to get wet," he said to himself, "I'd better protect this." He drew from his pocket a two-inch tube formed by folding his record of service and rolling it inside a thin strip of leather. He plopped it in his mouth and waded into the swift current. He sloshed from boulder to boulder. Halfway across, he could tell the water moved swiftest where the wheel had been built, and diving into that 10-to-12 foot wide stretch proved as risky as it looked.

Cale fought the current in a losing battle until his arm struck a chain. He grabbed hold and, hand-over-hand, groped the length of chain to an iron piling that anchored it on shore. He scrambled a few feet up the bank and stopped to shake water from his clothes. He removed the leather tube from his mouth and kept it in his hand. Once his eyes cleared, he realized he had surfaced a good 20 yards downstream from the waterwheel. He squished his way up the bank and surprised two men who stood beside the idle mill's big saw.

"We don't get many visitors from out of the water," the older man said. "Were you in that cold river on purpose?"

Cale shivered. "Only way I had to cross," he said. "Never would have made it without that chain."

"We put that there some time ago for our safety when we work on the wheel," the older man said. "Glad to know the other end must still be wound around a rock. Where you bound for?"

"I'm lookin' for a man... name of Caleb Morgan... worked here a while back," Cale got out between spasms of trembling.

The older man's stare did not ease Cale's shakes.

"I'm his grandson."

A barefoot Cale sat by the warm kitchen stove with a quilt wrapped around him and sipped hot coffee. The man who invited him in had returned from draping wet garments on the clothesline to sit at the kitchen table and resume his stares. A woman stirred the pots on her stove but found time to cast a suspicious glance now and then at the stranger in her kitchen.

"My name is Murdock," the man said, "Jesse Murdock. This is my wife, Rhoda. Are you the grandson that Caleb helped escape when the Home Guard put you in my shed out back?"

"Yes Sir," Cale answered quickly. "I want to find him and let him know I went back to the fight ... came through in one piece. I'll never forget Grandpa saved me from a hangman's rope."

Murdock's stare softened. He took a sip from the cup of coffee his wife placed on the table in front of him. "You should be thankful, young man. That act forced Caleb to leave this area ahead of some men who swore vengeance on him."

Cale's head drooped. "I've dreaded hearin' I caused him trouble," he said in a shaky voice. "All the more reason I have to find him and try to make it up to him" He lifted his chin, "Do you know where he went?"

"Not certain," Murdock shook his head. "Over a year ago, I received a short letter. He was working on a dredge boat at a place named Tishomingo. That's a ways west on the Tennessee River... in Mississippi. No word since."

"Thank you, Mister Murdock. Soon as them clothes are half dried out, I'll head for..."

"Well, you'd have quite a walk in front of you," Murdock interrupted.

Cale leaned forward and placed his emptied cup on the table. "No Sir... I don't mean I'd head *there* right now. My friend Dave's waitin' up at Decatur. He's dyin' to go west. I wouldn't start without him. This sidetrip down here's so I could see Grandpa before we left. What I meant to say... I'd start back where I came from."

"And swim the cold Hiawassee all over again?" Murdock asked with a hint of his own amusement.

Trapped by his own hasty words, Cale fell silent.

The older man put him at ease with a proposition. "Instead of going anywhere today, why don't you lend us a hand at the sawmill? I've got nobody else just now except for Wesley. We could use a stout young fellow like you. Dinner will be ready in a few minutes, and you can start with that. A good afternoon's work is all you have to give us in return."

The aromas from the stove inspired Cale to accept. "Be glad to, Sir."

"Then come on in the other room with me, and we'll find you something to wear to work," Murdock said and led the way from the table.

They worked efficiently through the afternoon. The two experienced men operated the saw. Cale applied muscle to support the sawyers when and where they called for it.

"You catch on quick," Murdock praised when he called a halt to the day's work. Wesley left for his home, and Murdock pointed to the shed in the back yard. "If you don't dread going back in that shed, you're welcome to bed down in there. Your grandfather spent many a night in it. We can use you again tomorrow, if you're willing."

"Don't know why not," Cale said. "It'll give me more time to plan what to do next."

"There's a store a few miles south of here," Murdock said. "Run by a man named Pickett... not far from Caleb's farm. Be sure to mention you fought for the South. If he's in a mood to talk, you might ask if he's heard any more than I told you. I can't

215

offer you anything but food in return for your labor, and I won't ask you to stick around more than another day or two."

They shook hands on it.

In Cale's dream he stood by a freshwater spring. A young woman appeared beside him, and he reached for her hand. He first thought it was Agnes, but this woman's hair hung playfully free of any bonnet. Long hair. Like Betsy's. He embraced her. She did not pull away. A tender kiss heightened his joy and convinced him the full lips he tasted, unmistakably, belonged to Betsy Gleason. An unseen dog barked somewhere close by. Then a man spoke in a commanding tone. McAndrew? What business was it of his? He had Agnes. He didn't even know Betsy. The voice became insistent, and Cale's arm flailed out when something brushed against his chest and separated Betsy from him.

"Hurry!" a male voice snarled in a loud whisper. "Get that rope around him."

Cale jerked awake and pushed back as hands tried to restrain him. He rolled to one side, drew his knees to his chest, and kicked at a figure on his right. A loud "Ohfff!" and a hard thump against a wall signaled he had made solid contact. A body pressed atop him from the left and began to force a burlap sack over Cale's head.

The dog barked louder.

Fully awake, Cale twisted his shoulders and scooted his buttocks and legs clear of the weight of the body of the attacker who used the sack. They rolled across the floor of the shed, upsetting a

216

wooden bucket and a row of garden tools that had been propped against a wall. By starlight allowed in through the opened door, Cale caught a warning glance as the flat side of a shovel came down from his right and crashed against his ribs with a stream of curses from the wielder.

"Dammit, drop that shovel and git that rope around his arms," commanded the voice of the one who had regained the upper hand with the burlap sack.

Cale swung wildly to resist the rope and thrashed the floor with his legs. He kicked so violently that the body atop him was forced to slide along or give up control.

"What the hell is this!" roared a voice from the door. "Leave that man alone and come out of my shed!"

"Now Jesse," said the man who forced the sack over Cale's head. "this man deserted. That was a crime against the people of the South! He got away once... he must be punished."

"Is that you, Abner?" asked the voice at the door. "Come out of there. Don't make me fire this gun. The war's over."

"Don't matter," the man protested as Cale wrestled free of his grasp. "Justice is still due."

"What kind of justice" And who are you to render it?" Jesse Murdock stood in the opened door, barefoot and in his nightshirt, the long barrel of a gun thrust forward.

The attacker who wielded the shovel backed away at the sight of the gun, but the one who held the sack struggled to keep Cale on the floor. The younger and more agile Cale wriggled away from him, got to his feet, and moved alongside Murdock.

"You're makin' a big mistake, Jesse," whined the leader of the duo from where he sat on the floor. "Your community won't like your interference."

Murdock motioned with the gun for everyone to vacate the shed. "I know this community as well or better than you do, Abner," he said. "This man went back to fight once he left here."

"Pshaw!" Abner blurted. "What fight would a coward have left in him?"

"Kennesaw Mountain... Atlanta... Jonesboro... with Hood in Tennessee..." Cale volunteered. "To the last days with General Johnston in North Carolina."

That brought silence from the men still in the shed.

"And how much fight did the Southern cause get from you, Abner?" Murdock asked in lowered voice. "Aside from helping yourself to crops raised by women and children while their men were gone ...and burning out some of them. How'd you know this man was here? Wesley must have told you."

"He'll never work for you again, Jesse... and you won't have many customers at the mill," Abner threatened.

"Get out of here before I use this gun, Abner. And take that man hiding in the shadows with you. I don't want either of you to set foot on my property again," Murdock ordered. "One... two..."

Abner leaped out of the shed with his accomplice at his heels. They fled across Murdock's yard and headed for three horses tied to a tree downhill from the tavern. Once mounted, they rode away at a brisk trot, leading the third horse.

"I'm sorry I caused this, Mister Murdock," Cale said. "I've done caused trouble here all over again.... and I sure didn't mean to."

"You'd better come in the house and get some sleep," Murdock answered as he eased the hammer of the shotgun into place. "We have work to do when daylight comes."

218

Murdock had just begun to acquaint Cale with the operation of the big saw when a nervous Wesley appeared. He seemed relieved to see Cale present.

"My wife told me what she done," he said to Murdock. "I made the mistake of mentionin' this young feller's arrival to her when I got home. She was a Suggins, you know.... first cousin to Abner. Right after supper she slipped off down the road and told him. She didn't tell me where she went til breakfast... said he went to get some others to come down here with him. Abner felt disgraced that time this feller escaped. If they caused you trouble, it's my fault. I'll understand if you don't want me to work here any more."

Murdock placed a hand on his workman's shoulder. "Wesley, if anybody disgraced Abner it was Abner. Make sure your wife understands that. Thank you for telling me what happened. I believe it's settled... and you still have a job, if you want it."

Wesley, obviously relieved, hustled into position at the saw.

They worked through the day, and Cale slept again in a spare room of the Murdock home. He stayed into a second week until assured the workload had been completed, thanked both Murdocks for feeding and housing him, and asked directions to Pickett's Store.

"Go right up that hill past the tavern," the mill owner directed. "Take the road to the left when you reach the fork. I believe Caleb used to say it was six or seven miles more to the store. If you learn anything, I'll appreciate it if you stop by and tell me before you head back up to Decatur."

"I promise that, Mister Murdock. You've been a mighty good friend."

The little country store would not fill more than a corner of Gleason's big place of business back in Gowensville, but the array of merchandise jammed inside its walls, stacked on the floor, and hung from the loft surprised Cale. A narrow passageway led through the maze to the big counter that served as the proprietor's command post. Behind it, a stooped, apron-clad man subjected his visitor to a long and cautious inspection.

"Mister Pickett?" Cale asked as he advanced.

The scrutiny continued in silence.

"I'm Cale Morgan.. new to these parts since the fightin' ended.. Tenth South Carolina, under General Johnston, then Hood, then General Johnston again to the finish. I believe my grandpa was a neighbor..."

"Are you the deserter that caused him to have to leave?" the storekeeper interrupted.

Cale swallowed his embarrassment but looked the man in the eye. "Yes Sir. I regret that I left my company for a short while. Grandpa took the blame, I'm sad to say. But I'm tryin' to find him and let him know I went back... like the soldier I vowed to be when I enlisted. I hoped you might have received some word about where he is now... and if his family is all right."

"How would I know you went back...like you said?"

Cale withdrew the leather tube from his pocket, unrolled the folded paper, and placed it on the counter. "You see it's dated May... in North Carolina... where General Johnston surrendered our army."

The storekeeper read quickly. He returned the paper and spoke in a less hostile tone. "After what happened to my good friend and neighbor Caleb, I'm cautious when anybody comes in here and asks about him."

"Mister Murdock told me Grandpa wrote him over a year ago," Cale said. "From Tishomingo... in Mississippi. Wonder if you can add anything to that?"

Pickett leaned on the counter, weariness plain in his face. "I think he went on from there. You ought to ask up at the Greers," he said. "Follow the road up the hill another mile... you'll see a house on your right. Sam Greer has been tryin' to sell Caleb's old place for him."

Cale spotted the house as easily as a phalanx of barking dogs saw and charged toward him. He raised his arms high and advanced with a memory of a similar reception when he first visited Caleb's cabin. "Anybody home?" he yelled.

A man came into view from in back of the house.

"Mister Greer?" Cale called. "I'm Caleb Morgan's grandson... Mister Pickett suggested I see you."

The drill of introduction and explanation had to be repeated, but Greer chased the dogs away and showed a willingness to talk. Before he said anything about Caleb's whereabouts, however, he had a question, "Why don't you buy his old place? He left it to me to sell for him."

"If I had any money, I'd sure do that, Mister Greer," Cale said. "Give it right back to Grandpa when I find him. Have you heard anything from him... lately?"

Greer invited him to sit on the porch and called into the house for his wife to join them. A grandmotherly woman stepped out, wiping her hands on a dish towel while her husband introduced their visitor. She echoed the land offer immediately. "Why that would please Caleb and Jenny," she said eagerly. "Keep it in the family. We'd be neighbors again."

Cale had to disappoint her with his confession of empty pockets. "I do want to find Grandpa, though. And I hope you have some notion of where I should start."

"Jenny wrote to me back in June," Mrs Greer said. "She told me not to answer until she wrote again. Mail's dreadful slow. They left Tishomingo with three other families in wagons bound for Texas. She wrote from a place called Helena...said they had a dreadful time crossin' the Mississippi River. Caleb had to repair the wagon before they could go on."

Greer spoke, "You have any knowledge of that part of the country?"

"Not much," Cale said. "Our army spent a little time in Mississippi before we went on to the Carolinas. If Helena's across the river, it must be in Arkansas... or Louisiana. I've got a good friend who's itchin' to go west. I'll convince him to go by way of Helena. Somebody there will know the direction settlers' wagons would take. We may not be able to leave til next spring, though. I'll be with the Pomeroys, up in Decatur. Will you write to me there if you get more word?"

The older man disagreed. "You'd find out quicker if you're right up the hill," he persisted. "Don't see why you shouldn't farm that land... it still belongs to your grandpa. I'd help you get started... raise a cabin and such."

"What happened to the house that was there?" Cale asked.

Greer left the porch and motioned that Cale should follow "You may as well see for yourself," he said. They walked a trail that led from one farm to another. One of the hounds tagged along. "That's Jackson," Greer said. "Caleb left him behind because he's so old. Tried to leave the other one, too, but the little boy squalled too loud. That old dog wanders over here most every day."

The sight of caked ashes and blackened ruins sent a shiver up Cale's back and reminded him of too many scarred battlefields. This one was personal. A lonely stone chimney towered over the heap of charred wood that had once been a home.

"Did the army... do this?" he struggled to ask.

"No, some devils did it when they discovered Caleb and his family had gone," Greer said.

"Oliver Pickett feels mighty guilty about givin' directions to Caleb's place when some men with faces covered threatened to burn his store. That bunch whooped and hollered so it woke me and the wife, but the whole cabin was in flames... barn, too... before we got outdoors and saw the devils ride away. Oliver went into town and told the sheriff, but nothing's ever come of it."

Cale bent and grasped a clump of ashes caked by rain. He crushed it between his fingers and watched the gray lumps fall across his boots.

"Caleb's land goes a ways back in the woods... good spring back there...and all the way down to the creek," Greer said and pointed downhill. "Real good bottom land down there. Why don't you look it over and stop by my house? We'll work something out, and you could plant these fields in the spring." Without waiting for an answer, he turned and retreated to the trail. The dog stayed to sniff the rubble in search of something familiar.

Two years earlier a confused and desperate Cale walked into this clearing in search of food. He found it, and a previously unknown grandfather to boot. That man made it possible for

Cale to be free to go on until he came to his senses. The ruins in these ashes testified to the penalty levied on a man who came to his grandson's assistance.

"Grandpa... I'm sorry," Cale said aloud. "The day I showed up sure meant trouble for you."

He looked at scattered chips on the ground that still marked the woodpile where he cut firewood and fields that once yielded harvests.

"I could farm this place again, all right," he said, as if the dog listened, "but the same men who did this to Grandpa would likely burn me out, too. Once word spread that a Morgan lived here, they'd be back."

He paced around the remains of the cabin and stopped to stick the toe of his boot into a mound of rubble before he moved on to the next. He kicked several charred stubs of timbers away from the base of the chimney and spotted what once had been a hearth. Shards of baked clay lay on the flagstone. He chose a smooth piece to slip into his pocket. The curious dog stuck his nose into the space the boot cleared to begin another inspection of his own.

Cale turned away from the burnt ruins and followed the trail back to the Greer home. He estimated he could make the Murdock place by nightfall, then start for Meigs County next day. He had a lot to consider, a wedding to attend, and a friend to help regain his freedom.

The dog stayed behind.

Chapter 13: A Wedding for Christmas

A crisp December wind carried sounds from the Pomeroy house even more unusual to Cale than the rare sight of a horse and buggy on the premises. The music borne by the air was a new experience entirely.

The singer's voice made him quicken his steps. It must be Agnes, he decided.

Thoughts of her competed with concern for his grandfather every step of the way from Murdock's. Yet this vocal phrasing was not smooth like her rendition of hymns, and sudden stops led to a line's being repeated once or twice. With each halt, a piano replayed the notes of the difficult phrase alone then accompanied the soloist in a second try to get it right. Cale could not identify the song that often made use of the words 'dreamer' and 'wake', especially in parts attempted again.

He strode past the bare crape myrtles at the steps and silently crossed the veranda to the front door, eased it open, and tiptoed into the hallway. A door stood ajar at left, providing his first sight of the interior of the parlor. The front part of the house suffered leaks before Cale and David put new shingles on the roof. The sisters explained they rarely used the parlor any longer, certainly not in months of cold weather when firewood must be conserved. The several chairs and a settee still wore their protective cloth covers. Only a spinet and its bench had been uncovered.

Agnes stood at one side of the bench, peering over Louella's shoulder at a large sheet of paper propped above the keyboard. A bonnet lay atop the spinet. Fully revealed, Agnes' golden hair fell short of her shoulders. Seated on the bench, Louella's hands busily stroked the keys. Their backs were turned, and Cale slipped in without being seen or heard.

When the line "Beaut-i-ful Dream-er... wake un-to me" had been repeated to Louella's satisfaction, she gave the keys a final flourish and reached for the singer's hand. "I think we have it now, Agnes."

Cale applauded.

Startled, they whirled to face him.

"Beautiful, all right," he complimented. "Miss Louella, that's the first time I've heard that piano played."

"Cale!" Louella squealed. "You're home!" She hurried from the bench to throw her arms around him. "Oh, we've missed you. You've come just in *time*. There's to be a *wedding*... in *this house*... and there's so much to do."

Agnes remained by the piano. She took the sheet of paper in her hands and studied its contents.

"I must tell Ada," Louella said as she rushed out of the parlor. "She'll want to know Cale's home. We must find David..." her voice faded as she hurried down the long hallway.

Cale advanced into the room. "Your voice matches that song," he said.

"Thank you, Mister Morgan," Agnes said. She did not look in his eyes. "It's the first time we've rehearsed it. It's a new piece by Mister Stephen Foster... or new to *me,* perhaps I should say.

Mister Tucker heard it performed somewhere. He mentioned it to Miss Ada and Miss Louella when they began to plan the wedding."

"So he did ask her, did he?" Cale said.

She seemed puzzled, but the remark made her look at him. "You knew?" she asked. "You must have learned a lot about us in the short time you've been here, Mister Morgan."

"I wish you'd call me Cale," he said. "Everybody else does."

"I think I should address you as Mister Morgan. We hardly know each other, and I *am* engaged to Joshua McAndrew." Her tone sounded the stiffness of formality.

"So I was told... some time ago." He added the last in a devilish twist to see how she would react.

Her fingers ran nervously along the edges of the big sheet of paper, her eyes hidden from him. "Our engagement has been prolonged... more than either of us want... by circumstances of the war," she said but with less firmness. She faced him again. "I realize you and Josh were on different sides, but surely you respect a promise made to someone I've known and loved since childhood... someone who suffered terrible wounds."

Cale boldly took one of her hands in his. "Of course I'm mindful," he began, "...won't ever forget seein' men on both sides tore apart... " When he saw her face reflect the weight of his words, he stopped. She did not withdraw her hand, and that encouraged him to continue. "Times when it got so bad, I shut my mind to all but them I wanted to live to see... Ma... and Grandpa... friends back home... Miss Ada and Miss Louella... and a young woman I heard sing a Christmas song one time. I never saw her then, but her voice was the loveliest I ever heard. I'd never want war or *anything* to harm her."

He could see the question form in her eyes, but he hurried on out of fear she would pull her hand away before he finished what he wished to say.

"Many, *many* men came home in bad shape. My arm healed up all right, but I yearn to see and be near something war did not spoil. The little bit I've come to know about you simply makes me want to know more. I thought about you every day I've been gone."

She smiled for the first time since he arrived. "You've heard me sing," she said. "And you saw me try on a new bonnet. I would hope you also see I belong at Josh's side. That was decided a long time ago... and it is where I pray to share a lifetime of happiness."

Cale released her hand. "How old were you when you made that promise?"

Agnes broke eye contact, but he pressed.

"You'll marry him because you love him? Or because...you feel sorry for him?"

"I.. love him, "she said at the sound of excited voices from the hallway. The Pomeroy sisters were on their way. "That's all you need to know," she whispered as she placed the sheet music atop the spinet and retrieved the bonnet. Her fingers deftly tied the laces beneath her chin just as Ada rushed in, Louella at her heels.

"Welcome home, Cale," Ada said as she embraced him. "Did you find your grandfather?"

"No, I'm sorry to say, Miss Ada. It's a long story that will take some time to tell."

"Well, we have plenty of that," she assured, holding his arm. "Let's all go back where it's warm. It's so *cold* in this room.

Louella, I don't see how you could move your fingers on the keys. Agnes, we surely can be more hospitable somewhere else. David went to the courthouse, Cale. He'll be back soon.."

"I really must go, Miss Ada," Agnes said. "But I want to rehearse again at least once more if that's all right, Miss Louella. I can study the lyrics in the meantime. Would next Monday afternoon be convenient?"

"We have it down pretty well but take the sheet music if you wish," Louella agreed. "I want you to be confident."

The foursome moved into the hallway. "I'll see you to your buggy," Cale volunteered.

"That won't be necessary," Agnes protested, but he was out the door behind her before she could stop him. He helped her into the buggy first then stepped to the hitching post, untied the horse's reins, and handed them up to her.

"I had to tell you how I felt, Agnes," he said. "You've been on my mind so much I had to say something."

She looked down at the reins instead of the eyes fixed on her. "I believe it will be best if we do not see each other again... alone," she said slowly. "Try to understand, Cale."

He gripped her elbow and sought to make her look at him. She glanced straight ahead, but her cloak did not hide the rise of her bosom in reaction to his firm touch. He did not let go of her arm. Instead, he placed one foot on the buggy step to narrow the space between them. With heads again at the same level, he leaned in and kissed her. She did not resist. Their lips joined, expectant and responsive. Seconds later, she bent her head away from him, pulled the reins taut, and signaled the horse to turn to the road. Cale released her arm, stepped down, and backed away when she called a firm "Giddy up!" to the horse.

He watched the buggy roll away. Her words hung in his mind but could not match the memory of the way she returned his kiss.

Cale's explanation of what he learned about his grandfather had concluded at the big kitchen table when David walked in and demanded to hear it from the beginning.

"In a minute, Dave... first I want to hear some good news." He addressed the sisters, "Tell me more about this wedding."

"Jefferson and I decided the afternoon of Christmas Day should suit those we wish to attend," a smiling Ada said. "Four o'clock. After refreshments, they'll be able to get home before dark. It will be a small group... about a dozen in all. Of course that includes the two of you."

"Oh, but Cale," Louella broke in, "there's so *much* to prepare! We have just a little over a *week!* I'm so glad you're back." She left her chair to begin supper preparations.

"Now," David insisted, "tell me about your grandpa."

"Not there, Dave. Some fellers didn't like that he helped me out of that shed. I learned he had to move his family to safety." When Cale got to the part about his grandfather's last known location, David shook his head and, with a loud sigh, stalked out.

Cale excused himself and went after him. David was halfway to the barn before he could be overtaken.

"Dave... stop!" Cale clamped a braking hold on his friend's shoulder. "At least we know his trail."

"Which you can follow while I'm stuck here," David snorted as he tried to escape Cale's grip. "Every week I go see that sorry excuse for a sheriff, and he still can't tell me if anybody's been captured or even seen! I'm 'bout ready to believe they ain't even lookin'."

"I'm not goin' anywhere right now so hush up," Cale scolded. "We'll be busy helpin' these folks through the winter. I'm sure Mister Tucker will like some help gettin' fields ready to plant. How are you feelin'?" he asked, squeezing David's bicep. "Got your strength back?"

David shook off the hand but stood still. "I'm as fit as you. Just need more time for this scab to heal." He brushed his fingers across the base of his neck. "Good thing we never got around to sharpenin' the blade of that knife of yours. Would'a sliced my jugular for sure."

"Well, let's go back in to the ladies," Cale said. "No point spoilin' their excitement. We'll make our plans day by day."

Louella orchestrated her own day by day countdown for everyone in the household.

The young men went to the woods each day and brought back an abundance of pine and cedar boughs, stems of holly, pine cones, and nuts with each sled load of firewood. The sisters dusted and cleaned the house. They removed all the covers from parlor furnishings and burnished the wooden arms, lamp tables, the spinet, and the mantel.

Since Cale had been in the parlor only once, he did not know the wall centered by the huge fireplace consisted of sliding doors that opened into a dining room with another fireplace backed up to the same chimney that served the parlor. The only drawback came when Louella called his attention to more windows that needed to be cleaned.

When the two rooms at last met her approval, she set Cale and David to affixing boughs and stems of holly above doors, across the mantel, atop the spinet, and dangled from the top of the parlor's framed painting of a fox hunt in the Virginia countryside. The pine cones were balanced on windowsills. From some hiding place, Louella produced candlesticks and red candles for the dining room table. The lamps held meager supplies of oil, but she wanted candles to complete the scene for Christmas and a wedding.

To their surprise, the young men found that the sisters had attacked what remained of their late brother's wardrobe. Waistcoats and dark trousers had been altered for each of them. "You won't need to be outside when the guests arrive," Ada explained. "The silk vests will look quite handsome on you."

Ada and Louella decided the former bedroom of their parents should henceforth be occupied by the newlyweds. Each sister had her own room in the large house, but the parents' bedroom was roomier and adjoined the study directly across the front hall from the parlor. Consequently, Cale and David were needed to shift heavy trunks and furnishings from room to room.

When Ada consented to apply her time on the morning of Christmas Eve to her bridal wear, Louella could give her own total attention to food preparation. "I wish there had been another tree filled with honey for you to find, Cale," she said. "We'll have to make do with the molasses jug's last drops. Still, we will have a few sweet treats, and we'll roast the chestnuts and pecans you boys found. A wedding without a cake, I'm afraid, but Ada understands."

Jefferson Tucker arrived at twilight with two jugs. Hard cider.

"Mister Pomeroy's whiskey must be long gone, and you need some spirits for the occasion," he said as if he dared any debate.

"But Jeff," Ada cautioned, "you know the preacher and his wife will be here."

"And I also know he takes a dram or two now and again, Ada. Why don't we taste a sample now? It is Christmas Eve."

Louella happily fetched cups while Tucker uncorked a jug, sniffed the contents, and flashed a broad smile. "Good stuff," he pronounced and poured generous splashes into each cup held before him.

When all had been served, Tucker raised his own cup high then clinked it against the one held by Ada. "This old year's been hard, but it's just about used up. Christmas is the right time to start some new beginnings. Merry Christmas, everybody."

They cheered in unison.

The flames in long-dormant fireplaces cast beams of welcome in both the parlor and dining room.

"It's such a joy to bring these rooms alive again," Louella said when she saw Cale and David's handiwork at the fireplaces. Excitement glowed in her face. She had chosen to wear a rose-colored gown with bouffant sleeves that reached just beneath her elbows.

When the first guests knocked at the front door, Ada emerged from her new bedroom and joined her sister to receive them in the hallway. The sisters had worked for hours to alter their mother's wedding dress, and Ada looked radiant in its whiteness.

A miniature shawl of delicate lace covered her shoulders. A small square of the identical lace rested atop her tightly-pinned dark hair.

Ada and Louella welcomed the guests and directed them into the parlor. Tucker, clad in a dark gray suit, waited just inside the door to greet arrivals and invite them to be seated and chat in comfort before the warmth of the fire.

Agnes and Joshua arrived first. Cale spotted the approach of their buggy and waited at the bottom of the veranda steps. McAndrew slowly managed his own dismount from the buggy but accepted Agnes's support along the short path to the house. When they reached the leafless crape myrtles, Cale stepped forward and offered to assist.

"Captain, why don't you lean on me to climb these steps? They're a bit steep."

Agnes avoided his eyes but motioned him to take her place and brace McAndrew's left side. "Thank you, Mister Morgan," she murmured. McAndrew said nothing until they reached the front door, where he mumbled a succinct "Thank you," and nodded for Agnes to take over again.

Inside the parlor, McAndrew insisted they sit close to the door. When she removed her wrap, Cale saw Agnes had chosen a violet dress with encircling flounces of the same fabric descending in three tiers from waist to toes. A cluster of tiny violet ribbons was pinned at the back of her hair. She would not look at him but greeted other arrivals pleasantly by name. Stung by her evasion, he turned to replenish the logs in the fireplaces.

When the big clock on the mantel chimed four, Louella seated herself at the spinet and began to play a medley of Christmas carols. Ada sat by Tucker; Cale and David stood in back of them.

Agnes rose when the carols ended, crossed to stand alongside Louella, then turned and faced the gathering. The few introductory chords brought a calm expression to her face, and she began to sing, "Beautiful Dreamer... wake unto me..."

A vision formed long before became a reality to Cale.

He could not see Ada's face but could tell her upper body lost its customary rigidity while she listened. The song captivated her, plain to see, and she leaned against Tucker's shoulder. He took her hand in his, where it remained until the last notes sounded.

Louella nodded to the silver-haired preacher. He got to his feet, cleared his throat, and signaled the bridal couple to stand before him at the front of the hearth. A few words about Christmas and the sanctity of marriage preceded his quick recitation of vows to be repeated before witnesses. At "Mister Tucker, you may now kiss your bride," Louella's spinet broke into the joyous bars of Mendelssohn's "Wedding March."

The best wishes and congratulations flowed with music as escort into the dining room, where cider glasses were filled, rounds of toasts ensued, and guests feasted on Louella's tempting assortment of sweet nibbles along with the roasted chinkapins and pecan halves served up from an iron skillet Cale had positioned at the edge of ashes in the dining room fireplace just before the ceremony.

When Agnes left a seated McAndrew to chat with Ada, Cale sidled to his chair near the dining table. "I did rejoin my company, Captain... right to the day things were settled in North Carolina," he said quietly but audible at such close range.

McAndrew did not give a sign he listened.

"War's been over some time now," Cale went on, "Your side won. I don't regret what I did to try and keep that from happenin', but I don't mean to spend the rest of my life fightin' it...."

"So you wound up in North Carolina did you?" McAndrew interrupted.

"Yes Sir... it was a long walk." Cale managed a chuckle.

McAndrew looked him in the eye for the first time since their meeting in the sheriff's office two years earlier. Still absent from the stoic facial expression, however, was any hint of cordiality. "I'm sure you have been of some assistance to the Pomeroy sisters, Morgan, but see that you don't annoy Miss Woodson."

Cale recovered quickly. "Never meant to annoy...any time I've seen her, Captain. She's beautiful. She sings beautifully. The South needs all the beauty we can find."

McAndrew's eyes scanned the room. "See that you admire it from a respectful distance," he said out of the side of his mouth.

He must have caught Agnes' eye because she excused herself and hurried to McAndrew's side.

"Are you about ready to leave?" he asked, placing his empty glass on the table.

"Yes, let me say goodbye to the others and get my cloak."

When she rejoined them, McAndrew first declined Cale's offer to provide escort down the front steps. "No need for that," he shrugged. But he did not resist while a stout host made sure their slow descent was safely accomplished. Cale heard Agnes murmur "Thank you" when they reached the ground though he could not see it in eyes she hid from him.

As if on cue, other guests began to depart. The preacher and his wife were last to leave. His cheeks and forehead showed a brightness that suggested he had enjoyed the festivities, the cider in particular.

Cale could not decide who looked happiest, Ada or Louella.

He saw Ada leave Tucker's side for a moment to embrace her sister. "It was all so lovely, Louella," she said. "You saw that everything went perfectly. I can never thank you enough."

Louella prolonged the hug, her joy effusive. "Wasn't it *wonderful* to have life in these rooms again, Ada? Just like the happy times before Mother became ill. We must do it again for your first anniversary!"

"Then we'd better scrimp on firewood the rest of this winter," Ada laughed. "We've burned a week's supply in two hours."

"You've got plenty more where that came from, Miss Ada," Cale volunteered. He was about to add that new trees need room to grow but caught himself. "Meant to say *Miz* Ada... or should I call you Miz Tucker now?"

She laughed again. "I like the sound of the last one, Cale. But it's a bit too formal for you and me. Thank you for all *you've* done to give us this happy day."

Chapter 14: Turning Points

On the third day of the new year 1866 David Appleby learned a man suspected of being one of the two who attacked him and murdered Euclid Pomeroy had been arrested.

"They got him down at Chattanooga," David announced when he returned to the Pomeroy house after another trip to the courthouse. "Sheriff and his deputy both went to bring him here for trial. Clerk won't tell me any more than that. Sheriff's office is locked tight." His normally pale face rivaled a sunrise.

"Then I 'spect you'll soon have your day in court, Dave," Cale said. "Let's ask Mister Tucker when he comes home. He knows all the procedure... how long it takes to get a trial goin'... pick a jury... all that."

As it turned out, Jefferson Tucker was a step ahead of them. He still had sources around the courthouse, and word reached him at the harness shop almost as fast as the sheriff and deputy rode out. "A rider was sent to tell the judge," Tucker announced to all assembled at that night's supper table. "He'll likely hold a hearing a day or two after the sheriff brings in the prisoner."

The wheels of justice rolled swiftly in Meigs County once tipped in motion. Inhabitants in the town of Decatur and the surrounding countryside gladly put aside their postwar irritations for the drama of a murder trial. The little courtroom was packed to capacity when the judge rapped his gavel and seated the jury on the first Tuesday of February. David was sequestered along with Ada and Louella in another part of the courthouse until called to testify. Cale squeezed in when friends made room for Tucker on a back row bench. The prosecuting attorney decided against calling Cale as a witness since he could not offer a distinct recollection of the rider who yelled up to the roof of the Pomeroy house.

A surprise awaited when the judge ordered the prosecutor and defense attorney to stand and identify themselves. The familiar back of Joshua McAndrew rose alongside that of an older man at the prosecution table a few feet opposite from another attorney who stood by the seated accused man.

"What's McAndrew doin' here?" Cale whispered in Tucker's ear.

"He's a lawyer now.... likely assisting the prosecutor to gain trial experience," came the whispered reply.

"How'd he get wounded?"

"Horse shot out from under him. The fall broke his leg... shattered an elbow, too."

The prosecutor briefly summarized events of the fateful Sunday and explained the accused had been apprehended in Nashville, where a suspected accomplice was shot when he tried to evade arrest. The man who surrendered was sent by train to Chattanooga, where the Meigs County sheriff took custody and brought him for trial. The man stood at the judge's direction, identified himself as Tobias Fisk, and entered a plea of not guilty.

Testimony began with Sheriff Early. The lawman showed his nervousness but managed to describe what he found when he first arrived at the Pomeroy home with the subsequent discovery of the body of Euclid Pomeroy. In no part of his account did he credit the assistance provided by his predecessor in office. The knife found at the base of the oak tree was presented into evidence, followed by Early's boasts of how quickly he notified sheriffs in adjacent counties.

Ada was the second witness summoned. Composed, as if she sat in a witness chair every week, she gave an unemotional account of her late brother's reappearance after several years' absence and what had been discovered on the return from church.

Louella came next. She wilted before the defense attorney's questions about Euclid and his past. The lawyer pounced with a rapid sequence about the young man found wounded in her house, his background, whether he exhibited a violent streak, showed any resentment toward her brother, and so on. When the judge permitted her to step down, she fled the courtroom in tears. The defense attorney's upraised chin suggested he was pleased with himself.

When his turn came David strode in with the bearing of a man eager to be heard. The prosecutor held up a wide-brimmed, black leather hat and asked if David had seen it before.

"Yes Sir.. it was on the head of one of the men who beat Mister Pomeroy half to death. When I heard the commotion and run to the house to see what caused it, one of 'em jumped me from behind. They took a knife from me... tried to cut me to pieces with it.

The knife was produced. He identified it and explained how he had been asked to hold it while its owner went to church. "Got his initials on it... Cale Morgan."

The prosecutor handed the knife to the first juror, who looked it over and passed it on for the entire jury to examine.

Cale marveled as his friend commanded the jury's attention. He made the entire courtroom audience hang on his every word.

David turned the witness chair into his personal stage, where he delivered a masterful performance. When called to identify the man seated at the table, he calmly asked if the judge would have the defendant stand.

"That's the man who wore that hat," David said slowly but emphatically. "He and his partner attacked Mister Pomeroy and me."

The defense attorney bore in with questions about how David came to be at the Pomeroy house, his time in the war, and what his mental state had been during that experience.

"Never got hit in the head... No Sir. Not til that rascal set in to kill me."

So it went. To each of the soon-frustrated lawyer's questions, a composed David gave an unhurried reply that caused heads in the courtroom audience to nod in satisfaction. When he was allowed to step down, the defense asked the judge to declare a noontime recess. The judge seemed relieved to grant it.

"He did well," Tucker said to Cale as he excused himself on his way to the harness shop where a customer was due to meet him. "Hold my place, I'll be back in about an hour." Cale stood and stretched a while, lending an ear to comments others made as they exited the courtroom in search of midday refreshment. "That young feller sure put that suspect's neck in a noose," said one man; "Don't see how that lawyer'll keep him from the gallows," agreed another. "I never liked Euclid Pomeroy," said a third, "but I'd trust that young feller... he fought for the South."

The witnesses were told to return to the room where they had been assigned in case one or more needed to be recalled when court resumed. Since Cale would not be able to talk with them until the end of the day, he decided to wait right where he was and secure a spot on the bench for Tucker and himself.

Tucker returned before the judge banged his gavel and recalled the jury to the packed courtroom.

The defense called David back to the witness chair for another attack on his credibility. The witness did not crack. Cale noticed looks of empathy on faces of men who made up the jury, but those expressions grew solemn when the defendant was heard.

Fisk admitted he gambled at cards – he was in the midst of a game when arrested. He conceded Euclid Pomeroy had partici-pated at tables in Nashville and at least one of the riverboats Ada testified her brother mentioned. Fisk said an acquaintance – one Cedric Hays – claimed Euclid Pomeroy owed him hundreds of dollars, and he meant to collect it. He, Fisk, agreed to ride with Hays but stayed with the horses, never entered the house, and did not take part in any beating or murder.

On cross examination, the prosecutor handed Fisk the black hat and asked that he try it for size. The defendant placed the hat far back on his head. "This is the way I wear a hat," he main-tained when questioned.

"Pull it forward please," the prosecutor said, "like you want to keep the sun out of your eyes."

"Objection!" shouted the defense attorney.

"Overruled," the judge growled.

Fisk stalled The prosecutor stepped closer and tugged the front of the brim. The hat fit the man's head perfectly. "Gentle-men of the jury," the prosecutor intoned, "here you see the man who an eyewitness says attacked him and the late Euclid Pome-roy. Euclid Pomeroy was murdered, the witness barely survived. We hold this man responsible."

243

As a closing summation, the defense attorney set out to get the jury to accept that the murderer, Hays, had paid for the crime when he resisted arrest. He portrayed Fisk as an unwilling accomplice and cited the risks in convicting a man on the testimony of a young stranger such as David Appleby. "He's not one of you," he pleaded with the jury.

The prosecutor used few words in resting the state's case. "You can believe the eyewitness because he was there. They thought they left him to bleed to death. But he survived to identify one you see before you, one who is just as guilty as the man shot when he resisted arrest. We await your decision."

The jury retired but deliberations did not take long. Tobias Fisk was found guilty on all counts. The judge handed down a sentence of death by hanging and ordered that it be carried out before the end of the week.

The courtroom walls echoed the raucous conversations among the audience as the sheriff led Fisk to the jail and the beaming prosecutor made his way to the door. A silent McAndrew hobbled along behind, bracing himself on a succession of outstretched hands.

"Let's go find the ladies and take them home," Tucker said. "You may need to throw a rope around David to keep his feet on the ground."

Cale followed the big man to the crowded courthouse foyer where Ada, Louella, and David enjoyed their release from confinement. Tucker embraced Ada, then spread an arm about Louella's shoulders as well. David excitedly pumped the congratulatory hands extended to him as people left the courthouse.

"Well done, Dave," Cale called out once he managed to get close. "I bet you could swap a wore out mule for a horse right now with any man on that jury, and he'd brag about what a good deal you gave him."

"Cale, you don't know how *good* it feels for this waitin' to come to an end. *Finally!*"

Tucker, Ada, and Louella joined them. "Let's go home," Tucker said. "I got paid with some venison sausage for mending a bridle. We'll have meat for supper tonight."

"First let me find the sheriff," Cale said. "He won't need to hold my knife any longer... I want it back. I'll meet y'all outside the courthouse."

While most of the South including Meigs County entered a second year of Reconstruction under military occupation and a heightened sense of gloom, spirit rose at the Pomeroy house. Jefferson Tucker's addition to the household brought stability. Ada welcomed his suggestions for the farm. Louella happily embraced the security of having so many men around and performed small miracles from dwindling reserves in the cellar to keep them fed.

Cale and David made themselves useful in wintertime chores. They added to the supply of firewood, replaced fence rails, repaired farm implements needed for spring planting, then cleared bushes and vines from fields left idle in years no one cultivated them. The unpleasant task of shoveling out the cow's stable produced mounds of manure that made good fertilizer.

Tucker bartered his blacksmithing skill for supplies of seed from a few willing farmers. That led to after-supper sessions around the kitchen table to determine how to expand the vegetable garden and which fields were to be planted in corn, cotton, sorghum, peas, and potatoes.

Cale thought no farther ahead than planting and tending the new crop to a midsummer point when it could be expected to grow and ripen on its own. Being on the scene a while longer accommodated his constant notion to change Agnes Woodson's intention to marry Joshua McAndrew. To his surprise, David had not mentioned going west since the trial. That suited Cale's reason to let the subject rest.

All five members of the household went in to attend church services, but seeing Agnes and hearing her sing without an opportunity to talk with her outside McAndrew's presence tortured Cale.

Seeing his discomfort, Louella offered words to console. "I'm afraid you arrived years too late to compete for Agnes. Her mind was set on Josh while they were children. Everybody could see. If anything could have changed that it would have been when the Union side removed her father as judge. He had been like a second father to Josh til that happened. Judge Woodson wouldn't speak to him again. Poor Agnes was torn between them, but she would not break the engagement as her father wished. The judge passed on before Josh came home. When she saw him crippled up, I believe it only deepened her love for him."

She allowed him a moment to swallow his disappointment, then continued. "Josh has long been considered one of the county's most promising young men. He took advantage of opportunities to get an education. That means a lot to Agnes."

Cale sat in silence. It had not been said in so many words, but Louella hinted he could not match the material things even a handicapped Josh McAndrew would provide. That brought to mind the way he felt when Willingham cousins lorded it over him.

He thanked Louella for her insight and went back to his chores, still short of an idea how to arrange to see Agnes alone. He simply knew he must try.

He hunted any excuse to go into town. One day's explanation had to do with a visit to the store that served as Post Office to see if the Greers had written as promised with any late word about his grandfather's location. Disappointment awaited, however, and he could only collect two letters for the sisters. When he opened the door to leave a sudden rainbow appeared. Agnes was on her way inside. The proprietors were busy with other customers, and no one paid attention to two young people who lingered inside the front door.

"I hoped if I kept comin' to town there'd be a chance to see you again," he whispered.

She did not seem displeased to see him, but caution showed in her eyes. "I really don't think we ought to see each other," she said, matching his low tone of voice.

"That's not what that kiss said," he countered. "I can't get it off my mind. There was hunger in your lips, too. Look at me, Agnes."

She glanced about the store's interior before she met his eyes again. "We can't ever do that again, Cale. You are a nice young man, and..." her voice trembled, "things might have been different if we'd met earlier. But I promised to marry Josh."

She started to move away, and he clutched her arm. "Agnes," he whispered, "please let me see you again."

"I can't dare that," she said as she left him and moved quickly to the store's big counter. He watched her engage another woman in conversation. Head bowed, he walked home more dissatisfied than he had been on arrival.

Cale burned his energy in woodchopping expeditions. Repetitive swings of the ax blocked out deep thought until David fired one of his questions.

"Wonder how a feller goes about becomin' a lawyer?" he asked one day in the lighthearted, indirect way he often tossed up subjects for speculation or debate between them.

Cale rested the ax on his shoulder. "I reckon it takes a lot that we don't know about, Dave. Why?"

His friend leaned against a tree and reflected aloud. "Guess there's college... and all that. College means books. Any smart feller can read a book. So that might not matter much if a feller got real interested and determined."

Cale swung the ax before he replied. "And just where would that smart feller get his hands on one of them books?" he grunted. "If he didn't go to college, that is?"

David scratched his chin and considered the obvious. "Doubt there is such a thing as a store that sells law books. Not in these parts, anyway. If a feller lived someplace near a college town, he could get hold of one, I bet."

"Yep, if a feller's in the right place with money to spend he can do a lot of things," Cale said, leaning on the ax handle. "You're fallin' behind stackin' firewood on the sled," he reminded.

David bent to his task and said no more about it that day. But he raised the subject again the next morning as they pulled the empty sled into the woods.

"That feller McAndrew ought to know," he said. "Cale, I been thinkin' a lot since that trial. It opened a big world to me... helped me understand how a lawyer on either side of a case has a certain job to do. Before, I just thought lawyers sat around in big chairs and schemed up ways to take money from people. Sure

248

wish I'd been able to hear all that happened in that courtroom before and after they called me in."

"Well, you've asked enough questions about it, you should have a pretty good idea by now."

"Next time I hear there's a trial..."I'm goin' in and spend the day. You'll just have to work by yourself whatever day that is."

"Might not be too hard to handle.".

David's bold approach when he spotted McAndrew seated in the buggy after the next church service caught even Cale off guard. He could not overhear their conversation but the look on his friend's face when he walked away said it did not go well.

"What bee stung you?" Cale asked.

"I tried to find out if I could come talk to him 'bout the law," David mumbled just loud enough to be heard. "He said he didn't have time. Time's all I got."

"Don't quit on your first try," Cale counseled. "You got to know that sheriff fairly well. He ought to have a good notion who to see around that courthouse."

The sneer that suggestion ignited told Cale it would be wise to drop the subject.

The weeks that followed bulged with preparations to plant the Pomeroy farm and left few minutes for Cale to think about Agnes. At first Tucker bartered for a mule to pull the plow, but the arrangement proved unsatisfactory with the animal available only one or two days per week. He persuaded Ada to accompany him to meet with a man in neighboring McMinn County. A promissory note took shape with proceeds from the 1866 crop pledged as security for a loan. That purchased a mule and bulk supplies of seed immediately. Then the planting spread quickly from field to field. By the first of May, Tucker returned to his shop in town, leaving Cale and David to put in the last rows while Ada and Louella completed the garden.

Tucker came home one night carrying a private message for an astonished Cale. He read the note as quickly as the older man slipped it to him.

"Dear Cale, I have something to suggest to you. Please meet me at Mister Tucker's shop Friday at 4 P.M. I remain, Agnes Woodson."

Elation and befuddlement fought for the upper hand of his emotion. She continued to avoid him at church, and there had been no other sightings since the occasion at the post office. He was not about to let new opportunity slip away. He had no idea what her suggestion might be, but he was determined to hear it. The promise of seeing her alone lightened his body's weariness from farmwork and quickened his feet for the walk into town.

The familiar horse and buggy in front of Tucker's shop signaled she had arrived first. Cale walked in to witness Tucker demonstrate the hinges he had replaced on a folding tea cart. Agnes seemed delighted with the workmanship.

"Mother will be so pleased, Mister Tucker," she said.

"Let me fold it and put it in the buggy for you," Tucker recommended. "I'll go on around back to tend to something." He nodded to Cale while in the act of collapsing the little cart and was out the door without another word.

"I sure am happy to see you, Agnes."

"Thank you for coming, Cale."

He waited, hesitant to disrupt the order of an apparently arranged meeting. Tucker obviously knew more of what this was about, but if sworn to secrecy he had certainly kept it. The opportunity to see and talk with Agnes again was well worth granting her the first move. She stepped to one side of the small room and then retreated as if uncertain where she wished to stand. The only sounds came from the swish of the long black skirt above her footsteps. His heart pounded in anticipation, and he could bear the silence no longer.

"Agnes, there's so much I want to say..."

Her upraised palm stopped him.

"Please, Cale. Not now. Let me explain what this meeting is for."

He positioned himself in front of her so that she had to look at him. "Go ahead. I'm listenin'."

"Josh knows I am here." She paused, as if awaiting reaction to that statement, then rushed on. "It is my idea, however. I must tell you that your... presence... makes me uncomfortable. I want to marry Josh, and be a good wife to him. You are a temptation I cannot risk. As long as you are here..."

Cale reached for her hand, but she locked her fingers to prevent it.

"I wish you had never come here, Cale. That's hard for me to say... but you don't know..."

"I don't know your feelins' are mixed up? And you don't like standin' at the water's edge any more than I do?"

His interruption broke the awkward delivery of what must have been rehearsed. He could tell she bargained for time.

"You told me that when we kissed, Agnes. I had already said it,,, out in the open... how I feel about you. I just want..."

"I'm sorry, Cale, but I cannot accommodate what you want," she retook the lead. "I will marry Josh." Her fingers parted for a second then nervously sought each other again.

"...for you to be happy," Cale interjected, finishing his sentence. "If you'll give me a chance, you'll see. And a grown man is tellin' a grown woman what's in his heart. It's not a promise between two children."

He saw tears form before her eyes turned away from him. Silence settled within the shop, save for uneven clangs from the forge out back. Agnes walked to the lone window that looked out on the courthouse square and stood there for a moment before she faced him again. The voice from the face cast in shadow carried a flat tone of finality.

"Your attentions may have shaken my confidence for a time, Cale, but I will keep my promise. And my keeping it will be more certain if you go... someplace else... and stay away from here. If you will do that, and allow my happiness, I am prepared to do something for you in return."

The sour taste of disappointment stuck in his throat and dulled his curiosity for the second half of her terms. He had dared to think that, once he had won her love, he would persuade her to go on to a new life with him.

His slow response evidently led her to decide to spell out the remaining conditions. "Your friend David has asked to study some of Josh's books on the law and discuss how to prepare to become a lawyer. Josh is in the midst of establishing his practice. He would find it hard to spare the time. He will do it, though, as a favor to me. So you see the arrangement has equal benefits."

"And my leavin' benefits Dave, too... is that the way you see it?" Cale concluded for her.

"I hoped you see that," she confirmed. Her lips formed a hint of a smile.

He braced his hands on the back of the only chair Tucker kept in the room and let emotion course through the muscles of his arms. Years of woodchopping had taught him to release anger or confusion through physical exertion. The act gave him time to sort out thoughts and form them into words. He wanted to be very sure of what were likely to be his last words with Agnes.

"How do I know Dave will ever see one of them books?" he demanded.

She managed a full smile before she answered. "You have my promise. And when I make a promise, I keep it."

Cale took time to study her face and commit it to memory as if he were carving her likeness into a cameo. Locks of blonde hair escaping the brim of a customary bonnet. The soft, pink hue on her cheeks. The fullness of her lips, and the clear blue depth in eyes set between long eyelashes.

Satisfied, he released his hold on the chair and spoke from the first calmness felt since he walked in.

"Then the captain has to tell Dave it's his idea. When I know that's been said and agreed to, I'll leave as soon as the crops can make it on their own."

Her puzzled expression showed she had not anticipated alternate terms. He met her questioning look with one of unflinching resolve.

"Very well," she said once an awkward moment passed. "I thought you... would want to be the one to tell your friend, but... it will be done. Soon."

Cale saw no reason to linger. "Then I'll bid you good day, Agnes. I won't cause you any more discomfort with my presence. But it may not be as easy for you to be rid of the feelins' we stirred up in that kiss. I know it won't be for me."

He started for the door, but she stopped him.

"It will look better if I leave first," she said and moved past him to the outside, closing the door behind her.

Cale left the shop without telling Tucker anything from the conversation. He did not trust himself to confide in anyone, not even David. The tight-lipped change in him was apparent to everyone at the Pomeroy house in the days that followed, but they granted him the right to examine his mind to his own satisfaction.

To his relief, David talked so much about a recent trial he witnessed that he did not need a conversational partner. Cale could immerse himself in the work at hand and let his friend chatter on without agreement or contradiction. The character trait had been amusing when they first met. It eased the boredom of wartime days when they waited for someone to tell them what to do.

The insistence that McAndrew be the messenger grew from Cale's reluctance to confront David with the choice of their longstanding plan to go west or a personal opportunity to read up on the law. If Cale presented the offer, David might think he was unwanted as a travel companion when the time came to depart. Better that the offer come from the one who would be obligated to keep it. That action did not come as fast as Cale wished, but it did come.

McAndrew summoned Appleby to the side of his buggy on the sunny first Sunday in June. It could not be described as a conversation because McAndrew talked while David's head bobbed repeatedly. But from the excited expression on David's face, there could be no doubt that a deal had been struck.

"He's reconsidered, Cale! Said for me to come see him at his office, and he'd show me a book that he says will be a good introduction. He wanted to know if I knew about the Bill of Rights! Must think we forgot all we learned before the war."

"Now don't go correctin' the captain, Dave," Cale joked. "He got used to givin' orders. Besides the law is his territory, and if you want him to tell you how to go about preparin' for it, you'd better listen til he says it's all right to talk."

The buggy's departure drew his attention, and he turned just in time to see Agnes, seated in her customary place beside McAndrew but with eyes fixed solely on Cale. With a slight nod of her head, she smiled to him before she looked ahead to the road.

"Wonder why he changed his mind?" David asked.

Cale fought back his own dismay and slapped his friend's back. "Guess that's one of the mysteries of the law you might be able to figger out on your own someday."

The next move would be his to make. It, too, required preparation time.

Chapter 15: Departure

Fortunately, the crops had reached a sufficient stage of growth to withstand any drain of nutrients from grass or weeds. Sunshine and nourishing rains had the corn, potatoes, peas, and sorghum well on their way to produce a good harvest. The cotton plants struggled, but eastern Tennessee was not good for growing cotton in the first place. As he looked out over the fields, Cale's years of working cotton in South Carolina's better conditions suggested that the yield on the Pomeroy farm might amount to one bale at most. But that could be turned into cash, which with sale of some of the corn and potatoes should see the promissory note paid on time.

The Tuckers and Louella knew he intended to go in search of his grandfather, and a midsummer departure did not need to be explained. With David, on the other hand, the subject of leaving had to be approached with caution. Cale took comfort in hearing his friend reconstruct each session with McAndrew. One lengthy account ended with David's complaint that he had to do his reading in the office without being allowed to take a book for study at home.

"He may have spent a lot of money on his books," Cale suggested. "How does he know your interest won't die out with you forgettin' to bring one back?"

"Oh, my interest gets stronger by the day, Cale. I read and reread every page I have time to see."

The opening was there for the taking. Still, Cale felt reluctant to rush the inevitable.

"Becomin' a lawyer... not a railroad man... is that what you really want to do?" he asked.

"I sure do.... I don't care how long it takes. I believe he's startin' to see how serious I am. It'll take time. There's so much to learn..." His words slowed and he seemed less certain of what he wished to say. "Trouble is... I guess it means... I won't be goin' west... with you." He drug out the words, and his face confirmed the sad sound to them.

Their friendship, rooted in the face of enemy fire and fed in the resulting disorder that encouraged ideas of westward exploration, thrived on assurance that one understood the other even when agreement was unspoken. Cale sensed that his friend realized, as he did, that taking separate paths would be difficult for both, at least for some time. David had made his choice voluntarily. The moment had come for Cale to put him at ease.

"Well, Dave, I don't know how far west I'll ever go. You know I want to find Grandpa Morgan. That sets my destination right there. When I find him... *if* I find him... I may want to stay around a while, or I may not. Don't know where that place *is*, or anything about what goes on there. When you saw it you might not care to stay two minutes. But you've always understood why I want to find him. And I understand that the law has become just as important to you as the notion of goin' out west used to be. I'll miss havin' you around, but I wouldn't want you to walk away from something that important just to go off on my hunt."

The relief that spread across David's face settled the matter to Cale's satisfaction.

258

But his friend had more to say. "You know... it's funny. A while back, I thought *you* would likely take a notion to stay in these parts once you charmed that little Agnes, and *I* would be the one itchin' to leave. Sure is i-ronic the way it's workin' out."

Cale forced himself to grin. He didn't think there was anything funny about the arrangement he had accepted, but he chose not to dampen the mood.

"I never have been sure what i-ronic meant, Dave. Knowin' how and when to use words like that ought to give you a head start becomin' a lawyer."

He asked Tucker to walk with him and survey the state of growth in the fields as June became July. "I agree things look pretty good," the big man said. "We should do well with most, and whatever we get out of the cotton will come in handy, too. You and David have done most of the work... Ada, Louella, and myself are much obliged."

"Well, I wanted you to be satisfied before I think about headin' out," Cale said. "Will you and Dave be able to take care of the harvest?"

Tucker took a few steps between shoulder-high stalks of corn for a better view of distant fields then returned to stand beside Cale. "Yes, it won't matter if the shop sits idle a few weeks. And you know by now these ladies are not too proud to do fieldwork when it means survival. Gathering this crop is all important. If we make it through this year, we'll have enough to eat and be in much better shape for what's ahead. A lot better shape than most folks around here."

"I wouldn't be leavin' if I thought there was a need for me to stay longer. You folks have been mighty good to me. And I 'preciate Dave's havin' a place to stay while he finds out if there's a way for him to become a lawyer. That is *if* Captain McAndrew keeps his word." Cale seized the confidence of the conversation to ask the question that troubled him. "Tell me, Mister Tucker, do you think he'll ever get around to marryin' Agnes?"

Tucker ended his inspection to give undivided attention to Cale.

"I think he'll do both things. I know you got serious about her yourself. Most men can see why... she is a pretty little thing. From the way she asked me to carry that note to you, I could tell that you were on her mind. Besides her father and Josh, no other man has lingered there for more than a fleeting minute, I think I can safely say. And I have a notion what was said between you two gave a mighty shove to Josh's agreement to help David."

"You figger things out as good as any man I ever met," Cale said with respect.

"Well, let me give you some more opinion," Tucker volunteered. "I believe there's another reason Josh decided to do it. A lot of local people sat in that courtroom and listened to David's testimony. Since then, I've overheard more than one comment favorable to him. Some of that's bound to get back to Josh. Here's why that's important. This county... probably this entire state,... is still just as divided as it was during the war. We're not big enough here to support more than a few lawyers, and some people won't have anything to do with a lawyer known to have favored the other side. Josh was a popular young fellow before the war. Everybody wanted him to do well. But some feelings changed when he took the Union side. He won, but now he's trying to get a law practice on its feet. Some Southern sympathizers avoid him because they won't forget. So... when it becomes known that he's allowing a former Confederate soldier to read up on the law... in *his* office... that might cause some people to reconsider. That's the sort of gesture and the kind of thinking we need if we ever pull this country together again."

Tucker waited for reaction, but the points seemed too well laid out for Cale to question. The big man turned to begin the return walk to the house. Cale fell in step.

"He'll marry Agnes pretty soon," Tucker continued. "Josh is a proud fellow. I believe he needed some time to get used to the aftereffect of his injuries. He may be stiff-legged from now on, but he knows Agnes made a great sacrifice for him when she went against what Judge Woodson wanted her to do. Josh won't let his manly pride make that devotion go unrewarded."

The night he prepared to leave, he explained to David why he would not walk into town with him next morning. That conversation kept their parting words in the hallway brief and light.

"Try and forget that he wore a blue coat," Cale suggested. "Listen to him."

"You know I like to talk more than listen," David quipped. "But I'll try it your way. Since I won't be there to do it for you, watch out for yourself."

Cale wrapped him in a bear hug then pushed him out the front door. "You'll make a good lawyer, Dave."

With no other men around, Cale joined Ada and Louella at the kitchen table where they had talked so often. The threesome dawdled in their enjoyment of a rare time of leisure instead of the usual daily routine. Cale purposely sought it because he wanted to spend one more private hour with the sisters.

Their reminiscences blended memories, frequent laughter, and some crying. The latter furnished by Louella, whose sniffles took over in the middle of each recollection she wanted to contribute. Ada's voice kept its familiar even tone, although Cale saw a tear glisten in the corner of her eye more than once.

"We understand how important it is for you to go and search for your grandfather, Cale," she said when the conversation began to wane, "and you have delayed it to see that we get this farm... our livelihood... back into production. We will never forget the many ways you have been helpful to us. We hope you'll send word to us when you've found him."

"I'll sure do that, Miz Ada," he said.

"Wherever you are, we'll know God is with you," Louella said as she caressed his hand. "And I hope there'll be someone who'll reward you and share the feelings you've had for Agnes."

Mention of the name gave Cale a moment's uneasiness, but he suppressed it and seized her fingers. "Not only did I get here too late to have a hope with her, I was born twenty years too late to be in the race for you!"

"Oh, *Cale,*" Louella shrieked then collapsed in laughter.

Ada laughed along with them as she went around to help her sister conquer the spasm of glee and get to her feet. "Cale, there's one more thing we want you to do for us before you go."

She guided Louella to the kitchen doorway. "Do you have your knife?"

"Yep, right here at my waist."

With her free hand, Ada touched the door frame. "Carve your initials... right about here."

"Are you sure you want to put a scar on that nice wood?" he asked, surprised by the request.

"Oh, yes," she said quickly and Louella echoed. "If it's right about here," Ada continued, "we can touch it anytime we want and remember you were once part of this home."

He drew the knife and stuck the point of the blade in the wood to test its hardness, then proceeded to etch a small "c" and an "m" in the surface while they watched.

"There!" Louella sighed and eagerly became first to trace the grooves with her finger. Ada followed suit immediately.

He tucked the knife away and spread his arms about them. They paused to share a long embrace, no one speaking a word. When he lowered his arms and reached for his pack – stuffed by Louella with corn cakes and fruit – he made a request of his own.

"Come with me out to the front steps."

"Well, of course," Ada said.

They walked up the long hallway arm in arm, passed through the front door, and crossed the veranda. At Cale's direction, all three stepped down to the first step above ground level.

He released their arms and stepped to the ground. "Please stand right there," he directed, "I want to carry with me the memory of you standin' in front of this house."

He backed a few feet away and gazed for a moment at the two women he had come to regard as beloved aunts, framed between pink blossoms of the crape myrtles. He raised his right palm in a wave, and they did the same. Then, with long strides, he left the front yard and began his westward journey.

A hundred yards or so down the road he began to talk aloud.

"I'm on the way, Grandpa.

"Twenty-one years old... two strong legs... our knife at my waist... spirit not even bent!"

Chapter 16: Unlikely Alliance

The crowd wanted to see blood spilled. Whose blood did not matter. The thrashing given the first challenger made few think the reigning champion would be the next bleeder. Cale knew the odds when he handed his pack to the barker for safekeeping and swung his leg over the rope that bordered the ring. How long he could last would determine the worth of his effort.

"Five dollars to any man who can go a full round," the barker shouted. "Five more to the hero who can stand after two... and ten, I said *Ten more dollars*... if the man will give Baalem the Bull three rounds of competition. Ah... I see we have a second contender. Place your bets, gentlemen."

Cale sensed the stares from men who crowded round to witness another man's humiliation or improbable triumph. When he shed his shirt, they appraised him as if he were a hog bound for slaughter. He heard them exchange opinions and saw several approach the barker to wager on the outcome. He did not care how they judged him. He needed the potential payoff.

The man who could keep it from him strutted about the opposite side of the ring, fists raised above his head. His chest and shoulders glistened and bulged with muscle. Baalem the Bull looked to be shorter than Cale's own six-foot height, but the heavy upper body suggested a weight advantage of 25 to 30 pounds. Any would-be survivor of blows from those powerful arms must evade them or deflect their full impact, at least.

When satisfied he had coaxed all the bets the crowd would willingly give, the barker ducked beneath the rope and made his way to where Cale waited inside the ring. Strips of cloth were produced and wrapped across the knuckles of each of Cale's bare hands. "Tuck the ends inside your fists," the man said as he exited the ring.

"The challenge has been accepted," the barker called to the crowd then turned to address Cale. "We don't want these people to be disappointed. The first round will be five minutes' long. If you are still game, there will be a three-minute rest period before the second round of another five minutes. In the unlikely event you are still standing, another rest period will precede the third round... if there is to be one. No biting is allowed. Now, prepare to be rushed by Baalem the Bull!"

True to his name, Baalem charged as if bent on goring another victim in one rush. Cale shifted his weight quickly and danced to his left. The bull braked himself on the rope and whirled to launch a second strike.

Cale managed to elude being flattened by shoving against the onrushing man's shoulder. Disrupting the attacker's balance became his primary tactic, and he survived lunge after lunge until the enraged Baalem finally forced him into a corner. Cale weaved and ducked the swings aimed at his head and began counterattacking Baalem's midsection. Combat at close range, though, placed him well within the grasp of those powerful arms, and he soon found himself entrapped. Baalem applied crushing pressure in a bear hug unlike anything Cale had experienced before. With the breath being squeezed out of him, he struggled to get hold of some part of the oiled and sweaty body of his opponent. They remained locked together until Cale's own sweat helped loosen their clamped skins, and he slid free to one side.

The bull charged again, aiming successive punches at the challenger's head. Cale discovered an advantage in the length of his own arms. The fists of those heavily-muscled arms fell short of Cale's jaw when Baalem could be kept from toe-to-toe range. The extra reach allowed Cale to land an occasional blow himself. They circled the ring time and again, each landing a punch now and then between misses, and Cale avoided a repeat of being crushed for the remainder of the round.

He leaned against a ring post and gulped air during the rest period. His heavy breathing meant he scarcely heard the barker call for wagers on the next round, but he was determined to continue. He vowed not to quit before he was assured of no less than 10 dollars.

When the second round commenced, he realized Baalem had used the rest period to apply another layer of oil to his upper body. Their first brush of contact told Cale the reigning champion had become more slippery than a fish. Confident no hand could grab hold of him or push him to one side, Baalem chose to head-butt his way past Cale's flailing arms and secured the prey in another bear hug. Instead of a frontal crush, he slid an arm past Cale's shoulder and twisted his neck inside a headlock. The free arm then began to pound Cale's head with punch after punch until the victim wriggled out of the trap and backed away.

A dizzy Cale staggered to the rope and slid first one way then the next to avoid being wrapped in another brutal grasp. Baalem's method of attack left him open to the challenger's superior reach, and little by little the number of punches landed began to draw even. Not without cost, however, and Cale tasted blood from his own cut lip. He felt his brow swell at his right eye, but Baalem's grunts told Cale some of his own licks had taken a toll He lost all track of time as the struggle continued. It seemed a different day had come when he finally heard the call "Time."

There being few bets on a third round, the second rest period went quickly. Cale summoned all his stamina to meet the maddened Baalem's next charge. The so-called bull abandoned wrestling moves entirely and struck furiously with his fists. Cale managed to duck or parry most of the blows until a punch thrown by Baalem's left made solid contact with the side of his head. He dropped as suddenly as if he had been shot.

The next thing Cale realized was the taste of dirt. He tried to raise his groggy head and spit out the blood-and-dirt mixture. His nostrils seemed to be bloodied as well, and he almost choked before he could lift his chin high enough to rid his mouth of what did not belong there. When he could see, he made out a trousered knee bent close to his head. Above the knee, the eyes of another man peered down at him.

In spite of an aching head and blurred vision, Cale could tell this man was neither the barker nor Baalem.

"Welcome back to consciousness," the man said. "That was quite a blow to your head."

Cale struggled to a sitting position, but the effort made his head hurt worse. He groaned aloud and found it helped him breathe.

"Here," the man said, "take a sip." He inserted the opened neck of a silver flask between Cale's lips. Good brandy overpowered the taste of dirt and blood. Cale gulped a second swallow.

"The first thing you should do when you get to your feet," the well-dressed man said as he slipped the flask inside his coat and rose to the full extent of his short stature, "I suggest you collect your ten dollars from that barker. Men who stage these performances have a habit of disappearing. Then I'd like to talk with you."

That is how Cale met Adam Blaine.

Nothing in Cale's experience compared with the changed life he led as an employee of Adam Blaine.

After final visits with Jesse Murdock and Sam and Beulah Greer provided word of his grandfather's location, Cale pushed onward to reach that place identified as Promise, Texas. He subsidized his journey cutting crossties for railroad repair and expansion from Chattanooga, working on a crew of a snag boat to clear stumps and similar underwater hazards for traffic along the Coosa and Tennessee rivers with stints as farm hand or woodcutter according to season as he moved westward across Alabama and Mississippi. That year-long progression placed him at the sprawling city of Memphis in September 1867, where too many hands competed for the too few jobs available. His lack of funds dictated Cale's decision to face Baalem the Bull at the traveling tent show and circus.

Once he stuffed the hard-earned 10 greenback dollars in his pocket, reclaimed his pack and felt within to be sure his knife was still there, Cale accompanied Adam Blaine to his hotel, where soap and a wash basin removed most of the nicks from hand-to-hand combat.

"You may have taken the measure of that fellow," Blaine commented as Cale toweled himself in the washroom just off the lobby, "had he not slipped something inside his left fist before that third round. I saw him place his hand inside the waistband of his tights but could not tell you what he extracted. It's not uncommon in these shows. Just as the duration of the round depends on the stamina shown by the challenger. No doubt you noticed that second round ran longer than the first. But let's get a piece of raw meat for that eye then talk further over lunch, shall we? We'll take one of these small towels for an eyepatch," he said as he pressed a coin in the hand of the washroom attendant.

The stately dining room would have intimidated awkward Cale, but Adam Blaine's manner put him at ease. His host rated a table by a window, and they reached it without crossing through the well- populated tables filling the center of the big room.

Once Blaine had ordered for them, he got down to business.

"I admire your strength and skill in combat," he said "No doubt you were in the war. Which side doesn't matter to me. The fact you risked injury the way you did this noontime tells me you need employment... possibly no one else... a wife or children... to prevent you from travel. Am I correct in these assumptions?" The smaller man reached across the table as he talked and adjusted the cloth above Cale's right eye to secure the small slice of raw beef the waiter produced.

"You're right... I need work," Cale said. "I'm on my own. I want to go to Texas and find my grandfather." He slowed and took time to choose his next words. "I don't know what sort of work you have in mind. I'm not wanted by the law, and I aim to stay that way."

Blaine smiled easily. "I assure you the work is legal. I, too, respect the law and obey it. You would become my personal assistant and bodyguard on my journey to New Orleans. If you agree, and arrangements can be completed this afternoon, we board a steamer tonight. Tomorrow, at the latest."

The offer overwhelmed Cale. He welcomed the patient expression in the gray eyes studying him, but a nagging question had to be asked. "You're not one of these men who..." he stammered, "well, cheat... down-and-out Southern storekeepers and farmers?"

"I'm no carpetbagger, " Blaine interrupted. "My reputation is respected in both New Orleans and Saint Louis. The uncertainty of the times has made me realize a gentleman who travels a great distance must exercise caution beyond what law enforcement can provide. You will know more of what it is that I do when we reach New Orleans."

Cale nodded that he understood and forced his sore lip into a twisted smile. "I will do whatever it is you'd like me to do, Mister Blaine. And I can leave whenever you say."

Adam Blaine extended his right hand across the white tablecloth. Cale shook it.

They finished lunch and adjourned to a haberdashery nearby, where Cale was outfitted in the first full dress suit of his life. And a second suit including waistcoat and trousers for good measure. Blaine made sure the tailoring was to be done by the end of the day, then oversaw Cale's selection of new shoes, three shirts, two cravats, underwear, and a hat with a narrow rolled brim. From the haberdashery, they stopped to purchase a valise for Cale's new wardrobe. Their return to the hotel included a visit to the barber shop and bathhouse where Blaine issued instructions for grooming Cale's thick beard and thatch of hair before he left to purchase tickets for the evening steamboat to New Orleans.

Cale shed the beefsteak poultice before they returned to the haberdashery. The bath at the hotel eased his adjustment to new clothes. He emptied his pack of everything except his knife, the shard of baked clay, and a jacket Louella Pomeroy altered for him, added the shirt and trousers worn earlier that day, then stuffed the pack with the remaining items of new clothing inside the valise.

They rode in a hired hack to the riverside, where experienced deck hands hoisted Adam Blaine's two enormous trunks on board the *Empress of Ohio* with much less effort than Cale, the driver, and two porters exerted to depart the hotel. During the ride, Blaine made Cale aware the clothing investment and shipboard accommodation would constitute salary until after business in New Orleans concluded and future terms discussed.

On board, they were shown to a suite on the second deck. Blaine and the trunks took the bedroom; a cot was brought in for Cale to sleep on in the small sitting room. Then it was on to dinner in the gilded salon and dining room just as the big side-wheeler left the pier and night descended on the river.

Blaine ordered shots of bourbon for each of them, and conversation came easily. Cale's background seemed to interest the older man, who kept the subject away from the mission or himself. Generous servings of red wine with their food loosened Cale's tongue to share a full account of his rescue by the grandfather he did not know he had as well as pleasant recollections of time spent with the Pomeroy sisters and the friendship formed with David Appleby. From time to time, Blaine interrupted with a question about Cale's pronunciation or a polite correction when the wrong word had been used. He did it in such a manner that Cale did not feel embarrassed.

"Morgan, I'm glad to see that your personality does not change when you drink," Blaine confided as they walked back to the suite. "That became the problem with your predecessor. His belligerence left me no choice but to discharge him the evening before you and I met. Good drink is meant to be enjoyed... in moderation."

Blaine retired early, and that suited Cale. The gliding movement and sounds of the big steamboat lulled him into deep slumber, and he did not stir until he heard Blaine unlock the outer door next morning. The little man stood before him in a dark dressing gown. Several articles of apparel were draped over one arm, and that hand clutched a small leather kit.

"Get dressed and come with me," Blaine instructed. "While I am in the bathroom, you are to keep watch outside the door. When I have finished my morning ablutions and we have returned to this room, you may then use the bathroom yourself."

Cale slid off the cot and did as he was told, all the while wondering what threat his new employer took such precaution to avoid.

Late in the afternoon of the second day out of Memphis, the *Empress of Ohio* put in at Vicksburg. Many passengers disembarked, but Blaine chose to remain on board for the night. They went ashore the next morning.

More than four years after the siege in which Federal troops wrested control of the town, the scars of war could not be overlooked or maneuvered past. What business establishments survived, revived, or changed hands could be reached within a short walk from riverside. The wooden sidewalks were clogged with wares displayed by shopkeepers and watched over by sturdy types to prevent theft or discourage the destitute from lingering near the shop entrances.

Blaine remarked that he had seen Vicksburg on previous journeys but insisted they climb the hill for a better view of the battlefield. Trenches, remnants of abandoned artillery, and barricades thrown up to identify unexploded ordnance quickly spun Cale's mind back to his own wartime experiences. Memories still too raw to be shared, and he simply nodded acceptance with whatever Blaine said.

They walked back down amongst the shops, where Blaine rummaged through a stack of books at the front of one establishment then went inside for a conference with the storekeeper. He rejoined Cale on the sidewalk a moment later, book in hand.

"A gift for you," the short man said as he thrust the book so that Cale was forced to take it. He looked down at the worn but legible stiff cover and suppressed a grin.

"Mister Webster's dictionary will be your friend," Blaine said, "if you will but turn to it now and then. I think we've had a good morning's outing, now let us return on board in time for luncheon."

Cale fell in step with him and mumbled his gratitude. The dictionary should help him follow Blaine's talk when things like ablutions and predecessor were mentioned.

The routine became familiar. As instructed, he stuck close to Blaine and accompanied him on strolls about the upper and lower decks of the *Empress*, lingered at the rail to study the farmland and forests they passed, or when they retired to the suite to read or nap before another feast in the dining room. At table Cale watched his host carefully before he chose a fork from the many alongside his own plate. That close inspection made him notice the strong hands that seemed odd for a man of Blaine's small stature, but he dismissed the thought as he sampled his first tastes of roast pheasant and Beef Wellington. "Wait until we reach New Orleans to sample the raw oysters," Blaine advised.

The *Empress* called for overnight stops at Natchez and again at Baton Rouge as the days went by. Blaine's anxiety to reach New Orleans became obvious. To Cale, the lazy life of traveling by steamboat seemed too good to be true. He found it easy to put out of mind the hard times when he stumbled along uninviting roads and across dark, mysterious valleys, never sure where his next meal was to come from or where he was to find a safe place to sleep.

The only thing about his newfound way of life that Cale disliked was the isolation from everyone else on board. Adam Blaine was not an unpleasant fellow to be around, but he expected Cale's undivided attention. Tables near their own in the dining room were surrounded by people of all ages and outward signs of success. Their dress and mannerisms convinced Cale he had stepped into a world beyond the stark postwar conditions which had been so familiar. The number of lovely young women of Cale's own generation left him bedazzled. More than one, he noticed, was in the exclusive company of a well-dressed older man or a Union officer. He was one of only three or four young men on board who were not members of the crew, yet duty at Blaine's side forbade an attempt to strike up conversation with any young woman not hovered over by a dinner partner. Likewise, he could not take part in any after-dinner socializimg and could but listen as the sounds of orchestra music and gaiety wafted over the decks and crept into the suite until he tired of reading his dictionary, blew out his lamp, and dropped off to sleep.

An air of excitement swept through the passengers as the *Empress of Ohio* nudged her way alongside the pier in New Orleans. Cale, seeing the city for the first time, caught himself drawing shorter breaths in expectation. Seasoned travelers such as Adam Blaine merely showed their confidence for what awaited them on shore. To them, arrival had a purpose. To Cale, another veil of uncertainty needed to be lifted. Soon he expected to know why Blaine had recruited him for this mission and how it might fit his own quest to find his grandfather.

As they rode with the trunks to a hotel, Cale could see one reason why a man of Blaine's size and obvious means would want protection. The boulevards, though narrow, were open and well-populated, but side streets hinted of menace with figures darting in and out of shadow. They did not have to travel far to their destination, the Hotel Royale on Royal Street, where Blaine customarily booked.

After effusive welcomes from the staff, they were shown to a second floor suite. Again, Blaine and the trunks took the bedroom; this one even more spacious and well-appointed.

The sitting room doubled as Cale's accommodation at night. The suite did include a small private bathroom. When Blaine had familiarized himself on how to secure the French doors that led to the iron balcony overlooking Royal Street, he arranged for a message to be sent at once to an address on St Charles Avenue. A reply came within the hour.

"We are to dine tomorrow night with friends," he told Cale. "Summon a porter to have our clothing pressed."

That night they dined at a small French restaurant near the hotel. The proprietor gushed delight at his good fortune to serve Blaine once again. Cale managed to hide his amusement watching each diminutive man vie to outdo the other in gesture and in words of praise.

"Morgan, you must... *we must* have the oysters here," Blaine instructed. He demonstrated how to enjoy the icy cold delicacy, presented raw on open shells, with generous dollops of sauce. They finished off the meal with filets mignon, then it was on to a sporting house, an ordinary three-story townhouse when judged by exterior appearance but lavishly furnished within. And it was immediately apparent that Blaine and the middle-aged madame knew each other well.

Cale blinked at the array of beautiful women who moved about the parlor and paused to chat with well-dressed men who nursed drinks and considered the many options available to them. A small combo of piano, cornet, and guitar kept the mood upbeat. Beyond the bar, card games could be seen through open doors. As Cale accepted the drink a waiter thrust in his hand, he realized the real show took place on the staircase. Each woman led her patron up the stairs in sensuous invitation sure to be seen by other eyes in the big room.

Blaine was deep in conversation with the madame who seemed eager to fulfill his request. She excused herself, and the little man turned back to Cale.

"Amuse yourself down here for a while, Morgan, and wait for my return." The implication was clear – look, but don't touch. Blaine did not wait for confirmation.

The madame reappeared, and with her came a young woman who looked to be about Cale's age.

Her low-cut gown swayed rhythmically with each step. She smiled as the older woman took her hand and extended it to Blaine.

A wallop of recognition equal to the last punch from Baalem the Bull hit Cale when he heard the madame say "Adam, I'd like you to meet Betsy."

The couple had moved halfway up the staircase before Cale recovered his senses. He fought back a powerful urge to shout "No!" and turned away to keep from witnessing more. He stumbled to the bar and asked for another drink. "What?... whatever I had the first time. Mister Blaine's payin'."

He stared at the fresh drink before him but did not raise it to his lips. Stunned in disbelief, he slouched on a lacquered wooden stool. He sat in morose silence for several minutes and barely felt the touch of a woman's hand on his shoulder. "I haven't seen you here before, Handsome," a soft voice said.

Cale looked into the inviting face of a redhead bent next to his own. "I'm Portia," she said, "and I'd like to be your friend. If you let me," the last words softly purred.

"I'm here with Mister Blaine," he stammered. "He's with... Betsy."

Portia pressed her cheek close and breathed into his ear, "And he won't let you have a little fun of your own?" When Cale did not reply immediately, she started to move away.

"Wait...," he said. "Do you know Betsy?"

"Of course... I know every girl here."

"I used to know her... before the war."

Her expression grew solemn. "You *knew* her, then decided you'd go off to battle rather than stay to marry her." Her inviting tone had flattened. "Am I right?"

"No, that's *not* right," he said quickly. "Her family 'spected... better than me, for her."

Portia's face registered surprise at his honesty. She drew close again. He could not tell if that meant sympathy or simple curiosity, but he seized his chance to say more.

"Would you give her a message?," he whispered. "From me?"

She looked to see if anyone else might overhear then turned back to him. "We're not supposed to," she said softly. "Why don't you come back tomorrow night and ask for her?"

"I can't... I have to go someplace with Mister Blaine. I'm his... protection."

The bartender leaned in to warn Portia, "Madame's watching."

She placed her hand on Cale's shoulder and whispered in his ear, "Write a note.. quick. I'll try to pass by in a few minutes. That is, if I'm not busy. If so, you're out of luck." She moved away.

He found it was easier to talk the bartender into supplying a slip of paper and a pencil than it was to decide what to write. He crossed out his first scribbles, turned the paper over, and began anew.

"Dear Betsy. I work for Mr. Blaine. We stay at the Hotel Royale. Can you leave a message for me? I want to see you. Can we meet some other place? Your friend, Cale."

He reread what he had written then folded the note to a quarter-sized wad and covered it with his palm. He glanced over his shoulder between sips of his drink. Several minutes went by before he saw Portia again. He sighed aloud when she headed for the stairway, a man at her heels.

The bartender saw Cale's head droop. "Did you write something for Portia?" he asked. "I'll see that she gets it... for a price."

"No... it's not for her," Cale said. "I wanted to get a message to the one named Betsy."

"Same offer, same price," the bartender replied as he swiped a towel across the bar. "If you want, I'll add it on your friend's tab. He won't know how many drinks you've had, will he?" The man's wink tempted Cale to accept.

"No, I 'druther pay myself," he said. "Five dollars suit you?"

That surprised the man. "Hell, for that I'll even bring her reply to you. Where will I find you?"

"First let me change part of what I wrote," Cale said. He unfolded the paper, crossed through the words "can you leave," scribbled "give this man" above them and marked out the question mark. He folded it again and spoke to the man behind the bar. "Hotel Roy-alle... my name's Morgan. Tell them at the desk to hold the message til I ask for it." He dug in his pocket for one of the hard-earned five dollar bills, wrapped it around the paper wad, and passed it to the bartender as if they were shaking hands.

The man deftly slipped his hand in his pocket, nodded to Cale, and turned to clear the empty glasses left on his bar.

Cale seethed with resentment toward the little man as they left for the walk to the hotel. He choked back words because he did not want to invite Blaine to say anything about his hour of pleasure with Betsy. That singleminded concentration kept Cale from seeing the arm thrust out when they passed the corner of a building.

"Morgan!," the little man cried as the arm attempted to pull him into a dark alley. "Help me!"

Cale lunged and rammed his shoulder between Blaine and the attacker. The bulky man stepped back, drew a thin knife, and waved it in Cale's face. "You want to get stuck?"

Cale pushed Blaine to safety. In the same movement, he slipped a hand inside his own coat and grasped the hilt of his knife. With no other use for the inner breast pocket, he had contrived a way to carry the big knife there with the blade dangled through a slit in the bottom of the pocket lining. He withdrew the knife swiftly, his first time to brandish it as a weapon.

"There's a lot more of you to cut on than there is of me," he confronted the would-be robber. "Where would you like me to start?"

The dim light did not prevent the man's realizing he faced a bigger knife. He backed away and broke into a run. His thudding footsteps and heavy breathing vanished down the dark alley.

"Thank you, Morgan," Blaine said with a loud sigh of relief. "Where did you acquire that knife?"

Cale slipped the knife back inside its hiding place before he answered. "From my grandpa."

They walked the rest of the way in silence.

Blaine made several attempts at conversation the next day, but Cale could not shake sour thoughts of his employer's time with Betsy. A night of restlessness instead of sleep almost provoked his resignation at the breakfast table. He thought better of it once he realized walking out on the little man meant he would never know her reply to his note, if it came.

A carriage sent by their hosts for the evening arrived at the hotel at 6 o'clock. Blaine insisted on calling attention to examples of New Orleans architecture they rode past. "Many Saint Charles Avenue houses," he explained, "feature galleries across the full front of the second floor." When they alighted from the carriage, Cale looked up at twin columns that soared three stories to a gabled roofline. Blaine described their destination as a Creole townhouse. "The Creole style has smaller balconies," he said and pointed upward. "See how they are centered on both the second and third floors?"

Cale's discomfort increased with each step he took inside what seemed, to him, a castle. A uniformed butler received them and led the way to a parlor where three men were seated. Blaine seemed to know them well. His brief introduction of "my assistant, Morgan," gave all the information about Cale the three men cared to know. They may as well have conversed in a different language for all that he could follow. That did not change when three mature women, richly gowned and holding tiny fans, joined them for the move into a large dining room. Stiff politeness prevailed under a massive chandelier throughout dinner, after which the women withdrew and Cale sat by while the three men joined with Blaine in a round of brandies and cigars. In Blaine's departing remarks, Cale learned that a second meeting had been agreed to for the following day at the hotel. He suspected that might lead to the opening of the second trunk.

However, it soon became clear the arrangement did not require Cale's presence.

"Why don't you enjoy a stroll about the Quarter?" Blaine suggested to him when a hotel porter came to the suite a little before noon to announce the arrival of guests. "We'll be at luncheon and then in conference here most of the afternoon. You won't need to return before five o' clock."

The suggestion chafed Cale's already bruised feelings, but he took a deep breath before he spoke.

"I would 'preciate some time to myself, Mister Blaine, but I believe I'll stay with you right now. You gave me your word when we left Memphis that I'd find out what we're doin' after we reached New Orleans."

Those gray eyes studied him closely, but Cale did not flinch. "I've done all you asked," he said. "You ought to know by now... you can trust me."

A thin smile began to crease Blaine's lips and then spread wide.

"Very well, Morgan," he said. "I think you should stay. If we are to make future plans we cannot doubt one another." His fingers smoothed Cale's lapels and straightened his collar. "Let us not keep our guests waiting."

Blaine hosted a long luncheon for the five of them in the hotel dining room. They entered the suite a little before 3 o'clock. The maids had finished the daily cleaning, and both rooms were quite presentable when the little man asked his guests to make themselves comfortable in the sitting room while he brought out items for their inspection.

"Morgan, you can help me," he said as he entered the bedroom.

Cale watched him key the padlock and swing open the upright trunk that dwarfed the little man. The first vision was of straw tumbling forth and forming a small mountain on the rug. Then the interior could be seen, divided into four sections of wooden boxes stacked upright in pairs and stuffed with more straw. The contents of each box remained hidden in padded material. Blaine carefully peeled the protective wrap away from the object in the lower left corner and signaled Cale to lift it. The weight of the object forced him to place both forearms beneath it for a better grip. The item Blaine then freed from the upper left corner looked small by comparison, although both objects were still enshrouded in dark velvet.

Blaine led the way into the sitting room and motioned that Cale should place the heavy object he carried at the feet of the man who hosted them for dinner the previous evening.

"Walter, here is the bust of General Grant that you commissioned," Blaine said. "Lift the shroud and see if it is to your liking." The little man kept the second article in his arms.

The man addressed as Walter removed the velvet and leaned back in his chair to better appraise the two-foot high marble likeness of the chest and head of the general. "Magnificent... absolutely magnificent, Adam," the man said. "I shall see that it has a place of honor in our museum. I believe he will be our next president."

Blaine bowed his head in gratitude and stepped close to personally deliver the second object. "And here is my attempt to recapture the beauty of your lovely Angela."

Walter's hands shook as he accepted the item, and that prompted Blaine to remove the velvet for him. A feminine head and neck had been carved in a warmer shade of marble than the stark whiteness of the bust of Grant. Walter let his fingers run slowly from brow to chin, then he cuddled the marble head to his chest. He raised his eyes and tried to speak but choked on emotion. Tears ran down the man's cheeks and prompted Blaine to gently rest a hand on the man's shoulder. "There, old friend," he said, "you honor me with such appreciative reaction to my humble effort to see that you have another likeness of your dear departed daughter."

The other gentlemen leaned forward in anticipation of what Blaine had for them. When the contents of the last two boxes were brought out and presented, one by one, Cale could see that one man unveiled a miniature racehorse in full stride, while the second man lifted the velvet from the stone likeness of an owl.

Blaine motioned Cale to follow him to the bedroom. "Now you know that I am a sculptor," he whispered. "I paint, as well. Please restore the remaining contents in the trunk, go to the lobby, and arrange for the staff to bring some tea that we may offer our guests.

The unexpected mission provided his opportunity to ask about a message, and the timing could not have been better.

"Yes, Mister Morgan," the concierge said. "It was delivered only a few minutes ago. Here is a message for Mister Blaine, as well."

Cale thanked the man and placed the small envelopes in the pocket that held his knife.

When the guests had been assisted with transfer of their heavy treasures to their carriages and Blaine said his goodbyes, he took the envelope Cale handed him and retired to his bedroom for a nap before dinner. Cale leapt at the opportunity to be alone in the sitting room and open his envelope. The folded page his eager fingers withdrew felt as smooth to the touch as some expensive fabric.

Betsy's flourishing script began with a "Dear Cale" lettered twice the size of any word on the rest of the page..

"I'm glad you did not die in the war, but I wish you had never come to N.O. I'm happy here, so much more than when I was married. I doubt you know I ran off from that Hawthorne School to marry an officer – Confederate, of course – who took me to Charleston and used me to advance himself. I couldn't go home after the war, so I accepted the offer to share a gentleman's passage on a ship to N.O. He introduced me to Mrs Delaprerre. I've been here a year and make good money. Please don't ever come here, Cale. Go have a happy life some place else. Your friend, Betsy."

He read it through three times. Disappointment grew with each reading, and the crushing blow near the end hit with force and finality, "Don't ever come here. Go... some place else."

At first he tried to convince himself Betsy was simply embarrassed at having been discovered. That premise weakened when he remembered his own hastily-scribbled note on scrap paper from the bar proved him to be no man of means. Time to her meant money. Evidently she could not spare the first because he did not have the second.

That evening Blaine suggested they dine at another favorite restaurant. On the walk there, the sculptor-painter explained his letter brought an invitation to visit next day at the home of a prominent matron who wished to discuss a new commission.

"Her son will call at eleven and escort me in his carriage," Blaine said. "After luncheon, I'll make sketches of the subject she has described and will not return to the hotel before six o'clock. You may spend the noon hour and the afternoon as you wish."

Cale perked up when he heard the last words.

Chapter 17: Portent

The sunny day invited exploration, and Cale sought to clear his mind. He strolled past shops and outdoor marketplaces clustered around the government house he overheard another pedestrian call the Cabildo. The streets of New Orleans teemed with their representative shares of idlers, peddlers, beggars, and shady types who appeared ready to resort to violence to satisfy their needs. But none so bold as the man who grabbed Blaine two nights before.

An artist like Blaine moved in a circle made up of those who either profited from the war or recovered rapidly. Yet, as daylight made clear, a larger circle of those who had not – many of them very likely former soldiers – were as plentiful in New Orleans as in any other part of the South. Cale had much in common with the "have nots," but time with the Pomeroy sisters and men like Jefferson Tucker and Jesse Murdock convinced him to seek his own path.

At St Peter Street, he headed toward the river and came into the wide square that fronted St Louis Cathedral. Hands in his trouser pockets, he wandered about the plaza with strangers who bent necks to view the cathedral's facade and three spires that towered high above the city. "Couldn't dare me to climb that," he muttered to himself.

He walked past an elderly reciter of lines from a poem who scattered crumbs before an audience of seagulls. A few steps farther, he paused to look over the shoulder of a painter who dabbed at a small square of canvas mounted on an easel. Nearby, a barker called anyone within the sound of his voice to examine the display of glassware and trinkets laid out across a tabletop.

The aimless ramble about the square brought Cale to a long crescent formation of benches; a couple occupied by men engaged in conversation, others by women watching small children at play in the late September sunshine.

A little girl skipped across his path, forcing Cale to halt in midstride to keep from tripping over her. A wide red bow bounced atop her brown hair, but long tresses in back swung loosely at her neck. Her cherubic face radiated excitement although she played alone.

A woman seated on a bench nearby called out, "Caroline." The girl skipped a few steps farther before she turned toward the summons.

Cale had not seen such innocent joy in a very long time. Captivated, he witnessed the child half-skip, half-run along the row and come to a stop in front of the woman who had called her. The woman reached out to smooth the brown locks and bow that bounced so freely a few seconds before. Then a second woman appeared and seated herself beside them. The little girl sidled close to the new arrival's long skirt and laid a tiny hand on the knee. That woman rested her parasol on one shoulder and helped the child to be seated The first woman got to her feet, said something, and began to walk toward Cale.

He stepped to one side, placed a foot on an unoccupied bench, and pretended to adjust a strap on his boot until the woman passed. He decided to sit with his arms spread across the back of his bench and take in the full panorama of the square. When he turned toward the child again, he still could not see the woman's face for the parasol kept her head in shadow, but whatever story she told held the little girl's rapt attention.

After a few minutes, Cale rubbed the back of his neck, stood up, and began a walk to the opposite side of the square along St Ann Street then moved on toward riverside to watch the big steamboats, the cargo ships, and the smaller craft anchored or at work. About 50 yards to his right, a ramp led down the bank to the piers.

The busy activity at dockside beckoned Cale to amble from one pier to the next. One boat, unlike the sidewheeled *Empress of Ohio,* had a wide single paddlewheel at the stern. From this boat's upper deck, a man called orders down to a crewman somewhere below.

"Where you bound, Captain?" Cale yelled when the man had finished giving instructions.

"Jefferson," the man replied once he identified his questioner, "Jefferson, Texas."

The name of the city did not mean anything to Cale, but the state certainly did.

"Ever hear of a place in Texas called Promise?" he asked. "Is it in parts you're headed to, or is it somewhere on the coast?"

The man took time to issue more instructions before he answered. "Promise is up north of Jefferson, young man. Never been there myself, but I hear it's within fifty miles or so. You want to travel up that way with us?"

Cale's heart picked up a beat at the suggestion. "I'd sure love to, Captain... but I can't this time."

"Well, there's a boat that leaves here most every week," the man called back. "We brought a load of cotton downriver, and now we're heading back for another." He waved and disappeared inside the wheelhouse.

Mind outraced feet as Cale strode back up the ramp and resumed his post at the rail. He had identified his next destination and learned a direct route to get there. A brief experience riding the river taught him that manner of travel sure beat months of walking across unknown territory. The problem lay in assembling the means if he ended his work for Blaine.

With so much to consider he lost track of time until he heard the bell in a clocktower somewhere behind him chime 4 o'clock. He glanced back at the crescent of benches. The woman who left had returned. She held the little girl's hand, and they appeared to be taking leave of the woman with the parasol, who placed it on the bench and knelt to embrace the child. She reclaimed the parasol, and with her back to Cale, watched the other woman lead the child away. The brown locks jostled as the little girl looked back across her shoulder at the woman beneath the parasol.

The child and her minder disappeared at a corner. Cale's eyes turned from following them to notice the woman with the parasol begin a walk toward the river, her sun protector raised high. When the distance narrowed to 20 yards or so, he could not fail to identify the face beneath it. He had to grip the rail to control his exhilaration when she crossed the street and took up a position at the rail not far from his own.

"Hello, Betsy," he said once he moved alongside.

She did not return so much as a glance. "Whoever you are, please go away," she said. "I want to be by myself." She kept her eyes focused on the harbor scene before her.

"It's Cale," he said and extended his hand along the rail as if that neutral fixture might serve as common ground.

"Have you followed me here?" she asked, still without looking at him. "I answered your note. I do not want to see you.... or anybody else right now."

He edged his hand closer. "I swear I didn't follow you, Betsy," he said. "I just happened to cross the square a while ago. That precious little girl skipped by me, and I couldn't help but watch her.... so playful and full of life. I saw you come to sit with her and that other woman, but I didn't recognize you... til you walked over here."

She would not face him, and that indifference stung him to act.

"Betsy," he said as his right hand seized her wrist, "Talk to me."

She did not try to dislodge his hand but kept her eyes on the water until she consented to turn her head slightly in his direction.

"The little girl is my daughter. She'll be four years old in December, That's all you need to know, Cale."

He grabbed hold of the rail with his free hand. His first shock had come with discovery that Betsy was in New Orleans. The second tremor developed with a slower numbing effect. Well over four years had elapsed since he and Betsy set out on their separate ways. He stared deep into those familiar dark brown eyes. When they did not reveal the answer he sought, he spread both arms and pulled her to him so quickly she almost dropped the parasol.

"Cale!" she protested, but he hugged tighter.

"She's *ours*, ain't she, Betsy?" he breathed in her ear. "That last time we were together..."

"Turn me loose, Cale," she ordered. "Who gives you the right to maul me out here? In broad daylight! I won't talk to you any more if you don't back off," she said and wriggled to free herself.

He dropped his arms and took a step back but kept his eyes on hers.

"I found out I was pregnant not long after I enrolled at Miss Hawthorne's school," she said after a pause. "The school hosted a soiree... lots of soldiers there... and I danced with this young lieutenant. He wanted to see me again, so I sneaked out to meet him. I guess he figured it all out pretty soon after we persuaded that Spartanburg preacher to marry us because... after my baby was born, he forced me to entertain any officer he thought might recommend him for promotion. He made it to major before the war ended. He drank all the time by then and hunted any excuse to beat me. I took the baby... got away from him as fast as I could. I met a man who brought me down here. Miz Delaprerre helped me find the place where my little girl stays. The woman you saw with us in the square cares for a few other children whose parents... have to work. She brings her to see me twice a week... different places... so don't camp out down here believin' you'll run into us again." A commanding glint in her dark eyes accompanied the last words.

"But, Betsy..." he stammered..

"No 'buts' about it, Cale. Do you hear me? I'm now able to see that my little girl is well cared for. Well fed, nice clothes. She'll go to school... things I want my child to have. I think I've managed pretty well... on my own." She broke eye contact and moved away from him.

Cale's jumbled mind could not separate and absorb her account as neatly as she told it. He tried to step close again.

"Betsy, I wish... Lord, I'd have..."

"Cale, stop it. We can't change what's gone. I've told you more than I should've. I know how to look out for myself... and my little girl, too. Go on... do whatever it is that you do for that little man. Just what *is* it you do?"

"He hired me to travel with him as protection. Keep vagrants off him so he can carve things out of stone and paint pictures. Hasn't told me how long he plans to stay. I may decide to do something else..."

"I knew he was an artist," she interrupted. "Miz Delaprerre told me he asked for someone to let him make some sketches. That's all he wanted... hardly said a word to me while he sat there... drawin' away in that little book he carried in his coat. Didn't he tell you?"

"No... and I didn't ask," he shrugged. "When I saw you that night... well I 'druther not say what I thought. Up to then, workin' for him hadn't been too bad."

She smiled for the first time. "The war didn't knock all that boyish charm out of you, Cale. But you shouldn't mix me up in your work for him. It's not likely I'll ever see him again. That suit looks good on you... he must do all right by you." She stepped farther from him. "I have to go. Goodbye Cale."

"Wait Betsy! Before you leave, tell me this... I thought I heard that other woman call your little girl 'Caroline?'"

"That's right," she said with a twist on the handle of her parasol . "Do you like it?"

"Pretty name," he agreed. "Pretty as she is."

"There's a lot of meaning in a name," she said as she left him, "if you think about it."

Blaine studied him across the flame of the single candle that lit their dinner table. The gray eyes expressed friendliness, but the squint suggested curiosity, too. The silent examination prompted Cale to elaborate.

"I'd just like to know, Mister Blaine... so I can figure something out and go on to find my grandfather. I found out today there's steamboat passage from here to Jefferson, the part of Texas where Grandpa Morgan's said to be. That's why I asked how long you plan to stay... and need me around. I might be able to find some work on the boat. I've worked on a snag boat and know how to..."

"Something disturbs you, doesn't it?," the little man interrupted He sipped from his wine glass while Cale tried to begin again.

"I just don't fit here, Mister Blaine," he finally chose to say. "This week and a half of... well, comfort... with you still don't seem real. So different from anything I ever knew. I've seen how your friends respect you... and your work. I don't think they'd allow anything bad to happen to you."

"While I'm in their presence, yes. I'm confident you're right," the little man said. "They could not have helped me that first night after our arrival, could they? Is there something else you haven't told me? Are you bored? If so, we shall find time for your own pursuits."

"No, Mister Blaine, more time on my own in New Orleans will just make it worse. There's somebody here... the girl you spent time with that night... that I used to know. I ran into her again today.

"She came to the square to be with a little girl that another woman keeps for her. I was in love with Betsy before I joined the army, but our circumstances... well that is, her family was much better off than my own. I believe the child most likely is mine."

The waiter appeared unsummoned to pour more wine in Blaine's glass. Cale declined the offer and held his words, but Blaine beat him to it once the waiter left their table.

"Did you speak with her? Did she ask anything of you?"

"Yes, I finally got her to talk to me... but no, she didn't want anything," Cale said, "'cept for me to go away and leave her alone. You see, bein' off in the war, I never knew 'bout her bein' pregnant. She told me she married this man who abused her and forced her into... the life she leads now. But she insists she's able to take care of herself and her little girl."

Blaine's tone softened, "The story is not uncommon. Many prostitutes secure the services of someone else to raise their children."

Cale's neck stiffened. "Well, it's not common for me to accept that it's somebody I care 'bout and I'm responsible." He heard the sharp edge in his own words. "I can't stay here without tryin' to do something about it. Trouble is... I don't know what I *could* do.. when she don't want me around."

"I now understand why you have this sudden urge to leave, Morgan," the little man said. He plunged into words like 'dilemma' and 'perplexing' that made Cale wish he had his dictionary at hand. "Absence can be a time for reflection," Blaine continued, "or a time to consider other opportunities."

He leaned back in his chair, summoned the waiter, and ordered coffee to be brought with their desserts.

"I've been pleased to have your company," Blaine said, "as well as your protection. You see, I suspected the fellow that I had to discharge would seek revenge. He knew my destination and could have connived his way on board our steamer. He had traveled with me from Saint Louis, knew the contents of my trunk, and something of their value to those who commissioned them. Thus I feared he would attempt to harm me or seize my work. I did not see him on board, nonetheless it was reassuring to have you close by at all times."

Chocolate tortes that oozed even richer filling between layers were presented. Blaine's commentary paused until the coffee had been poured and the waiter left them.

"When that man's arm came out of the shadows the other night," the little man said, "I first thought it belonged to the man I discharged. But Krueger is tall and lean, not heavy-set like that fellow in the alley. Still, he may be somewhere in this city. He knows the hotel I prefer. I trust this will explain why I've wanted you so close by. However, as you point out, I am blessed with friends. I'm sure one or more will offer me accommodation in their homes once I explain the need for your absence. In the morning we shall look into schedules. When we learn how often steamboats depart for and arrive from Jefferson... I believe that's Red River country... we can make informed decisions. If you can reach the far port in less than a week, proceed to locate your grandfather and visit several days with him before boarding another steamer for the return, you should complete the journey in about three weeks time. Time to reflect on other matters that concern you."

Cale did not try to conceal his gasp of astonishment at the way this little man's organized mind dealt with someone else's problem.

"All that sounds like it *could* work out, Mister Blaine. I 'preciate you for takin' time to hear my reasons for goin', but I want to be completely honest with you. When I find Grandpa, I don't know how long I'd want to stay. I may be of some use to him. I owe him a lot. Course I wouldn't want to be underfoot and create a problem for him or his family... I don't know that I'd stay very long."

Cale slowed to drain his coffee cup before he continued. "Am I to understand, Mister Blaine, that you would want me to keep workin' for you? Even when you leave New Orleans?"

The artist smiled. "Yes, Morgan," he said. "If you had not raised the subject tonight, I would have soon done so. I planned originally to be in this city for two to three weeks, but I'm in no rush to get back to Saint Louis. I shall advise Mrs Blaine by telegram that my stay has been extended. You will be invited to accompany me on that return, and we shall discuss further ways you may be helpful to me in my work. I am giving serious consideration to a voyage to France next year. A friend has put me in contact with Edouard Manet who, I am told, is a pioneer in a new method of capturing landscapes and personal likenesses my friend describes as 'impressionism.' I would like very much to visit him and see his work. That long voyage and the big city of Paris could very well harbor threats to a small stranger like myself."

Blaine's arm went up to signal for the check, and the gray eyes twinkled when he spoke.

"Mrs Blaine and I should have little need for concern with you in our travel party. And if that trip should not materialize, your employment will continue so long as you and I desire it."

When the check had been settled and the proprietor assured that everything exceeded expectations, they strolled back to the hotel. Blaine resumed discussion of an agenda.

"We shall go to the bank tomorrow and arrange for your travel funds. All I ask is that you give careful thought to what

I have said and how it might apply to your future. Send a telegram to me in care of the hotel with word of your return, or if you decide to stay. If there is no telegraph office available, the hotel will forward your letter to me if I have departed for Saint Louis."

Chapter 18: A Place Called Promise

For two years they traveled hundreds of miles by wagon from Tennessee, endured scorching heat and freezing cold, forded countless streams, hung together as a harmonious family unit without a significant disagreement until they reached Texas. Right where things were supposed to get better, a line of separation threatened instead.

Caleb paced around the campsite at the edge of the town of Promise, Texas while Jenny stirred the supper cookpot above the fire the Morgans shared with a family of Stewarts. The two families had traveled together since Mississippi. The noisy end-of-day play of the many children – three Morgans, six Stewarts – afforded each set of parents a few minutes of private discussion if needed, and such a time had come.

The crisis arose with Jenny's alarming suggestion that she remain in town when the two wagons rolled out the next morning, a departure agreed upon to settle 120 acres jointly purchased with Gabriel Stewart two days before. By pooling small amounts each man earned from odd jobs along their way, they secured a promissory note to buy land one of many east Texas farmers rushed to sell in the hard months that followed the end of war. The Stewarts were to occupy an existing house on the property and share it with the Morgans until resources allowed a second house to be built. The two men had agreed to work out, after the first harvest, an equitable division of land for two separate farms. The arrangement seemed a common practice among newcomers who hurried to establish homesteads with limited funds.

A drop-off in the noise level from play made Caleb realize the two smallest Morgan children had stopped to stand and watch him pace about. He motioned them to play on and rested his arm on a wheel of his wagon. He did not want to attract attention from either Gabriel or Sadie Stewart, who were sure to ask questions. That would not be convenient.

He decided he should rejoin Jenny and try to dissuade her. The evening meal would taste better if that could be settled first.

"Jen, I just don't like the notion of you stayin' on to work in that boardin' house," he said with an effort to make it sound less than a demand. "There's so much work ahead of us out there."

Lifting her ladle from the pot, she sought to console him with one of her smiles.

"I know, Caleb. I do nae like to think of the miles between us, but 'tis a grand opportunity to earn a bit of money.... wi' a solid roof above the children through the weather. Have our own room, we would. Mister Carmichael says I'm to run the place... not just toil there, like I've done these noontimes."

He still did not like the prospect, and his displeasure must have shown because she dipped the ladle into the stew that was to be the family's evening meal then raised it to his lips. "A wee taste might help the notion go down," she said with a wink.

He pushed the ladle away. "But Jen," he sputtered, "I won't be able to come back like I could from Murdock's mill... not nearly as often. It's a good fifteen miles to our land. Gabe and me will be workin' seven days a week for a long spell. There's no other way to build onto that house and prepare land to plant. Don't you see?"

She gave the stew a final stir before she turned back to him. "Yes, Caleb, I see that... but do ye nae see that every time ye *do* come back, I'll have money waitin' ? Money for supplies. Methinks that will do more to help our new home be built faster than me goin' with ye now."

Caleb had seen Fred Carmichael only once, three days after they reached Promise when he accompanied Jenny to ask about the note posted on the boarding house front door, 'Cook to help with midday meals. Apply within.' They had settled the wagons at the edge of town, and all the Morgans benefitted from the food she brought back to camp in return for her three hours' work each day. Carmichael, affable and well-suited to deal with the public, appeared to be as old or older than Caleb. According to Jenny, he lived alone in a ground-floor room but spent much of his time away from the house. He hobbled about on a gimpy leg attributed to a fall in childhood. That did not hamper his partnerships in two of the town's establishments in addition to the boarding house.

Where Carmichael's presence was a minor concern, the thought of comings and goings of younger lodgers revived Caleb's old fear that the difference in Jenny's age and his own might one day cause her to tire of him. Smooth-talking drummers who frequent boarding houses could tempt a woman. Caleb, miles away, could do nothing about it. The pacing had not relieved his concern. How was he to keep his mind on work with all that bothering him?

Jenny appeared ready to call the children to supper, and they would not have a private time to talk again until bedtime. One thing had to be made clear if Caleb consented. He had not mentioned it before, but neither had he been forced to deal with the circumstances of separation.

"It's plain I don't like it, Jenny," he said to hold her attention a minute longer. "I'll worry every day you're not with me. I'll go along with you though... if you're willin' to accept my decision 'bout something else."

She moved to his side, took his arm, and smiled. "And what may that be, Caleb?"

"Meg and little Tom will stay with you," he said slowly, "but William needs to go with us."

Her eyes narrowed as did the smile that soon vanished entirely. "He's a *boy*, Caleb," she whispered loudly. Alarm showed in her words. "I've nivver been apart from..."

"He's nearly eight," Caleb broke in. " He can fetch, water the mules, clear brush, do chores...same as he does now. I'll watch after him. We'll git by on what's left in Sadie's cookpot."

Head down, Jenny withdrew her arm to resume supper preparations.

Caleb felt the moment to close the agreement could not be allowed to slip by. "If you're 'bout ready for supper, I'll call the young'uns," he said.

She nodded in silence. He moved away from the campfire. The compromise had taken his appetite, but hungry children waited.

Caleb spent a restless night and welcomed the sound of the Stewarts stirring to prepare breakfast for an early departure. He kissed Jenny's cheek, rose from the quilt pallet they shared on the floor of the wagon bed, and stepped down to discuss the change in plan with Gabriel Stewart.

"Y'all go on soon as you're ready, Gabe. Jenny wants to stay behind and run that boardin' house a while. What money she makes can pay for supplies... to your benefit as well as ours. The boy and me will come on behind you after we see her and the littlest ones settled in."

Stewart held onto a stick of wood meant for the breakfast campfire.

"That's sudden strange, Caleb," he said. The dawn light behind him cast his face in silhouette. "When did that git decided?" From where she knelt by the fire, Sadie Stewart craned her neck so as not to miss anything said.

"Last night," Caleb said. "Carmichael made the offer yesterday. His housekeeper's goin' to live with her son in Clarksville. We ought to catch up with y'all soon after dark. And we'll be ready for work tomorrow mornin' just like we planned."

Jenny joined him to prepare their own breakfast and soon whispered more details to Sadie as the two women worked..

"Well, it sure is strange," Stewart said. He placed the stick where he had first intended. "I guess we'll work it out, unless... you won't try comin' back here every week, will you?"

"No, Gabe," Caleb assured, "I'll be workin' every day with you. When it's convenient, I'll grab what free time our work gives me."

Stewart nodded a silent acceptance, and the two men took up their individual tasks to ready each wagon for the day's journey.

Two hours later, Caleb remained in the wagon with the children while Jenny entered the boarding house to accept the position. Shrieks of excitement from the departing housekeeper carried through the walls. "At least one person's happy," Caleb muttered to himself.

"That's what I hoped to hear, Jenny," the woman gushed. "My son is on his way here today. Bring in your things, and we'll get you settled in a room for tonight. When we leave in the morning, I suggest you move into my room... it's light and airy. Room enough for you and your children. Mister Carmichael's gone somewhere, but he'll be back at dinnertime. I know he'll be pleased."

Before Jenny returned to the wagon, Caleb unloaded most of the items she said she would need. All the children scrambled down from the wagon bed to help or, like Calhoun the dog, get in the way. Caleb carried in the heavy objects and left smaller items to her or the children.

"You're sure that's all you'll need?" he asked when they reassembled beside the wagon.

"Yes, I think so," Jenny said in lowered voice. She pulled William to her side and repeated many of the motherly instructions the boy had heard all his life. He had accepted the news without complaint but showed his nervousness when the moment of parting came. She kissed his cheek and held him in a tight embrace.

Caleb bent to hug five-year-old Margaret, whom they had chosen to call Meg, and three-year-old Tom. "Mind your ma," he said. "We'll all be together again as soon as I can make it happen."

When Jenny released William, Caleb took her in his arms and kissed her. "I'll miss you, Jen... but if this is what must be, I'll be back soon as work allows."

She rested her head against his chest. "I'll pray the Lord watches over ye every day and night, Caleb Morgan. My heart goes with ye. Be sure ye bring it back."

They kissed again before he released her. He untied the mules from the hitching rail and motioned that William should mount the wagon seat. Unaccustomed to that high honor, the boy bounded up with Calhoun right beside him, but Caleb's strong arm pushed the hound to settle into a crouch at William's feet. Jenny stepped back as did Meg and little Tom, the first to wave goodbye. His mother and sister joined in as they watched Caleb, again in his customary driver's place, turn the mules and head into the street.

"When we're out of town, Pa," William's voice sounded above the wagon's rattles, "can I drive the mules?"

"Reckon so," Caleb said.

Except for a Christmas reunion, Caleb and William did not see Jenny, Meg, and Tom again that winter of 1865-66. That meant they suffered the pain of parting all over again, but the brief time together did much to reassure Caleb. Jenny's obvious happiness at her tasks warmed his spirit through the long ride back to the farm.

The farm's abandoned three-room house had been found to be in better condition than expected. Caleb and Gabriel soon brought the detached kitchen up to Sadie Stewart's standards, put the waterwell in good working order, and made the barn sufficient to their animals' immediate needs. Gabriel then wanted to take time to build a new corncrib, pigpen, and coops for chickens, but Caleb insisted that should wait until they possessed actual occupants for such outbuildings.

The earnings Jenny shared made it possible to put the first seeds in the ground in March, and the two men had a dozen fields of corn, potatoes, and cotton sprouts to admire by the first of May, with a vegetable garden well underway. William proved to be a useful helper, along with 13-year-old Clete and 10-year-old Barney, the eldest Stewart boys.

The best fields for planting lay on both sides of a creek that coursed through the approximate center of the acreage. As he worked, Caleb spotted a good place to build the new home for his family on the far side of the creek. Placing a house on the eastern side of the slope would allow it to face the east instead of the back of the Stewart house which sat near the road. Cedars grew in abundance on that slope and formed a natural brake to winter winds. He made a vow to build a cedar chest for Jenny to store her things. The trunk brought from Tennessee had been sacrificed one rainy night when no other dry wood was available to get a fire going.

In early July, Gabriel agreed the crops looked hardy enough to fend for themselves, and Caleb took William back to Promise to spend a month with Jenny. Carmichael, spouting praise for the way Jenny took charge of his house, supplied the name of a local sawmill operator who did not hesitate to add a man of Caleb's experience to his workforce, if for a few weeks only. The earnings allowed Caleb to pay half the first amount due on the promissory note before he left town and prevent that obligation from consuming most of the income from the first harvest.

He had to admit, when he returned to Promise in midNovember flush with rewards from a good harvest, their separation had a few compensations. Jenny brought such a system to her duties at the boarding house that she found ways to devote a good portion of each afternoon to him alone. His good mood flourished in these intervals so that he did not resist when she suggested that William should remain with her through their second Texas winter in order to enroll in school.

"Reckon you're right. He does need more than what we've been able to give him up to now," Caleb said as he stretched on the bed and watched Jenny brush her hair before the mirror. They had never known the luxury of such a bed to enjoy the bodily pleasures of their love. The contented expression in her face shone back to him from the mirror, and he silently vowed she would have an equally-equipped bedroom in their new home.

Jenny applied the final strokes to tresses that hung past her shoulders, laid the brush on the dresser, and began to pin her long brown hair into a tight bun. "He can read a bit and do easy sums," she said before she slipped her dress back over her head. "He should nae be far behind others his age if he begins now."

"I 'spect we'll manage without him til springtime," Caleb agreed. "Gabe will need convincin'. He's still annoyed that you're not there, but Sadie rules that house. She wouldn't let you move a thing from where she's put it... not in that kitchen. Y'all got along all the time we made do in separate wagons, but she'd never share that house with you now. I'll start on our place soon's I get back. Hope I can have it ready for you to move in before next year ends."

"Well, lie yeself there and think on it," Jenny said with a kiss on his cheek. "I need to get back out front."

Late that afternoon Carmichael returned from one of his frequent absences to see Caleb hammer a loosened stairstep back into place.

"I feared a body would trip on it, Mister Carmichael," Jenny said in explanation.

"Good for you, Mrs Morgan," the owner approved. "You're a handy man to have around, Mister Morgan," he said when he plopped down on one of the cushioned chairs in the big front room that served as lobby and office. "Matter of fact," he said, continuing to address Caleb, "I'd like to discuss something with you. Know anything about making brick?"

Caleb placed the hammer on the small counter that served as Jenny's desk. "Never done that, Mister Carmichael. I've only worked with wood. And a little rock," he added quickly. "Built a couple chimneys."

Carmichael rested his elbows on the chair arms, formed a church steeple with his fingers, and eyed Caleb across their tips. "Well, from what I heard about your work last summer at that sawmill, I have a notion you could handle most any chore you set your mind to. You see... I've taken over a brickworks that sits idle right now. Fellow owed me... couldn't repay any other way, so I settled for that. We could ride out tomorrow and look it over."

Caleb looked to Jenny before he spoke. Her eyes showed as much surprise as he felt inside. "Tell you the truth, Mister

Carmichael," he began, "I've got all I can do right now at the farm. Got a house to build this winter... then land to plant next spring."

"Won't hurt to take a look, will it?" Carmichael persisted. He dropped his hands and gripped the arms of his chair. "We can talk about it at breakfast." He heaved himself upright and began to wobble to his room. "At least, you might help me figure out where to start." He closed the door behind him while Caleb and Jenny exchanged questioning looks.

To please Jenny, Caleb consented to take the ride suggested by the boarding house owner.

Carmichael kept a buggy at the livery stable, and they were soon headed out of town. "The last owner prospered during the first years of the war," Carmichael explained while they rode. "Like a lot of people. Got in trouble putting all his money in Confederate paper. I'm Southern-born and proud of it... bought bonds to support the army, all that... but I make it a habit to keep from letting my sentiments get too tangled up with my money. I switched a lot over to Confederate bills, but I put some aside in gold and Federal bills, too. This fellow's entire workforce was in his slaves, and that went the way of his money. Still, after they learned they were free some wanted to stay and work for him. But he had no way to pay. I loaned him money to keep going. Gave him a year to begin to pay me back, and still he couldn't. He just lost heart... like so many others. When he signed the works and the ground it sits on over to me, he told me he'd head down to the coast to get himself a boat and fish for a living."

They reached the brickworks before Carmichael finished his narrative. "You can see... place looks to be in decent shape. Don't judge it by the little shack of a building. That's just the office.

Let's go around back to the mixing drums, the forms that shape and press the bricks, and the kilns where they're baked. You may have noticed clay is plentiful in the soil of this area."

"Certainly have," Caleb concurred. "Stuff sticks to a plow... wagonwheel...shoe..."

While they toured the layout, Carmichael remarked how the former owner's freedmen could likely be recruited to return to work. "I believe some will jump at a chance to earn some money." The words had hardly left his mouth when they saw a large man emerge from the woods in back of the works. His ebony face broke into a broad smile as he walked close to their position.

"Y'all gentlemen aim to fire up the works?" he asked, eagerness evident in each word.

"Thinking about it," Carmichael replied. "Did you work here?"

"Yessuh, Mista Varnado brought me and my mam here when I little. You prob'ly know he had lots slaves. Some took off oncet they freed. Some us stayed... and would kept workin' for him, but he couldn't. My little house back there in woods. Heard y'all talkin'... told my Florrie I had to go see. My name's Nathaniel. I kin git more folks to work... if you wants me to."

Caleb's eye caught the glance Carmichael directed his way, and the nod which followed.

"That's good to know, Nathaniel," Carmichael addressed the man. "Nothing's decided just yet, but I hope to start up pretty soon. Your experience should be... very useful. I'll let you know."

The freedman's second smile spread wider than the first. He bowed slightly before Carmichael when he spoke again. "Anything I kin show you now, Suh?"

"Thank you, no," Carmichael said. "We'll just examine the big ovens, check the condition of these forms, and see what's inside the office."

Nathaniel backed away in the direction he came but not without another bow and smile to show his satisfaction.

"When y'all come back, just call in these woods. I come a-runnin'." He waved a polite farewell and vanished in the trees.

Caleb ran a toe alongside one of the many wooden forms left on the ground. "Some of this wood's rotten, Mister Carmichael. Might need to build several new forms before you could start work. Why would a man leave mounds of clay out in the open like that? To git rained on and cake up like rocks? Need to put up some kind of cover back here."

Carmichael fished in his vest pocket for a key. "That's exactly the sort of suggestions I wanted to hear, Mister Morgan. You have a keen eye. Let's have a look inside." He unlocked the padlocked door and swung it wide.

Caleb realized he said more than intended and probably too much already. He reminded himself to stay uncommitted when he followed Carmichael inside.

"Jenny, I just don't see how I can do it," Caleb said gently because he had seen her excitement for the prospect. Carmichael had drawn a broad outline of an agreement as they returned in time for the midday meal at the boarding house. Once the three lodgers had been served along with two locals who took their midday meal at the boarding house, Carmichael went off on his rounds. Jenny restored order to the dining room, straightened the kitchen with the woman who assisted in cooking and cleaning the rooms. That done, Jenny encouraged the children to play outside, and accompanied Caleb to the bedroom for their private hour.

"I want to start buildin' our house soon's I git back," he said. "Winter's the time to do it without losin' time from plantin' season."

"'Twould be a way for us to be together every day," she said. "Nae more waitin'."

He sensed that the favorable considerations in Carmichael's offer filled her mind and left very little room for what he might say.

"But what would I say to Gabe? Jen, we made a *commitment* with him and Sadie."

"And keep it we will," she said. "Farm's up and runnin'... a house to live in... plant all they want in the spring. We'll help with supplies..."

"He won't like it," Caleb interrupted. "He'll see it as shiftin' all the work on him. He's our good friend... cranky in some ways, but he's honest and trustworthy. After all the miles we traveled together, I don't want to cause a fallin' out. And the farm's what we said we wanted... you and me."

"Caleb, I'm nae sayin' give it up," she put in quickly. "We'll pay our share of what's due, and our part of the land will be there waitin' for us. Meantime, tis a grand opportunity Mister Carmichael gives us."

Jenny sat on the bed and pulled his arm so that he sat beside her. She snuggled close and whispered "'Twould be more grand times like this."

He spread his arm about her shoulders and drew her backward across the bed. He realized another debate had been lost, but he wanted to unfasten the buttons of her dress more than fret about dealing with Gabe Stewart.

He found Carmichael seated at the big table in the dining room, pencil in hand, papers spread before him.

"Come look at this, Mister Morgan," he said. "Some ideas for a signboard."

Caleb peered over the man's shoulder at the penciled lettering. "Carmichael Brickworks," read one scrap of paper. "Carmichael Industries," another. A third had been thoroughly scratched out except for traces of the surname.

"Call it whatever suits you, Mister Carmichael," Caleb said. You own it. You have that right, seems to me."

"But what do you *think?*" Carmichael implored.

"The road that runs in front...where does it go?"

"To Clarksville," came the quick reply. "What's that got to do with it?"

"That'd be a main road in these parts, wouldn't it?"

"Yes. Make your point."

Caleb realized his every word was about to topple him forward from the brink of commitment where he had allowed Jenny to lead him. He walked to the side of the table so as to face Carmichael before he spoke.

"Well, it 'pears to me that the best sign will be... if you take the first batches and build a brick building to replace that shack out there. Show what business you're in. Them who pass by will notice that before they read any sign."

Carmichael slapped an open palm on the tabletop. The loud bang echoed through the quiet house. "I've got my man!" he roared. "I won't take 'No' for an answer, Mister Morgan."

Jenny's head appeared in the doorway to the front room. "Did something fall?" she asked.

"Everything's in order, Mrs. Morgan," Carmichael assured. "Please overlook my excitement. Come hear the good news your husband is about to give me. Well... is it agreed, Mister Morgan."

Caleb gave in. "I'll say 'Yes'... if you'll start callin' me Caleb."

Jenny rushed to his side and hugged him.

He found Gabriel Stewart at the woodpile.

"Let me spell you a while, Gabe," Caleb said and reached for the ax handle.

Stewart did not hesitate to relinquish the ax. With hands free, he mopped his forehead and greeted Caleb.

"Clete was supposed to do this, but Sadie talked me into lettin' the boys take some things she cooked to a family up the road... do some chores for 'em, too. Somebody sick up there, she says."

Caleb's arms, shoulders, and back quickly fell into the wood-chopper's rhythm he perfected over more than 50 years. The familiarity of repetitive strokes and dead-center gashes in wood comforted him. He wondered if he could ever come to feel that way about baking bricks. He kept working until a stack of cut lengths had grown knee-high. Might as well say it now, he decided as he placed the handle of the ax across the chopping block and wiped his face.

"I accepted a job in town, Gabe. But I'll keep payin' my share of our note and work with you on dividin' up the farm."

Stewart reacted with stone-faced silence. He shook his head twice before he said anything.

"You did *wha-a-t?*"

Caleb summarized his offer and his reasons for acceptance without allowing time for interruption. "I wanted to tell you now so you'd take it into account when you plan what and how much to plant. Jenny and me will help with money for seed and such in exchange for some corn and vegetables next season. Why don't we go in the house so I can explain all of it to Sadie, too. Tomorrow we can walk the property and set some dividin' lines. You keep what's on this side of the creek, we'll take the other. That gives y'all more acreage, but it's the simplest way to divide, fair and fair alike. For the time bein', you and your boys can plant the bottom land over there if you want. That sound all right to you?"

Gabriel cleared his throat several times. He looked away, then back before he turned away again. When he finally settled on the direction he wished to face, he showed he had listened.

"I reckon, Caleb. But all of it's.... sudden strange. Takes some time to get used to."

Caleb slapped him on the back.

"Believe me, Gabe... the decision wrung considerable time out of me, too."

Questions from the more inquisitive Sadie stopped him several times, but Caleb finally concluded his explanation. "All this time," her sigh broke the silence that descended afterwards, "I counted on havin' Jenny close by every day. You men don't understand. Y'all have your crops, and livestock, and concerns 'bout the weather... " She turned and removed a kettle from the fire to pour hot water over strips of bark and dried berries placed at the bottom of her teapot.

"Well, Sadie... as busy as she is," Caleb assured, "Jen has said more than once that she misses you, too." He did not add 'you might be surprised how confident she's become lookin' after that boardin' house. She might not go along to git along the way you were accustomed.'

A little smile on Sadie's habitually serious face confirmed that his flattery had scored.

"Y'all will just have to find time to come in for a visit sometime. I'm sure that would tickle her," Caleb said. He knew Jenny did not wish to harm the friendship they shared with the Stewarts any more than he did. The matter of immediate concern had been dealt with, and that's where he chose to let it rest.

An obviously pleased Sadie lifted the teapot and filled the three cups before them.

"Mmm," Caleb said after a sip from his steaming cup, "that's good tea."

It took but one shout to summon Nathaniel. The big man's face broke into a wide grin as soon as he recognized the callers, and he could not keep still when Carmichael told him the brickworks would be reborn.

"Glory to God!" he shouted. "Suh, I been prayin' somebody be sent to do it."

"Well," Carmichael said, placing a hand on Caleb's shoulder, "this is the man who will get it done. This is Mister Morgan. He's in charge. Show him how y'all used to do things 'round here. I'll go inside and see if I can make sense out of the papers Varnado left. I want to get word to some of his old customers right away."

Caleb and Nathaniel spent that first morning poking through cluttered remnants of materials, firing the kilns for a test, and assessing what supplies were needed to resume operations. Carmichael collected what records had not been destroyed and took them along when they returned to town at midday. They left Nathaniel with instructions to recruit two additional experienced brickmakers. By the end of the week, the little office building had been dismantled, new forms built to shape the water-softened clay and sand mixture into sets of individual bricks, and construction begun on a roofed, open-sided shed for storage. Carmichael paid for Caleb's mules and wagon to be housed in town in return for their use at the brickworks.

When the new year of 1867 began, Caleb saw the shed finished, new mounds of clay and sand hauled in, barrels for water and mixing set up, and some two dozen bricks baked in a test run. The Carmichael Brickworks was in operation.

When he returned to the boarding house to share the news with Jenny, she surprised him with a letter from Beulah Greer back in Tennessee.

"Yer grandson's alive, Caleb! Here, read it." She thrust the letter in his hands. "This part right here," her thumb pressed against the center lines on the page.

319

"...The second time he came I could give him your P.O.," Sam Greer's wife had written, "since your last letter came to hand the month before. He said he went back to fight and served out the war. He's been with some Pomeroys he knows up in Meigs County. He saw Mr. Murdock, too. He said he's coming to see you. Sam tried to persuade him to stay and farm your place, but he's bound to find y'all instead. May take him a while, so if you move on from that place leave word where you'll be...."

Caleb's hand began to shake. Jenny steadied his arm as she took the letter from him. "Tis joyous news," she said. She must have sensed the wave of emotion that swept over him because she did not look into his eyes and could not see they were wet. He swallowed hard before he tried to talk, but once he started the words tumbled out, filled with pride.

"Stood up to all of 'em... courage to face 'em all down. Them in his own lines as well as enemy in front. Ty Morgan all over again." He pulled Jenny to him and held her tight, then his amusement surfaced. "Clever rascal. I don't doubt he'll show up here one day," he laughed. She smiled as she looked up into his face. He felt no shame that she saw his tears.

By springtime 1867 a new brick building on Clarksville Road fronted daily whirls of activity as Caleb and his work-force of three turned out stacks of finished product for masonry.

320

Fred Carmichael was so pleased with their output he ordered a foot-high sign that read 'Carmichael & Co.' in modest lettering above the much larger 'BRICKS' and placed it above the road-side door. He hauled a rolltop desk from town for the office, but Caleb seldom sat in front of it because he preferred to oversee the work out back.

He left sales contacts to the gifted Carmichael. The man's quick wit and tongue extolled the advantages of using brick instead of frame construction to all who would listen. As Caleb predicted, the demonstrative impact of a single all-brick build-ing caused more than one who traveled the road to place an order right on the spot.

One party of travelers with other business in mind rode up one afternoon when Caleb had little time to talk. They did not dismount to enter the door of the office but walked their horses around back instead. One horse moved forward when its rider spotted Caleb, who shook a sifting screen above a wooden tub.

"You the boss 'round here?" asked the man who did not leave his saddle.

Caleb looked up. "Yes, I'm in charge. Can I help you?"

"I wanted to see for myself," the rider said. "Friend told me y'all had freed darkies workin' here. I see that's true. Don't you know there's plenty of white men who could use a job?"

Caleb finished with the screen, removed his hat, and wiped the back of his hand across his brow.

"Do you... or them... know anything 'bout makin' brick?" he answered. "These men do."

"That ain't the point. Folks got enough to worry about with these bastards runnin' free, much less findin' employment so as to stay put. Let 'em go someplace else." The man's mustache drooped past both sides of his mouth but did not conceal his scowl. He looked to be in his middle 30s, a possible veteran of the war, Caleb surmised.

"A business this size needs workers with skill," Caleb said, his tone even and measured. "Soon as we build up our trade, we'll likely add more men. Qualified, if we can find 'em.. Them that have to learn, if not."

"You think white men will work with this lot?" sneered the man on horseback. "You don't sound like a Yankee... where'd you come from?

"You name it," Caleb said. "Born Virginia, on to the Carolinas, Tennesee, all across the South til I got here. War's over, Mister. The South's all broke apart... goin' to need a lot of small businesses like this one..." Suddenly distracted by a throb in his left arm, he said nothing more.

The man pulled sharply on his horse's reins. "Listen to me, whatever your name is," the voice had been lowered but the words spat venom. "Plenty of men in this county won't put up with what you're doin'. You better take this fair warnin' and act on it.... before it's too late." He spurred his horse and jerked it around, scraping the animal's legs against a stack of brick-shaping forms. The other riders followed their leader out of Caleb's view.

When informed in private that night, Carmichael acknowledged he had heard such threats before. "Tomorrow, I'll tell the officer in charge of the military encampment in town. They're responsible. I'll ask him to ride out so you can give him a full description."

"Well, all this man's done so far is threaten. It'd be hard for even the army to do much 'bout that. Let's not mention it to Jenny," Caleb said. He chose to say nothing about the annoying throb as well.

322

Caleb's wagon reached the brickworks at his usual time next morning. He always arrived before the workmen, being seated in the office or outside appraising the work to be done when the first of the three reported. He kept to that routine, but when he remained alone for the better part of an hour he grew concerned.

He walked to the edge of the woods and called, "Nathaniel?"

That met silence except for the fluttering of birds' wings above him. He called again, louder.

Anxious to get the new day's work underway, he strode into the woods along a path he had seen Nathaniel use. The trees had a good start on new growths of leaves, and bushes crowded both sides of the pathway that looked well-worn. The serpentine trail prevented good visibility to what lay ahead wherever it ended. With each turn, he called again, "Nathaniel!"

"Mista Morgan?" a voice whispered at his right. "That you, Mista Morgan?"

Caleb stopped dead still to answer. "Yes. Where are you?"

Nathaniel appeared suddenly in a gap between two tall pines, and Caleb could see past him to a clearing with a cluster of cabins.

"I've been waitin', Nathaniel. Nobody's showed up. We've got work to do."

"Won't be comin', Mista Morgan," Nathaniel said slowly. "Nobody will... not after last night."

Caleb stepped closer, but the big man backed away.

"What are you talkin' 'bout?" Caleb demanded.

"Riders... 'bout midnight," Nathaniel blurted, "riders all 'round house...a-whoopin' and a-wavin' dem torches. My Florrie most tremble to death, and new baby 'bout due. I feared whole woods git set on fire..." His rush of words became indistinct.

"Listen, Nathaniel.... Mister Carmichael's reportin' what them visitors said yesterday to the army. An officer's comin' out here today, and I'll tell him what happened and answer whatever he wants to ask. You can tell him what happened here..."

"Too late, Mista Morgan," the big man protested. "Levi and Hezzie done gone. My Florrie got people at Clarksville... she want me take her there now... git away from here."

Caleb felt the throb return to his left arm. Not as sharp as the day before, but noticeable. He flexed the arm and began to rub it with his right hand while he sought time to hold Nathaniel until the military arrived.

"Will you wait til the officer gits here?" he implored.

He watched Nathaniel mull the question. That presented an opportunity to sweeten the request, "I need time for the money you're due from Mister Carmichael. You'll need it."

The throb advanced to his shoulder. He slid his right hand upward to massage the shoulder area.

"What time he come?" Nathaniel finally spoke.

"Soon... I'm sure. Mister Carmichael said he'd take care of it early today. He'll likely come out with the soldiers."

Nathaniel looked toward the clearing. Caleb presumed he lived in one of the cabins back there.

"I finish loadin' my cart and see if Florrie ready. Long way to pull that cart, Mista Morgan... can't wait long."

"I understand, Nathaniel. You do what you need to do. I'll go back and see if they've come already. I'll call you the minute they arrive."

Each man turned and headed to respective tasks. When Caleb emerged from the woods, he found the brickworks as deserted as he had left it. That did not help his frame of mind, nor did it allay the throb that had become a constant ache. He went inside, sat at the rolltop desk, and stretched his left arm across the papers to accommodate a more vigorous massage. When the throb eased a bit, he leaned back in his chair, sipped from his canteen, and pondered what to do next.

An order for 300 bricks was half-filled. With no one to help, he would have to mix and shape each set and stoke the kiln fires himself. At that slow pace, baking a dozen bricks at a time in each of the two kilns, it would take him a week to produce the rest of the order, after culls were discarded.

"No time to pamper this doggone arm," he said aloud, left his chair, and went out to fire up a kiln. He had moved on to sift clay and sand into a mixing barrel before he heard the sound of horses' hooves and the familiar voice of Fred Carmichael call out "Go around back." Caleb knew the ensuing conversation would take a while so he halted work..

Three men in Federal blue uniforms dismounted. Their leader approached Caleb. Carmichael's buggy came into view, and the owner scrambled down immediately.

"Morning, Caleb," Carmichael said hurriedly. "This is Lieutenant Oxford. Where are the men?"

Caleb shook the hand extended by the young officer but directed his comments to his employer.

"Gone, Mister Carmichael... 'cept for Nathaniel. And he's in the act of leavin'. I asked him to wait til you and these men got here, but he may be gone by now."

Carmichael stood open-mouthed.

Lieutenant Oxford took charge. "Mister Carmichael reported what happened yesterday. Can you describe their leader? Do you believe their visit had anything to do with your workers' disappearance?"

Caleb nodded. "Must have, Lieutenant. Best thing I can tell you 'bout the man who talked to me is... he had a thin mustache, sorta sandy-colored... curled down the sides of his mouth. Clothes looked fairly new. Gun in his holster. Rode a sorrel horse. Now... when I finally found Nathaniel this morning, he said riders came in the night. Circled his cabin wavin' torches... yellin' threats. I reckon the same must have happened to the other two. Nathaniel said they're already gone. Let me call..."

"Nathaniel!" Carmichael bellowed at the top of his voice, beating Caleb to the act. He limped toward the woods and repeated the summons.

"Might find out quicker if we walk back there," Caleb suggested. "I followed a path to where I found him an hour or so ago. It's not far... I'll show you the way."

Before he took a third step, Nathaniel's voice sounded from the road.

"We out here, Mista Morgan. We come 'round field road... that path too narrow...cart too wide."

"All right, Nathaniel," Caleb called out. "We're comin' 'round there."

"Good," Carmichael sighed and led the way to a shortcut through the office.

Caleb moved quickly to overtake him. "I hope you've got a little money on you.... only thing I could think of to stall him."

Lieutenant Oxford handed the reins of his horse to one of his soldiers and followed through the office doors to the road. They found Nathaniel in front of a two-wheeled cart at roadside. He had a rope looped across his chest and through his armpits to form a harness and pull the cart by his own power. A woman sat amidst lumps of possessions on the bed of the cart with two small children huddled beside her.

"We need you to tell this officer what happened 'round here last night," Carmichael said. He motioned for Lieutenant Oxford to move alongside him.

Caleb rubbed his left arm and listened to Nathaniel hurry through another frightened telling of events. Oxford pressed for details, but Nathaniel kept repeating "Torches all I saw... couldn't make out no face... just heard they yells... 'Better git out if you want stay alive'... such as that." Behind him, the woman's head drooped as she hugged the children.

In spite of the officer's pledge that he would attempt to find and punish the night marauders, Nathaniel could not be persuaded to stay. "Got to go... now," he said.

Carmichael withdrew his wallet and thumbed through the bills. He chose a few, folded them, and extended them to the big freedman. "You've been right helpful here, Nathaniel. I wish you wouldn't leave, but this covers what's due since last payday. If you decide to come back, come see Mister Morgan."

Nathaniel pocketed the money and bowed in gratitude. "Thankee kindly, Suh. You, too, Mista Morgan." He pulled hard at one side of his harness to turn the cart back to the center of the road and began his trudge without another word.

"There goes the best man of my crew," Caleb said as the cart moved away. He turned and entered the office. His arm hurt, but he had work to do. Behind him, Carmichael began to lecture the lieutenant. Once he paused for breath, Oxford seized the opening.

"I've got four men besides these two in my detachment. We can't be all over the county. I'll ride back to town and post warnings, but... without descriptions to connect with what Mister Morgan told me, I just don't know..."

Caleb caught Carmichael's eye. "I'll go back to what I started, Mister Carmichael. 'Preciate it if you'll find me some help. Right soon." He left them to finish their discussion.

Jenny fussed over how tired he looked when he returned to the boarding house that night. She brought his supper to their room and stood over him while he ate. He had managed to concentrate on work all afternoon because the throb lessened once he was alone again at the brickworks.

"The thing of it is, Caleb, ye can nae do everything out there all by yerself," she said when she gathered the dishes to return them to the kitchen. "That order will wait. Mister Carmichael will find ye some new workers."

"Won't be that simple, Jen," he said. "The men who've gone knew how to make brick. They showed *me* more than I showed *them.*"

"With a good teacher like ye, new hands will catch on quick," she said with a wink and closed the door behind her.

Caleb wanted to believe her, however pessimism over the loss of his crew rode an undercurrent of concern for his troublesome arm. Still, he did not regret his decision to leave that unmentioned. The afternoon's respite from pain convinced him to let it be. He kicked off his boots and stretched full-length on the bed.

He must have drifted off to sleep because his next moment of awareness came in the dark of night when she lay beside him. The throb awakened him, and it seemed worse with his body lying flat. He eased himself from her side and sat on the edge of the bed. The ache in his arm and shoulder began to subside, but his breathing became more difficult. She must have heard his gasp.

"Caleb?" her frightened voice asked... "what is it?" Her arm stroked his back. "Sit right there," she instructed, "let me light the lamp."

He heard her fumble for a match, then a soft light from her side of the bed penetrated the pitch darkness of the room.

"Sorry I woke you, Jen," he got out between short breaths. He knew he could not put off telling her. "This old left arm and shoulder's been actin' up now and then." He paused for another breath. "Pain got worse all of a sudden while I lay flat... had to sit up." Another pause, then "I believe it helps a bit 'cause I'm beginnin' to breathe deeper."

"Rest right where ye be," she ordered. "Let me find something to prop behind yer pillow." She dashed out of the room in her nightgown and returned a minute later with two stuffed cushions from chairs in the front room. She braced them against the headboard of the bed, commanded him to lie back against them, and placed his pillow in back of his head. After she lifted his feet and legs from floor to bed she stared down at him.

"Methinks ye'll nae go to that brickworks in the morning, or anytime, til ye've first been seen by a doctor." With that, her expression softened. She blew out the lamp, returned to her position beside him, and kissed his cheek.

"Yes'm," Caleb whispered. He felt decidedly better.

Dr Isaac Samuels, the only doctor in Promise, came to the boarding house soon after Jenny told Carmichael about Caleb.

"The rhythm of your heart is not as steady as I would like to hear," the physician said after 10 minutes of questions and examinations. "It's probably pointless to tell a man such as you to remain in bed for a couple days, but you must not exert yourself. Limit yourself to light work, or you may not be as fortunate when your heart acts up again. And it will, I assure you." He turned to Jenny and gave instructions about food and the frequency she was to spoon doses from a bottle he produced from his leather bag.

"I'll find some men, Caleb," Carmichael said when he returned from showing the doctor to the door. "From now on, you supervise."

"That won't work," Caleb protested. "Not at first."

"It'll *have* to," the brickworks owner retook control of the conversation. "I heard Doctor. Samuels... no shoveling, no lifting... definitely not bricks in or out of the ovens. You show 'em. They do the rest." He called back over his shoulder as he left the room, "I'll let you know when I've found somebody. We'll ride out there together."

True to his word, Carmichael produced two men the next day. Once the foursome traveled to the brickworks and Caleb walked the newcomers through a lengthy demonstration, he reluctantly agreed to give them a trial.

"We'll add at least one more," Carmichael promised. "Not as raw as these two, if I can help it."

The young man discovered several days later ranked higher in Caleb's evaluation right from the start. Tim Grogan was a recent arrival from Alabama. "Couldn't make it when I got back home after the war," he explained. "Told my wife we might as well give Texas a try."

Caleb liked the way Grogan paid attention and elevated him to foreman before that day ended. When he told Jenny that night, she shared his relief. "'Tis what I've prayed for, and what ye need" she said. "One ye can trust to see the work is done."

The delayed order was finally finished, and Caleb left it to Carmichael to arrive at what the aggrieved customer would accept as a fair price. They moved on quickly to new orders as summer settled in. Caleb left Grogan in charge while he traveled by wagon to scout the countryside for new supplies of clay and sand. He was about to depart on one such mission when visitors rode up to the office. One very familiar visitor, in fact. The man with the thin horseshoe mustache.

"I see you took our advice," he said.

Caleb bristled, but Jenny's admonition that he must not get upset rang in his ears.

"Your point bein'." Caleb said slowly, "the men who work here now, I take it. Glad we found 'em... but nothing wrong with the first ones, either. You here on business this time, or do you just ride around makin' threats?"

The man sat silent in his saddle. A cold stare spoke for him at first.

"If I was you," he began in a tone that dripped menace, "I'd show some 'preciation for loyal men of the South who mean to set things straight again no matter what the occupiers say. Let 'em post their orders and think they're in charge. We aim to restore the South like it was meant to be. You'd be wise to..."

"I'm considerably older'n you," Caleb broke in, "and we may well have seen different sides of the South. Maybe you came from a life of privilege. I did not. Mine's been hardscrabble... before, durin', and after the war. Didn't waste time complainin' 'bout it then, and I don't now." He forced himself to take a deep breath. "If you're so confident... like you said... why don't you go into town and tell it to that lieutenant? You may make him see the odds against him, and he'll just take his men with him and go. Might set things straight... like you said... a lot faster."

"Don't mock me, old man," the rider spat out. "You'd regret it. And you'd better not get in our way. Our organization is wide and growin'. You'll see," he predicted and spurred the sorrel horse into another fast departure.

Caleb called Grogan to discuss ways to secure the premises at night.

"Is all that necessary, Mister Morgan?," Grogan asked.

"'Fraid so, Tim" Caleb said.

That night he reported the incident to Carmichael, who immediately went to find Lieutenant Oxford. He returned just as Caleb finished the supper Jenny kept warm.

"Oxford believes it's somebody from the ranks of disgruntled former Confederates who've banded together to cause trouble," Carmichael confided. "Army's had reports of burnings and crop destruction all across the South. Freed slaves being the main targets, but sympathizers as well. Guess this fellow lumps us in the second category."

"Well, what are they doin' 'bout it?" Caleb asked. Jenny stood behind him and placed a protective hand on his shoulder.

"He wants you to come by tomorrow morning and repeat that description... add anything you can think of. He says he'll prepare a poster to be printed."

Caleb rested his palm atop Jenny's hand.

"Reckon he thinks local folks trust the Union army all of a sudden," he said half-heartedly.

"It's all the protection any of us has got, Caleb." With that Carmichael heaved himself to his feet and retired to his room.

The first poster went up in a few days, and the lack of attention paid to it or its duplications did not surprise Caleb. A state of overkill had been reached in the flood of ordinances and regulations posted across the occupied South. Any new notice suffered in that saturation, certainly if it urged readers to furnish information about one of their own.

With no flareup of the annoying throb or shortness of breath, he preferred to concentrate on Jenny, their children, and the brickworks' output as summer segued into fall 1867. The only other matter he allowed to dwell in mind was the anticipated arrival of his grandson. That day could not dawn soon enough to suit Caleb.

Chapter 19: A Mixed Reception

The sternwheeled *Pride of Dixie* arrived at Jefferson five full days after leaving New Orleans. Half a day had been wasted at the busy docks in Shreveport waiting for space to be cleared for offloading cargo before the steamboat could turn west into Big Cypress Bayou and reach the bustling port that served north Texas.

Cale hurried down the ramp at dusk in search of a stagecoach to transport him the rest of the way. He found the depot shuttered for the night.

"You'll need to go to Clarksville first, then take another stage to Promise," a man told him in between swipes of a broom outside the door. "Clarksville stage left at one o'clock. I'd open back up and sell you a ticket, but you can't go anywhere til tomorrow. Might as well wait at one of our hotels."

Cale thanked him but chose to go back on board. The captain agreed to let him sleep one more night in his vacant, spartan quarters. The willing assistance of a man with snagboat experience had earned the crew's appreciation when smokestacks had to be lowered and raised frequently for passage through narrows where trees overhung the Red River. With her single wheel at the stern, the *Pride of Dixie* rode higher on the water than heavy sidewheelers. Even with that advantage, an extra hand proved valuable for the small crew's tricky maneuvering on the Red's low water level.

Long nights aboard gave him time to consider many things with Betsy at the center of most of them. Finding her made his ill-fated infatuation with Agnes easier to forget. Though denied him once, and even if shielded in a different way when rediscovered, Betsy had never been displaced in his heart. He refused to dwell on her discouraging words in their most recent conversation because he detected hints of the old fondness they shared, particularly in the playful almost teasing remark about her little daughter's name.

Cale said the name "Caroline" over and over as he lay in bed each night on the journey upriver. He had never heard Betsy nor his mother mention a Gleason elder identified by that name. The connection to their home state was so obvious it did not suit his knowledge of Betsy. She had never seemed sentimentally attached to places or things. She bubbled with energy for what lay ahead and left dwelling on tradition to others. Betsy possessed too much originality to join their number.

"Reckon there's a code in there somewhere," he said aloud one night as if to invite some spectral being to furnish the answer. He began to break the eight-letter formation into individual parts, and that led him to sit upright suddenly in his bunk.

"There's the proof!" he yelled. "I *am* the father! Betsy chose a name that hid *my own* name in there."

A subsequent return to Jefferson for another steamboat to New Orleans became a certainty before he boarded the Clarksville stage with two older passengers, a man and a woman. He volunteered to sit with his back to the driver and thus allow his fellow travelers the forward view of countryside. They in turn did not object to his silence. He had too much on his mind to join their chatter. When not savoring the impending reunion with his grandfather or sorting ideas for how he would pursue another meeting with Betsy, he had to decide what he would say to Adam Blaine.

Neither of the latter issues had been resolved to his satisfaction before a second stagecoach pulled into the town of Promise in late afternoon one full week and a day after he left New Orleans. Cale finally set foot in the last known location of his grandfather. The opportunity that opened made all other matters wait.

Promise appeared smaller than either Clarksville or Jefferson, but business establishments filled both sides of the town's main street. Cale did not need to go far to find the post office because a lettered shingle tacked to the front of the stagecoach depot identified both services. When the proprietor and the stage driver concluded their drawn out conversation over delivery of a mailbag, Cale approached the counter.

"Sir, I wonder if you recall a man named Caleb Morgan," he said. "Moved here 'bout two years ago, I believe. This was his post office address in a letter shown to me by some of his friends. Does he still live 'round here?"

The proprietor stopped sorting the contents of the mailbag and faced his questioner.

"Would he know you?" he asked.

Cale grinned. "I believe he would.... I'm his grandson."

"Aim to settle 'round here yourself? Where you from?" The man clearly expected details.

"Well, last place I stayed very long after the war was Tennessee... been down to New Orleans.... then came straight here to see Grandpa. If I can find him soon, my visit's not likely to last more than a few days before I head back."

"You ought to find him pretty quick," the postmaster/stationmaster ended his interrogation. "His wife runs the boardin' house one street over. She told me somebody like you would show up one day. Turn right down at the corner past the hardware store... you're bound to see it. Your grandpa usually comes in a little past sundown. Stage passed right by his place of business, the brickworks, on your way into town."

Cale's sigh of relief was so audible the man behind the counter cracked a smile. He had enjoyed a moment of amusement at a newcomer's expense, but his hospitable self resurfaced.

"Stage runs back to Clarksville day after it comes through here. Doubt you'll want to leave tomorrow. Next one's Saturday. If you want to go, be here before noon. I'll be lookin' for you."

"That's mighty helpful to know," Cale thanked the man. "And I 'preciate the directions, but I'll walk back out to the brickmakin' place first. I noticed it when we came in. Wasn't much more than a mile out there." He started for the street but turned on his heel. "Can I send a telegram from someplace in town?"

"Not yet," the man said. "Army's been grumblin' to have one. Closest place to do that's Clarksville, I believe."

The sun would not set for another hour or so. Cale reckoned he could reach the brickworks on foot well before quitting time. He was not about to let a little thing like toting a valise delay the long-anticipated reunion with his grandfather. His feet never failed him in war or any of his miles of postwar experiences before Adam Blaine made it possible to travel by steamboat and stagecoach.

Well-rested and eager, he fell into a familiar pace and soon left the town of Promise behind him.

Open country helped him concentrate on what he wanted to say once he found Caleb Morgan. The circumstances of this visit could not have been more different than their first accidental meetings, but Cale felt responsible that his grandfather had needed to relocate in such a faraway place. An apology was long overdue. Choosing and rehearsing the right words made him unaware of approaching sound until a sorrel horse came to an abrupt stop alongside him.

Cale looked up at the face that towered above him. The man's eyes were shaded beneath a broad-brimmed hat, but that shadow did not hide a carefully-trimmed mustache above and at both sides of the mouth.

"Lose your horse?," the rider asked.

"Never had one," Cale replied. He stepped forward to resume his walk.

"Hold on," the rider said.

Cale ignored the command and took a second step before he realized two other riders moved past the first and occupied each flank. He heard a click and turned to see the gun pointed at him.

Perhaps he had been rash to set out on foot without regard for highwaymen who prowl open territory and fatten their pockets with whatever money and valuables a lone stranger might have on him. Facing the open barrel of a pistol, he regretted that he abandoned the caution used on the streets of New Orleans.

"You look like one of them carpetbaggers," said the mustached man with the gun. "No other fool would strike out on foot in a suit of clothes and draggin' a satchel like that. You headin' out to make some poor soul's life more miserable than it is already?" The eyes beneath the hat brim had become more visible. They did not offer friendliness.

"I ain't no Yankee," Cale protested. "I don't know that it's any business of yours, but I fought for the South. I'm in these clothes 'cause I just traveled here by stage. Now, while you point that gun somewhere else, I'll be on my way." He took a step, then another, and the riders began to walk their horses on both sides of the road. The man on the sorrel horse holstered his gun but maintained his close position.

"If you were one of us then, maybe you'd like to be part of our organization," he said. "You look fit... we can use more good men... and I'll see you get a horse. We're First Arkansas Cavalry men... rode with General Forrest. Why don't you mount up behind him?' he waved a hand at the rider at their left. "We can talk it over when we get to camp."

Cale continued to walk forward and spoke from the side of his mouth. "I don't intend to be part of any organization that means to start 'nother war. Sounds like that's what you've got in mind."

"No," the man sniffed, "we aim to protect white folks who've got nobody to stand up for 'em. Help 'em keep their farms... or find work that will go to freed darkies... like we had to set straight at that brickworks up ahead."

Cale stopped in midstride. "What's that 'bout the brickworks?"

A trace of a smile showed beneath the thin mustache. "Just one example of our usefulness. White men work there now instead of the first lot. Good riddance, too. Even a tough old boot like the one in charge there catches on."

The rider at the right side of the road crossed his horse in front of Cale, and the rider on the left turned to follow toward a cluster of pines. The rider who had done all the talking halted his horse at Cale's left side.

"So...do you want to reconsider... and ride with us?"

Cale stared up at him without fear. "That tough old boot at the brickworks is my grandfather," he said with emphasis. "If you've caused him harm, I'll hunt you down."

"Easy there, rooster," the man snickered. "Just see that your grandpa keeps hirin' the right kind, and we won't need to visit him again. Mind what I've told you... our organization's gettin' bigger every day." He jerked the rein, and horse and rider disappeared into the pine thicket.

Chapter 20: Reunion... and Peril

Caleb sat at his desk, head bent low in a study of scribbled figures, when a sudden dimming of afternoon light from the lone window by the front door made him turn to see the outline of a man who peered inside.

He pushed his chair back from the desk, walked to the door, and pulled it open.

"Can we help you?" he asked.

A dark hat with a narrow, rolled brim topped the dark-bearded young man who grinned at him. "Howdy, Grandpa," he said once he dropped his valise and thrust out his right hand.

"Well... I'll be damned," Caleb said. He seized Cale's hand and yanked him into the open doorway. "Come in here, Son! Never expected you'd arrive...out here... but I'm sure proud to see you."

"I rode right past here on the stage not more than an hour ago," Cale laughed. "I'd a jumped off if I'd had any notion of you bein' here. Postmaster told me... so I hurried back quick as I could. I'm sure relieved to find you."

Caleb placed a palm on each of his grandson's shoulders to appraise him head to toe. "Looks like you prospered once you got through with that war. I can't tell you how glad I felt... Jenny, too... when Beulah Greer wrote us that you made it, and we might see you one day. Sit down there at that desk," he said, releasing his hold. "What's it been... four years now?"

"That's my count, too, Grandpa," Cale said. He spotted a stool beside the back door. "I'll drag that stool over... it'll do fine. I sat still a long time on that stagecoach. You sit back down at your desk... I saw you there through the window. If you're busy, I'll wait."

"Not atall, Son. Let's see... I believe you said folks call you 'Cale'... that right?"

"Yep....Ma told me Pa said he liked the sound of it. Couldn't have been as much as I liked hearin' him say it."

Caleb took time to clear his throat. Cale sensed a flash of recollection for his grandfather's sudden show of discomfort when told of Ty Morgan's death. He slid the stool close to the desk and clasped his grandfather's wrist..

"Grandpa, I'm so terribly, terribly sorry that my showin' up back there in Tennessee caused you to lose your home. I can't *ever* thank you enough for savin' my life... how what you said inspired me to be a man. When I saw what they did to your place, I got mad... but I felt shame, too. Because of me, you had to leave...force your family to travel all these miles... find a place to start over in these hard times. Grandpa, I *had* to find you somehow, and... apologize."

Caleb placed his free palm atop his grandson's clutching hand. He stroked the back of the hand without speaking until the exact words he wanted took form.

"No more than the hardship I brought on my son Ty... and later on you... when I left like I done. When you told me he left you and your ma and went off to the army, I realized my thinkin' the Willinghams would treat him better if I left must'a made them go even harder on him. You never threw that in my face when I told you who I am. You're a bigger man, Grandson."

"Grandpa," Cale rushed to put in, "Ma told me Pa said he came to understand why you left. She said he talked a lot 'bout you. I hope that's some comfort to you."

Caleb swallowed before he could say more. "It is, Son... Cale," he said as he squeezed the back of his grandson's hand. "It is."

"So I was overjoyed to discover who it was who helped me," Cale hurried on. "I went back to see Ma soon as the war ended and confided in her before I set out to find you again. I think she was more amazed than me."

Caleb released his grip and leaned back in his chair.

"I'm amazed myself," Caleb said, "that you actually got here."

Tim Grogan entered by the back door. "I didn't realize you had a visitor, Mister Morgan," he apologized. "Wanted to let you know everything's closed up. Anything you want before we leave?"

"Yes, Tim...a very special visitor. This is my grandson... Cale Morgan... the son of my late son Ty. Cale, shake hands with Tim Grogan, our foreman."

Introductory remarks aside, Caleb handed the paper with his scribbles to Grogan. "Before you go, Tim... take a look at this and tell me if I added wrong." He turned to Cale and winked. "If Fred Carmichael ever finds out who really runs this place, I'll be out of a job."

Grogan scanned the paper quickly and returned it. "Looks right to me, Mister Morgan. I'll say good night to you both... see you tomorrow."

"Good night, Tim. Come on Cale.. Let's head to town. Some folks there'll want to see you."

A grand night of reunion ensued. Caleb proudly introduced Jenny and the children, one by one. Carmichael overheard the commotion and popped out of his room to be included. "Fine looking young fellow," he whispered to Caleb out of Cale's hearing, "what does he do?"

"Haven't found that out yet myself, Fred. Said he came up here from New Orleans."

Throughout supper Jenny apologized the evening meal was less than she would have liked. "We'll do better tomorrow, tis a certainty."

"It's delicious," Cale assured her. "But whatever you cook couldn't taste better than that stew you served me back in Tennessee. Kept me goin' for days."

He tousled the hair of nine-year-old William, seated beside him. " I remember this little man brought me a drink of water." The boy blushed from the attention, but his pleased look immediately aroused envy in seven-year-old Meg and almost five-year-old Tom.

Jenny headed off trouble by insisting the children say goodnight and prepare for bedtime. Caleb and Cale adjourned to the big front room to relax in comfortable chairs, where Jenny joined them later. They took turns in sharing accounts of separate paths over the preceding four years until the lady of the house reminded her husband of the hour.

"Tis long past time for yer nip from that medicine bottle," she chided gently.

The health concern had not been mentioned in their conversation, and Cale pressed for details. Caleb brushed the inquiry aside as "nothing but a little inconvenience."

Cale saved the telling of his discoveries in New Orleans for the wagon journey back to the brickworks the next morning. As he rode side by side with his grandfather, he bared his innermost feelings.

"When I saw Betsy again.. even before I realized that little girl was undoubtedly mine... Grandpa, my whole outlook started to change. I've got to find a way to get Betsy to let me back into her life."

Caleb listened without comment until he was sure his grandson had said all he wanted to say.

"From what you tell me, the child's mother seems to be convinced she can provide what's needed. The life she's been forced to lead makes her think of money first, and her mind will be hard to change. I'm afraid however deep your feelins' for Betsy may be, they'll come second to what she's already decided 'bout the welfare of her child."

"I can't disagree," Cale said grudgingly. "But, Grandpa, I have to go back and *try*. It's as important to me as... findin' you."

"I'm sure you won't rest, Cale, until you do. You've faced some big odds before..."

Caleb stopped in midsentence when three riders emerged from a pine thicket at the side of the road ahead. The riders turned to approach Caleb and Cale head-on. When he saw they meant to block the road, Caleb slowed the mules. "Whoa.. whoa," he called out.

The sorrel horse and its rider looked familiar. "You got nothing better to do than block men goin' to work?" Caleb shouted.

"Glad I saw you, old fellow," the rider said. "Would have been up to see you at the brick place, but this does just as good.

I see your visitor found you yesterday. Still feel feisty this morning?" the last directed to Cale.

"Depends," Cale answered.

"What do you want?" Caleb demanded, his irritation showing.

"A few words is all," the rider said. "A message you might pass on back in town. Count it a warning. Like the one I had to give you."

"Git out of the way!" Caleb yelled.

"Now hold on," commanded the rider as he placed a hand on the butt on his gun. The sorrel horse began to prance. "Let people back in town know," the man said while he jerked the head of his horse to control it, "we had to clear out another nest of trouble last night. Not far from here. The same treatment's waitin' for any and all who get in our way."

Caleb shook the reins to his mules. "Deliver your own threats," he yelled. "Right now you're in *our* way.,"

"Well, go on," the man on the sorrel horse shouted and fired a shot at the feet of the mules. The startled team flinched and veered toward the rider at Cale's right, who drew his own gun and fired. His horse bolted, and the rider fired a wild second shot.

"Whoa! Whoa!" Caleb bellowed as the mules lurched ahead in a frantic run through the opening given way by the horse on the right. He fought to keep the panicky team from leaving the road. Only when he brought the mules to a stop did he notice the weight of his grandson slumped against him on the wagon seat.

"Cale?...you all right?" brought no response. Caleb freed an arm from the reins to brace Cale's shoulder and prevent his falling off the wagon seat. His grandson's eyes were open, but his efforts to talk brought gasps instead.

"Mister Morgan... is something wrong?" The voice of Tim Grogan called from the road ahead. "We heard shots."

"Come help me, Tim," Caleb pleaded. "My grandson's been shot."

Grogan closed the distance between them at a fast trot. He jumped into the wagon and helped Caleb place Cale in the open bed behind the wagon seat. They spotted blood seeping at his upper chest when they laid him flat.

"What happened?" Grogan asked.

"Fools! Damn sorry fools!" Caleb cursed as he sought to stanch the flow of blood with a wad of Cale's shirt. "Same bunch that run off the first workers we had. More threats of what they'll do to anybody who hires freed slaves. Help me turn the wagon around, Tim. I need to git Cale to the doctor. Come with me...I'll need your help."

He forced that mule team to a breakneck pace to reach town. Jenny had insisted he see Dr Samuels for a new supply when the first bottle of medication ran out, and Caleb knew how to find the residence which also served as the doctor's office. But a wagon hurtling through town attracted considerable attention. Bystanders took note when Tim Grogan jumped down and waved for assistance in getting Cale inside.

The doctor ushered them straight into a room where Cale could be placed on the examination table.

"Please sit down, Mister Morgan," the doctor counseled. "You must not aggravate your own condition."

"Well, it's pretty damned aggravated already, I tell you!" Caleb protested. "Please help my grandson, Doctor. Don't worry 'bout me. Tim, go find the sheriff … or one of them Union soldiers… whoever you see first."

The doctor consented that Caleb could remain for the examination but pushed him to be seated on a chair beside the wall. When Grogan left them, Samuels bared Cale's chest to inspect the area of the wound. He worked without speaking for what seemed an eternity to Caleb. When he finally turned his head, the doctor's countenance was grim.

"I'm afraid the bullet may have penetrated his lung, Mister Morgan. There's so much internal bleeding that I must operate. Mrs. Samuels will assist me, however the procedure will take a while. Please go to your residence and lie down. Perhaps it will be best if Mrs. Morgan comes to see me after another hour. I'll make her aware …"

"Doctor," Caleb interrupted, "I'll wait in the room outside, but I won't leave my grandson. Please do whatever it is you need to do."

Dr. Samuels agreed to call it a draw, and Caleb retreated to the waiting room. When he sat down he became aware the throb in his left arm had resumed. No more than two minutes later, Jenny rushed in.

"Oh, Caleb!," she said in a rush to embrace him. "A kind man came to tell me something's bad wrong over here. Don't say a thing til ye've had a wee sip of yer medicine. Brought it with me, I did. Forgot a spoon, but ye can sip from the bottle. Here, let me help ye."

He started to protest but knew she would never relent until he swallowed the bitter liquid. He slid his right arm out of her embrace and began to stroke his left above the elbow.

Grogan returned with the sheriff, and Caleb addressed the lawman. "Same bunch I told that lieutenant 'bout some time ago. Same leader on the same sorrel horse. Bragged they took care of some trouble not far from here last night. I'm sure that meant somebody got run off their place. They came out of that pine thicket... a quarter-mile or so this side of the brickworks. May be camped back in there someplace."

"I'll take it up with the lieutenant right away," the sheriff pledged. "Threats are one thing... shooting people's another."

"Well, you'll likely see more of both if that bunch ain't stopped."

"We'll do out best," the sheriff said. "The army will spread word." He left the room. Grogan followed, but not without saying "I'll be outside."

Jenny knelt at Caleb's side and urged him to drink water from a glass she had appropriated from somewhere. He sipped and continued to stroke his troublesome left arm without speaking. They huddled together until the door to the examining room opened.

"Your grandson will recover, Mister Morgan," the doctor said. "The bullet lodged against a bone dangerously close to a lung but did not penetrate as I first feared. I've removed the shot and stitched him up. You may see him in a few minutes..."

Caleb did not hear more of the doctor's words. Cale would live. That was all he needed to know. Or so he thought until he noticed the object the doctor held in his hand.

"This fell from the inner pocket when I removed your grandson's coat," Dr Samuels continued. "My first attentions went to him, naturally, but when I retrieved this from the floor just now... I saw this chip in the wooden handle. Seems an unlikely place to carry such a weapon, I'd say. This knife appears to have prevented that bullet from striking your grandson's heart. You can see the mark of the ricochet...."

Caleb reached for the familiar knife. He ran a thumb slowly across the gashed edge of the handle then raised his eyes to make contact with the doctor's own. "Sure looks that way to me, too, Doctor. There's a long story 'bout how he got this knife... meant to protect him then... must have done so today."

He stood and seized the doctor's hand. "Sure do 'preciate you, Doc," he said, "much more than whatever money's due for all you've done."

The doctor smiled. "Let's wait and talk about that after I've looked in on him tomorrow. I'm glad you got here as quickly as you did, Mister Morgan. The force of that bullet may have flattened that lung. Talking may be difficult for a few hours. He lost a bit of blood. But he's young and strong. I expect a full recovery in a matter of days."

Jenny kissed Caleb's cheek. "I'll be leavin' ye now to prepare his room," she whispered. "Bring him home the minute the doctor says tis safe to move him."

Caleb saw her out then stayed right on the doctor's heels for a return to the examination table. Cale's body lay inert, but his eyelids fluttered and lips twitched noticeably.

"Young man," the doctor spoke gently, "we're right here, your grandfather and I. You stopped a bullet, but it's been taken care of. Your grandfather wants to talk with you, but don't force yourself to say much. Not for a while."

The doctor moved aside so that Caleb could approach the table.

"By Golly, Cale..." He choked up and was forced to swallow twice before he could continue. "Ain't this a sorry way to treat a man who comes for a visit? We'll do better, I vow. And thanks to Doctor Samuels here, we'll have you back on your feet in no time."

"Grandpa," Cale rasped, "my coat pocket... knife... paper..."

Caleb raised the knife into view and placed the other hand on his grandson's shoulder. "We'll talk about this after we move you over to the boardin' house. Rest right where you are. I'll fetch Tim to help put you in the wagon."

Within the hour they settled Cale into the room Jenny had prepared and waiting. A round-the-clock showering of attention ensued with either Jenny or Caleb looking in on the patient at 30-minute intervals. Even the children peeped in when he dozed. By late afternoon, Cale's grogginess had run its course and he wanted to talk.

"Grandpa, with my knife... did you find a paper ...in my pocket?"

"Yes," Caleb assured him. "Adam Blaine, Hotel Royale, New Orleans. That right?"

"I need to... send telegram," Cale grunted, "let him know... I'll be back."

"We'll do that, Son. Tomorrow. You can tell me what to say. We'll talk 'bout it in the mornin'."

After breakfast the next day, Caleb brought paper and a pencil to Cale's bedside.

"Why don't you write out what you want to say," he suggested. "I'll take care of the rest."

Cale spread the paper across his thigh. After opening words of success at finding his grandfather, he wrote "I will return. May be late. Stagecoach & steamboat schedules slow. Please see Betsy. Ask her to see me when I get back. Thank you, Sir. Morgan.' He handed the paper to Caleb.

353

"Never sent a telegram before, Grandpa. Mister Blaine's 'spectin' to hear whether I'm comin' back. He said this is fastest way. Man at the stage depot told me... closest place to send one is Clarksville. Will that be a problem?"

"Not if Tim's willin' to ride over there and back," Caleb assured. "I'll see 'bout a horse for him. I'll let you know."

"Thank you, Grandpa. It means a lot to me. There's money in my clothes."

Caleb lifted the knife from where it lay on the bedside table. He ran his thumb across the handle's splintered edge, "Want me to smooth this off for you,?"

"No, Grandpa... not if it's still mine to keep. I've looked it over. I think it ought to stay like that. I've rubbed them initials dozens of times. They always remind me of the man who saved my life. That scar shows... his knife did it again."

"Give all the credit to the knife this time," Caleb said. "Hope there's no third time, but you keep it... just in case. Means more to me that way."

Dr. Samuels voiced satisfaction when he saw his patient. "Why a dying man would rally from all this attention, young man," he teased. "You only came close. You may stretch your legs for a few minutes at a time. Don't push yourself, but you should feel much better by tomorrow. Continue to take the medication I'll leave with Mrs. Morgan, but let me know if I can help you further."

"Thank you, Doctor," Cale managed to say without grunting. "I need to board a stage in two or three days... then a steamboat to New Orleans. That all right?"

"I should think so," the doctor smiled and accepted Cale's offer to shake hands.

The next day Cale accompanied Caleb to the brickworks. The journeys there and back proved uneventful the second time, and the hours between provided grandfather and grandson ample time to talk. They shared separate reminiscences but found their opinions had a lot in common.

The day of the next stagecoach departure for Clarksville the entire family trooped with Cale to await its arrival. William insisted on toting the valise. Meg and Tom settled for the honor of holding each of Cale's hands during the walk.

The stationmaster was outside and hailed their approach.

"I see you found the whole Morgan family, young fellow," he said. "You're right on time. Stage'll roll in pretty soon. Looks like you'll be the only one to board here."

Cale followed the man inside to pay the fare, Meg and Tom still at each side. They returned to join the others just as a dust cloud at the end of the street announced the impending arrival of horses and wheeled conveyance.

"I hate that we didn't have time to ride out to the farm," Caleb said. "That's where I'll build a house someday. This land's different from South Carolina and Tennessee, Cale. Low hills, fewer hardwood trees, but the soil's rich. Makin' bricks is all right for now, but I want to be back where I can work the earth. It's a hard life sometimes, but there's reward in it, too. I reckon I'm a simple farmer at heart."

"You'll do it, too, Grandpa. I'd bet on it. I'm sorry that I ran into that bullet and caused so much trouble, but I've sure enjoyed spendin' time with you again. And really gettin' to know y'all." He stopped short as the clattering stage rolled to a stop. He made a move to take the valise, but William protested.

"I want to give it to the driver and have him put it up top for you," the boy pleaded.

"Then go right to it," Cale said, gave a gentle slap to the boy's back, and watched him approach the driver. He bent to share a hug with each child before final words with Caleb and Jenny.

"I'll let you know if Betsy..." he started but couldn't finish.

"You can't tell 'bout that til you see her," Caleb advised.

Cale embraced Jenny as the driver called out "Board!" "Remember, rub that salve on yer wound," she whispered in his ear. "God be wi' ye."

Caleb's hand reached out. Cale gripped it hard.

"I feel Pa's touch in your hand, Grandpa." He squeezed Caleb's hand harder a second time.

"You said it better than I could, Cale." Caleb was too choked up to say more, but he broke the handshake to lift his right arm. That part of him spoke convincingly when it swept around his grandson's shoulders.

They walked together to the waiting coach. Cale climbed in but turned back for a farewell wave.

Five upraised hands returned his gesture.

He settled into the one unoccupied corner seat as the stage departed with another flurry of dust. Life came close to an early end for Cale at a place named Promise, but the family he regained there shared healing love and inspiration for the challenge that awaited in New Orleans.

He slipped his right hand inside his coat pocket for a reassuring touch of the familiar.

Chapter 21: Decisions

Seven days later he walked into the Hotel Royale and found a message from Adam Blaine.

"The concierge will see that you are assigned to a room and notify me that you have arrived. I shall join you there as soon as possible. Adam Blaine."

He found the artist/sculptor waiting in the lobby when he returned from a short walk the next afternoon.

"I'm glad to see you, Morgan," the little man said. "I can only spare a few hours this afternoon because my hostess insisted on a farewell dinner party this evening. Tomorrow, I shall transport my trunks to the hotel and join you here to make our plans."

"Thank you for your patience, Mister Blaine. Do you want to talk here or up in my room?"

"We'll have privacy in the room. Let's go there now."

Cale tried to summarize his adventure briefly, but Blaine wanted to hear all of it in detail. "You accomplished your quest to find your grandfather, and I'm sure that had great meaning for each of you. The altercation you described, however, is frightening. It's wonderful that you received such excellent medical attention. The incident is another sign of the terrible unrest that besets our nation. I fear we will find evidence of it in Saint Louis as well.

"Did you see Betsy," Cale hurried to ask before another subject could be introduced.

"Yes, I persuaded Madame Delaprerre to arrange it," Blaine said. "The young lady was unwilling to consider a meeting with you. She insisted that you knew her decision, and that it is final. But she softened a bit as we conversed. I believe your perseverance impresses her favorably. I suggested that I contact Madame again when you return, and we agreed to leave it at that. The house is closed on Sundays... New Orleans being a very Catholic city... and a further inquiry must wait until tomorrow."

"Thank you, Sir," Cale said with a great sigh of relief. "I'm grateful for all you've done so that I could find Grandpa, and I just don't have words to tell you how I 'preciate your help with Betsy. I hope havin' to wait around on me has not been a hardship on you or your friends."

"Far from it, Morgan, in fact I gained two more commissions. I have done the initial work. You can assist me in securing the canvases for the return to Saint Louis, where I shall finish each one in time. We can attend to that when I return tomorrow."

They ate once more at Blaine's favorite French restaurant on the night preceding their departure from New Orleans. They had come to an agreement on Cale's duties once they reached St Louis, where his position was to be elevated from bodyguard/personal assistant to attache with responsibility for maintaining Blaine's studio, serving as intermediary at functions where the artist's work was to be exhibited and sold, arranging transport and accommodation for Blaine's lectures at art galleries and museums, and freeing the artist to concentrate mind and talent on his work. Housing would be provided apart from a monthly salary which seemed generous to Cale.

"You should find that to be more than adequate for a family man," Blaine observed over their final glasses of wine. "Let us go now to keep the appointment. Madame Delaprerre suggested we be there precisely at the stroke of ten."

Cale's nervous tension mounted anew, and the walk to the sporting house did not do much to relieve it. He fidgeted, hands in his pockets, while Blaine asked the doorman to announce their arrival to Madame.

"Say what you feel," Blaine whispered when they were alone again, "and make sure she understands the time our steamer leaves tomorrow."

The elegantly dressed Madame received them in her private salon. Cale could not tell if the expression on her face signaled hope or hopelessness in his case. She dispatched a servant to notify Betsy then asked Cale to accompany her to a small room containing a card table and leather chairs. "She will join you here in a few minutes. I shall return to Mister Blaine." With that, she closed the door and left him to fidget.

He tested the comfort of a leather chair, but he could not sit still. Each minute he waited made him more nervous, as did the stillness in the room. He began to pace, hands clasped behind his back, between the table and the wall farthest from the door.

The doorknob turned, and Betsy hurried in. A stole of black silk covered her shoulders, its ends forming an X across her bosom. Her gown of pale blue matched the coolness of her silence. She pulled a chair away from the table and seated herself before she even looked at him.

"I've had second thoughts all day about this, Cale," she said.

He moved toward one of the chairs at her side, but she stopped him.

"No. Please sit on that side of the table. We're here to talk, correct?"

"Whatever suits you, Betsy. I'm so grateful you agreed to let me see you again. I must tell you what's in my heart... Betsy, please let me back in your life. I want us to share our lives together... be a family with our daughter."

Her brown eyes studied his own through every word but the set of her mouth and chin did not encourage him to believe he persuaded her. He plunged ahead, determined to leave nothing unsaid.

"Like you said, there's a lot of meaning in a name, and I realized... with joy... why you chose Caroline's name. I wish I could have been with you and her a long time ago, but she's not the only reason I'm so glad to have found you again. Betsy, I think I've always loved you... since childhood."

Her silence could not deter him.

"I remember the first time I ever saw you... it was in your grandpa's store. I must'a been 'bout six... you 'bout five. While Ma was makin' some little purchase, I dawdled in front of the candy display. That candy always mesmerized me. So many kinds.

"All of a sudden I heard you say, from behind me, 'You better not steal any of that candy.' I blurted out 'I don't steal, I'm just lookin',' or some words like that. You walked away. I remember you wore a big golden bow at the back of your hair. Later I recognized you when you started to school.

"But that day... when Ma told me she was ready to leave and took my hand... before we reached the door I felt something pressed into the palm of the free hand at my side. I didn't look at it til we were out in the daylight. It was a piece of hard toffee. You *had* to have put it there, Betsy. I've never forgotten."

The reminiscence seemed to stir a flicker of amusement in her eyes.

"But a Morgan was no suitable match for a Gleason back where we came from," Cale continued. "We both knew that. Yes, we had some good times together... prob'bly meant a lot more to me than to you... but we had to hide, even though some people likely saw us a time or two when we slipped away. Still, we couldn't change the circumstances. You went away to school, and I went to the army."

When he paused for breath he thought he saw a hint of a smile on her lips.

"Things are a lot different now. Mister Blaine has made it possible for me to be more than a woodcutter and hardscrabble farmer.... a man of some means who can provide for a family, and have time left over to love and protect them. Back home, I could never offer you anything but my love, Betsy. We're grown now...it's a different world."

She raised her hands from her lap and rested them on the table. "Cale, can't you see the world that's right in front of your eyes? We can't deny *any* of it. Yes, we had feelings for each other long ago, and even if we stir those feelings again, there'd be something. Somebody will say something... and you'd throw my past up to me. And poor little Caroline would be right in the middle of it. We can't do that to her."

Energized to have her join the discussion, he rushed on. "Betsy, I understand why you did what you did better than anybody you'll ever know. You *survived!* It's what life calls us to do.

Since that last night we had together, I've been bullwhipped, shot twice, knocked unconscious by a wild animal in a man's body, but I got back up... and *none* of it changed me from the Cale you used to know. And I see in you the same spunk I remember you had when I first saw you in your grandpa's store. That Betsy won't linger to call my attention to something I do wrong, and I'm sure I'll slip up once in awhile. But our love can survive it."

Her facial reaction had not softened much, but she continued to listen.

"What I want you to consider is this.... our steamboat leaves for Saint Louis tomorrow at four o'clock. It's the *Missouri Maiden...* Dock Three. Mister Blaine has booked a room for you and Caroline next door to his suite. He may have told you that he has a home in Saint Louis. He says he'll create an apartment for us, separate entrance and everything. It'll be a new life in Saint Louis, Betsy. Entirely"

Cale dared to stretch his open palm across the tabletop, but she did not take it. Instead she rose from her chair. He quickly did likewise when he saw her approach his side. They embraced without a word spoken. She rested her head against his shoulder for a moment before she stepped back.

"I won't get a wink of sleep tonight, Cale... you know that?"

"You can sleep on the boat," he said with a grin. "Four o'clock. Don't forget. Matter of fact, I'm sure Mister Blaine will let me bring the carriage for you after we put his trunks on board."

"I haven't said I'll go anywhere yet, Cale. *I'll* make the arrangements... *if* any are necessary."

She smiled then quickly left the room.

The efficient loading of Blaine's trunks allowed him to settle into the suite he was to share with Cale a half-hour before 4 o'clock. The little man busied himself unpacking and arranging the order of furnishings in the big bedroom to his liking. Once he heard the words, "There... we'll try it like this for a day," Cale excused himself to wait outside the suite.

"Yes, yes... by all means," Blaine said. "I understand your anxiety."

Cale chose a position along the rail of the upper deck that give him a clear view of the rampway from street level down to the river. The ramp teemed with passengers and porters' dollies making their way to either the *Missouri Maiden* or the *Star of Pittsburgh* at the adjoining dock. As each minute ticked away, the line to the *Maiden* became a trickle compared to the numbers headed to the *Star*'s later departure. The busy port required captains to keep a tight schedule and show little mercy when would-be boarders ran late.

He realized Betsy did not have much time to prepare for the little girl's departure as well as her own, but her smile when she left the cardroom emboldened him to believe she would find a way to keep it. That confidence tempted him to use the last hours at the hotel writing letters to his mother, his grandfather, and everyone at the Pomeroy house, but better judgment suggested he wait to be certain of the news he wished to share. There would be plenty of time for that on the journey upriver. Still, he fought back any doubt of her coming until he heard the cathedral bell begin to chime the hour.

His heart sank when he saw a uniformed messenger run down the ramp, waving a paper in his hand. A message to someone, Cale knew. He prayed it was not for him.

Then a fringe-shrouded carriage stopped at the head of the rampway, and a porter hurried to push a dolly to meet it. He saw two veiled women seated in the carriage. One woman embraced the other who remained seated, stepped out of the carriage, and assisted a child to follow her. The porter signaled for a second dolly to be brought quickly. The woman and child began to walk down the ramp.

Cale bolted from the rail and raced to the stairway amidship. He wanted to be there when they stepped on board and throw his arms around his future.

Carvings

Caleb Morgan relinquished management of the brickworks to Tim Grogan in 1868. Caleb spent more time at his farm adjacent to the Stewarts but returned to share several days with Jenny and the children at the boarding house at least once each month. He devoted most of his time at the farm to the construction of a five-room house that faced the dawn of each day.

The family had prepared to join him there until Fred Carmichael died suddenly in 1870. He bequeathed the boarding house to Jenny; the brickworks to Caleb and Tim Grogan, who bought Caleb's share within three years. Caleb agreed that Jenny remain in Promise, and a pattern emerged whereby he continued to return to town as before while she and the children joined him for short stays once the new house was built. The adjustment might have strained an ordinary couple, but Caleb and Jenny made it work. Their children thrived.

Caleb died at the boarding house in 1879 at the age of 74. They buried him in the town cemetery. A young Methodist minister, who two years earlier became the husband of Meg Morgan, led the graveside service.

Jenny ran the boarding house with her customary diligence. Although a larger hotel opened when the railroad came to Promise, the hospitality and comfort at the Morgan House ensured its recommendation by townspeople to any traveler. Young Tom

Morgan assisted his mother and sister there until his 22d year, when one distinguished guest – the district's Congressman who rested there while campaigning for re-election – persuaded him to relocate to fast-growing Texarkana and manage the district office while the representative was in Washington.

When William Morgan completed his education at the Promise School, he moved in with Caleb at the farm. He became a proficient farmer, residing in the house that faced east and competing with his friends Clete and Barney Stewart to see who could grow the tallest corn and tastiest vegetables.

- - - - - -

A group of six gathered in front of a single-story building on the courthouse square in Decatur, Tennessee at noon on a September day in 1872. The youngest of three women in the group lifted a cloth that concealed a sign tacked to the building's front door. The other women, more advanced in years, joined her in applause once the cloth had been removed.

Fully revealed, the sign read "McAndrew & Appleby, Attorneys."

The young woman who unveiled it kissed one of the younger men. The other young man stepped back, admired the sign for a moment, then voiced an opinion.

"A comes before M," he mumbled. "Ought to be 'Appleby & McAndrew.'"

A man who looked to be more than 20 years senior to either young man touched the speaker on the shoulder.

"Quit while you're ahead, David," he whispered aloud.

—   —   —   —   —   —

A young brunette soprano concluded her debut performance on an evening in 1885 to resounding applause amid shouts of "Brava" from the St Louis theatre audience. The standing ovation awed the young singer, but she regained composure quickly and curtseyed in gratitude.

The sounds of approval intensified as the soloist bowed to her accompanist and again to the audience in front of her. She then looked to a loge box at her right, flashed a broad smile, and blew a kiss to the four people seated therein.

In the box, one man spread his arm about the woman seated beside him, and they rose to acknowledge the high honor. The man joined the sustained applause with vigor but whispered in the woman's ear.

"Congratulations, Betsy," he said.

"Congratulations, Cale," she answered. "There's a Morgan we'll have to share with the world."

The End

Made in the USA
Charleston, SC
23 November 2013